THE VAMPIRE WAR

MELISSA CUMMINS

ALSO BY MELISSA CUMMINS

CHRONICLES OF THE OTHERWORLD

Part 1. The Vampire War

Dark Vampire and Witch Romance (Interconnected Standalones best read in this order)

Night Shade

Night Fury

Night Fall

Part 2. Feral Wolves - Coming Soon

Dark Omegaverse/Shifter Romance (Standalones read in any order)

Carnal Claim - Coming Soon

Bitten To Obey - Coming Soon

Primal Hunger - Coming Soon

Savage Embrace - Coming Soon

Part 3. Fae - Coming Soon

Dark Fae Romance (Standalones best read in any order)

Fae Book 1 - Coming Soon

Fae Book 2 - Coming Soon

Fae Book 3 - Coming Soon

STANDALONES

My Brutal Beast

Crowned In Blood

My Vicious Beast - Coming Soon

NEVER MISS A RELEASE

To get information on works in progress, new releases, and receive exclusive discounts, giveaways, and bonus content, make sure to subscribe to my newsletter!

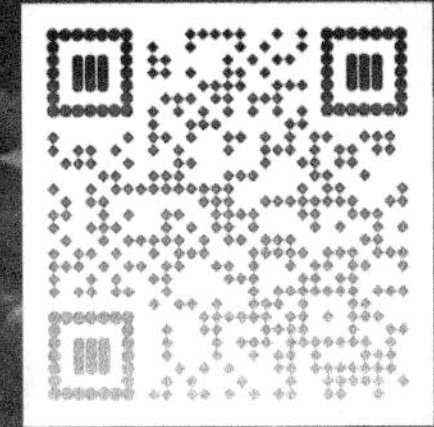

DEDICATION

Remember, no matter who you are, where you are in your life, or what you've gone through, you deserve to be loved. You deserve someone who puts you first, makes you their priority, and knows how to make you scream.

AUTHOR'S NOTE

This series has been an incredible journey for me. It's taught me so much, not only about being an author, but about myself. It's changed my life.

In the same ways it's been a journey for me, these three books will be a journey for you. You're going to have a lot of questions, and I promise they'll all be answered as you read along. But the best thing I can tell you to remember is not everything is always as it seems.

<u>Welcome to The Otherworld</u>

These books get darker as they go on. Please read the content and trigger warnings below for more information.

General content warnings for the bundle: The Vampire War is intended for mature audiences. This bundle contains mentions and detailed depictions of physical, emotional, mental, and sexual abuse, explicit language, sexually explicit scenes, extreme violence, murder, and blood drinking.

Night Shade Triggers

One magical dub-con scene, mentions of drug use and suicide, as well as detailed depictions of sexual and physical assault.

Night Fury Triggers

Mentions of rape, sexual harassment, as well as and detailed depictions of suicidal thoughts, and torture including sexual and physical assault. This book also heavily discusses negative self-talk, feelings of unworthiness and inadequacy, criticism, depression, PTSD, manipulation, trauma, amnesia, and therapy.

The following kinks have also been included in this work: agoraphilia, begging, breeding, praise, primal, Dom and Brat behavior, breath play, and spanking.

Night Fall Triggers

Mentions of rape and torture including castration and sodomy. Detailed depictions of suicidal thoughts and attempts, and sexual harassment and assault. This book also discusses and depicts grief, deaths of love ones, near death experiences, war, negative self-talk, feelings of unworthiness and inadequacy, criticism, depression, and amnesia.

The following kinks have also been included in this work: begging, praise, degradation, Pleasure Dom and Brat behavior, breath play, and spanking.

FULL BUNDLE PLAYLIST

Want to listen along while you read? Search The Vampire War on Spotify or scan the QR code below:

Streets - Doja Cat
Telepatia - Kali Uchis
Off Limits - BAYNK, Glades
Horoscope - Young Cereal, Baby Frankie
Surrender - Cash Cash
Throwaway (with Clairo) - SG Lewis
Always Been You - Jessie Murph
Crazy In Love - Sofia Karlberg
Sweater Weather - Kurt Hugo Schneider, Alyson Stoner, Max S
Middle Of The Night - Elley Duhe
Into You - Ariana Grande
Excuses - Audrey Mika
Alone (feat. Brielle Von Hugel) - NERVO, Askery

Bring Me To Life - Evanescence
Feel Good - Gryffin, ILLENIUM, feat. Daya

A Little More - Alessia Cara
One Night - Christina Perri
Light Me Up - RL Grime, Miguel, Julia Michaels
Not Giving In - Tom Walker
Waking Up - MJ Cole, Freya Ridings
Mind Is A Prison - Alec Benjamin
Artistry - Jacob Lee
Good Enough - Evanescence
Courage To Change - Sia
Hollow - Submersed
Distance - Yebba
Shadows - Canyon City

Iris - The Goo Goo Dolls
Can't Help Falling In Love - DARK - Tommee Profitt, Brooke
War of Hearts - Ruelle
Good Enough - Evanescence
Hurts Like Hell - Fleurie, Tommee Profitt
Still Here - Digital Daggers
Falling Apart - Skylar Grey
Dancing With Your Ghost - Sasha Alex Sloan
First Thing To Go - Hayley Williams
Razors Edge - Digital Daggers
Letters From The Sky - Civil Twilight
Far Away - Nickelback
Heal Over - KT Tunstall
Inside Out - Zedd feat. Griff
Royalty - Egzod, Maestro Chives, Neoni
Never Stop (Wedding Version) - SafetySuit
Queen Of The Night - Hey Violet

NIGHT SHADE

CHAPTER 1

The mattress squeaked underneath them. Sweat glistened off Daniella's skin as she rode Alexander, working them closer to ecstasy. Alexander gripped her hips hard as he fucked her, bruising her skin, slamming into the slick heat of her body. She knew he was close.

Daniella ground her hips in response, her eyes drifting shut as her head fell back. No longer did she see the pale man beneath her, with his curly, sandy hair sticking to his forehead, and his heated brown eyes. Instead, he shifted in her mind, changing into the one she truly desired. Her fantasy lover. It was his silky brown hair, his darkened eyes, his smell, his taste.

Yes, yes!

His was the body beneath hers, filling her, bringing her closer to climax.

The familiar shiver started at the base of her spine, circulating throughout her body, and then it snapped hard, making her cry out as she came. In three quick strokes, Alexander joined her with a loud, guttural moan.

DANIELLA DRAPED HER DARK BROWN LEGS OVER THE EDGE OF THE bed. Her orgasm left her feeling warm, relaxed, until the man behind her stirred.

"Another go?" Alexander smirked as he thumbed a new condom.

She cringed. Her stomach knotted, a deep weight settling within as her intuition flared to life. It demanded he leave. If it weren't for the few glasses of wine she'd had before he called, she would have never allowed him into her home, or *her*.

Daniella stepped away from the bed to retrieve her robe. "No, I've got to get ready for work."

Alexander purred. "It could wait."

She could feel his gaze. It roamed over her like a slithering snake ready to strike.

Daniella narrowed her eyes. "No, it can't." She lifted her dark curly hair from the collar of her robe and tied the sash tight around her midsection in finality. "I'm sorry if you're confused, but nothing about our deal has changed. I came, you came, and now it's time to go. I have things to do, and I'm sure you do as well, *elsewhere*."

Alexander's feet hit the floor and she breathed a sigh of relief. She turned to give him privacy while he dressed, but her body refused to relax as the feeling within her gut grew heavier.

He's leaving. Just give him a couple of minutes.

Daniella pressed the button to open the long pink and gold drapes covering her floor-to-ceiling windows. Her gaze settled on the breathtaking view from her penthouse floor, unobstructed by the surrounding New York skyscrapers. The soft rays of the sun were low against the horizon, but still magnificent in the way their rosy tints contrasted through the early morning blues.

The scene almost calmed her, but then a noise shattered the serenity. Daniella turned and found Alexander behind her, still naked and much too close. She took a step back, and he took another forward, caging her against the glass.

He smirked as he grabbed ahold of her chin, his lips hovering near her own. "Now come on, Daniella, we both know you didn't mean no."

She narrowed her eyes and quickly slapped his hand away. But before she could speak, he covered her mouth and pressed against her. "Or do you just like it rough, pet?"

Her fight-or-flight response went into high gear, flooding her with adrenaline. Daniella opened her mouth and bit his hand, hard. Alexander chuckled at the pain as if it were nothing, but he pulled back just enough to give her an opening. Daniella used the space to twist, and then flew forward, throwing a punch at his head.

Alexander jumped back and threw up his hands, but that asinine smile was still on his face. "Alright, I'll go. No need to be so hasty. But just remember, I'm only here because you agreed to let me in. I don't know why you're playing hard to get now when I was deep inside you not even ten minutes ago."

"And I think it's hilarious you think it's an act." She glared at him, clenching her fists. "You're right, I let you into my home, but you know what? Everyone makes mistakes they wish they could take back. So, let me be perfectly clear since you didn't understand the first two times. You have two choices.

Either you leave my house willingly, or I will haul you out myself."

He let out a low whistle and backed away, grabbing his clothes and shoes. "Whatever you say, babe. Whatever you say."

IT WOULDN'T GO AWAY. THE NAGGING, SOUL-WRENCHING FEELING that something was wrong had buried itself deep in Daniella's gut. If she was being honest, the feeling had been there for the past two weeks, but it had never been this intense.

Before, it was a whisper, something she could turn a blind eye to. It didn't worry her; it wasn't even a blight on her day. But today, everything felt drenched in the icky, sinking blackness. Even after her cup of coffee, warm bath, and meditative session, she still felt filthy.

Perhaps the situation with Alexander had bothered her more than she'd realized. He'd never acted that way before. But today ... Daniella shook her head. It didn't matter. She would never see or speak to him again, and if he tried anything, she could always rely on the guards in the lobby.

Daniella blocked his number, and on her way out she had a quick chat with both security guards. Under no circumstances was he to enter her floor, or the building, without her authorization. After confirming she was all right, they replied with a sincere, "Of course, Miss Ismania."

But despite that, the feeling remained, and if her intuition was right, she was in for a hell of a day. With a sigh, Daniella thanked the guards, before she scurried out the door and set off to work.

CHAPTER 2

The Novak Firm was Daniella's home away from home. She loved her work, the company, and, most of all, the people. Yet the moment she entered through the double doors, she almost vomited.

Panic and dread crept up her spine, making her shudder. She labored her way to her office and stashed her breakfast in her mini refrigerator. After she logged into her computer, she saw an urgent email calling the executive team to meet in Conference Room B for an emergency meeting. Taking a deep breath to steady her nerves, she made her way to the room, pen and paper in hand.

The moment she opened the door and saw Luke's face, some of her tension eased. Luke had been her best friend for the last four years. They met in college as dorm neighbors and bonded over their differences. She appreciated his out-of-the-box thinking, creative spirit, and how it directly contrasted with her analytical and serious personality. He loved to laugh, to make others smile, to throw caution to the wind. Luke taught her how to have fun, to balance her dedication to work while still appreciating life. He'd introduced her to his cousins, Gregori and Mya, and they had embraced her as if she was a missing part of their family.

When Luke told her that he and Greg wanted to start a business, it didn't surprise her. But when he asked her to help with their accounting part-time, she'd nearly fallen out of her chair. Wanting to support her friends, she said yes, but she never imagined that decision would have put her on the path to becoming the CFO of a now multi-million-dollar agency.

"Good morning, sunshine," Luke said with a small smile.

"Good morning to you too." She paused, taking in his ruffled copper hair and slightly wrinkled clothing. "Is it still going to be a good morning after this meeting?"

"I wish I knew, Dani. I wish I knew."

Before she could respond, the door opened behind her and the air rushed out of her lungs. Her nerve endings awoke, firing so fast that goosebumps erupted over her skin. She shivered from the sudden change in body temperature and bit her bottom lip to keep from gasping. The expansive energy washed over her and spread throughout the room—dark, hot, seductive. Daniella didn't need to see who was behind her. There was only one person who had ever made her feel this way.

"Good morning, Ella." The deep baritone of Greg's voice rolled over her in waves.

She straightened in her chair, trying to disguise her body's natural response to him. "Good morning, Greg."

He walked to the head chair, coming to stand between herself and Luke. While he conversed with Luke, she looked him over. Gregori Novak was breathtaking. He was a six-foot-six

Adonis covered in toned bronze skin that made his Spanish heritage proud. His russet-colored hair fell to his ears, complementing his sharp jaw and strong facial features. While Greg considered his eyes to be brown, she had stolen enough glances at him to know they were, in fact, hazel. They took on a life of their own, becoming lighter or darker depending on his mood, sometimes even light enough for her to see their pale jade depths. They drew her in, enticed her, while his lips could—and often did—convince her of anything. And if that wasn't enough, he also had a perfectly shaped ass.

Luke cleared his throat and she blushed at being caught ogling. Luckily, the door opened once more, saving her from any additional embarrassment.

Once the rest of the executive team arrived, Greg took his seat, drawing their attention. "Now that you're all here, let's begin."

The room fell silent when Greg uttered the single word "embezzled".

"Embezzled? What the fuck do you mean, embezzled?" Mya snapped.

His eyes narrowed. Mya's anger was second to none and she was about to unleash it in full force. "Mya—"

"Do not 'Mya' me right now. How the fuck did this happen?"

"We don't know. But this is a time for solutions, not anger."

"I go away for two weeks, two fucking weeks, and this happens?" she grumbled.

Greg's eyes bore into Mya's, warning her to keep her mouth shut. She sat back in her chair with a frustrated sigh, crossing her arms while still glaring in his direction. That was as good as he would get, and he'd take the small blessing.

He scanned the room, observing his team. Merida and Dominick appeared calm and collected, even though he knew they were brimming with rage. Luke had also known of the news prior to the meeting, which was the only reason he hadn't lashed out like Mya.

Greg's gaze lingered on Daniella, who concerned him the most. Her amber eyes stared down at the table, unblinking. She may have hidden it well, but the death grip on her pen told him exactly how upset she was. She took her job seriously and was devoted to not only the company, but his family as well.

"Aren't there accounting principles and security measures in place to prevent things like this from happening?" Johanna asked. "I'm sorry, but I'm with Mya. I don't understand how this could have occurred."

As his Chief Human Resources Officer, Greg knew she had a right to this table. He could understand her concerns, especially if anything might affect funds for wages and benefits, but he did not appreciate her subtle accusation of blame toward Daniella and Merida.

"That's an excellent question, Johanna," Merida said as she laced her fingers together. "The security and accounting protocols that we have in place are why we made this discovery so quickly. This is a jarring and confusing time for all of us, but we will collaborate with the pertinent parties to find the perpetrator and fix any security issues in our processes. If you have any questions regarding this incident, please be sure to come to my office and I will do my best to explain everything to you."

"Thank you," Johanna responded, giving Merida a curt nod.

Greg continued, holding the gaze of each person around the

table as he spoke. "I know this is a stressful time for everyone. Your behavior here shows how much you care about this corporation and the dreams that Luke and I founded this company upon. We thank you and are confident that we will overcome this setback."

He motioned to his security team. "Merida and Dominick's team will be speaking with each of you and your departments. We trust that if you have seen anything suspicious, you will be forthcoming with any information you may have. As Merida has already stated, if you have any questions, please direct them to her. Thank you."

Greg watched as Daniella stood, her expression tight as she left the room. Johanna followed after her, leaving him, Mya, Merida, Luke, and Dominick behind.

The moment the door shut, Mya sat forward, and slammed her hands down upon the table. "Now that the fake bullshit is over, tell me what really happened."

CHAPTER 3

Greg paused outside of the door to Daniella's office, his fingers clutching the brass handle. *You have to. Just keep it together for a little longer. Remember, you're keeping her in the dark to protect her. She can't know, not yet.* He took a deep breath, rolled his shoulders back, and stepped across the threshold.

Daniella froze, her fingers hovering above her keyboard. Trepidation flashed across her face when she saw him, and even though it was only for a moment, it made his heart ache.

Greg cleared his throat against the emotion as he closed the door behind him and shut the horizontal blinds. "I didn't mean to startle you."

"No, it's all right." Her voice was tight, clipped, and he hated it.

Greg sighed. "Ella, come here."

They met in the middle, somewhere between him reaching out to pull her into his embrace and her curling herself around him. "It's not your fault."

Daniella trembled in his arms. "But it is." She lifted her face from his chest. "It's my job to make sure that the company's finances are squared away, and I failed. Someone stole money from here, from us!"

She moved away from him and began to pace, her hands flying wildly in the air as she spoke. "I've been backtracking through all of my reports, trying to make sure this has never happened before. What if I missed something? What if that's the cause for all of this? They got away with it once and thought they could again?"

He caught her hands in in his own. "Ella, this is not your fault. You are brilliant and an incredible accountant. Because of you, we know exactly how much was taken. If your reports were not as detailed as they are, or if your data was not up-to-date, we would be screwed."

She looked away, but Greg grasped her chin, forcing her gaze back to his. "Give yourself some credit. You saved us. You, no one else. I see it that way, we all do. None of us blame you, and I'm not going to sit here and let you blame yourself either."

She shook her head with a sigh. "I just don't know, Greg, I just don't know."

"Well, I do," he replied with a tap on her chin.

Greg forced himself to step away from her, and led her to her office chairs, where they sat facing one another.

Daniella tucked a loose strand of hair behind her ear, an action Greg wished he could have done for her. "Thank you for comforting me, but you're the one who had your money stolen. How are you doing?"

"I'm okay. Disappointed, but okay."

"But how are you so calm? Why aren't you angry or frustrated?"

Greg rubbed the center of his forehead. "Because someone has to be. Luke was only calm because he knew beforehand. Without that, between Volcano Luke and Hurricane Mya, someone would have lost their head."

Daniella hiccuped a laugh, clamping her hand over her mouth to keep the sound contained.

He chuckled at how effortlessly adorable she was and then reminded himself to mask his emotions, because he wasn't joking. But that didn't matter, right now, all he wanted was to see Daniella laugh, see the way her mocha-colored eyes twinkled in delight, and how her shoulders relaxed as the stress left her body. He wanted his mate to be safe.

"I'm sorry, I'm sorry. It's just, those two are something else. I don't know how any of you survived to this age," she said with a smile.

"It was difficult, I can tell you that."

Daniella looked him over, then leaned back in her chair, and crossed her arms. "Greg, there's something you're not telling me. What are you hiding that kept me from finding out about the embezzlement before that meeting?"

His smile wavered. "Sometimes you know me far too well."

"Maybe, but I also know when you're trying to change the subject. What is it?"

Greg ran his fingers through his hair before clasping his hands together. He slouched forward, elbows resting on his knees. "A security alert was released early this morning. Since Mya was on her way back from her vacation, she didn't receive the notification, but her team and the security team did. They looked into the matter quickly and found that the bank transfers were initiated internally. Both teams scanned the system three times." He paused as his gaze met hers. "The credentials that were used to log in last night and triggered the alert were yours."

Daniella gasped. "What?"

"Ella, we know it wasn't you. But the person who did this, they were smart. They left almost no trace. Even Mya is having a tough time tracking them down, but they left that information, which means they did it on purpose."

"Oh my God!" Daniella squeezed the bridge of her nose as she held her face in her hands.

He leaned forward and stroked her forearm. "Hey, what did we say? This was not your fault. I need you to understand that. A competitor could have done this. You are one of the founding pillars of this company. It wouldn't have been hard to get your name. Our entire team's roster is up on the website."

"But my fucking credentials aren't!"

"No, they're not, which makes me think it was an inside job."

"I don't leave my credentials lying around the office, Greg," Daniella bit out.

"I know you don't," he said softly, "but anyone on the IT or security team with enough know-how could have stolen them. We're a growing company. We're interviewing and filling positions that we have never had before."

"So it could literally be anyone?"

He nodded. "Yes. I have an idea of how to figure this out, but I need your help."

Daniella looked up at him. "Greg, whatever you need, just ask me."

"I need you to take a vacation."

Her eyebrows rose. "I'm sorry, what?"

"There are only so many reasons someone would want to go after you here, one of which would be to steal your position. If you were gone for a couple of weeks, that person would think things were working in their favor. Then they'd start rumors, try to help more than necessary, and we would find out who's really responsible."

"Case closed."

"Exactly." He could see the wheels turning in her head as she pondered the plan.

"Greg, if you think this will work, I'll do it, but it doesn't feel right to me. Why go this far just to get me fired? There are plenty of easier ways to try. It feels like they're not only going after me, but the company as well."

"I don't think they're only after you, either. But I do think you're a part of their plan and this was the only way they could try to get rid of you. You can't reason with someone's irrational logic, and we won't know exactly what is going on until we catch them."

Daniella took a deep breath. "Okay. I'll stay out of the office for a few weeks. But I'm going to monitor every transaction that comes in or out of the corporate account. While I may be willing to cooperate with this ruse, there's no way I'm letting the accounting get that far behind."

Greg smiled as some of the tension left his body. "Yes, ma'am."

ANYONE WHO WATCHED GREG WALK OUT OF THE ELEVATOR AND down the hall—his steps measured, back straight, head held high—would think he was having a nice, calm day. But that calm was a practiced lie. The moment he shut the door to his office, the deep-seated rage and need for justice broke out of him. His fingers curled around the mahogany desk, tightening to the point that he left impressions in the thick wood.

Breathe, he commanded himself. *Breathe before you lose it.*

Today was a nightmare, and it wasn't over yet. As the president of this company, it was his job to make sure that he appeared professional at all times. But as the current leader of the Novak Clan, the reigning circle of vampires in the Northeast United States, it was his duty to be ready at every moment. He did not get peace, he did not get pity, and when his people died, he took it personally. Greg carried the weight of his title with his muscles tense and ready for battle at every turn, and now they sensed a new opponent charging towards his door.

Luke stormed into his office, shouting a millisecond after the door had slammed against its frame. "Gregori, what the hell do you think you're doing?"

"Lucas," he warned, but his cousin was clearly in a red haze and did not understand how close Greg was to losing control.

"You sent Daniella away? What the fuck is the matter with you? How could you ever believe she's the reason for any of this?"

Greg's anger was feeding into his power, his need to unleash, to break, to destroy. He counted backward from one hundred, trying to tune out the accusations.

"Did you not see how hurt she was? None of this would have happened if you had taken the proper steps to ensure her safety!"

"Enough!" Greg's eyes flashed red and he slammed his fist so hard against the desk, it buckled under the blow. His power surged around him like a shock wave. The room darkened, shadow seizing light as Greg's powers expanded and grew. The black was so dense that it blocked out the sun's strong rays.

Luke froze, his mouth hanging open at his explosion.

Greg's voice was low, dark, when he said, "Do you think to question my judgment?"

"Most days," Luke replied, his retort earning him a growl.

Greg closed his eyes again. *Breathe in, breathe out.* He balled his fist and called his power back to him. His family meant everything to him and he would never hurt them, but there were times when they pushed him too far. He could only take so much, and today was not the day to test him.

As Greg spoke, the glowing red of his eyes dimmed. "Let me connect the dots for you. Daniella's credentials were used to log into the system."

Luke's eyes narrowed. "I already know that."

"Then let me tell you something you clearly missed while you were busy berating me. They left them there on *purpose*. The attack on our finances was done directly after the attack on our people, by Zachariah. Not because he needed the money, but because he knows, Luke. He knows Daniella is my mate."

His cousin gasped. "That's impossible, the only people who know—"

"Work in this building." Greg rubbed the corner of his eyes and sighed. "They're the only people who have seen us together, and only an immortal would have been able to sense our connection. We have a mole, Luke. Daniella is not safe here, nor is she safe at her home. That is why I sent her away."

"Greg—"

He shook his head. "I know how much you care about her, and you know how I feel about her as well. But we lost twenty-two people last night from the attack." Greg clenched his fists again. "I have already failed those people. I am responsible for their deaths, and when I catch Zachariah, I will enjoy watching the blood drain from his body. But Daniella…" He shuddered at the thought. "I will never, ever risk her life or her safety. I can't."

CHAPTER 4

Daniella kept her head down as she exited the building. She'd been successful in avoiding everyone until she ran into Luke at the elevator. She told him about Greg's plan, knowing he'd be upset if he wasn't included. He was quiet at first—never a good sign with him—but when his jaw ticked, she knew he was about to erupt.

She tried to explain it to him once more, but it was like talking to a brick wall. Luke could be over-protective and he wasn't one to change his mind, or listen to reason when he was seething. He ignored her, cursed, then set on a warpath towards Gregori's office. She felt bad for Greg and the whirlwind barreling in his direction, but if anyone could handle Luke, it was him.

She sent Luke a quick text to call her once he'd calmed down, and then another one to ask him if he'd grab her laptop and drop it off at her house tonight. It killed her to leave it there, unattended for the afternoon, especially after her credentials had been used, but she needed to keep up the ruse of a questionable probationary period. She tried to convince herself that they would find the perpetrator, but the task seemed incredulous.

Go home and relax. Take a nice long bath, order an extra-large pizza, and drink a tall glass of chardonnay. That's all you can do right now.

Yet the moment she thought of her home, her stomach churned.

Glancing at her watch, she realized it was noon. She hadn't eaten all day. Once she had some food in her, she'd feel better. That was the only thing that made sense.

Daniella stopped at a little corner café and ordered herself a delicious steak and horseradish melt with a generous portion of avocado, and a raspberry lemonade. She chose a seat outside, where she could enjoy the warm sun and cool breeze. Nature always helped to balance her out. But when she thought of going home again, her stomach cramped so hard she almost vomited.

What was going on? She'd never felt this way before. And to be this sick, especially all day? She knew not to disregard her feelings. How many times had her foresight helped her to avoid the worst? But this? Now? Her home had always made her feel safe, so this had to be something else.

Instead of going home, Daniella stopped in every store she could think of and even took a trip to the museum, trying to enjoy the many sculptures and extravagant paintings. But then the sun began to set, and when she checked her watch it was after 6:00 p.m. Luke usually left the office around that time, and if he'd gotten her message, he'd be on his way over with her laptop. Thinking of him made her feel better. Maybe she'd entice him with the pizza and he could stay and have a bite too.

Maybe I should call and ask him to pick me up? Daniella shook her head at the ridiculous notion. She was fine, everything was fine, and yet with every step closer to her home, she felt worse.

With her building in view, she heard the familiar soft tones of a violin. Daniella used the opportunity for distraction and turned past the topiary and towards the melody's creator, Stacy.

Her friendship with Stacy had begun strangely. Stacy played outside of tall complexes and skyscrapers, handing out flyers for her performances to anyone she could. She always went for the "big fish" and had figured Daniella to be one. But somewhere between Stacy's over-energetic and pushy nature, and her beautiful way of enthralling someone with her music, Daniella had grown to love her, even if she hadn't been given much of a choice. Stacy simply felt good to be around. She was a positive force in Daniella's life, but the moment her eyes landed on Stacy's small blonde form, bile sputtered from her mouth and she turned to vomit into a bush.

Stacy ran over to her and placed her hand on Daniella's back. But instead of a feeling of comfort, Stacy's touch felt like daggers piercing her skin. Daniella pulled away as more bile and unrecognizable chunks spat from her mouth. *It's never been this bad.*

"Dani, are you okay?"

"Yes," she gasped, begging her stomach to stop dry heaving. "I-I'm fine," she lied. "I think I have the stomach flu. I'm sorry for worrying you. Go back to playing, I'm okay."

Stacy reached out to her. "Dani, you look horrible. Come on, let me help you—"

"No!"

Stacy jerked back and Daniella stumbled to her knees. She wiped her mouth with the back of her hand, eyes watering as she looked up at Stacy. "The stomach flu has been going around the office. I guess I'm its next victim." She braved a laugh, but Stacy still seemed skeptical. Daniella noticed her clasp her hand tightly to her chest, as if she'd been stung or wounded. "I'm sorry, did I hurt you?"

"No, no. I've probably just been playing too long. But are you sure you're okay? I can help you back to your house?"

Daniella winced at the instant headache brought on by the mention of her home. "No, it's okay. I don't want to make you sick too. Plus, someone will try to take your spot if you're not here."

"Yeah, they're a bunch of vultures." Stacy sighed, turning to check and make sure that no one had touched her violin or taken the money in her case. Then she shifted her focus back on Daniella. "I am going to watch you and make sure you make it into your building, and when you get upstairs, take some medicine and call me after you've rested a little, okay?"

Daniella smiled, but shook her head when Stacy offered to help her up again. "I've got it."

She stood and closed her eyes for a moment. Taking a deep breath, she focused on her mother's mantra, one of the few traditions she had left of her. *I am one with the earth. I am one with the Mother. She flows through me. She offers me her guidance, and I can make it through anything.*

After the third time, Daniella opened her eyes only to meet Stacy's crystal blue orbs clouded with concern. "I'm feeling better. Don't worry," she said, hoping she sounded convincing enough.

Stacy mumbled something in German and rolled her eyes.

"I will always worry about you. You're always working. You don't take care of yourself." She threw her hands in the air. "I work on the street and I'm healthier than you. If I find you passed out in front of your building, I'll call an ambulance for you, only after I knock you upside the back of your head."

Daniella gave a real laugh this time. "Yes, mother. But you may want to save that for the man getting a little too close to your money."

Stacy turned and stomped towards the stranger, all five-foot-three of her yelling in a mixture of English and German.

Daniella shuffled to her building, counting the steps. Anything to draw attention away from the familiar blackness. The war between her physical body and whatever was bothering her intuition was so intense that she felt lightheaded. Opening the door to her building, she looked around for the night guard, but his post was vacant.

That's odd.

Stacy played right outside of her building, and she had been shouting obscenities. He must have just gone to make sure that everything was all right, and Daniella had missed him by the time she made it to the door.

Her stomach lurched again and she rushed to the elevator. She scanned her keycard, entered, and felt triumphant the moment she pressed the penthouse floor. She'd made it!

Slouching against the golden mirrored wall, her relief was replaced by a buzzing under her skin, as if a second beat had started in her heart, renewing her strength. Her body flooded with a mixture of bliss and energetic adrenaline, and for the first time she questioned if everything that she'd felt had been some sort of anxiety attack, or a mixture between that and her normal intuitive feelings. After all, she'd had a horrible morning, barely eaten, and had been on edge for the entire day. Perhaps what she'd believed was her intuition was really an ugly ball of fear and stress, and she had simply made herself sick. Maybe she really did need to take a vacation, get out of town for a couple of days. Maybe Stacy was right. Maybe she was overworking herself.

As she touched the handle of her apartment door, it shocked her. Daniella wrung her hand from the zing of static electricity and tried again, her fingers still tingling from the jolt. This time, the handle moved and she entered her home. Yet, instead of feeling relief, a fresh wave of dizziness hit her so hard that she rushed towards the half bathroom in case she was going to hurl. Her body stopped mid-motion, held back by something she couldn't comprehend. She tried again to move forward, to no avail.

Someone chuckled behind her, and her hair stood on end.

"Oh, Daniella, I'm not going to let you get away that easily. I have to punish you for making me wait."

CHAPTER 5

Daniella gasped. What was Alexander doing in her house? She had made sure he left this morning. How did he get in here?

"What the fuck are you doing in my house?" She thrashed, trying to break out of his hold as he tightened his arms around her from behind.

"Not so fast, sweetheart." He grabbed her chin, forcing her head to the side. "You love to think you're in control. It's a bad complex that you have, really, but you're not, nor have you ever been."

Daniella squirmed and fought against him, but his arms held her in place. No matter how hard she tried, he was unmovable.

Her heartbeat thundered in her ears. *Calm down and think! Remember your self defense lessons. Focus on your opponent.*

He was stronger than her, so she had to be smarter than him. She had to wait for her chance. Daniella couldn't reach her phone, and no one would hear her scream from here. Alexander would give her an opening, eventually. She just had to wait. By then, Luke would find them and she'd have an ally in her fight. Hopefully. She just had to wait.

Keep him talking, your life depends on it. "What do you want?"

Alexander shrugged behind her. "It depends on the day. Some days it's world domination, other days to feed, others to fuck, and, occasionally, to take everything away from my enemies. I appreciate you for assisting with all of them."

Daniella shuddered. World domination? To feed? *What the hell is wrong with him?* "You're sick."

He snickered. "No, I'm driven. Besides, you only have yourself to blame for the situation you're in." His hand slid over her breast and he squeezed it hard.

Daniella's body recoiled in disgust.

"If you had let me get inside of that thick head of yours earlier, I would have spent the rest of the day fucking you. Then, who knows? I might have been able to spare you. But alas, you were too stubborn for your own good." Alexander purred. "Although, there's no reason I can't have fun with you before I rip out your throat." He bent his head to her neck, sucking at her skin.

Daniella held back the bile that rose in her throat.

Just a little more, she told herself.

His hold on her torso loosened as he moved his hand to grip her through her pants.

Now! She bent forward and then snapped back as hard as she could, slamming the back of her skull into his nose.

Alexander yelped and his arm dropped. Daniella fought against the dizziness and stumbled toward the door, but she wasn't fast enough. Before she knew it, he grabbed her by the neck and slammed her against the wall so hard she saw stars.

"Oh, I'm going to enjoy this," he said, and when her eyes focused, she could see a smirk playing on his lips.

The door to her home blew apart. Alexander swung her around, using her body as a shield from the debris. Daniella's heart stopped when she saw the cause. Greg. He looked furious and his eyes were ... red?

Gregori moved toward her but stopped when Alexander tightened his grip on her neck.

Alexander tsked. "Now, you wouldn't want me to break your mate's neck, would you, Gregori?"

Mate? She didn't have time to focus on the word as Alexander's nails dug into her throat.

"Let her go," Greg demanded.

Alexander chuckled. "I don't think so. That was never going to happen, not when I found out this tasty little morsel was your mate. She's quite delicious, really, and a fantastic fuck."

She could see the wheels turning in Greg's mind. Daniella wanted so badly to reach out to him, to connect with him, her salvation, but she knew she couldn't, not until she was free of Alexander's grasp.

His grip tightened again, forcing her to gasp for air. She tried to claw Alexander's hand from around her neck, but her eyes filled with tears and her vision clouded. Even though she couldn't see Greg, she could feel him. Her body responded to his, nerve endings firing under her skin even as breathing became difficult. She fought recklessly, struggling, gasping, writhing to break free.

Please, I don't want to die here.

Greg snarled, and a dark, deep-seated rage filled her. Something crawled beneath her skin, ripping her apart. The chains of her consciousness rattled until they snapped, and a single certainty filled her mind. She would *not* die here.

"Ella!" Greg yelled.

Daniella's hands fell from Alexander's grip around her neck as her body hummed with energy. "Let me go," she choked out.

Alexander laughed. "This one's a handful! She really thinks she can take on a vampire. Cute. Does she know that you and your little family are vampires? How weak and pathetic you all are? You've spent centuries trying to stop the vampire wars when so many lives could have been saved, including hers."

"I said, let me go!" Purple sparks of electricity shot out from her, attacking the thing that held her hostage. She no longer saw it as a human, no longer recognized it as a lifeform. She wanted it to bleed, to suffer, to no longer exist in this world.

Alexander screamed, throwing her away from him as he fell back against the wall. Daniella clutched at her throat, coughing, spasming with each new full breath.

Greg leapt onto her attacker. They tumbled, and hissed curses and growls came from their tangled bodies that moved much too fast. The blurs careened back and forth, crashing against the walls and into objects, shattering glass and wood, denting metal. But then their bodies flew, smacking against the glass in such fury that it shattered and the blurs were no more. They had fallen out of her window and into the night.

Her vision darkened and she collapsed with one final thought. Alexander couldn't have survived that fall, and neither could Greg.

CHAPTER 6

Daniella shifted under what felt like an enveloping cloud. She was so warm, so comfortable in the weighted softness that she never wished to leave. But her mind pleaded with her to open her eyes.

When she did, she saw two forms in the darkness. They were speaking in hushed tones so low she couldn't hear. One opened a door and light illuminated their silhouettes and she realizes it was a man and a woman. Immediately she felt safe, loved; they were familiar to her. Yet, when she tried to lift her head to greet them, it pounded with such violence that she fell back onto the pillow and groaned.

"Dani?" a familiar voice said. "Hey, hey!" They rushed to her side and pressed on her shoulders. "Don't try to get up, okay? I don't want you to pass out again."

Even though she heard and understood what the voice was saying, she tried with more determination to rise. Something important had happened. If only she could fight through the pain to understand, to remember.

Please stop, Daniella begged the pounding in her head, and her eyes grew wide when it did. *What the fuck?*

She heard the soft click of a light and shielded herself from its luminescence. Once her eyes adjusted, she could finally see the face beside her. "Luke?"

His shoulders sagged. "You remember me, that's good."

Daniella shook her head, smiling. "Of course I remember you, silly. Why wouldn't I?"

And then she remembered everything else.

Her mind shattered into a million pieces, just as the glass in her apartment had done when Greg flew out of it.

"Greg," she hiccuped, a sob trapped in her throat. "He ... He—"

Luke smiled and patted her hand. "He's fine."

"No, I saw him. Luke, I saw him!"

"Shh." He squeezed her arms. "Who do you think brought you here?"

"But he couldn't—"

She clutched at her chest. Her body shook, pulsing unnaturally as the room swayed in and out of focus. Alexander had said they were vampires. Vampires weren't real. They were nothing more than a fairytale. But Greg couldn't have survived that fall unless...

She stared at Luke, wide-eyed. "He's...you're all vampires."

He grimaced. "Dani—"

Static electricity surged around her. "Please get away from me."

"Dani, please, let me explain—"

She struck out her hand. "Stay away!" The walls seemed to

be closing in around her. Gasping, she pleaded, "Please, I-I don't want to hurt you."

Luke nodded, taking several steps back until he stood in the middle of the room. "Just breathe, okay? Inhale and exhale. You can do it, Dani."

But she couldn't. The room felt heavy, out of focus, spinning out of control. She closed her eyes, clutching at her chest. It was an anxiety attack. She used to have them as a child after her mother died, but it had been so long ago that she couldn't remember all the steps to calm down.

Breathe, she commanded to no avail. She clawed at her skin, begging her body to pull in more air. But each breath felt stale, unmoving, like sucking in cement.

The door slammed open, the noise so loud that it shocked her. A gust of cold air was the only warning she had before strong, warm hands squeezed her arms.

"Ella." Greg's voice pulled at her, connecting to something beneath the panic, something strong, wild, "It's okay, everything is okay."

He's here! Daniella chanted internally, but her mind couldn't rationalize it. How was he here? Confusion changed to fear, and she began to lose control.

"Get away, please. Something's wrong." She pushed at Greg's shoulders, but he wouldn't budge.

"Listen to me. Look at me." He cupped her chin.

Daniella obeyed, her eyes meeting his own, and it felt as if he was peering into her very soul.

"You're not going to hurt me. Whatever is going on, whatever this is, release it."

"Greg—"

"Let me help you. Trust me, Daniella."

He leaned so close that she could smell his unique scent, spicy wood wrapped in cinnamon and musk. Her eyes drifted shut as she breathed him in, trembling. When she breathed out, the room blew apart.

A window exploded as air forced its way in, whipping around her. Large vines traveled through the opening, winding around furniture and electronics, crushing them, breaking them apart under their heavy weight. They poured and poured and poured so fast, until they suddenly stopped.

Daniella gasped, drawing back and taking in the carnage she had caused. Her eyes darted around the room, and the vision made her skin pale. In less than three seconds, she had destroyed everything.

This is impossible. How could I have done all of this? This can't be real, there's just no way—

She gasped. "Wait. Luke. Where's Luke? He was here when—"

"He's fine," Greg interrupted. "He came to get me when you started having an anxiety attack. Do you feel better?" he asked, rubbing her cheek.

Daniella splayed her arms wide. "Greg, look at what I did!"

"But do you feel better?" He smiled, cocking his head to the side.

She couldn't figure it out. Was he really here, kneeling in front of her, smiling, after everything that had happened? But she knew how those hands felt against her skin, how connected she felt to him when their eyes met, how he made her feel safe. A million different people could act, look, and seem like him, but there was something deep within her that would always know the difference.

Daniella took another deep breath, letting his warmth seep

into her skin. She stared into Greg's eyes, searching for answers to questions she couldn't comprehend. They were jade now, reminding her of a pale moonstone, and yet glowed from within with a power she could almost feel.

"He hurts for you. Hunts. Protects. He waits," voices whispered to her.

Daniella drew back. She searched for whoever, whatever, had spoken to her, but couldn't find the source. As strange as it was, the voices soothed her panic, leaving a welcomed feeling of reassurance.

"He waits," they said again.

Greg frowned. "Ella? Are you okay?"

She needed to be here at this moment. Whatever this was, it would figure itself out along the way and she would get a handle on it in time. Daniella bit the inside of her cheek. "Is it weird if I say yes?"

Greg slumped forward, a small smile teasing at his lips. "Not at all. It's been a weird day." He stood and lifted her in his arms, cradling her to his chest.

She squealed at the sudden movement and wrapped her arms around his neck. "What are you doing?"

He chuckled. "Exactly what it looks like, carrying you."

Daniella scowled. "I can walk, you know."

"Not barefoot on vines and broken glass. Plus, you don't know your way around here yet."

They emerged from the room into full light and her mouth fell open in awe. Floor-to-ceiling windows covered an entire wall, providing a glorious view of the mountains. *Mountains?* She gripped his shoulder. *This isn't New York City. Where am I?*

She took in the walls, paneled in a deep royal blue that reflected the warm light from the golden sconces. The ceiling lights behind them dimmed as those ahead brightened, activated by each step Greg took. Turning her head over his shoulder, she could see a black ornate banister that wrapped the landing and led downstairs just before Greg shuffled her into a new room.

This room had a similar ambience—dark yet warm. The walls were painted a walnut brown. As he moved, she took in two doors—both closed—a black dresser, matching nightstands, and a large bed with a black padded headboard. Greg pulled the bedcovers back with one hand and then laid her down with care.

She sighed and let him pull the covers over her, but when he went to move away, she stopped him. "This is your house, isn't it?"

His gaze flickered away from hers, but then he nodded.

Daniella's eyes narrowed. "I thought you lived in the city."

Greg squatted beside her. "I kept this house off record so that anyone who stays here will be safe."

"And what happened to me earlier happens so often that you need to have a safehouse?"

"I know of this place, my family knows of this place, and now you do too." He moved his hand, holding her own, rubbing his thumb over her skin. "I just want you to be safe. That's all I've ever wanted."

"I suppose I should feel special," Daniella said sharply, "but, I'm beginning to understand just how much I don't know you at all. I didn't know where you lived or what you were. Are you even thirty?"

He winced.

"Right." She pulled her hand away from his, but he reached out to grab it again, trapping it between his palms.

"Ella, I know. I know I hid things from you, but that was never my intention. It was never what I wanted."

"And yet you did it anyway. Greg, we have been friends for years! I thought I knew you, and now I'm finding out that I don't. I just went through the worst experience of my life with someone who is apparently a complete stranger to me. How else am I supposed to feel? You lied to me, not once, not twice, but multiple times. How am I supposed to trust you?"

He cupped her cheek. She desperately wanted to pull away from his warmth, to let him know it wasn't that easy. But it was, and that made it even more infuriating.

"I never, ever wanted to lie to you. I never wanted to hide anything about myself from you. It has been one of the hardest things that I have ever done, but I did it to protect you."

Daniella scoffed, rolling her eyes.

"I'm serious, Ella. What happened to you today could have been much, much worse, and it happened to you because of me," he croaked. "I know you don't understand that right now, but when I explain everything, you will. I have to live with that on my conscience. I failed you. All the lying and hiding I've done didn't stop that from happening. Knowing that will bring me more despair than anything else in this world."

She gazed at him, at this strong man who seemed so vulnerable right now. She desperately wanted to believe him, to forgive him. But she couldn't, not without honesty.

"I asked you earlier today what you needed from me, and now I'm asking you, what do you want from me? How do I know everything you're saying isn't just pretty words, Greg?"

"Because you know me better than anyone." He tucked a strand of her hair behind her ear but froze at her bitter laugh.

"Then you clearly have some work to do."

"Maybe you're right. But I am being honest with you, right here, right now. Yes, I'm a vampire, and there's a past filled with history and knowledge that comes with that. I didn't give you the opportunity to learn those things about me, and that was wrong of me." He sighed. "But that's all they are. Things. They're just pieces of who I am. Do they make up a part of me? Yes, of course. But you ... I've never been like this with anyone but you. I have to be calm enough to make decisions, to protect my people, and to do that I have to leave my heart out of it. But I can't do that with you. I can't leave my heart out of it."

He kissed her hand, making her skin tingle. Greg stood, staring down at her with a saddened expression. He had never looked so lonely. The feeling washed over her with such strength that she had to grip the side of the bed to keep from reaching out to him.

"I'm sorry for the hurt that I've caused you and for betraying your trust. I understand if you can't see me the same way you used to, or if you can't trust me again, and while I will do everything I can to fix this, I understand it's not enough. The only thing I'm asking of you is to let me resolve this situation. After that, I'll leave you alone, if you wish. Please, rest, and when you're ready, come downstairs and I will explain everything to you."

"Greg—" Daniella called out to him, but he was already gone. She groaned and laid back on the bed, staring up at the ceiling.

Vampires.

Tears gathered in her eyes, but she forced them back, refusing to let them fall. He wasn't the only one who had betrayed her. Luke and Mya had done so as well. Her friends, people who had become her family, had lied to her. They'd broken her trust, and that hurt pierced through her heart, leaving a wide hole. Yet, the thought of not having them in her life was worse.

Leaving them had never been a possibility for her, and everything in her fought against the thought of it. She struggled, battling between the hurt they'd caused and the love she felt for each of them. The happy memories they'd had, birthdays they'd spent, the company's grand opening, the times they'd laughed, the times they'd cried, how they cared for one another, how they'd cared for her, was that all a lie too?

Daniella shook her head, knowing it couldn't have been, especially not when she'd known them for so long. There was some semblance of truth there, and she held onto it like a lifeline.

No matter how angry she was at Greg, Luke, or Mya, they meant everything to her, and did she really have a choice in the matter? The man who attacked her was a vampire. These people, her friends, were vampires, and she was a literal natural disaster in the making. They were the only stable thing she had, the only ones who knew what was going on.

The emotional and mental toll the news had taken on her left her exhausted. She needed to rest, to reset herself before she approached anyone. Arguing was not the right path to truth, and she wouldn't accept anything less.

Rolling to her side, Daniella took another deep breath, inhaling the scent of spicy wood, cinnamon, and musk. The scent of Greg. This was his room. It fit him, she decided, with its warmth and darkness and how it stayed hidden away from the world. But she was here, wrapped in its depths, and—much like Greg—she would only stay if he shared his secrets with her.

CHAPTER 7

The room was still dark when Daniella awoke. It took her a moment to remember this wasn't her house, or a place she was even familiar with, but at least she was safe.

The rest had served its purpose, giving her enough of a reprieve to focus on the questions circling in her mind. What did she really want? What was most important to her right now? How could she wrap her mind around all of this? All questions she needed answers to before she approached Greg.

Following the small stream of light that filtered through the curtains, she discovered the balcony and took a seat outside. But the lack of skyscrapers, foot traffic, honking of cars, or scents of street food just served to remind her of how little she knew. Taking a deep breath, Daniella did her best to accept her new surroundings and this situation. She listened to the soft sounds of birds chirping in the background as animals foraged in the brush and nearby woods, and eventually she saw the peace of this place.

A light knock caught her attention. The silly little girl in her heart jumped at the thought of it being Greg. She wanted to hold him in her arms. Hadn't she almost lost him, or was jumping out of a twenty-story building a regular walk in the park for a vampire? But her skin didn't tingle and her body didn't feel alive like it did when he was near. The disappointment she felt was enough to make her heart ache.

"Come in," she called out.

After a few steps, Luke came into sight, carrying a plate of food. "Are you hungry?"

Daniella nodded and took the plate from his hand. "Thank you."

"You're welcome," he said as he joined her on the balcony.

They sat in silence for a moment before she spoke. "I'm sorry for earlier."

"It's okay. Greg told me what happened. I'm happy he was there for you."

"He tends to do that a lot, doesn't he?" She couldn't keep the anger out of her tone.

"It's his way. Dani—"

Her eyes bore into Luke's. "You should have told me. I know you all believed this was the right way to protect me, but it still hurts."

"I'm sorry, Dani. I really and truly am."

"How much do I not know, Luke?"

He winced.

"A lot then. Got it." She sat back in the chair, picking at pieces of her sandwich.

"Dani, there is a reason why Greg thought this was the best way to go about things, and why I agreed with him."

She snickered and then opened her mouth, ready to snap at him, but she stopped herself.

Give him a chance to explain before you bite his head off. He's at least willing to give you some information, but you can't get answers if you won't listen.

Luke sighed. "Vampires are broken into sectors depending on how many are in the community and the leaders they select."

She nodded quietly, digesting the information as she took a bite of her sandwich.

"Most leaders can only manage a few hundred, others a thousand or more. They're sectioned into different jurisdictions by states, or state clusters. However, as it stands today, Greg is the leader of the Northeastern Circle, the largest circle of vampires that exists within America."

Daniella gasped and drew back in shock. "What? How?"

He stared into her eyes. "Because of how he is. Greg turned us, me and Mya, and as time went on, we took in others. Merida and Dominick, for example."

"They're vampires too?"

He nodded. "They are. If it weren't for Greg, they would be dead right now and their baby Iris wouldn't be here."

Her gaze shifted downward. She was grateful for the actions that kept all of them alive today, but the news still shocked her. How was Greg responsible for all of them, and how many vampires were under his reach? Millions? How did he keep them a secret? How did he not lose his mind?

"Leaders are elected because they lead, Dani." Luke leaned back against his chair. "Greg doesn't just manage the firm, he manages everything. He has bought countless houses for vampires to live in, created businesses, and established full corporations just to make sure that they have jobs. He's even vouched for mates to the council."

Sensing her confusion, Luke clarified, "They're like our government. Normally they sit on the sidelines, but every so often they cause chaos, and Greg deals with them. He does a lot. Greg does more good in a year than most people can in a lifetime."

Daniella's heart beat erratically at the news. It was all too much, especially for one person to bear. What had he sacrificed? Who took care of him when he was busy protecting everyone else? She gasped as the answer hit her. No one. No one knew him, not really. That was his sacrifice.

"But that ... takes a toll, eventually." Luke stared off into the distance. "I give Greg a lot of shit because he's constantly doing things for other people but never for himself. But the only person—the *only* person—who he will drop everything for is you. He almost did when he fell out of that window."

"But h-he ... Why did he?" She swallowed against the mounting panic in her chest. "He looked okay earlier. Is he okay? Is he hurt? I should have—" Daniella made to get up and leave, but Luke stopped her.

"He's fine. We heal faster than you do, and even faster than normal vampires."

She shook. "But—"

He stroked her arm. "He's fine, I promise. My point in telling you all of that was to explain how important you are to all of us. We all care about you, *especially* Greg. But unfortunately, that makes you a target. That's why we tried to hide everything from you, and that's why Zachariah went after you."

"But I don't understand!" She threw her hand to the side.

"He told me his name was Alexander. How would he know to go after me? Why am I important to Greg?"

Luke sighed. "He may have told you his name was Alexander just in case you overheard some information and put two and two together, but Zachariah is his birth name. He's been around for a while, not as long as we have, but long enough, and he's been a thorn in our side the whole time. Zachariah's a determined fucker, but he's also smart and difficult to kill. Unfortunately."

She steadied herself against that information, forcing herself to be open-minded about a world that spoke so easily about killing someone. But then she remembered how badly she wanted Alexander's—Zachariah's—hands off of her, how she didn't care that he was a living being. She'd wanted him dead, and a part of her still did. To judge Luke, or anyone else, would make her a hypocrite.

Luke twiddled his thumbs, pressing them together repeatedly before exhaling into his clenched hands. "Zachariah went after you because you are Greg's mate."

There's that word again. "What? What does that mean?" Daniella cocked her head to the side. "Is that like a soulmate?"

"Sort of. Vampires and other species"—at her raised eyebrow, he smiled—"yes, there are others, have genetic rules. Much like humans, we can have sex, but we can't procreate nor share our immortal essence with anyone unless they're our mate. Since vampires are immortal, watching the people we love die over and over hurts, so every vampire searches for their mate. You are Greg's."

Was that why she'd always felt so connected to him? Why she'd grown to care about him so deeply? She bit her lip. How many times had she fantasized about them being more than just friends?

"What does that mean for me?" Daniella asked.

He shrugged. "Nothing really. You're not a vampire, although based on the powerful magic you cast earlier, you're probably a witch or something like that."

A witch? She shook her head, unable to even think about that possibility right now.

"But either way, you're not governed by the same code we are. You're free to do as you wish," Luke explained.

"And Greg?"

"Being a mate, or finding your mate, doesn't make them automatically fall in love with you." He stared at his hands. "It's a delicate process. Human mates can reject their immortal one if they choose to. They just won't share that special connection with anyone else. For the immortal though, it's an entirely different process."

"How so?"

Luke's face grew grim. "Imagine your worst heartbreak and then amplify it by one hundred. That is what the immortal will feel. It's a pain worse than death."

Her eyes widened. "What?"

"Yeah, I suppose that was nature's way of controlling our population."

Daniella shuddered at the thought and then blocked it out. She couldn't deal with that level of cruelty, not now. Not ever. She forced herself to focus on the conversation once more. "But how would Zachariah know that I'm Greg's mate?"

"He'd know the moment he saw you and Greg together. The two of you are like magnets, constantly attracting one another.

Someone else who had seen the two of you together could have also told him."

"But that would mean you have a mole."

Luke drummed his fingers on the chair's arm. "That's what we're trying to figure out. After the embezzlement, Greg realized Zachariah knew about you. That's why he asked you to go on a vacation. He thought keeping you away from the office would keep you safe since it was a clear, direct attack against you. Unfortunately, he was wrong."

She sighed. "I knew there was more to the story, but I would have never thought this was the reason."

"I know you're upset that we lied. I know you wish we would have told you about this before. But honestly, how could we? Would you have believed us if we'd walked up to you one day and said, 'Hey, I know you barely know us, but we're vampires, and we'd love it if you could spend the rest of eternity with us. What do you think?'" Luke pressed at the corners of his eyes before facing her.

"Vampires tried to be open about their existence before and that resulted in wars founded on humans' fear. And while I have a much higher regard for you than that, this is a lot of information. So, we did what we could." He shrugged. "We focused on taking care of you, keeping you safe, and protecting you as much as possible. Knowing that you were in real danger gave us a huge reality check."

A violent shiver ran down her spine as Daniella remembered what happened in her penthouse apartment. Zachariah mocked and toyed with her, held her hostage in her own home. She'd been stupid to believe she could save herself from that. What would have happened if Greg hadn't come to save her?

"Dani? Are you okay?" Luke reached out to her and squeezed her shoulder, zapping her back to the present.

"Yeah, I'm fine. I just realized how much danger I was in earlier. Greg saved my life and I..."

Never even said thank you, she finished internally.

"I'm sorry. I wish—"

She squeezed his hand in return. "No. Please don't. I asked for honesty and you gave it to me. I have so many other questions, but I assume I'll need to get those answers from Greg, won't I?"

He nodded. "That's where I leave you two." Luke patted her hand. "But before I go, Dani, you're one of the best people I know. It makes me happy that I can finally share these secrets with you, even though I hate the circumstances. It's a lot all at once, so just breathe through it and follow your heart, okay?"

He took a deep breath. "I know some things may have changed about how you see us, but for us, they haven't. I want you to be happy, to feel safe and treasured. I want you to smile, and whatever makes you feel that way, even if you decide not to speak to me tomorrow, will be something I support. I will always support you, *always*."

Daniella hugged him. "Luke, I'm confused, shocked, and still pissed off"—she slapped his shoulder—"but I'm also curious. You guys are like a family to me. You're the brother I never had. Plus, I could never hate you. You would pester me until we became friends again."

Luke laughed. "Damn straight."

"It's going to take some time. I have a lot to learn and I feel like I'm playing catch up. But I still love you, even with all your ridiculousness. Just keep being honest with me, okay? I'm in this now, so don't try to take me out."

He grinned. "You got it."

CHAPTER 8

Daniella paused at the base of the stairs to take in her surroundings. The front door was large, made of solid wood, and in a black frame similar to the windows and balcony doors. A lamp cast a yellow glow over the space from a hallway, and the same motion-triggered lights lit her path as she walked. The house was vast and open, with columns and furniture sectioning each room into its own unique space.

The foyer had a bench and a small table to the side of what she assumed was a coat closet. Daniella could imagine Greg sitting on the bench, lacing his snow boots before braving the cold weather. *Do vampires get cold?*

The living room was filled with paintings of different styles from different time periods. The heart of the room was a gigantic fireplace covered in one continuous slab of black marble. There was no TV or apparent electronics, just a grand piano in the corner which faced more breathtaking views of the mountains. She didn't know Greg played the piano. *I guess when you're immortal, you have time to pick up new skills.*

But each room, each color, each piece of furniture and its placement, said something about Greg. He said she knew him emotionally, and even with everything that had happened, Daniella thought that was true. This place felt like his real home, more personal and lived-in than his apartment in the city. It was filled with antiques and artifacts that spoke directly of him and his interests. She wanted to know more, wanted to compare the details to see if she'd find the same version of Greg she knew at the end of all of this.

Daniella turned down a hallway lined with vibrant art pieces. Arched built-in shelves held delicate sculptures made of clay, bronze, marble, and polished gold. Her eyes flickered to them, but it was the man she found inside the next room who captivated her. Greg stood shirtless, staring out of a window. As she crossed the threshold, his back tensed and rolled. The tendons in his neck became more pronounced. He turned his head to acknowledge her presence, but otherwise stayed silent, as if bracing for the worst. It took everything in her to resist the urge to wrap her arms around him and breathe him in.

"Can we talk?" she said quietly.

His jaw ticked. "Of course."

She took a seat on his blue velvet couch. It was comfortable under her body weight, and the motion provided a much-needed relief from the tension threatening to snap between them.

He joined her with a harsh breath. "Ella—"

She held up her hand, stopping him. "Wait, please. I need to clear this up with you first. Greg, I'm not happy that you lied to me. It hurt me, but only because I care about you. This thing where you and Luke think I'm going to hate the two of you and never want to speak to you again, it needs to stop."

She reached out to grasp his hand, needing to erase the distance between them and reestablish their connection, whatever it may be. "People learn about one another as time goes on, right?"

"Right." He exhaled and some of the sorrow in his eyes dissipated when he smiled. Greg kissed her hand, causing a jolt to race up her arm and settle in her chest, easing her worry.

"I want to learn about you, Greg. About everything, all of this," she said softly. "Maybe I won't agree with some things, and maybe I will, but I am in this now whether you're ready for me to be or not, so I want to know. I deserve to."

Daniella twined her fingers through his and he embraced her hand in kind, his thumb caressing her skin, and with each stroke her heart felt full of him. "You all have always been there for me. You've made my life more ... colorful. I'm not just going to give that up because I'm upset with you, especially when I can't fault you for what you've done. After all, it's not like I told you I could electrocute vampires, did I?"

They shared a small laugh.

"No, no, you didn't. But I don't think you knew before either," he replied.

"But I knew I wasn't exactly normal. I have a strong intuition. I can always tell when something bad is going to happen, but I can't always connect the dots." She looked down at their linked hands. "To be honest, I'm not quite sure whether it's a good thing or a bad thing right now."

Greg kissed the inside of her wrist, drawing her gaze there. "Vampires have different abilities, and as they get older, they get new ones. One day they're used to the life they have, and the next their world is turned upside down and filled with chaos. But eventually, they master it by being understanding and offering themselves kindness and compassion. You just need to master this new shift in your reality, and you can do it. I know you can."

Daniella blushed at his belief in her. "Thank you. Those were some very wise words there, Mr. Novak."

He chuckled. "I do what I can. I have a friend who specializes in helping people with their abilities, and I think she can help you. If you're okay with it, I'd like to call her and see if I can set up a meeting between the two of you."

"I'd like that. Thank you."

Greg nodded. "You're welcome."

They grew quiet again, sitting together in an awkward silence. Greg's eyes were downcast, leaving her with the opportunity to look him over. While he was here physically, it felt as though his mind were miles away. His shoulders tensed and bowed, weighed down by some invisible force that she didn't know.

She sighed. "Greg, what is it?"

His fingertips froze on her skin, so she moved hers instead.

"We're trying honesty today, remember?"

"It's not that. I'm just trying to figure out how to say this, to help you understand."

Daniella squeezed his hand. "Don't. Like you said before, I know you on an emotional level. I'll understand what you're trying to say."

His eyes flared to life with hope, much like a bird rattling against its caged door. But then, with the flip of a switch, it died down to a thin flame and left a pained darkness that threatened to break her apart.

"Before you came down here, my mind was in a million different places, focused on what everyone needs, including you. I need to finish fixing your room. Your clothes and items are in there and I want you to feel at home here. I also want to be more open with you, but there's just so much." He shook his head. "What you said hit me hard, but it's a little difficult when you've been stuck in your ways for over seven hundred years."

"Seven hundred?" she exclaimed.

Greg smiled and half shrugged. "Give or take a few decades."

"Damn, I didn't realize I liked them that old."

A laugh rose deep from his gut. The vibration spread throughout his body, down their linked hands, and over to her. She couldn't remember the last time she heard him laugh like that, but she craved its richness and how its joy transformed his face.

Greg rested his arm on the top of the couch, bending it at the elbow to support his head with the side of his hand. "You've never said that before."

"What?" she mimicked the motion, resting the side of her head against the couch.

"That you liked me."

"I mean, you're all right," she teased.

"You're not too bad yourself." Greg chuckled.

"I do a little somethin' somethin'." Daniella shimmied her shoulders and he laughed again. There was something in his eyes now, like rays shining through the clouds. *Hope*, she realized. He was hopeful, open, embracing something here, committed to whatever magic they were spinning together in this moment. She had to take advantage of it, to get the answers to the questions she needed to better understand him, so that he could truly believe she wanted to.

"Can I ask you some questions?"

Greg smiled. "Of course."

"Where are you from originally?"

"Spain. That was my mother's homeland. She met my father, Henry, there. He was Dutch-English, but we mostly took after my mother, Eleta."

"That's a beautiful name."

"Thank you." He ran his fingers over her hand again. "The plague had spread to small villages, such as ours. Countries were pointing the finger at one another, blaming each other for it, and I was conscripted into their fight. While I was gone, my father fell victim to the plague, then Amani, Luke's mother, and lastly, my mother. Mya and Luke did the best they could for her, but they were too young and it wasn't a responsibility they should have had to take on."

Daniella knew that feeling, how it could warp a child's persona, contributing to lasting trauma. It was terrible, and she felt for him and his family. No one should have to watch their parents die, much less in such horrible circumstances, and to know he never got to say goodbye devastated her. She inched closer to him and kissed the hand absentmindedly trailing circles on hers. "I'm so sorry."

"It's okay. It was a long time ago." His voice was thick with emotion and he had to clear his throat to continue. "There was a rumor that someone found a cure in one of the nearby villages, so I went, hoping to get it for Mya and Luke. But there wasn't a cure. Men were spreading that information to lure people there and steal from them. They attacked me and left me for dead." He breathed out slowly. "That's where I met Lord

Erik Devereux, a vampire who resided in England. He took pity on me and turned me, and then I turned Luke and Mya before they died from the plague."

"That's—" She stopped herself, wanting to focus on the positive. "I'm happy he saved you."

Greg smiled, but it didn't make it to his eyes. "Me too. He taught us how to be vampires, the fun things, what our new duties and responsibilities were. We stayed together for a long time, but he ... lost someone very dear to him and decided not to live on."

Daniella remembered Luke's words. *Worse than death.* A chill went down her spine as she realized the man had lost his mate.

Greg frowned. "I'm sorry. I wish those tales were more pleasant. Life was just harder back then."

"No, it's just ... all of you have been through a lot."

"We have, but it hasn't all been bad. I could show you some of the good times, if you like."

She cocked her head to the side. "How?"

"One of my abilities allows me to pull memories from a person. It also allows me to share my own with them. Like seeing a vision through another person's eyes."

Daniella eyes grew wide and she nodded rapidly. "Yes, please! That would be amazing!"

He chuckled at her eagerness. Letting her hand go, Greg cupped her cheek. He leaned forward until his forehead was almost touching her own.

Daniella's breath rushed out of her lungs as he neared her. "Greg—"

His voice dropped to a graveled whisper as he caressed her skin. "Don't worry, I won't do anything unless..."

"Unless..." she breathed.

"You want me to."

Goosebumps spread over her flesh and she suddenly found it difficult to swallow. Daniella's lips parted as she forced a breath into her now heavy chest. The action drew his gaze and he licked his lips.

Greg murmured something as her eyes drifted closed. His breath tickled her lips, and for one glorious second she thought he would finally kiss her. But instead, he rested his forehead against hers. Something wrapped around her, a pressure that made her hair stand on end. The energy spun around the two of them like a cocoon of fine silk, and then his memories played behind her eyes.

The first was a vision of three children. Greg, *Luke, and Mya.* They were playing, throwing bits of mud at one another, rolling around until they were covered head to toe in the thick substance. A woman yelled from the doorway. Based on her golden skin, long, flowing, dark hair, and resemblance to them, it must have been Eleta. She was beautiful, even more so when she laughed at how dirty they were.

The scene changed to a tavern where Mya, dressed in outlandish clothing for what appeared to be near the Victorian era, worked as a bartender. Luke, the ever-present playboy, had a lady on each arm while Greg sat at a table, speaking to a man. *Erik,* she realized, based on Greg's love for the man—a cross between a father figure and a good friend. His cream skin contrasted with Greg's warm tone.

Erik's silver eyes gleamed as he leaned towards Greg and whispered, "That sister of yours is about to cause a scene again."

The direction of the vision changed to a man who stood a

little too close to Mya. He whispered something he must have thought was flattering, but based on how Mya punted him clear across the room, it was not. The patrons stopped and stared as if Mya had grown a second head, but she simply shrugged and yelled, "Who wants another drink?" Everyone cheered, and Mya graced Greg and Erik with a large smile.

The next visions came one after another: a tiny English cottage that they'd called home, followed by the moment they set sail to America. The purity of those memories was evident, but the love they'd shared as a family touched her the most.

The vision faded as Greg sat back, and when she opened her eyes to meet his own, they were glazed over with unshed tears.

"Thank you for sharing that with me."

"Thank you for wanting to see them." He blinked a few times to clear his vision, but his voice was a deep rumble as he spoke. "It can be so easy to forget the good times. Days can blend between one another and sometimes they seem ... endless. It's good to remember." As his fingers left her cheek, they brushed against her shoulder-length hair. He tilted his head to look at something and grunted. "I didn't realize they were that deep."

"Huh? What?" Daniella tilted her head to the side.

"The marks that bastard made on your neck." His fingers traced over each one and her heart beat faster. "Do they hurt? Do you have any other injuries?"

She wanted him to continue his inspection, to undress her, slide his hands over her, under her, inside her. She wanted to feel him everywhere, to drown out everything, anything, from before.

Focus, Daniella chastised herself. To keep her hands from

reaching out to him, she felt around her neck and found the four indentations made by Zachariah's nails, and a fifth on the other side of her throat. "I'm sure I do, but when I woke up, I asked my body to stop hurting and it listened. I haven't felt any pain since."

Greg gave a small nod. "That's good at least, but these are going to turn into some nasty bruises."

Daniella groaned. "Fantastic, just one more thing to remember him by."

Greg froze. The tendons in his neck tensed and his Adam's apple bobbed as he swallowed. "I know I don't have a right to ask you this, but seeing your physical injuries made me think about other, deeper ones you may have. I want to help you. If you need it, that is. Zachariah said the two of you were together before, and—"

Daniella laughed at his nervousness. "There is nothing for you to ask or worry about there. I'm fine, that wasn't..." She paused and felt her face grow warm under his quiet scrutiny. "Zachariah and I had been together before, yes, but we weren't in a relationship—"

"Oh." Greg's eyes narrowed as he spoke through clenched teeth. "I see."

Rejection and jealousy flickered over his features until dejection settled over him, and she hated it. He had been all she'd ever wanted for so long. Did he really not know what he meant to her?

Of course not.

She'd never told him from fear of losing him or making things awkward between them. But now, if there was a chance, she had to try. She had to fix this.

"No. I don't think you do." Daniella shifted against the

couch and took a deep breath to settle her nerves. "Sometimes, being around you is too much for me. I ... Fuck," she croaked. "This is harder than I thought it would be." She wrung her hands, then sighed loudly.

Just say it.

"I want you, all the time. It's ridiculous and all-consuming. Even when you're being distant, or you're states or even an entire country away, and you call me on the phone for us to talk about our days, it drives me crazy. I know we've only ever been friends, but I-I can't help how I feel," she sputtered. "And lately it has gotten to a point where I needed to resolve my ... desires so that I didn't throw myself at you like a wild animal. I needed to scratch an itch temporarily. That's all that was. There were no feelings, no emotions, nothing." She breathed. "And there never could be with anyone else but you."

When she finally looked at him, she saw a boyish smile on his face, but his eyes showed something else: a deep-seated intensity and hunger that made her heart pound. She couldn't take that look. The way it shot through her, setting her body on fire as if it had just awoken from a long slumber. And awoken it had—her nipples peaked under her clothes and the inner walls of her vagina clenched with need.

He still hadn't said a word, hadn't moved a muscle. He just stared at her as if he were taking her in, savoring every word she'd said.

This is too much. I can't. She shook her head and crossed her arms over her breasts, creating a safety net for herself. Her confidence may have been as shaky as a piece of straw in the wind, but she'd fake it if she had to. "I don't think I've ever seen you speechless before."

Greg chuckled, but his voice was so low that it sounded like a growl. "That's not why I'm being quiet, Ella."

"Then why are you?"

"Because"—he hooked his hands under her knees, dragging her to him until he was seated directly in between her thighs, making her gasp—"it's taking every bit of my control to not rip off your clothes and bury myself so deep inside you that you won't know where you end and I begin."

She moaned at the thought. Greg's skin was warm and firm under her palms, and she could imagine how it would feel to have him moving within her, on top of her, below her, consuming her, making her his. She wanted to be his.

Greg gripped her thighs and his hands slid to her hips as he pulled her until there was no space left between them. His eyes turned the molten amber, like that of a raging fire, and his erection rubbed against her, seeking what she was so desperate to give.

She bit her lip and whispered, "then do it."

CHAPTER 9

Never had Greg been undone before, left so open, so helpless, and then tantalized and set ablaze with such honesty. How would it feel to caress her silky skin? Was it just as soft on her breasts? Were her nipples as dark as her soft brown hair? He hoped. By the gods, he hoped. How would she taste? He salivated at the thought. And her blood? How rich would it be as it flowed into his mouth, as he bit her, mated with her?

He rubbed her cheek, following the line down her jaw to her neck. Then he saw the reddish-purple marks again. They reminded him that even though he yearned for her, like a plant for sunlight, or a fish for water, he could not have her, not yet. His fingers, featherlight, traced back up her skin until he could take hold of her chin.

"Ella," he whispered, "I want you more than I could ever express. I've wanted to touch you like this for so long." His fingers wandered again, starting from the base of her neck and traveling lower over her spine. She curved into his touch and shifted, rubbing against him. He hissed and squeezed her hips to keep her still, eliciting a whimper from her.

He cursed. "We can't, not yet. Not when I want so much from you."

Daniella's shoulders dropped as she looked away, but Greg cupped her face, drawing her gaze back to him. "I'm not rejecting you. Don't you know what you are to me? What you mean to me? You drive me crazy, Daniella." She was so close. So close that if he just leaned in, just an inch, her lips would be against his. He'd swallow her breaths, her moans, her cries as he plunged inside of her ... *Fuck.*

Greg shook his head. "One night isn't enough for me. I wouldn't be able to stop myself from making you my mate, and that's not right. It's not fair to you. Not with everything going on."

She cupped his face. "But—"

"I am not a good person, Ella," Greg said sharply.

"Isn't that for me to decide?"

"Do you always have to make sense?"

"You know me well enough to know the answer to that question." She smiled.

He took her in. The way she watched him, how deeply she seemed to want to understand, and her fierce determination to do so. She was so gentle, yet so strong. He finally understood that stepping around the issue would get him nowhere. Greg had promised her honesty, and if she could be open with him, he should do the same for her.

"I am in the middle of a war that you have, unfortunately, been drawn into."

Her eyes widened, and he wrapped his arms around her, bracing her for what he had to say.

"I don't use that word lightly, Ella. This is not the first time, and unless certain people are dealt with, it won't be the last. Zachariah has caused me and my loved ones a lot of pain, and I need you to understand what that means. We don't police in my world, certainly not at this stage. The next time I see that vampire, I am going to kill him with my bare hands."

His gaze shifted downward. "If you can still want me after you know I've done that, then you will have all of me for the rest of our exceptionally long lives. But without that, I can't. It's not fair to ask you to spend forever with me while I hide parts of myself away from you. I know that now."

"Greg," she whispered, but he shook his head and looked away from her. His heart was too exposed, and if she rejected him now it would destroy him. In all actuality, he deserved it.

That bastard had touched her, scared her, put his hands on her. Greg wished he could erase those marks, replace every fiber of her being with his own so that she would never remember that monster.

His voice was gruff as he struggled to push his rage and jealousy aside. "I can heal these for you, if you like."

She cocked her head to the side. "How?"

"I have a healing agent in my blood and saliva."

Daniella's eyes narrowed slightly. "And what would I have to do?"

"Nothing. Just sit here. But try not to squirm around too much. You are still on my lap after all." He tried to lighten the mood with a smile, and while her lips tilted upwards, he could tell she was still irritated with him.

"All right." She lifted her hair, brushing the strands behind her shoulder.

Greg bent toward her hesitantly, giving her time to change her mind. He paused, breathing her in, the soft perfume that still clung to her skin barely noticeable under her own scent—something mild and warm, like apricots and berries drizzled with honey from the sweetest of flowers. He steeled himself.

Stay in control. You don't want to scare her.

He licked her pulse, felt it spike against his tongue. She took a breath as his tongue slid upward, following along each mark that scarred her beautiful maple skin. A whispered moan escaped her lips when he sucked her neck.

Daniella slid her arms around him, burying her hands in his hair. He squeezed her back, tugging her closer until he could feel the rise and fall of her soft breasts pressed so perfectly against his chest.

Her breath caught when he kissed a spot below her ear. He traced the lobe with his tongue and when he nibbled on the flesh, she hissed, a shiver running through her body. She shifted, wrapping her legs around his waist. Her hips circled, then rolled against his own, and Greg's eyes drifted closed as pleasure soared through him. This time, he didn't stop her. Instead, he cupped her ass, urging her to keep moving in such delicious sin.

Daniella gripped at the strands of his hair, panting, moaning with each move. He spread his legs wider, desperately wanting to fit his erection more firmly against her core. He could smell her desire, her wetness, could almost see her swollen lips in his mind's eye, feel her as he slid inside of her.

Greg was frantic now. He tugged her hair just enough to pull her head back, to leave every inch of her throat accessible to him so he could kiss, lick, and suck at her skin. He felt her swallow, the muscles in her throat moving, and it reminded him of her blood, of how it would feel to drink from her. His fangs extended.

Greg pulled his head back, stopping just short of biting her, conflicted. He feared how close he'd come to breaking his promise, and yet he was still so desperate to continue. But when he stared into her eyes, there was no shred of fear. Instead, she met his gaze with wonder and unabashed need.

"Ella?"

She trembled against him and her voice was hushed when she spoke. "I understand what you said and I know why you said it. I know you still want to protect me, to keep me safe. But I've always felt safe with you. Greg ... I thought I lost you." Daniella swallowed hard. "I destroyed that room because I thought you were gone. If you have any question about my feelings for you, or what I think about you, remember that."

His eyes widened as her confession squeezed at his heart, making it beat faster.

She rubbed his cheek. "Kiss me, please. It doesn't need to go further. I'll respect your wishes but just ... Please, I'm so tired of pretending."

Greg cupped her chin, his finger trailing over her bottom lip. The moment her lips parted and her eyes fluttered closed, he surrendered. He brushed his lips against hers and let out a blissful sigh. He was so damn tired of pretending too, especially when she tasted this good. When her lips were so soft, so warm, so perfect. Again and again he kissed her, trying to be gentle. But then he couldn't take any more. Not of her moans, her hands as they ran over his body, or how she felt against him. He needed more.

Daniella clenched her thighs around his hips as he lifted her and laid her back on the couch, his lips never breaking from her own. She pulled at him when he tried to keep his weight off of her, and finally he gave in, pressing every bit of his body against hers.

Their kiss heated, became wild. He squeezed her back, kneading the plump curves of her ass. Greg licked her lips, nibbled and sucked until her mouth opened. Taking the invitation, he slid his tongue inside and they waged a battle together, one they both won.

Her feet crossed at the base of his back and pushed at his hips. Answering her call, he rocked against her, swallowing her moans, drinking her in. His fingers slipped under her shirt, following the lines of her spine. He circled his hips, pressed against her clit, and she hissed. Greg smiled in the kiss and did it again.

Daniella pulled at him, her hands stroking his skin, squeezing, clawing at his back while they soared higher. When Greg finally lifted his mouth from hers, he felt as if he'd been drugged. He was mindless in his desire for her. Needing to taste her again, he leaned toward her lips, only to be stopped as she placed her fingers against his mouth.

"I promised to respect your wishes," she panted, "but if you touch me like that again, I will make sure you won't stop."

Greg nibbled on her finger. "You're a dangerous woman." He slid his hands out from under her shirt and used their position to roll until he could cradle her beside him.

Daniella's head came to rest under his, while her hand laid right above his racing heart. "I've been called a lot of things in my life, but never dangerous."

"Good," he said darkly. "I like knowing I'm the only person who has seen that side of you."

Her eyebrow shot up. "Was that possessiveness I heard?"

"Yes." He turned his head towards hers. "If that's okay with you."

"Yes, it is." Her fingertips swirled over his chest as a blush stained her cheeks. "It's a relief to hear you say that. I was worried that you'd want our relationship to stay the way it was, and I don't think I could go back to that, not after tonight."

He captured her hand and brushed his lips against hers. "Neither could I. I'd planned to try and stay away from you. I wanted to give you space, to help you feel comfortable here. But now, when I know I can lie here beside you? I could never give up that chance."

"That makes me really happy to hear." She smiled and her blush deepened. "While today was … difficult, I don't regret it."

He sighed. "I wish things would have happened another way. I never want to see you hurt, and the fact that you were will haunt me for a long time. But I am happy you're here. I'm happy that I've finally gotten to share this part of my life with you." Greg twined his fingers in her hair, his voice deep with emotion as he spoke. "Ella, you are my heart. There is so much more I have to tell you. But please know that I won't rush you. I don't want to ruin the possibility of us growing into more."

She lifted her head to meet his eyes. "Why are you so afraid that something is going to ruin us when I want to be with you? I'm happy with you."

"Because the supernatural world is different. The monsters told in fairytales exist here. My life has afforded me many luxuries. I've visited many places, met incredible people, but the history I've gone through and the current events of today, they're not easy. This world isn't easy, and you deserve better."

Her eyes softened. "I get to decide that, Greg. You care about me so much, and it means the world to me, but I get to decide if I can accept your world. Plus, I believe you're forgetting about the mess I made upstairs. I may be a little late to the game, but I'm still a contender."

He opened his mouth to argue, but upon seeing her glare, he picked the safer option and agreed. "I suppose you have a point."

"Thank you. Now, tell me about vampires. Do you drink blood?"

"Yes," he drawled, taking in her reaction. "I do."

Daniella raised an eyebrow. "Human blood?"

"Yes, typically, although sometimes animal blood."

She frowned. "But I've seen you eat normal food. Does it provide nourishment to you, or do you just eat it for appearances?"

"I enjoy normal food. I can still taste it and eat it, but it doesn't replace the nourishment blood provides. There are some exceptions to that though, such as a raw steak, but it's the difference between eating a snack or a meal."

"What is it like? Does it have a taste? Do you have a favorite kind?"

Greg chuckled at her. He loved to see her mind work, the joy in her gaze as the puzzle pieces began to fit and paint a picture. "All blood tastes different. Different blood types have different nutrients. I suppose I don't have a favorite." His eyes drifted down to her neck. *Yet.*

"So, you ... take blood from people? You bite them often, I mean?"

He chuckled. "No, I haven't drunk blood from another living being since we established blood banks. And I only need to drink blood every one to two weeks."

"Vampires established blood banks? I guess that makes sense." Daniella laughed, and then a soft blush tinged her cheeks. She bit her lip, drawing his gaze. "Do you want to drink my blood?"

His humor left him with her question. Greg ran the back of his hand over her cheek as he whispered, "I do."

Her eyes widened, but she didn't pull away from him.

"Taking someone's blood can be a sexual experience. And when a vampire finds his mate, it's required to cement the bond." He stroked her cheek with his thumb, scared she may fear him now. "It doesn't hurt. I would never, ever hurt you or do anything without your consent. Please don't let that thought scare you. I don't want you to be afraid of me."

Daniella leaned into his touch. She cupped his palm against her skin and nuzzled it. "I'm not scared of you, Greg." She kissed his hand. "I know you would never hurt me. I trust you."

"You're taking this all very well."

Her gaze turned mischievous. "I just keep reminding myself, everyone has their kinks. Who am I to judge?"

A bark of laughter escaped him. "That's true, although"—his voice deepened as his hand slipped down the back of her neck, pulling her to him—"I'm curious what yours are."

She smiled as her lips neared his own. "If you treat me right, I'll tell you."

Greg flipped her onto her back, fitting his body against hers once more. Daniella gasped at the sudden change but wound her arms around him as he kissed her temple, her cheek, his lips brushing against her skin with every word. "I will treat you like the goddess that you are. Like the core of my universe. I will give you anything you want, every part of me, just for this."

And then he kissed her as if he were starving for her taste, because he was. He would never get enough of her. His body exploded and he drank her in. Every whimper, every moan, every caress pulled him under, until the world around him completely disappeared and all that was left was her.

CHAPTER 10

Daniella was nervous. Even the fresh cool breeze hitting her face, and the scent of the sea as they drove along the coast, couldn't fully erase her worries.

They were on their way to meet Astrid, an immortal who specialized in understanding and assisting with abilities. While it was true that what she had experienced last night was other-worldly, Daniella had done her best to remind herself that this was her new reality, and nothing could change that fact. But she'd heard the voices again, like an internal alerting system that buzzed when she needed guidance, and even though they were helpful—caring even—they reminded her of her mother's demise.

Yes, she wanted help to manage her new abilities, but what if there was more to all of this? What if something was actually wrong with her mentally? What if she was having some sort of psychotic break? What if—

As if sensing her thoughts, Greg reached over and squeezed

her hand. "It's going to be okay, I promise. You don't need to be nervous."

"Am I that transparent?"

"To me you are." He kissed her hand, bringing a small smile to her lips. "Astrid is a good person. I've known her for a very long time and she's helped many of my people. I know all of this has happened pretty quickly and, while you're handling it exceptionally well, it has been a huge shock. But think of this as a chance for answers. She'll be able to help you and give you some peace of mind."

Daniella rubbed the back of his hand as she took a deep breath. "Okay."

It took another half an hour before Greg came to a stop down a narrow brick road lined with oak trees and cottage-style shops. Astrid's storefront was picturesque. Its bright sky-blue exterior, sandwiched between cedar paneling and flower boxes, made Daniella smile. It was nothing like the tall skyscrapers of New York City. She liked it immediately.

Greg opened the door for her, and the first thing she noticed was the smell—fragrant but mild spices that paired well with the fresh scents of wood, citrus, and pine. Dried lemon and orange slices hung from the window with chimes, along with drying herbs. She knew one of them was rosemary, and another looked like lavender, but she couldn't identify the rest.

The shop was covered with crystals, cards, and books, so many that she couldn't count them all. It should have been overwhelming, yet the space felt welcoming, serene. She'd gone into occult shops before, but never one so peaceful.

A curtain moved in the distance, revealing a beautiful ebony woman. Her black curls reached past her shoulders and down her waist, contrasting with her silver eyes that seemed to swirl. She was ethereal, beautiful.

"Ancient", the voices whispered in her mind.

The woman smiled at her, the greeting warm and genuine. But when her gaze settled on Greg, she laughed. "Greg! It's been too long." Moving forward with silent steps, she gave him a tight hug.

He returned the embrace. "Hey, Astrid. Thank you for seeing us on such short notice."

"Of course!" Astrid patted his back.

It warmed Daniella's heart to see the exchange. Knowing Greg had friends, people he could rely on in between the multitude of the responsibilities he'd shared with her last night, made her hopes rise. Perhaps these people had helped to ease his loneliness.

"And you're his mate!" Astrid pulled Daniella in for a hug. "I'm so happy to finally meet you! This has been a long time coming."

A nervous laugh escaped Daniella's lips. She wasn't sure how this woman knew their situation, but she answered honestly. "Yes, it has."

She caught Greg's jubilant smile over Astrid's shoulder.

The woman chuckled. "I like her, she's got spirit. Come on back. Greg tells me you need a little guidance with your gifts."

Daniella followed after her with Greg in tow. "Thank you, I'm not sure how to deal with them."

Astrid closed the curtain behind them and motioned for them to sit down at a table. "Now that's not true. They may seem new to you now, but you've always had them. You've just forgotten how they work is all. Give me your hand."

Daniella hesitated, but placed her hand in Astrid's. She clasped their hands together, her hold strong but gentle.

"Every person on this planet has an ability," Astrid began. "Painting is an ability; singing is an ability. Humans have just backpedaled to only understand and believe in things they can see and study. They've forgotten the old magic that exists around them. But you, I, and even Greg can access that. Magic is in you, always has been and always will be."

Daniella jumped as a book moved, flying from behind her and coming to a stop beside Astrid. The pages turned of their own accord.

"I'm sorry, I didn't mean to scare you," Astrid said.

Daniella looked from the book, to Astrid, and back. *Flying books. It's just a flying book. This is the life you have to get used to. With everything you've done, this should seem like child's play.* She took a steadying breath. "No, it's okay. How did you do that?"

"My ability is to connect to things by threads. Have you ever heard the saying 'cutting ties with someone'?"

Daniella nodded.

"It comes from old magic. My ability is to create threads and use them for things I need. Anything I touch or come in contact with creates a thread, and when I need something, such as a book"—Astrid waved a hand and the book spun—"or to read another person's ability, I use that thread to do so."

"But doesn't that get tiring after a while? I don't know a lot about the occult or magic, but I thought you cut ties to keep people from bringing your energy down."

Astrid smiled. "It can, and it will if I'm not careful, but I take care to protect myself. Think of it like a type of residue. By touching your hands, I've left a little on you which I can use to create my thread. When I'm done, I'll remove it. If you want it to stay, then it will."

Daniella stared at the book and then at the impressive, eccentric woman in front of her. "That's incredible."

She laughed. "If you think that's amazing, wait until you see what you can do."

Daniella gasped. "You already know?"

"Mhmm, but I like to learn the history of things. It makes sharing the knowledge with you easier. When was the first time something seemed different? I get the idea that you went searching for answers."

Greg, who so far had been silently leaning against a wall, moved behind her. He rested his hand on her shoulder, giving it a small squeeze, lending her his strength.

"My intuition has always been strong. But I'm beginning to think that's not really what I thought it was. I know when bad things are going to happen. Not what, but sometimes where. It feels ... dark and heavy, depending on the warning. Sometimes I can ignore it if it's just a small inconvenience, like being a few minutes late to work or an event. But other times, like yesterday, it makes me sick."

She looked up at Greg for a moment, and at his nod she continued. "Everywhere I went, I felt sick. I couldn't figure out why, and then I was attacked when I got home."

Astrid's eyes widened and her gaze shifted to Greg's.

"It was Zachariah," Greg bit out.

"That bastard." Astrid crossed her arms. "I should have castrated him when I had the chance."

Daniella choked back a laugh at her outburst.

"He pisses me off. Sorry, continue."

"No, it's okay. I'm right there with you. After Greg got there, I became overwhelmed. I just felt this deep rage build inside of me, and then I electrocuted him."

At Astrid's raised eyebrow, Greg chuckled. "Don't get excited. He survived."

She huffed. "We'll have to work on that. Anything else?"

"I also destroyed a room in Greg's house. I was having an anxiety attack and needed to breathe. Then Greg's window shattered and vines poured into the room. And I've started hearing these voices—"

"Voices?" Greg asked.

Daniella fidgeted under his stare. "Yes. I wasn't sure how to tell you. It started last night. I only hear them sometimes, normally when I'm around you."

"Interesting." Astrid sat forward. "What do they say?"

Daniella's gaze flickered back up to Greg's. "Well, whenever you're struggling with telling me something, or hiding something from me, the voices tell me what you're going through. It's almost like they're trying to help me understand you or reach you somehow." She shook her head with a sigh. "It's difficult to explain."

"And what do they feel like?"

She paused. The question should have been strange, but Astrid was right. They had a feeling. "Each one is different," Daniella said finally. "Some are grounded, others vicious, but they are all ancient. The first time I heard them, they sounded external, like if I turned around there would be these ... things standing there. But now they feel as though they're inside of me, like they're a part of me. Does that make any sense?"

"It does."

The book beside Astrid moved, laying on its spine in front of Daniella. She hesitated to touch the enchanted object, so

Astrid leaned forward and tapped on a paragraph. "Your abilities are elemental."

Daniella read over the short blurb about people who could communicate with the elements and call on them to use their powers. It seemed impossible. "But that doesn't make sense. All I've ever felt is darkness, and how would the voices come into play?"

"When most people think of something dark, they become afraid. Monsters under the bed and all that nonsense." Astrid waved her hand dismissively. "Because of that personification, what you were feeling was the being of darkness. It was warning you of someone's intent to harm you. As you became more connected to it, that expanded to any general negativity or minor annoyance. The other voices are attached to the other elemental beings. As for you"—she pointed to Greg—"because you were hiding something from her, they revealed it."

Greg chuckled nervously. "I'm not sure how it feels to know I'm being spied on."

Daniella shrugged, a small smile teasing her lips. "Don't blame me. I'm just a conduit." Her attention shifted back to Astrid. "Why do you think they're talking to me now?"

"Did your parents ever teach you anything, any odd phrases?"

The mood of the room changed immediately. Greg went to speak for her, but she stopped him with a squeeze of his hand "I don't know my father, and my mother died when I was a child."

"I'm so sorry to hear that." Astrid reached across the table and squeezed her other hand.

Daniella couldn't tell if it was the shop, Astrid's abilities, or her own, but she could feel the comfort, sincerity, and strength radiating from both Astrid and Greg so strongly it brought tears to her eyes.

Greg bent down beside her and wiped one tear as it escaped. "Baby—"

She shook her head, wiping her eyes. "It's okay. I could feel both of you. Your compassion was so strong it was ... breathtaking. Thank you both for that. I'm sorry for worrying you, but I promise I'm okay."

Greg sighed and nodded as she turned back to Astrid.

"To answer your question, I don't remember much about her, but she had some odd phrases and a habit of talking out loud to voices. When I was a child, I would ask her what she was doing and she always said she was talking to her friends. People just thought she was crazy."

There was a somber look in Astrid's eyes when she responded, and Daniella wondered if she had experienced the same cruelty. "It sounds like she had the same ability as you, just not developed. Long ago, beings reigned all over this land. Some of them were real, and some of them were created by humans who worshipped them. Take fire, for instance. That was the best discovery to man at the time because it was something new, so they worshipped it. When their crops were dying, they worshipped rain. When their plants were fertilized, they worshipped the earth to keep them healthy. While those beings may have come from others, they eventually took on a whole life of their own and grew into their own power."

"Much like I can create threads, they can be called upon. When witches in movies and shows 'call the corners', they're communicating to the beings in those elements. You can do the same thing, just without all the hoo-ha. Here."

The book lifted, shut, and went back onto a bookshelf behind Daniella.

"Close your eyes and try to create something with your magic."

Daniella's eyes darted around the room and the various objects and items that Astrid clearly treasured. "I don't know if that's a good idea. I don't want to break anything in your shop."

"You won't." Astrid smiled. "You did that because you were scared. Are you scared right now?"

"I'm hesitant, but no, I'm not scared."

"Good. Being nervous can be a positive type of energy. It means you're willing to embrace possibility. Now, close your eyes."

Daniella did so, taking a deep breath to calm herself.

"Now think of something you wish you had in front of you, something from an element. Earth, fire, water, air, light, dark, it doesn't matter which, just pick one and then visualize it coming to you."

There was still a bit of fear deep within her. With each breath, she tried to work through it, knowing she would need to calm her doubt to focus properly. Then it dawned on her that wasn't what she needed. If darkness was what she was used to, maybe what she needed the most right now was peace. With that idea in mind, she tried to think of how to bring it to fruition. Did she just call on a being? Speak to them? Daniella gave herself a mental shake. When she'd attacked Zachariah, or needed to breathe, she didn't vocalize the need to anyone but herself. It was instinctual, and perhaps that need, the ultimate desire for something, was how she communicated.

What does peace look like to you? What makes you calm?

Daniella took another deep breath.

Air.

A vibration started within her as she focused. She searched for air, for fresh, clean air. A window unlatched, letting a breeze into the room. But she wanted more. She wanted a connection, a physical touch to the earth around her.

A thin vine wrapped around her wrist, making her eyes snap open. It grew, swirling over her skin. A bud erupted, revealing an iris, and then another and another. They slid between her hands, crossing and spreading up her arms until she laughed from the joy of it all.

When she lifted her head, the lights in the shop glowed yellow and she knew it was for her. She settled back in the chair and smiled in childish delight.

Astrid squeezed her hands. "See? There's nothing for you to be afraid of. You and the beings are connected, and as long as you keep your head straight, there's nothing you can't do."

DANIELLA'S EUPHORIA CONTINUED, LEAVING HER WITH AN EXTRA bounce in her step. After saying goodbye to Astrid, Greg draped his arm around her shoulders as they walked side by side. They talked briefly, spending most of the time enjoying the beautiful weather, neighboring shops, and each other's company.

He took her to get ice cream, where she got a cookie dough and cream concoction and he a sea salt caramel pecan flavor. She decided later, when their mouths and bodies were crushed together in a heated kiss behind the store, that the flavor tasted much better when combined with his lips. Today was good. Today felt right. Being with him felt right, and nothing could take her down from that cloud.

Daniella had been so focused on her time with him, on being there and present in this space, that she hadn't felt it. She hadn't realized the darkness was back—hard, cold, and spreading through her body—until they pulled into the driveway of Greg's house and parked beside two other vehicles.

"Greg," she forced through labored breaths, "something's wrong."

He took one look at her, followed her line of sight, and leapt from the car. She trailed behind him, unable to keep up with his vampiric speed. When she caught up to him, he was in the foyer with Luke and Mya. These were her friends, people she loved and cared about. Normally she would have embraced them, laughed, and felt love at their nearness, but their expressions were too sad, and it only served to heighten her fear.

Greg turned toward her, his skin pale. "Ella..."

"What is it? What happened?" When no one spoke, the ball of panic in her chest squeezed her heart in an iron grip. Shaking, she yelled, "Just tell me!"

Luke glanced at Mya, who sighed. Mya took a sheet of newspaper from him and handed it to her. "I'm sorry," she said.

Daniella's gaze shifted from hers to the page in her hand, scanning the title "Animal Attack Leaves Woman Dead". Confused, she read on, then stopped, her eyes moving to a small picture of a beautiful blonde woman. A familiar blonde woman. Her eyes moved between the picture and the article, taking in more information, the words ricocheting around her mind. *Ripped throat, bloody, teeth marks, teeth.* And then she saw the name.

Daniella broke. She shattered because she knew. She screamed, setting the page on fire because she knew. It was Stacy, and she was dead.

CHAPTER 11

Daniella struggled to open her eyes. The lids were glued shut, puffy and swollen from the tears she'd shed a few short hours ago. Greg had done everything he could for her. He'd brought her upstairs to his bedroom and held her until she'd cried herself to the point of exhaustion. He'd run his fingers through her hair, telling her it wasn't her fault and apologizing for her pain over and over. Then he'd just hummed to her while she wallowed in her grief.

The room felt cold without his presence, darker than normal. She searched through the emptiness as if it would give her answers. Then she remembered the last time she had seen Stacy and how the darkness had reacted to her touch. The way it had morphed into something ugly and horrid under Daniella's skin, like daggers piercing her heart. She had simply dismissed it as a fluke, because at the time, Stacy didn't fit. She shouldn't have fit in this world of chaos and darkness, but now she did, and that was on her. Stacy's death was on her.

If Daniella had known more, she could have warned her. If she would have listened harder or believed, if she would have been more focused, maybe things would be different. But none of that mattered now. Stacy was gone, a young woman taken long before her time.

Daniella came to the obvious conclusion that Zachariah had killed her. Everyone who knew of her friendship with Stacy was on the first floor of this house, and none of them would have ever hurt Stacy or her. Questions swarmed in her mind. If she had gone with Zachariah, would Stacy still be alive right now? Was he planning on killing her just for sport, or did he kill her because he couldn't get Daniella? Was this just another way to hurt her? Was this how he taught her that he was still in control, that he could get to her at any place, at any time, and would keep going until he got what he wanted?

"Stop! Enough!" the voices shouted, but the damage had been done.

Energy swarmed within her, powered by her rage. She glided towards the balcony, forcing the doors open without moving a finger. As she neared the railing, she looked down, needing to feel the earth at her feet. There was no room for doubt or fear as Daniella used the air to float over the railing and down to the ground. She had split herself away from reality, from the human constructs of what was possible and impossible. Instead, there was only need, the ultimate desire to shake the earth, to unleash her wrath. The air howled, crashing around her like the wild sea. Distant shouting came from behind her, but the words were sucked into the void she'd crafted. She couldn't hear them now, and she didn't care to. Her fury, her rage was all-consuming.

Raising her hands outward, Daniella called the clouds to

her as the wind grew harsher, wilder. It whipped around her and she called for more. Turning her gaze upward, she gathered energy and felt renewed in her vengeance when lightning flashed. One bolt, two bolts, three, the sky turning a violent white-blue at every spark. As the rain cascaded from the sky, frozen balls of ice followed. Large hailstones cracked against tree branches, snapping their stems from the force.

Strong arms wrapped around her. Greg held her, shouting that it would be okay, that she had to stop. But she didn't. She couldn't stop, not now.

Greg turned her roughly but paused at the fresh tears falling down her face.

"It's all my fault! He killed her because of me," she cried through the storm she'd created.

He didn't respond. Instead, he gathered her in his embrace. Daniella twined her arms around him, clutching his shirt as she buried herself in his chest.

The lightning stopped and the wind ceased to scream, but the rain continued to fall over its mistress, mixing with her tears.

AFTER TAKING A SHOWER, DANIELLA PUT ON THE CLOTHES MYA pulled out for her. While she was grateful for her care, it didn't ease the bitterness that had settled within her. She held the feeling around her like a protective shield. This wasn't the end of her journey or her fight. There was still the embezzlement, a war, her powers, her feelings for Greg, this family, immortals. There was too much. She couldn't slow down, not yet. She had to keep going, and if that were the case, she would do so by turning every bit of pain she felt into a weapon.

Daniella walked into the study to see Greg dressed in his business attire. Her heart skipped a beat when he focused on her, and then she took in the sadness in his eyes. "What happened?"

"Nothing. The council has summoned me for an emergency meeting and I'll need to go into the office. I'm sorry." His voice was full of remorse. "I don't want to leave you."

She breathed a sigh of relief. "No, that's okay. I've taken up enough of your time over the last few days."

The flash in his eyes was her only warning as he stormed toward her. She gasped, but before she could retreat, he pulled her toward him and crashed his lips against hers. For a moment, she hesitated, and then fell vulnerable to his touch, his taste. Her arms wrapped around his neck as he devoured her. He took all that she was and gave just as much of himself back.

At the clearing of a throat, they broke apart from the kiss.

"I'll wait for you by the cars," Luke said, grinning like a complete and utter idiot.

Her cheeks warmed as Greg nodded.

At Luke's fading steps, she smoothed the small wrinkle in his jacket. "You should get going."

He ran his finger under her chin, forcing her to meet his gaze. "Not until I address what you just said. You could never take up too much of my time because you are worth every second of every day. Eternity is not long enough for me to spend with you. It does not even compare to how long I want to be with you. Nothing expresses the amount of joy and happiness you bring me, or the depths of my emotions for you, but you are worth them." He brushed a strand of hair behind her ear. "You are worth everything, Daniella."

"Greg," she stuttered, drowning in the mess he'd made of her heart, "I-I don't think—"

"I know you don't. I know why, and I will prove that you should not feel guilty for your existence. You have positively affected so many more lives than you know. You have been my strength without even realizing it. Don't forget that, Ella. Don't forget the lives you affect, the good you've done and still have left to do. Don't forget what you mean to the people around you, those that love you."

He kissed her again, bursting her fragile heart open under the spell he'd woven. She clung to him and the light he gave her in the face of her despair.

"Mya's going to stay here with you. But when I'm done with the meeting, I'll pick us up dinner and then we'll talk, okay?"

"Okay."

He kissed her cheek before finally slipping out of their embrace, and she held onto his parting words to keep herself sane.

CHAPTER 12

When Daniella first met Mya, she'd reminded her of a wolf: big, fluffy, and able to bite your head off in less than ten seconds. But after she'd gotten to know her, she understood it was just her outer shell. Daniella had always suspected Mya used it to protect herself, although she'd never quite figured out why. Now it made more sense.

Mya had lived through periods of times where women were believed to be worthless, where they needed to dress and behave in ways that modern women found demeaning. Daniella had a new-found respect for Mya and her strength. That strength was admirable, and an inspiration for what she desperately needed to maintain, a semblance of balance right now to keep her grief at bay.

"On a scale of one to ten, how mad are you at me?" Mya called out before Daniella entered the kitchen.

She thought for a moment while taking a seat beside Mya. "Around a two."

"Huh, I would have assumed at least a six."

"No. One, because I know if anyone hated keeping me in the dark, it would be you. You don't have patience to deal with stupidity, much less lying. Two, because it's rare for you to be apologetic. I barely made Greg or Luke grovel for the transgression. You wouldn't bother."

Mya tapped her fingers on the table. "Well, you're not wrong there, but I am sorry. I never wanted to hurt you. You're like a sister to me, and I adore you."

Daniella smiled. "Same here." She nodded towards the laptop as automated numbers moved on the screen. "Is that about the embezzlement?"

Mya sighed, fussing with a dark brown strand that had fallen from her high bun. "I still have a lot to investigate. For some reason, the answer to all of this is eluding me, and it's pissing me off."

"I should have asked Greg to bring my laptop from the office. I also don't know where my purse or cell phone are. Could I borrow yours to text him?"

"Don't worry about that. Greg had me look at your phone to see if it could be tracked, which it could. He's getting you a new one and a card tied to his account while he's in NYC."

Her eyes widened. "Wait, what?"

Mya smirked. "The man's got it bad, and from the looks of it, so do you. Word of advice: don't say anything stupid like he doesn't need to do this, or shouldn't do this, yada yada. Just accept it. It's easier that way."

Daniella opened her mouth to respond but couldn't form any words. A blush spread across her cheeks as she tried to hide her shy smile. Greg's kindness and the strength of his feelings warmed her heart. He made all of her wishes for a future with him seem not only attainable, but actively reciprocated.

The computer chimed and Mya cursed, hitting the table with a sigh.

"Can I help somehow?"

Mya studied her for a moment. "How much do you know?"

"What do you mean?" Daniella cocked her head to the side.

"I mean, what do you think happened at the office?"

Her brow furrowed in confusion. "Well, I found out about the embezzlement at the same time you guys did. Greg initially told me he wanted me to stay out of the office for a few weeks on a fake vacation because he thought someone was trying to blame me for the theft. I now know that's not one hundred percent true. I know Zachariah was the one who did it, but he had to have inside help. He wouldn't have been able to commit the crime otherwise."

Mya raised an eyebrow. "Why?"

Daniella sighed, shoving her fingers through her hair. "Because he may have been at my apartment."

Mya whistled. "Sleeping with the enemy? Damn girl."

"Please don't tease me about it. Alcohol led to very poor decisions that night."

"A vampire booty call. I'd be proud of you if it were anyone else."

Daniella elbowed her. "Hush. It was not one of my finer moments."

Mya typed rapidly now. "Do you know what time he arrived and what time he left?"

"Somewhere around 1:30 a.m., and he left a few minutes after sunrise."

"Hmm. So he killed them first and then triggered the security alert."

Daniella drew back. "Killed them? Killed who? What are you talking about?"

Mya muttered a curse under her breath and faced her. "Fuck, Dani, when you said crime, I thought..." She sighed. "Zachariah didn't just steal money from the company. He killed twenty-two vampires before he did it."

"Oh God. Oh God, I think I'm going to be sick."

"Shit—"

Daniella barely made it to the trash can before she vomited. Mya held back her hair as she heaved. When Daniella became more stable, Mya brought her a glass of water.

"Thank you."

"It's okay. I'm sorry. I should have let Greg tell you. He would have," Mya insisted as she led Daniella to the bar stool.

"No, it's okay. I'm close with each of you, and I want you all to fill me in if I don't know something." She stroked the glass with her thumb. "I know Greg would have told me, but we just haven't had a lot of time. Every day something else happens." Her eyes slid to Mya. "Has it always been this way?"

Mya shook her head. "No. Things were good and had been good for a while. There were some terrible times, of course, and sometimes I don't know how we made it through, but we did. The war picked back up about a century ago. Each time, it's someone new. Someone always thinks that we shouldn't live beside humans, that our proper place is to reign over them. It's always a new vampire, one that doesn't understand what we've gone through and seen. That even though we are stronger, there are simply more humans."

Mya rested her head in her palm and shrugged. "It's not

about conquering or being the top predator. It's about creating a peaceful co-existence. Whenever vampires appear with those ideals, we shut them down. But Zachariah? I don't know. He doesn't even seem smart enough to do all of this, but every time we think we'll catch him, he slips through our fingers." She rubbed her temples. "He's caused more carnage and erased more of our history than anyone else."

Daniella shook her head. Her voice wavered as she spoke. "So much pain, so much death ... I'm beginning to understand why you all kept this from me."

Her thoughts turned to Stacy. Stacy wasn't a vampire. She shouldn't have been dragged into this mess, but she was. And the others. How many people had died in these useless battles, especially over the course of a century?

She didn't realize she was shaking until Mya squeezed her shoulder. "What about the lives of the vampires who were killed?"

"We have something of a cleanup crew. They tidy up any loose ends. Any work that needs to be done, investigations, housing payments, moving furniture, pets, they handle all of that. Dominick and Merida review their work to make sure nothing was missed and provide a final report to Greg."

"But what about family?" Her voice rose. "Don't vampires have families?"

Mya sighed. "When they become part of our circle, they leave all of that behind, Dani. They have to, for the same reasons you're seeing now."

A pained expression flashed in Mya's eyes, but she continued. "We take care of our own, but that doesn't mean there aren't casualties, and to keep everyone safe, only immediate family is brought in. Greg meets with each victim's family. If a vampire had a mate, we will take care of them, make sure they're kept afloat, and watch out for them. It's the same if they had children. Some vampires have extended family, grandchildren, or great-grandchildren who were born long after they became a vampire. For their protection, the vampire has to stay away. They may send anonymous presents or donations, set up funds for their education or life, which the cleaners make sure continue, but otherwise they have to keep that life separate from their vampiric one. No visitations, sharing anything traceable, and so on."

Mya grimaced. "It's not an easy life, but any vampire that comes into any circle agrees to those terms before they do. It may sound cruel, but—"

"It's not cruel. It's lonely." Daniella lifted her gaze from the counter and the look in her eyes made Mya draw back. "How do you kill a vampire?"

"That's not something you need to worry about."

"But it is. All of this is because of one vampire. I understand others may follow his ideals, but he's the one killing people right now, and it affects everyone. I mean, didn't you stay behind just to protect me?"

Mya's eyes narrowed. "It's not the only reason I'm here."

Daniella glared back at her. "Fine, but it's still one of the reasons. I need to learn how to take care of myself. Teach me how. Neither Greg nor Luke would ever show me, and even if they did, they'd go easy on me. You won't. Greg will be out for a while, so we have plenty of time."

Mya sighed and tapped her fingers on the counter again.

"Please?"

"You have a point, and it would be good for you to know how to defend yourself. But I have to be straight with you." She shrugged. "I have two abilities. One is to heal. Greg and Luke have a fraction of it because I shared it with them, but it's only a fraction. Even if you get a hit in, and that's a *big* if, it's not going to slow me down enough to stop me from countering. The second is speed. I'm fast. You aren't going to be able to keep up with me, end of story."

"You're also ruthless, competitive, and clearly not humble," Daniella said with a grunt.

Mya smiled and raised her hands in mock agreement. "I call it how I see it. But my point is, the you sitting next to me right now is not ready for this at all. If we're going to do this, I need your complete focus, and right now it's elsewhere. So, go deal with your friend's death, however you need to. Pain will get you far. It will motivate you, it will give you strength when you think all of yours has faded, but it will also eat away at you until you are nothing but a vast dark hole that crumbles under its own weight. If you need to scream, scream. If you need to throw a tree, cause a tornado or whatever that was earlier, then do it. Just don't wreck the house."

THE GROUND WAS DAMP UNDER HER FEET. THE PUDDLE SHE'D stepped into splashed back at her, but she paid it no mind. Daniella's thoughts had faded to a whisper. There were no voices, no darkness, no emotions, just a pull. An invisible string that connected her to somewhere she knew intimately, so she let it lead her.

Three days ago, she would have been scared, concerned about her irrational childish behavior. She loved the woods, loved nature, but she never had time for it, much less embraced it like she did now. She would have wondered where she was going, if she knew how to get back, thought of meetings she might be late for if she couldn't, set numerous alarms, and turned on the location on her phone to make sure she would be safe. Those were all things she had to do in NYC.

There was a certain necessary control required when navigating the bustling streets. It's how one avoided collision, a spilled drink, assault, or stolen property. It was how she kept herself out of danger. Keeping a tight, level head was how she made it through, combined with constant momentum, moving one foot in front of the other until she reached her destination. That had always been her belief, but now she realized her life never had to be that way.

The earth had freedom, something she never knew she needed. Yet here, surrounded by the forest, the scents of pine, maple, and even the poison ivy, she realized this was where she belonged. She knew it would take care of her, that it would keep her safe, as long as she relinquished control, as long as she listened.

Daniella went deeper into the lush forest until she found a break in the trees. Rocks jutted in a circle, irregular yet smooth. They surrounded a bed of wildflowers. Weeds to other people —tiny, insignificant things that would have been plucked from the earth for their unsightliness. They now felt like her greatest treasures.

Careful not to step on them, she wove through the rows before coming to stand in the center. Lifting her head up to the sky, she breathed in and basked in the sunlight, letting it warm her. Then she sank to her knees and cried. She cried for Stacy, for the murdered vampires. She cried for Greg, Luke, and Mya, for the torture and turmoil they had experienced. She cried for their responsibilities, the weight on Greg's shoulders.

She cried for herself, for never knowing she could be this version of herself that craved so much more but expected so much less. For the toxic ways she had lived her life, the busyness she no longer craved, the distractions, the peace she compromised, the abilities that had hidden within her for such a long time. Had she always lived this way, as half of a person, fearing that if she let go even for a moment, she would turn to drugs like her mother?

She cried for who her mother had been during her good times, who she had been during her bad, and who she could have been with guidance, with someone like Greg in her life. Someone who could sympathize and guide her abilities. Someone who had just listened.

A part of her wished that could have been her, but she was only a child back then. That was far too great of an ask, but now it became a driving force. In three days, her life had completely flipped on its head. She had these abilities, this knowledge, these people, this life, and she realized they were all things she wanted. All things she needed.

Daniella brushed her hands on her knees, wiping off the dirt, and swiped at her eyes with the inside of her shirt. Weaving her hands through the flowers she'd crushed, she spoke softly.

"Maybe I'm crazy for trying this or saying it out loud, but I don't care anymore." The air seemed to hum as she spoke. "Spirit of darkness, whatever, whoever you are, I don't know if you are connected with death, or if you can carry this message there, but if you can, please, wherever Stacy is, let her know I'm sorry. I'm sorry she died. I'm sorry for whatever role I played in her death. I know I'm not to blame. I know things happen for a reason, but I also know she was targeted because of me. I loved her." She sniffled. "I still love her. I can still picture her smile, I can still hear her violin, I can still think of all the times she worried about me. She was a great friend, and if she's somewhere out there, please let her know that. I'm going to do better. I'm going to finally listen, to take time for myself. I'm going to stop pushing so incredibly hard to just be okay, to be this person I think I'm supposed to be because I shouldn't need anyone." She released a shaky breath. "I'm going to let go of this idea that if I'm not in control, I won't know what to do."

A sad laugh escaped her. "Clearly, I haven't known what to do for most of my life, but I want to learn." More tears rolled down her cheeks as she trembled. "Let her know that, please, and please, you, the others, the spirits in the elements, help me. I don't want to be half of myself anymore. I don't want to be blind to these abilities or this world anymore. I just want to be whole. I want to be happy instead of temporarily existing and being content with that. I can't go back to my old life, where all my plants are in pots and I live in a polluted and overpopulated city. Where I can't see the tops of mountains or breathe in clean fresh air. I can't be diluted. This world, this place where vampires exist, where I have abilities, where I can figure out who I want to be, not who I think I need to be, is the world I'm meant to live in. I want to learn to have faith in that. I want to learn to have faith in this." She brushed the flowers in her hands. "So please, help me."

The flowers grew, their stems sprouting and rising higher and higher until they reached her chest. It delighted her so much that she laughed, the sound mixing with a new stream of tears.

Daniella made her way back to the house when she was done and paused when she saw Mya waiting for her outside.

A knowing smile touched her lips, and Mya adjusted her hair in its bun. "Better?"

"Yeah." Daniella stretched her arms outwards and then up, rolling her shoulders back. "Are you going to teach me how to fight now?"

"Yep, but when I whoop your ass, don't say I didn't warn you."

CHAPTER 13

All Greg wanted was to get back home to Daniella. He'd always hated being away from her, but never more than now, when she was in so much pain and distress. She needed someone to comfort her, and he wanted to be that person. But instead, he was stuck here.

The council meeting had taken almost four hours, much longer than he had initially expected. All because of Zachariah's bullshit. While many of the council members held Greg in high regard, they weren't known for their patience or sympathy. Some members went as far as to state that the vampires Greg lost were a sign of his weakened power and authority. He knew what they were up to. They just wanted his territory and were willing to use any means to get it, even unsubstantiated rumors. Fuckers.

Fear and greed were nasty emotions, but together they were destructive. If he wasn't careful, everything that he built and everyone he protected would end up torn apart. But he wouldn't worry about that now. The future was tomorrow's problem; the present was today's, and he had more than enough issues here.

That Stacy's death had been publicized was a huge issue for their world. This had not been the first time Zachariah—or another otherworldly creature—had taken the life of a human, but they were trained to keep these things hidden from the normal world. As long as Greg kept that from happening again and dealt with Zachariah within the next year, he would be fine. And he would get him sooner rather than later.

It was clear Zachariah had set his sights on Daniella, and the knowledge made Greg's blood boil. He would come after her again, and the moment he did, Greg would delight in ripping his spine out of his body. Then the war would be over.

His muscles rippled under his shirt, veins squeezed and tensed as rage rushed through him. He needed a distraction, to either let his powers flow through him, or to feed. But he couldn't here or at home, not in the way he needed. He didn't want to scare Daniella. But he was teetering on the edge. There had been too much, too soon, too fast: the events, his guilt, the racing of his mind, Daniella's pain, and the deep desire to mate with her, to make her his *forever*. His fist clenched. He was losing focus.

Greg forced himself to relax a moment before the door opened and a tiny bundle of brown curls awkwardly ran towards him.

"GG!"

He laughed, picked Iris up, and gave her a tight hug. "Hello, angel!" He looked at Dominick, still chuckling. "I didn't know she was coming here today."

Dominick smiled and took a seat in a nearby chair. "We're

taking her out of day care for a few days. With everything going on, she's safer with us."

Greg nodded and pushed through the tightening in his heart at the thought of his goddaughter being hurt. He tickled her as a distraction. With a kiss on top of her head, he sat her on his lap. He turned to speak to her father but stopped when her tiny fists pounded on his chest.

"GG!" she demanded.

"Yes, sweetie?"

Iris tried to stand and Greg held her under her arms to keep her steady. She grabbed his face with her tiny hands and stared right into his soul. "Why sad?"

He blinked, wide-eyed. Iris' ability as a born vampire was to see the emotions of others, but he hadn't realized they'd gotten that strong. He smoothed his hand over her head. "I'm okay, sweetie."

She twisted her lips and stomped her foot on his knee. "Stop sad!" she demanded, then gave him a hug and squirmed until he guided her to the ground.

"Did I just get told off by a two-year-old?"

"Yep." Dom picked up his daughter and tapped her on the nose before turning his gaze on Greg. "What's up, boss?"

"There's just been a lot going on and it's getting to me this time, that's all."

Dom raised an eyebrow. "I don't think I've ever heard you say the pressure was getting to you. Nice to see that even though you're old, you're not set in your ways. Growth is good, my friend."

Greg glared at him. "I get no respect around here."

"Was never a part of the deal. Now, what's going on?"

Greg used his ability to pick up several paper clips and a

pack of Post-it notes, floating them around Iris in a circle. Each time Iris tried to grasp one of the flying objects, Greg would pull it away from her. Again and again she tried, until she jumped off of her father's lap to chase them around the room.

"There's more at stake this time." He sighed. "Zachariah, this war, all of it ... This is the longest it's taken to resolve."

Dom's gaze softened. "We're doing everything we can to stop him, Greg. You know that."

"But that doesn't matter to the people he's hurt, or to the vampires he's turned against their will. If I can't rehabilitate them, that means more death on my hands." Greg shuddered and took a deep breath. "Those are people who could have been saved had I been able to catch him sooner. And what then?" The muscles in Greg's neck strained, his righteous anger brimming under the surface. "There's always another war, always someone else who wants to raise hell for their ideals. I just want to see it end and stay that way. In the old days, it was easier. Humans were scarcer. A bloodbath could be happening in the village next to them and they wouldn't even know. But now? All of these cities, all of these people?"

Dom shook his head. "It's not the same."

No, it's not. I took on this role to save vampires, not kill them. I don't want to see the people I love hurt. He slumped forward, tired of holding onto this weight, and watched his goddaughter. She ran around the room in joy and delight. Iris warmed his heart, and he thought about the days he wished to have children, the times he'd fallen asleep to those fantasies, to a life with Daniella. But now, he felt as if the chance for that piece of happiness was dangling in front of him, that his fingertips could touch just the end as it threatened to fly away.

"Sometimes it just feels like it's never going to happen," he whispered.

Dom leaned forward in his chair, drawing Greg's gaze. "I can never know the weight of your burdens. You're mindful about keeping them to yourself. One can appreciate that in a leader, but sometimes you need a release. You're not a machine. And I think you're feeling these things because for the first time, you can't stay objective."

Greg's eyes widened at that revelation and the spark it lit with him.

"You know how my life was before I met Merida." Dom's gaze shifted to his daughter as he watched her play, so close to the spitting image of his wife.

Greg nodded. He did. It was the reason he'd picked Dom and Merida to be his seconds-in-command. They knew first-hand what it was like to have the fate of millions resting on their shoulders.

A serene smile graced Dom's face and his eyes were overcome with love for his family. "Somehow, despite everything, I got lucky. I get to call Merida my wife. She has always made me feel alive, and for her I would give the world. She is at the center of my universe, and I'll bet Daniella is at the center of yours."

Greg's gaze shifted away. "She is, but I ... Dom if anything ever happens to her." His voice shook.

Dom's eyebrows drew together. "Why are you so sure something will?"

"Because it already did!"

"But that's where you're wrong. She was in danger, but she's not anymore."

"But she could be in the future."

A noise sounded in the corner, drawing both of their gazes as Iris jumped on the floor angrily. "Too loud! Stop mad!" She planted her hands on her hips.

Definitely her mother's daughter. They both chuckled and Iris smiled. Apparently satisfied, she went back to playing.

"Does Merida not have the possibility of being in danger in the future? Especially when she refuses to miss a single battle where we're involved? What about me? What about Iris? Is there not a possibility that someone could hurt her one day? What about my future children? What about yours, Greg?"

Greg's throat tightened at the thought.

"You see, you're stuck feeling afraid of the future because of a horror you experienced in the past. I get it, I understand it. You know I do. But the future isn't set in stone. If you need a reminder of that, think of us," Dom said.

Greg's gaze settled on his clasped hands. *Dom's right, you know he is.* If Greg had been one second later, Merida and Dominick would have died on the docks where he found them with bullets still lodged in their chests. They had believed their lives were going to end that day, but their lives had just begun. The future was always changing for everyone, even him and Daniella.

Dom's voice drew him from his thoughts. "You said you want to build a better future for all of us, and you have. Would it have been lovely if that bastard was dead right now? Of course. But that is not solely your decision. The job you signed up for can seem thankless and difficult, because it is. But do not forget all the people you saved by believing in yourself and the team you've created around you. That was all you, and it will continue to be with your woman by your side."

A beat of pride swelled in Greg's chest. He liked the sound of that. "Thanks, Dom."

Dom shrugged and stood with a smile on his face. "All in a day's work. Now please, cut yourself some slack. I expect you to have the same amount of faith in yourself as we have in you. And if you can't find it, I will be happy to go let my wife know so she can, rightfully, tear you a new asshole."

Iris wagged a finger at her father. "Daddy, bad word! Momma!" she screeched, running towards the door and down the hall.

"And now *I'm* going to get torn a new one too." He smirked. "Don't let my pain be in vain."

Greg laughed as Dominick raced after his daughter. Then he relaxed against the chair, feeling both exhausted and renewed from their conversation. He needed to speak with Daniella, to hear her voice and just ... connect with her. He grabbed his phone and called Mya, surprised when Daniella answered instead.

"Greg? Is everything okay?" she asked.

"It is now. I missed you."

He heard her shuffle in the background and then the gentle slide of a chair. "I missed you too." Her voice dropped lower. "It's different without you here."

"I feel the same way." He ruffled his hair. "The meeting took longer than expected. I'd hoped to be on my way back to you by now. I didn't want to leave you, Ella. I'm sorry for not being there when you needed someone."

"No, please, it's okay. I know you didn't want to go, but you had to. And even though you weren't here, you still helped me. What you said before you left ... it meant a lot to me."

His heart felt lighter at her words. "It's the truth, you know."

"Greg." She hesitated for a moment. "Come home soon. There's a lot I want to talk to you about, and so much I need to say."

He grabbed his keys in a rush and began packing his bag. "Is everything okay, baby?"

"Yes, I didn't mean to worry you. I just ... I'd really like to see you."

He smiled. "You still like the lobster ravioli from Orizzco's, right?"

Daniella laughed, and just hearing the sound warmed his heart. "I do, why?"

"I'll call in an order and pick it up on my way home. It'll take around two hours, but I'll be there as soon as I can."

"You don't have to do that. Plus, it'll be cold by the time it gets here."

He chuckled. "Well lucky for you, I know a thing or two about heating things up."

Her throaty giggle reminded him of how badly he wanted her naked, and he realized too late what he'd insinuated. "Well, I'll be the judge of that when you get here."

"Woman—" he warned.

"Goodbye, Greg." She was still laughing when she hung up.

CHAPTER 14

Greg nearly collided with Dom as he opened his door to leave. He took one look at Dom's panicked face and asked, "What's wrong? Did something happen to Iris?"

Dom shook his head. "No, she's fine. Elaine is watching her right now. It's Johanna." Dom motioned for Greg to follow him, and they took the stairs two at a time. "She's the one working with Zachariah."

"What? That doesn't make sense." Johanna, their CHRO, was human, not a being of The Otherworld. And if she had been turned, they all would have sensed it.

"Iris' ability gave us a hint," he said in a hushed tone as he opened the door to the administrative level of the building and began checking the offices to make sure they were clear of personnel.

"Merida was checking our HRIS software and scanning employees. Iris saw Johanna's profile and said she didn't like us anymore and that she wasn't 'real'."

Greg unleashed tendrils of his power, using his ability to manipulate matter to check the energy levels of the floor. It was empty. He nodded to Dom, and they approached Johanna's office.

"Merida called Mya. The two of them put their heads together and found a backdoor that had been used to gain access to our databases. The entry point was Johanna's computer."

Greg used his ability again to scan the office. At his confirmation that nothing was out of place, they entered together, and Dominick accessed her computer.

"You know I trust both your judgment and Merida's, but this still doesn't seem right to me. How would she have known how to hack the network and bypass our defenses? We're talking access to the server room, logins, and passwords, and what type of hacking software would we not have been able to catch? All of the tapes were damaged that night. She would have had to know the codes and commands to get into the recording center." Greg shook his head. "Are we sure no one else was helping her?"

"We're sure now." Merida came in with Luke behind her. "Dom, open her inbox and play the last file from her sent email, please."

He nodded, and they huddled around the screen as Dom double-clicked on the file.

The video started at the front door. A red light flashed as someone swiped their approved keycard to enter the building. It was Johanna, her blonde hair and round glasses reflecting in the overhead lights. Zachariah followed behind her. He smiled directly at the camera, meaning Johanna must have told him where they were.

Zachariah took off in front of her, a blur on the recording, but they all knew what would happen next. The first person murdered was Tony, his body left in the lobby, blood coating the walls. Zachariah moved floor to floor, killing anyone he got his hands on in the blink of an eye. They'd all been newly-turned vampires. They never stood a chance.

Johanna stepped out of the elevator on the fourth floor, missing the carnage. Zachariah dragged Nigel behind him, his face beaten and bloodied. Zachariah's lips moved and Johanna nodded in response before turning away. Zachariah tore into Nigel's throat, ripping apart his skin before he snapped his neck and tossed him to the ground.

Together, they rode the elevator to the eighth floor, the same one Greg and the others were on now. His stomach dropped. He knew who their next victim was. They all did.

Leo, a five-hundred-year-old vampire and one of Greg's battle officers, exited the stairway. He rushed toward Zachariah, knife in hand. Leo was almost on him before he froze mid-assault, paralyzed by an invisible force.

Zachariah placed a small object in Johanna's hand and waved her away. Her steps were robotic, with no trace of recognition for Leo nor sympathy on her face.

Zachariah took a step towards Leo. His grin spread as he spoke. Then he raised his hand to his throat, and they watched on in horror as Leo mimicked the motion, the knife gleaming in the light. Zachariah then pressed two fingers into his skin and smirked as Leo took his own life. He stepped on Leo's crumpled form as if it were nothing more than a rug and entered Johanna's office after her. Taking a seat behind her desktop, he slid his hand near the side.

Dom's voice wavered. "I think he's putting in a USB." He

nodded to the side of the computer where three ports were located. "Whatever is on that device is how he got into our systems."

"It's almost over," Merida whispered, her voice laced with grief and fury as she squeezed her husband's arm.

Zachariah and Johanna left the office shortly after. They took the elevator to the lobby, but before they left, Zachariah made a call from his cell phone. When a cocky smile appeared on his face, Greg knew exactly who was on the other line.

Daniella.

He'd *visited* her after killing vampires. Greg's vampires. People he cherished and cared for. Greg's body shook with rage. His incisors lengthened and his eyes turned red in fury. The cords of his muscles tightened in preparation for a fight, a battle he waged within himself. This was not the time nor the place, but still it tore through him.

A voice on the computer snapped him back to the present. He focused on the new frame and ground his teeth as he stared right at the face he wanted to crush and burn.

"I hope you enjoyed that little cinematic experience. I have to say, I found it especially compelling." Zachariah tapped his chin. "Ah yes, where are my manners? Greg, how are you doing these days? I assume you're pretty pissed off right now. You know, as a leader, you really should have more security. Or is that the best you could do? That group there was pretty pitiful. It was almost like you left the door wide open for me. Oh, and I must thank you for my fifty-million-dollar gift! Who knew you could be so generous!"

"I'm going to kill him," Luke spat.

"And Johanna, she's such a *doll*. It really is so nice to have friends. It wouldn't have been half as easy without her. Because of her, I now have the addresses of every single member of your little circle. But you know, Greg, killing your vampires gets old after a while. I'd rather convert them, show them the good things in life." Zachariah sat back in his chair. "So, I'll tell you what. You come to these coordinates, offer your head up on a platter, and I'll leave them be. You have twenty-four hours to decide." He sneered. "Don't make me wait."

The video clicked off, and Luke turned and punched the bookcase behind him, sending glass and splinters of wood crashing against the wall.

The action didn't faze Greg, Merida, or Dominick. Greg felt like breaking something himself, but he had to keep it together. They needed to make a plan, and fast.

"Everyone upstairs, now." He turned on his heels and left Johanna's office with his team in tow.

When they reached his office, Greg leaned against his desk. Luke stood near the door, his neck corded, nostrils flared. Greg shook his head, giving him a silent command to behave before addressing Merida and Dominick. "Is there any concern that he got into our offices?"

"No," Merida answered. "Nothing shows that any of the other offices were compromised."

"Good. Since he was in Johanna's office and various areas of the building, I want this building closed tomorrow. Send out a notice to everyone to keep their teams away. Have a sweeper team check for bugs or anything that he could use to gather information."

She nodded.

"As for the addresses—" Greg began.

"The ones in the system are fake. He didn't retrieve anyone's personal information," Dom replied.

"Actually, he could have." Greg drew in a slow breath. "You saw what he did to Nigel. I think he's able to get information by drinking someone's blood. If so, he could have pulled that information from anyone he killed that night."

"And what the fuck was that?" Luke shouted. "What did he do to Leo?"

Greg fought to keep his voice calm, controlled. "I don't know, Luke. I don't know."

"Is there any possibility that those are his new powers?" Dom asked.

Greg shook his head. "No, it's impossible. Zachariah is younger than all of us here. Powers are discovered around every vampire's two to three hundredth year. He would have just come into his second ability. We already know his first power turns him into a tank. He couldn't have two additional powers right now."

"Maybe they're not separate powers?"

They all turned their attention to Merida.

"He took information from Nigel through blood. Maybe that's his ability. Maybe part of the information he can take is their power. Or he can copy it. Whatever he used on Leo was some sort of mind control."

"But that wasn't Nigel's ability," Luke spat.

"No, it wasn't," Merida acknowledged. "But if he could control people's minds, including a vampire's, why would he need to threaten Greg? He'd be able to reach any of us at any time. I don't think that ability belongs to him. I think it's something he stole."

"Greg, your ability works similarly, what do you think?" Dom asked.

Greg tapped on the desk in thought. "Whenever I look into

a person's memories, it's temporary, and I can't go from one person to another repeatedly without expending a lot of energy. If he's able to control someone's mind, I'd assume the effects would be similar since all of our abilities are tempered in some way." He paused. "I don't think it's a vampire's ability, at least, not one we know. It could belong to a witch, fae, anyone. There are too many variables to guess. But whomever that ability belongs to, they're someone he keeps close. He wouldn't kill them and he wouldn't put them in danger. That ability would be too valuable to him."

"Is it possible," Luke snarled, "that it's Johanna's?"

Dom shook his head. "I don't think so. You saw how she looked throughout the video. I think she was under his control, not the other way around."

"But that doesn't make sense either. She could speak and move around just fine during the meeting on Monday, and she was working today. How would she be able to do that if he was controlling her?" Merida asked.

The door slammed shut as Luke stormed out of Greg's office. Merida and Dominick exchanged looks before turning to face Greg.

"I'll figure out what that was about later." Greg ran his hand through his hair. "For now, let's work on closing everything down. Merida, Dom, I need the two of you to work with Mya on expanding the list of known associates of the vampires that were killed. I know we have their immediate next of kin, but I want all family and friends included. Anyone they could have been in contact with within the last six months needs to be moved to another location for their safety. Also, choose a member of your team to investigate what Johanna was working on before she left. Check her employees too."

"And you?" Merida's eyebrow raised. "You're going to the meeting tomorrow, aren't you? Even though you know it's a trap?"

"Of course I am. We've never shied away from a trap before, why start now?" Greg said.

Merida and Dominick stood together. "What time are we having the strategy meeting?"

"Noon, at my house, for now. I'll let you know if that changes."

CHAPTER 15

Greg sorted his tasks into a mental list as he drove home. He would call Mya first. She was best at crafting the most effective routes, entry, and exit points, and would be key in ensuring their team would arrive safely at Zachariah's coordinates.

It was also an excuse to speak with Daniella. His mind was going a mile a minute, and he needed to hear her voice, to feel something of her wash over him. He dialed Mya's phone number and, just as before, Daniella answered first. Her voice filled his ears and everything else stilled.

Greg explained they'd found out Johanna was working with Zachariah, and he apologized for yet another delay. She absorbed the information and told him to take care on his way home, that she would be there, waiting for him.

Waiting for him. Against the odds, he smiled.

He relayed the same information to Mya. She had already

received the coordinates from Merida and had begun her analyzation.

After their call, Greg contacted each of his battle officers and provided them with the details of their emergency strategy meeting. He did all of this while monitoring the road to ensure he wasn't being followed. That was part of the reason why he'd chosen a property so far away from the office. The long drive meant many side streets and alternate routes home if needed. It also provided him with plenty of ways to lose someone if they were tailing him, including using his ability to flip their car and kill them without ever leaving his seat. He hadn't been followed in quite some time, but after the stunt Zachariah had pulled at his office, Greg couldn't take any chances.

Finally, he called Luke. It had been over an hour since he'd walked out of Greg's office, and he hoped his cousin had calmed down by now.

"Hey," Luke said.

Greg breathed a sigh of relief when he answered. "Hey. Is now a good time?"

"Yeah." There was a small rustling on the other end of the line before Luke continued, his voice heavy. "I'm sorry for storming off on you. That was inexcusable."

Greg ran his fingers through his hair. "Luke, I love you like a brother, but I cannot help you if you do not tell me what is going on. I understand your anger, but that was something else."

He sighed. "I know. But I can't, not yet. I'm confused. None of it makes any sense, and I just … I don't know what's going on Greg. I just don't know."

"Is it Johanna?"

Luke drew in a harsh breath.

"I know you thought she would be a good fit for the team," Greg said, remembering his feedback after her interview.

"That's not ... it."

When Luke chose not to explain further, Greg tapped the steering wheel and let out a deep sigh. "Whatever it is, I won't push you. When you're ready, come to me. We'll sit down and work this out together, okay? But whatever is causing you to feel however you do, it's not your fault. What is that ridiculousness you're always preaching to me? 'I can only control what I do or don't do, nothing else'."

Luke laughed. "The world must have gone to shit if you're quoting my advice back to me."

Greg shrugged, chuckling. "Nah. I just wanted you to realize I do actually listen to you, so you would quit your whining one of these days."

"Asshole."

"I learned from the best." Greg grinned. "We're having the meeting tomorrow at noon. I'll see you then."

"Okay. And Greg? Thanks for always being there for me."

"Of course. We're family."

THE SOUND OF LAUGHTER GREETED GREG AS HE ENTERED HIS home. It brought a smile to his face, which widened when he noticed the lights were on, welcoming him inside. Daniella really had waited for him, and that knowledge squeezed his heart, sending warmth through his chest.

When he entered the kitchen, Daniella's eyes met his and lit up. A smile formed across her lips and her shoulders visibly relaxed. "Welcome home."

Greg set the bags of food on the counter. With them out of the way, he could finally see all of her. He stopped dead in his tracks. Her t-shirt and shorts combination left her skin exposed, and he could see the new wounds that marred her skin: a cut on one arm, another across her chest, and her knuckles were purple, a bruise already forming.

What the fuck? Greg didn't hear Mya's sarcastic remarks, didn't even see her as his vision homed in on Daniella.

He pulled her to him and then lifted her over his shoulder. Daniella squealed and yelled his name, but it didn't deter him. He carried her out of the room and sprinted down the hall. When he reached the bathroom, he slammed the door shut and pinned her against it.

Daniella gasped and placed her hands on his chest, but he responded with a snarl, a warning. His breathing was rapid, harsh. Greg lifted one of her legs, holding the base of her foot as his eyes raked over her skin. His hand slid up her ankle, then her calf, following the path to her thigh before pausing at another wound. He ground his teeth but continued until he reached her hip. He did the same thing to her other leg and found a bruise on her foot and another on her hip.

When he spoke, his tone was low, threatening. "Where did these come from?"

Daniella shifted her gaze from his. The scent of her arousal washed over him as she trembled and clutched at his shoulders. Greg's nostrils flared as he continued his inspection under her shirt. His heartbeat was so loud that he almost missed her answer.

"I was training with Mya."

Greg froze. "You were what? Daniella, you are a human. We

are vampires. There is no need for you to do any sort of training."

She pushed against his chest, but he refused to allow any distance between them and instead pressed his body harder against hers. The way she moaned his name made him growl.

"Greg," she tried again. "I have to learn how to protect myself."

"God damnit, Daniella! No, you don't. You are mine!" He snarled, pinning her hands above her head. "You are mine to protect, mine to take care of, my priority. You are my mate. If you wanted to learn how to protect yourself so badly, you should have come to me!"

Daniella shivered, but even her haze of desire couldn't hide the defiance in her eyes. "If I would have gone to you, you would do the same thing you're doing *right* now. The moment I got hurt, you'd call the whole thing off. I needed to learn something!" Her voice softened. "You shouldn't have to take care of me. I can't be your priority. Your circle is your priority, and I want to help you with that, not hinder you."

Her words hit him like a blow, taking all of his anger and rage and leaving him scared and broken. He curved until his forehead rested against hers. "You are my priority."

"Greg—"

"You're my priority because the circle can survive on its own, but I can't survive without you."

She gasped, her body still against his.

"Ella, is it so wrong for me to want to be everything you need? Everything you want? To give you everything you could ever desire?" He cupped her face. "Seeing you hurt destroys me."

"No, it's not wrong." She wrapped her arms around his neck, and her smile could have rivaled the sun. "But you've forgotten one thing. You already are all of those things for me, *my* everything."

Greg's lips clashed against hers. He pulled her to him, pushed against her. They twisted, yanked, fell against one another like a rising tide, but it wasn't enough. He'd gotten a taste of her, the way she felt when she'd allowed him to wander, and now he wanted more.

He kissed down the contours of her neck. Daniella held him close as he sucked and nibbled on her. When he bit her neck, stopping himself from puncturing her skin, she moaned.

"Soon," he whispered against her flesh, a promise to the both of them.

Daniella fisted his shirt, clutching him to her. "Greg, please."

"Don't worry, love. I'm not going to stop, not yet." He licked down to her breast and traced the already fading scar with his tongue.

She sucked in a breath, tangling her hand in his hair. "But Mya—"

He pulled his head back for a moment, and her whine of protest made him smile. Greg lowered the straps of her top and bra until her beautiful breasts were free for him to savor.

"When I'm inside of you," he began, trailing kisses around the mound as his hand slid over her stomach, "I will make you scream my name. But for now"—his fingers slid under her shorts and pressed between her lips, tracing her core through her underwear, making her gasp—"I need you to stay quiet for me. I don't want anyone to interrupt us, not until I make you come. Can you be quiet, Ella?"

She bit her lip, nodding in response as he pushed her

underwear to the side and circled her clit. He sucked her nipple into his mouth and watched as her head fell back against the door. Over and over, he thumbed the engorged nub, adding pressure slowly while he teased her breast, switching from one delicious mound to the other.

Greg slid his finger down lower and then pushed inside of her. She covered her mouth, moaning against her palm. He thrust inside, rubbing her sensitive bud, keeping his movements in sync. When she rocked her hips, he slid another digit into her wet heat. Daniella gasped, sinking down, taking him deeper.

He let her breast go and claimed her mouth. Using the new angle, Greg curled his fingers, increasing his speed as he devoured each and every single one of her cries.

She clung to him, wrapping her legs around his waist, her arms squeezing his back. Greg rolled and pinched her nipple, and she grew wilder at the mixture of pain and pleasure. She was so fucking wet that it took everything in him not to ram inside of her. But he needed this, needed her, needed to give her pleasure. It was the only thing that would appease the animal inside of him.

She shivered as her movements became chaotic and disjointed. "Yes, yes, *yes!*" Daniella cried into his neck, sucking on his skin as he groaned. Then she trembled. Her head snapped back and she froze, suspended in bliss. He kissed her, swallowing her cries as she came, her liquid drenching his fingers as her pussy spasmed around him. Still he moved his fingers slowly, in and out, until her body relaxed, and then he withdrew them from her.

With a smile, he sucked them into his mouth and moaned at her taste. "I always knew you would be delicious."

THEY SHUFFLED BACK INTO THE KITCHEN TOGETHER. GREG'S HAIR was out of place, still a mess from Daniella's fingers, and she'd ripped several of the buttons off his shirt, but he didn't care. They were his own personal gifts, brands from the woman he loved.

Mya's gaze went from his face to Daniella's and back before she cackled. "You guys could have at least waited until I left to have sex, jeez."

"Come on, sis, you know I don't do anything half-ass."

Mya was still chuckling as she left the kitchen, and Greg used the opportunity to spread his fingers over Daniella's stomach and whisper in her ear, "You wouldn't be able to walk if we did."

A blush crept over her skin and she shivered, and smacked his hand away. "Arrogance doesn't become you."

Greg smirked as they sat at the table. "It isn't arrogance if it's the truth." He grasped her chin in his hand. "If you like, I'd be more than happy to prove it to you. Right here, right now."

He kissed down her neck while his hand slid up her thigh. "Would you let me bend you over this table and fuck you, Ella?"

Her pulse raced under his lips, but when he pulled back, he saw her devilish grin. She grasped his wrist, stopping his advance. "Two can play that game, Gregori. After all"—her fingers fell to his lap—"with how hard you are, it would be so easy to make a mess out of you."

He squeezed her wrist before she was able to touch him. "I'll remember that for later, vixen."

Mya returned with two large maps. "If you two are done

doing whatever you're doing over there, I pulled up those coordinates you gave me." She unrolled the maps and arranged them on the table before tapping on an area west of NYC. "I believe it's an unmarked cavern. I don't have a lot to base that hunch off of, but there's a cave system less than two miles away."

"So we have no way to determine how many entrances or exits there are, which means they can attack from anywhere." Greg paused, making a mental note of the roads in and out of that location and how easy it would be for a vampire to travel on foot. "I think Zachariah would attack from inside the cavern where he'd have more control. If he swarms from the outside, we'd have an easier chance to either overwhelm him or flee than if we're stuck in a tight space or driven further into a location we know nothing about."

Mya nodded. "What's the plan?"

"The same as always. We go in."

She raised an eyebrow. "Even though we're sure it's a trap?"

The air around Daniella tingled, calling Greg's focus. Small, almost invisible lines curved and rubbed against themselves, creating a type of pulse in the air that shimmered. His gaze shifted back to Mya, but she seemed to be entirely immune to the experience. Perhaps he could only feel it due to his abilities, or his proximity to Daniella. It wasn't a negative feeling, the opposite, in fact. It felt comforting, like a mother's hand on her child guiding them down an unknown path. Perhaps it was the voices she had mentioned. Could they be revealing something to her about the location? About him? Unsure of what to do, he carefully wrapped his arm around her to remind her he was there if she needed him. But she didn't move, didn't even blink, her blank stare focused on the map.

With a sigh, he finally responded to Mya. "Yes, especially since we're sure it's a trap. We have a reason to make sure we can keep him and his vampires in that space as well. If they get out, we'll lose them. The best strategy we have at this point is offense. He wants a battle, so we'll bring it to him. That's our chance of victory."

Daniella blinked, coming out of her trance, and Greg shifted as she leaned against him. "Are you okay?" he asked.

Her eyes had grown red and her heartbeat thundered so loud he thought she was going to have another anxiety attack. She grabbed hold of him and pulled him towards her until she could meet his lips. Her kiss was desperate, as if she were begging the gods to freeze time right at this moment.

When he pulled away from her, breathless, he saw fresh tears in her eyes. "Ella? What's wrong?"

"I'm okay. I'll tell you tomorrow." Her gaze slid from his to Mya's. "Can we talk about all of this tomorrow? Please?"

Mya, just as confused as he was, tilted her head to the side but nodded. "Of course."

Greg cradled Daniella, and she clung to him, grasping his back in her tiny hands.

Mya searched Greg's eyes for answers, but all he could do was shrug and shake his head. She folded the maps to clear off the table. "Why don't we eat and try to enjoy the night then?"

Daniella's shoulders slumped in relief. "Thank you."

They ate and fell into an easy conversation around the table with light teasing and small laughs, but eventually the night came to an end.

They stood and Greg pulled his cell phone out of his pocket. "Do you mind if I make a couple of calls?"

Daniella smiled. "No, I'll see Mya out. I have a few things to discuss with her anyway."

Greg looked between the two of them. The smirk on Mya's lips did not bode well for him.

"There's no need for you to worry, big bro. At least, not yet." Mya's smile spread and Daniella laughed.

"I wasn't until you said that, little sister." He gave her a hug. "Be careful on your way home. Text me when you get there, and if you can, please don't corrupt my mate's mind before you leave."

"I can't make any promises."

Greg chuckled and dropped a kiss on Daniella's head. "I'll be in the study when you're done."

CHAPTER 16

Greg was on his last call when Daniella entered the room, dressed in a floor-length silk robe. Everything faded away as he took her in, catching the mischievous look in her eyes and the teasing smile that played on her lips.

She had tied the robe around her waist loose enough for it to fall open and give him a generous view of her skin. He followed it with his eyes, devouring the path between her breasts, over her stomach, and down to her navel, disappointed when the sash obstructed his further progression.

With each step, the robe opened, revealing her long legs. The soft fragrance of her shower gel as it mixed in with her natural scent wrapped around him, tantalizing his senses. Saliva pooled in his mouth and he barely caught himself before he drooled.

Her smile grew, and his cock hardened. His vixen knew exactly what she was doing, seducing him.

There was a murmur on the other end of the phone with an uptake at the end. A question. "What?" he asked Michael.

"I asked how many people you want to watch the Tompson building."

"Five." Greg swallowed hard as she sat on the couch. The robe draped open around her as she crossed her legs and folded her hands over her knee. He wanted to be in between those legs, to feel them wrapped around his waist, or better yet, his head as he teased her clit.

Is she naked under that robe? Please, gods, let her be naked.

She had his sole focus, and he knew he had to give up when he missed something else Michael said. "I think we're having some interference. I'll conference you in at noon, alright?"

"Okay, Greg. Talk to you then."

"Bye." He hung up and rose from his chair, dropping the phone onto his desk.

Greg's hands slid to the top of his shirt, releasing the first button from its closure, then the next, and the next, smirking as Daniella watched him. Her eyes heated, darkening to near black, and when she licked her lips, he almost groaned.

"Were you really getting interference?" she whispered huskily.

"Yes, due to the gorgeous woman who walked into my office." He unbuckled his belt and ripped it free from the loops, throwing it on the ground as he prowled toward her.

She bit her lip, trying to suppress her whimper. But he caught its melody in the air as he grasped her chin, forcing her to meet his eyes.

"I am going to worship you like the goddess you are."

Greg pulled her onto his lap. Her gasp turned into a moan as he kissed her neck, tracing her skin with his tongue. Her arms wrapped around him while he pulled at the ends of the robe, desperate to feel her, touch her anywhere, to sate his curiosity.

His hands slid up her calves, caressing her skin. She was so soft, so smooth, like butter, and he was starving, famished for a taste of her. Then he reached her thighs, pulling the material caught from between their rolling hips, and when her heat brushed against his pants, he nearly lost his mind. Daniella was naked, wet, and wanting, all for him.

Her hand slid down his body, following the panes of his chest, over his abs, reaching the waistband of his pants where his cock strained to break free. That was his last barrier, after that ...

"Daniella, I won't be able to stop."

"Who said I want you to?" Her fingertips brushed over the closure and he hissed as she lowered the zipper.

"You'll be immortal." He growled as she licked her beautiful, heart-shaped lips, drawing his gaze. Greg had to say this now, while he still could. "You'll be stronger, faster, you won't age—"

She palmed him through his boxers and he cursed, a moan escaping his lips.

"On my first night here, you asked me if I could accept you, all of you, and my answer has never changed. Not once. It's always been yes to everything, including becoming immortal if it means I get to be with you."

Her hands left his body and he mourned the loss until they moved to her sash. Greg's breath hitched as she pulled it free.

"I've always been yours, Gregori." Daniella rolled her shoulders and the robe dropped, pooling around them and leaving her glorious body on full display. "So take me."

He crushed his lips against hers and pushed her back onto the couch. He wallowed in the softness of her skin, in the warmth of her body. Greg brushed her hair back, his fingers buried in it as he grasped her head and kept her lips lined against his while he consumed her. His tongue entered the warmth of her mouth and he moaned as she met each stroke.

Her hands were restless over his body, moving, groping, squeezing at his skin. Daniella branded him with each touch, and he reacted the same. He nestled between her legs, forcing them wider, and she cradled him there. His erection, already pulsing and heavy, fit against her as he ground his hips. He drank in every moan, felt dizzy as her wetness seeped through his boxers.

Fuck. He was drowning, and he hadn't even touched her yet.

Greg slid his hands down her body and she curved into his touch. He loved her moans, loved how responsive she was. When he reached her clit and circled the nub, she moaned and spread her legs wider to accept him. She *accepted* him, and it drove him crazy.

His teeth scraped over her nipple before he closed his lips around it, sucking it into his mouth, toying with it. Daniella writhed beneath him. He slid one finger and then another into her wet heat, moaning at how she drenched his hand.

She cursed and moaned as his fingers rocked inside of her. Daniella tilted her hips to draw his fingers in further as she ground against his palm, begging for release, and when he curled his fingers and thumbed her clit, she did.

Her cries urged him. He needed to see her orgasm again, to leave her a sweaty, disjointed mess for him to touch, taste, tease. *All for him.*

By the time his mouth made it down to her hips, her

breathing was erratic. He paused at the junction of her thighs and watched with heated fascination as his fingers slid in and out of her, coated in her juices. The sight was beautiful, and he couldn't stop himself from sliding them into his mouth and sucking them clean.

"Greg," she panted, watching him with glazed eyes.

He traced the inside of her thighs with his tongue and she squirmed from his touch. As he grew closer to her core, her breaths became shallower, rushed, and he smiled in pure satisfaction. Then he blew on her pussy before taking the lips into his mouth. She clung onto the arm of the couch, arching her back as he sucked once, twice, before spreading her lips with his tongue and sliding inside. He moaned at her taste, even more so when her climax hit her again.

But he didn't stop, couldn't. Not until she was grasping at his hair, both pushing and tugging the strands as she went wild underneath him. Not until her thighs squeezed tightly around his head, until her pelvis moved in perfect harmony with the strokes of his tongue.

When he touched her engorged clit, applying the familiar pressure she loved before easing away, she hissed and he chuckled. He enjoyed teasing her, especially when he knew she was so close. Leaving her sweet pussy, he kissed her clit, drew it into his mouth and sucked, sliding two fingers inside of her again.

Daniella's hips lifted off the couch when she came hard, tensing every part of her body as her release flew through her. She cried out, moaning his name.

I want to hear her scream it.

The single thought pushed the rest of his blood to his cock. Greg tore at his clothes, desperate to free himself and finally ram inside of her. Daniella gasped at the sight of him. Her eyes roamed over his form, pausing at his dick.

When he settled himself in between her legs, she sat up and stopped him. "I want to taste you." She coated her fingers in his pre-cum and spread it over his dick, before gripping him in both hands.

His head fell back as pleasure soared through his body, and when she took him inside of her perfect little mouth, he swore he saw stars. "Fuck, Ella."

She looked up at him, her eyes dark and devious as she sucked more of him in until he hit the back of her throat. His eyes closed, hands fisting the couch as she relaxed her throat to take him as deep as she could. Greg used every shred of his control to resist fisting her hair and thrusting inside of her throat, but when she clutched at his ass and pushed, he gave her what they both wanted.

She moaned, the vibration wrapping around his cock, and he shuddered as he thrust again. Daniella cupped his balls as she let him use her mouth, moaning with him, deriving pleasure from his own.

She made him crazy. He couldn't take it anymore. Daniella whined as he pulled away from her. Greg dragged her hips to his, and she gasped as he forced her onto her back. With one deep thrust, he was finally, *finally* inside of her.

"Is this what you wanted?" he growled.

"Yes! *Yes!*"

"Then hold on, baby."

Greg angled her hips, stuffing a pillow underneath her as he rammed home again. Her hands kneaded his back, nails raking over his skin, and he squeezed her hips, pounding faster. He pushed into her, driving them higher as she clung to him. "Mine!"

He sucked her neck, his fangs dancing along her skin. He'd hid them for as long as he could, but now he was too far gone. The need to slip them into her skin and taste her, *claim* her, make her his, was irresistible.

When she tilted her neck to the side, gripping his hair, he surrendered. He bit her, moaning as her blood flowed into his mouth and he sucked her life's essence into him, completing their bond.

Daniella cried out, chanting his name as he picked up pace. The world had disappeared, and it was only them, only this feeling. Nothing existed outside of their bodies. The way her walls spasmed around his cock, taking him deeper, the way her fingers gripped and slid over his skin until she scratched his back, how she held him, how the scent of their sex permeated the air, was everything. Nothing could ever match this feeling, nothing could ever make him feel so damn whole, so damn *good*.

He fucked her until he was senseless, and then he felt it for the first time. The shiver that coursed through her body, the way her breath caught in her throat as she prepared for one last scream, and it was his name on her lips as her pussy spasmed around his cock. His eyes rolled back as she dragged him over the edge.

Greg pulled his teeth out of her neck a moment before he shouted, his orgasm rolling through him like a freight train as he filled her to the brim.

CHAPTER 17

When morning came and she'd finally left Greg's warm embrace, Daniella felt relaxed. One could even say sated, as long as she managed not to stay too close to him, think about him too often, or what they had spent most of the night and early morning doing.

Making love with Gregori was everything she could have asked for and more than she could have ever imagined. According to him, it had also made her immortal. She was still human, but taking Greg as her mate gave her certain vampiric abilities, such as enhanced strength, speed, and immunity.

Daniella didn't feel any different, although Mya's movements seemed slower to her, like if she focused just enough, she could catch them out of the corner of her eye. Sometimes it even seemed like she hit harder, but true to Mya's word, even if she did, Mya would still have the upper hand. She was trained and honed for battle in a way Daniella was not, but she would be. She *had* to be.

"Remember to widen your stance. If you don't, you'll leave your left side open," Mya said, pulling her from her thoughts.

Daniella grunted and spread her legs further apart.

Mya spun to kick her again. Daniella knew she wouldn't be able to miss the attack, so she crossed her arms and blocked it.

"Good." Mya nodded. "You're faster. Mating with my brother agrees with you."

Daniella blushed, but stayed focused. She threw out a jab, and then another.

Mya evaded both and returned the attack.

Daniella ducked, escaping the first two punches, but Mya's elbow hit home. Her connection with the water spirit may have kept her from feeling pain, but the hit would definitely leave a bruise tomorrow.

Daniella's magic was where her strength laid. With it, she could unleash devastating long-range attacks. But she had to stay balanced and could only do so if she learned how to defend herself in close combat. If someone could incapacitate her, she would be nothing but a liability.

They practiced for another hour before switching techniques.

"Do you want to work on the boiling my blood thing again? I'm quite amused by it."

Daniella side-eyed her. "You're a masochist."

"Don't judge." Mya winked and they shared a laugh. "Plus, if I remember correctly, you had fun setting me on fire yesterday."

Daniella scrunched her nose. "Please, you know how much I hated that. No one likes the smell of burnt flesh."

Mya shrugged. "You'll have to get used to it though. Setting a vampire on fire may save your life in the future, and at least it's something if you can't figure out how to get blood boiling to work, especially on such short notice."

Daniella sighed. "You're right."

They'd spent a large part of yesterday planning and testing her powers. While her abilities were strong enough to rival a vampire's, she was not all powerful. Daniella could only affect an area she knew or could see. Because of that, a cavern with unknown, winding tunnels would hinder her, and she could not use any type of field magic or else she may injure their allies during the fight. Her only option was individualized magic that focused on the vampire's body.

"Are you sure that your healing ability will counter my magic?" she asked.

Mya laced her fingers, pushing at her wrists for a stretch. "I'll be fine, just try it already. But remember, focus on the brain. Anywhere else won't kill us."

Daniella nodded and closed her eyes. She connected to her surroundings and pushed deeper, past the cool breeze that dried her sweat, the warmth of the sun, and the wetness that hung in the air. Past the skin, outside of the natural world. There she pondered. What was she missing? Why couldn't she affect Mya's blood and heat it?

Perhaps it was her doubt and fear. Fear of hurting her friend, fear of this not working, the small voice that told her this was too sudden and much too new for her to be an expert at. While her fears may be justified, they frankly didn't matter. If she couldn't figure out how to defend herself and kill vampires, Mya would never help her make it to tonight's battle, and she had to be there, or else ... *No!* She could not think about that now.

With renewed determination, she focused on her intent.

Another deep breath released any lingering emotions, leaving her open to receiving and listening to the spirits. Then an idea popped into her head, single and certain. *Dehydration!* If she removed water from Mya's body, it would overheat.

Daniella called to the spirit that ebbed and flowed, equally calm and yet able to rupture and crash at any moment. She gasped at the surge of power, at how it wound around her and merged with her desire so seamlessly that it felt like a part of her consciousness. She was so engrossed in this feeling that she missed Mya's groan, the way she couldn't lift her tongue to speak, and how she swayed in the yard, until she heard a loud *thump.*

Daniella opened her eyes to see Mya on the ground. She rushed to her and cradled Mya's head to her chest. "Mya? Mya! Are you okay?"

Mya groaned in response.

Daniella released the breath she'd been holding. "Fuck, I'm so sorry."

Mya waived her hand dismissively and began to sit up on her own. She let Daniella help her to her feet, and they moved to a nearby bench. Daniella offered Mya her bottled water, but she shook her head, bracing her hands on her knees.

After several deep breaths, Mya slumped back against the seat with a sigh, eyes closed. "Well, it's good to know that works."

"Are you sure you're alright? Do you need me to get you anything?"

"No, I'm okay. I've almost finished healing." She opened her eyes to peer at Daniella. "Stop worrying before you end up with a permanent crease in the middle of your forehead. I'm fine. Now, do you think you can do that on a massive scale?"

She scowled. "Yes, Madam Dickness."

Mya's roar of laughter made Daniella smile, easing a bit of her guilt. She sat back against the seat and stared at the sky. Hurting Mya like that, so easily, shocked her. The spirits didn't operate on the same scale as humans, where everything was black and white, just or unjust. Death didn't harm them, nor did life bring them joy. They had no qualms about peace or destruction, and the more she connected to them, the easier it was to succumb to their force and forget the world existed. Daniella had to be clear about her boundaries when working with them, or else she may hurt someone she loved in the future.

Her gaze shifted back to Mya, who was staring off into the distance, toying with something on a small chain around her neck. The object shone in the light and Daniella realized it was a ring, a simple golden band that seemed too big for Mya's long fingers.

Noticing she was being watched, Mya stopped and laid the ring flat against her chest. "Greg is going to fight you with everything he has when you tell him you want to join us at the battle tonight. I want you to understand why."

Daniella cocked her head to the side but nodded. "Okay."

Mya struggled for a while to find the words, and when she finally did, she seemed broken. "I wasn't ... always this way. Cruel and brash, I mean. I've always been stubborn, hard-headed, a pain in the ass." She gave a sad smile. "But this, who I am today, was born out of pain and loss."

"I never agreed with Greg keeping you in the dark about us, because you should value the time you have with your mate. You never know when you might lose them." Mya picked up the ring again, grasping it in her hand. "This belonged to him, my mate, but he's gone now. This is one of the only things I have left of him."

Daniella's eyes widened. She reached out to hold Mya's hand as a tear slid down her friend's cheek. "Mya, I—"

"It's okay. I don't talk about him often, but it's nice to remember." Mya sniffled. "My parents were the epitome of love, and they did everything they could to teach us those values, to keep us connected. But when I was a child, they contracted the plague, and I lost both of them."

Daniella nodded. "Greg told me about the plague. That you got it as well, and how Erik turned him into a vampire, and then Greg turned you and Luke."

Mya's face warmed and for a moment her eyes brightened. "When I met Erik, he looked like an angel. I was dying. I knew it. I could feel the energy slipping from my body. When Erik taught Greg how to turn me into a vampire, he said Greg should be the one to do it because I had the greatest connection with him. But that wasn't true." She squeezed the ring again. "The person I had the greatest connection with was Erik. I just didn't know it at the time."

Daniella shook her head. "I don't understand."

"Erik was my mate, Dani."

She gasped and drew back. "But how? Greg told me he lost his mate. How could you be his mate?"

"Erik saved us. I was only a child when I met him. He helped me grow, not only as a vampire, but as a person. I treated him like a father figure at first." She laughed. "I'd cling to him constantly, always begging for him to play with me or carry me around town. When I was scared, I'd run to him. He was my safe place." The tears flowed freely now, but she wiped them away and took a deep, shuddering breath. "That changed when I became older. Erik taught us everything about life, about being a vampire and how to survive. He talked to us about our powers and abilities. But even though our bodies had matured as humans, we still had a lot to learn as vampires. My feelings for him were inappropriate, I knew that, and yet I couldn't let them go." She breathed.

Daniella wished she could take a piece of Mya's pain, but she couldn't. Its claws were too deep into her for Daniella to begin to help her heal, but still she tried as she rubbed her back, sending her all the comfort and light that she could through her touch while she listened to her story.

"We went through many wars together. That's why we came to America. We believed that it would be easier here, and over time Erik and I continued to grow closer. But there were other beings here, ones that did not appreciate all the turmoil humans, and some immortals, had brought. Two of them could shape-shift, mimic another person's body and their mannerisms perfectly, and that's what they did. They tricked him into thinking I'd rejected him completely, and it broke his heart."

Mya's lip trembled and she bit it to keep from sobbing. "I didn't even know! He never told me about mates. I had never even heard the term before. I just ... I just knew I felt something different with him than anyone else did. I wanted something more with him. He left me a journal filled with entries about me. About how I'd grown, how hard it was to stay away from me, how happy he had been that we were advancing toward a relationship, all the hopes and dreams he had for a future with me. He left me this"—she kissed the ring softly—"and then he left me." Her eyes hardened. "That's what happens when your mate rejects you as an immortal being. The emptiness is too much to bear, and it's easier to die."

Tears had already gathered in Daniella's eyes, but it wasn't until Mya shut down that they began their descent down her cheeks. Mya brushed away her lingering tears, straightened her back, and held her head high. Not a trace of the vulnerable woman who had been crying and talking about the love of her life was left. She had been replaced with a warrior, someone who could kill without consequence. It shook Daniella down to her core.

"I killed them. I killed every person who helped take him away from me, who burnt down his house and left me with nothing. Their lives for his, and I would do it again in a heartbeat," she spat. "Had it not been for Greg and Luke holding me back and nursing me through the pain, I would have followed Erik in death. Our bond ran that deep, and we had never even consummated it, unlike you and my brother."

Daniella's heart jumped, the ache reverberating through her body leaving her speechless as her eyes widened.

"You understand what I'm saying, don't you? I agreed I would bring you to tonight's battle, even against my brother's wishes, because your spirits told you he would die if you were not there to prevent it."

"Zachariah's newly turned vampires will be no match for you. He forces the change on his victims, making them crazed. They can't think for themselves and can only follow his orders," she sneered. "Even a human could take down a few of them if they're lucky. But you are kind, sweet, *honorable*, and if you show up to this battle tonight that way, you'll die. There will be no room for sympathy. Nothing will exist except for action and instinct. The only mentality you should have is kill or be killed."

Mya's voice wavered for a moment but she continued. "If

you cannot watch the life slip from someone's eyes to save your own, or my brother's, then it's better that you let him die in peace. Because if he survives you, he will do exactly as I did. He will destroy everything, and he will choose to follow you to the grave. Nothing I, or anyone else, could do will convince him otherwise." She squeezed Daniella's shoulder and stood. "Make sure your heart is in the right place before you leave with us tonight." Then she was gone.

Daniella broke apart. Tears muddied her face as she sobbed at the cruel honesty of Mya's words. She was right. Hadn't Greg confessed the same thing yesterday? That he couldn't survive without her? And after last night...

She shook her head, wanting to drown out the thought, but she couldn't escape it. Greg wouldn't survive her death. He wouldn't even try to, and she couldn't accept that. She knew how she felt about Greg. She loved him with everything in her. Wasn't that the reason she was going through with all of this? If Mya was asking her if she could kill someone to protect Greg, the answer would always be yes.

But didn't that make her a monster?

What was the point of no return?

When did justice and protection turn you into a murderer?

Zachariah was a murderer. He took people's lives for fun. He didn't care about anything other than himself.

And her? What did she care about?

The answer was simple. Greg. Daniella cared about the man she loved. She cared about Luke and Mya. She even cared about the other vampires, people that she didn't know. There was no reason for them to be involved in this madness.

Was that it, then? Was that the line between good and evil?

The phrase 'for the greater good' came to the forefront of

her mind. Daniella had always hated that phrase, yet never understood why until this very moment. The choice of what was the greater good was always subjective and thus selfish. But that changed nothing for her.

She may be partial. She may be selfish. But to her, the greater good was Greg and his family. It was what he was doing, what all of them did. No matter the circumstances, on any day, at any part of her life, she would always choose him over another. And if that made her evil, so be it. If that meant watching somebody die in front of her, no matter how difficult that may be, no matter how hard it may be for her to wrap her mind around, he was worth it. They were worth it.

CHAPTER 18

Greg's voice rang strong and clear as Daniella entered the house. Luke said something, and he laughed, a deep masculine rumble that danced over her skin. The thought of never hearing his voice again—

Her power ripped through her with such strength that she barely stopped herself from setting his home aflame. Shaken, she wrapped her arms around herself. She couldn't fall apart here, not with so much on the line.

Daniella raced upstairs and peeled off her clothes. She made it into the shower before she curled into a ball and smothered a scream with her hand. Her thoughts had turned into a chaotic web of despair. What if she couldn't convince him? What if she couldn't stop whatever was coming? What if she lost him? What if, what if, what if?

Stop! Stop, this isn't you. You always push through, you always do, and this isn't any different.

She repeated her mother's mantra in her head, let it fill her with peace as she grounded her energy. *I am one with the earth. I am one with the Mother. She flows through me. She offers me her guidance, and I can make it through anything.*

Her breathing calmed and her pulse slowed until she could think straight. She had suffered a great deal of hardship and loss in her life, and that unresolved pain had created a chasm of fear. Fear that she wasn't strong enough to protect someone she loved, fear that she'd lose someone else. But if she was willing to risk her life for Greg's, and even kill someone if necessary, the least she could do was believe in herself and her magic. The spirits said she would bring him home, and she *would*.

As she washed, Daniella imagined each negative thought leaving her body, swirling into the water and spiraling down the drain. When she finished, she wrapped herself in a towel and cleared the mirror of condensation. Brown eyes stared back at her, red where the whites should be and somewhat shifty, but otherwise clear and determined.

Tingles raced down her skin when Greg entered the bathroom, and her body hummed a soft melody of completion when his arms came around her. She couldn't resist melting into his embrace as he pressed himself against her.

"Hi," he whispered in her ear, eliciting a wave of goosebumps over her body. His eyes were dark and hungry in the mirror as he nestled the bulge of his dick between her ass cheeks. "I missed you."

Liquid heat pooled at her core and she sighed. "I missed you too."

She slid her nails down his arm and he hissed. His fingers brushed over her neck, tracing the path down to her shoulder and over the wound Mya had inflicted during their training. "I hate seeing these on you," he said gruffly, softly licking the wound, healing it.

Daniella whimpered. Her head fell back as he trailed kisses over her shoulder and back up her neck. Greg's hands roamed over her body. He squeezed her breast, and even through the towel she could feel the heat of his palm. She moaned and clutched at his hand. She could get lost in him, *lost*—

"Wait!"

He let go of her breast and loosened his grip as she turned to face him.

Daniella rubbed her hands over his chest. "We need to talk."

"What's wrong, baby?" Concern filled his eyes as he smoothed her hair, brushing the loose strands behind her ear before his hands fell to her hips.

"I'm going with you tonight."

"No," he said flatly, "you're not."

"Greg, please listen to me."

"No, Daniella." His hands tightened on her waist. "As much as I hate to admit it, you were right about learning how to defend yourself. But I will not let you follow me or anyone else into battle. I will not let you willingly put yourself in a position where you could get hurt. I love you too much for that."

Her heart stopped. He'd told her in so many other ways, but hearing those three little words took all of her fight and replaced it with a gentle understanding. Daniella slid her hand up to his cheek. "My love—"

Greg's eyes widened and he shook his head as if tormented. "No, please ... please don't call me that. It's already too hard to say no to you. Please don't tempt me this way."

She smiled and cupped his cheek. "My love, I need you to listen to me, please."

He treated the soft caress as if it was his salvation. His eyes drifted closed and he nuzzled her palm, tickling her skin with his stubble.

"I love you," she whispered.

His eyes snapped open.

"We're in the same boat. We feel the same way about one another, and I don't want to lose you. But if I don't go with you tonight, I will, and I'm not willing to let that happen."

Greg chest rumbled as he spoke, his tone low, dark. "And how do you know this? Why are you so sure?"

"Because the spirits told me last night when Mya opened the map. They warned me you would not come back to me if I did not go with you."

His jaw clenched, but she continued on before he could protest. "I did not agree to spend my life with you, only to lose you so quickly. I understand you want to protect me. I also understand why you refuse to budge, but you need to understand that I will not either. Compromise with me." She stroked his cheek.

"Ella—"

His eyes were kind now, but she knew he wasn't ready to give in, so she pushed harder. "Greg, you spent so much time trying to shield me, more than I will ever know. But I don't want that to be the basis of our relationship. I do not want to be in a relationship where you are constantly defending me while I sit back and do nothing, nor do I want the opposite. I want to walk beside you." She cupped his face with her other hand. "And I think you want that too. I think you want someone who can be your partner and teammate. I want to be that, so let me."

He hung his head, his forehead resting against hers as she wrapped her arms around him. Greg clung to her and his voice quivered as he spoke. "What you're asking from me is impossible. I want you to be my partner, but to know that you might get hurt ... I can't."

"But I would rather be injured and heal tomorrow than lose you today. You need to learn to trust me."

Greg's hands slid up her back. "I do trust you. It's never been a case of me not trusting you. It's been a case of wanting more for you, of caring for you, and worrying about you. That is my love for you." He pulled her closer. "But I do trust you, I've always trusted you."

"Then if you trust me, let me be with you, please. We will be better together than apart. You need to realize I can take care of myself. You need to have faith in me, just like I have faith in you to help me if I need it. Letting me stand beside you doesn't mean that you can't still protect me. It means that you believe I will be capable enough to tell you when I need help, and when I can defend myself and stand on my own. I also have to believe the same thing with you. You may be immortal, but I know that doesn't mean you're invincible." She ran her fingers over his nape. "I will not lose you Greg, I refuse to." Her voice wavered. "Please don't make me rely on someone else to take me there because you cannot believe in me."

His eyes hardened. "You would go that far?"

"To bring you back home to me, yes. I can deal with your anger. I can deal with hurting you, or even betraying you, but I cannot deal with losing you."

He balled his hands behind her back and spoke under his breath. "If only tying you up would work."

"It wouldn't be any fun if you weren't here to enjoy it with me." Daniella smirked. Her hands traced the strong muscles of his back as the smile died from her lips. "Please. *Please.*"

Greg cupped her cheek as he leaned forward, placing a soft kiss on her forehead, then the side of her face. He breathed in her scent. "It seems I don't really have much of a choice."

"You do." Daniella traced the waistband of his pants, drawing a small gasp from him. "It would mean the world to me to have your blessing."

"Vixen," he grumbled as he nibbled on her neck.

Daniella sighed and surrendered herself to him. She made quick work of his pants and boxers, pushing and kicking them off. Greg ripped her towel away and they fell into one another.

She moaned in their kiss as he spread her thighs, fitting himself between them. He sucked her nipple and she arched, pushing her breast against his lips. Her hands were full of his body, scratching his back as she tried to pull him closer. Daniella rolled her hips forward, but he stopped her.

"Please," she said, needing both his answer and his body.

He took her lips again and she wrapped her legs around his waist as he carried her into the shower. Greg turned on the water and pinned her against the wall. His fingers found their way to her slick core and he grunted at her wetness.

Daniella moaned, tearing her mouth from his to smother kisses over his skin. "Please," she begged again. When he said nothing, she bit his neck.

Her only warning was a growled moan before he shoved himself into her with such force she lost her breath. Her eyes rolled back. He snarled and rammed inside her over and over. She clung to him as he filled her so completely. He was ruthless with her, and she loved it. She wanted this, him, forever, always.

Greg gripped her hips hard as he drove deeper, and she chanted, "Please, please, please."

He moaned and kissed her, sliding his tongue into her mouth, flicking, rubbing, wrapping it around hers just as his cock drove her insane. Daniella gripped his back, her nails scratching, biting into the flesh. She needed more. He hissed, squeezed her breasts, rolling and pinching her nipples between his fingers, drawing long cries from her lungs.

"Please! Please," she begged, one last time.

Greg tugged her head back before plunging his teeth into her neck. She held him there, her body writhing, jerking against his, her hips moving and circling uncontrollably as he drove her higher. Then she screamed, clamping down on his cock as her orgasm soared through her. He gripped her ass, angling her hips, pounding faster, *deeper*, and then he threw his head back, shouting as he filled her with his come.

For a long time, neither of them moved. The only sounds were those of their harsh breaths and the steady stream of water. Eventually she rubbed his back, drawing spirals on his skin. He nuzzled the crook of her neck and pulled out of her.

"Greg—"

"I trust you," he said softly, "and I love you." He laced his fingers through hers, holding their hands beside her head. "Do you feel this?"

Something wrapped around their hands, tingling. It was similar to what she felt when he was near her, except stronger, more potent. "Yes."

"Can you connect to it somehow?"

She held onto the way his ability felt, a vibration that was purely Greg. It bonded to something at the very core of her being. Calling on the spirit of darkness, she morphed her energy, allowing it to twine around his own.

He gasped, staring at their clasped hands in wonder. "Amazing."

"What does it feel like?"

"It's odd. It feels like mist, but energized, like it's wrapped in an electric pulse." His eyes focused on her now. "This"—he squeezed her hand—"this is ours. If you need me, you call me this way."

"But, if you're in the middle of a fight—"

"You call," he said sternly, his fingers tracing her cheek. "And if I need you, I will reach out to you. Okay?"

"Thank you." Daniella pulled his head to hers and kissed him.

He sighed when they broke apart. "Have you come up with some sort of plan of how to use your abilities?"

She nodded.

Dropping a kiss on her palm, he turned toward the soap. "Good, we can go over it together, after this."

Greg poured the soap into his hands and ran them over her body, working it into a lather. She melted into his hands. His touch wasn't sexual, but it was intimate and warm. When he finished and she had rinsed, she washed him, bringing a serene smile to his lips.

Greg rested his forehead against hers and closed his eyes. Daniella wrapped her arms around his neck. "I don't know what's going on in your mind right now, but remember that I love you and I'm happy here with you."

"I know," he said. His muscular arms enveloped her and she sighed in his embrace. "When this is all over, I want to take you somewhere, just you and I." He rubbed his nose against hers. "We have a lot to figure out together."

She grinned. "I'd say we've made a bit of headway with that though, haven't we?"

"Fucking finally," he breathed, a moment before his lips met hers in a sweet kiss.

CHAPTER 19

The house filled with boisterous energy as Greg's battle officers arrived. They shouted over one another, clapped their hands while they laughed, and teased each other endlessly. Under different circumstances, Daniella would have been overjoyed. But for now, the most she could muster was a small smile. Perhaps when she had lived a hundred years and fought countless wars beside these people, she, too, would value camaraderie over impending chaos.

The room quieted to a few murmurs and the soft buzz of a speaker as she and Greg entered. Sixteen people sat in attendance, many of whom Daniella had never met. But it was clear they respected Greg as their leader by how they straightened and gave him their full attention. It was also clear in how their eyes wandered over her skeptically.

That reaction pleased her. Greg had found an excellent group of people, and their love and loyalty filled her heart with a sense of pride for her mate. She didn't want them to welcome her because Greg commanded them to, or out of respect for him. She wanted to earn it.

"Everyone." Greg paused and kissed her hand. "I'd like to introduce you to Daniella, my mate." The smile on his face was just for her, tender and kind. It spread through her body, leaving warmth in its wake.

Greg took a seat at the head of the table while she took her place beside him on the arm of the chair. His hand came to rest on her lower back and he caressed her spine, sending small tingles of energy through her system.

"She's human," one of Greg's warriors challenged, his near black eyes unforgiving.

Daniella read the message loud and clear. *You don't belong here. You'll break far too easily.*

Her eyes narrowed as she answered. "Yes, I am human, but that will not stop me from joining tonight's battle."

The man gave her a cruel, twisted smile that made Daniella straighten in the chair.

Greg's fingers paused on her back as he tensed. "Darius—"

Daniella squeezed his thigh under the table. *Let me*, she projected to him as their eyes met, and then she turned back to his people. "It's clear to me you all share a close bond. You work as a team, a family, and I recognize it may be strange for me to be here, as many of you do not know me. So let me take this opportunity to make myself and my presence here very clear."

Her gaze flickered to Greg's and she couldn't stop the smile that spread over her lips. "I love Greg, and while I am new to the way your world works, I am not ignorant of its dangers. I do not expect any of you to respect me, or treat me the way you treat Greg, as a proxy. However, I expect you to work with me because I am here for the same reasons you are. Now, are there any more questions of my loyalty or assumed fragility, or can we focus on why we're all here today?"

Darius held up his hands in a small retreat, and Luke and Mya gave her cheeky smiles of approval.

Greg squeezed her hip in pride. "Mya, if you'd please," he said, not wanting to dwell.

Mya pulled open the map on the projection screen. "The coordinates lead here." She tapped on an area full of foliage. "There's one road in and out. The location is only accessible on foot, so we'll have to leave our vehicles behind. This"—she traced a path on the map—"is the route we'll take. It leads to an unmarked cavern where Zachariah will be waiting for us."

"I believe their plan is to force us into the cavern and overwhelm us from there. Because we're unsure of the structure or size, your teams will stay behind. If we have too many people, we'll risk losing someone during the fight," Greg said in a measured tone, but Daniella felt him tense. She laced her fingers with his, lending him her hope and strength as he continued.

"Daniella will be our first line of defense." The temperature of the room dropped a few degrees, but Greg pushed on. "Her abilities will help weaken the vampires if she doesn't outright kill them. After that, you all can have your fun."

"What do we do if Zachariah runs? Will you hunt him down like usual?" someone asked.

"No," Greg answered, making everyone's head swivel in shock, including Daniella's. "While I would like to rip his arms from their sockets and use them to bash his head in, this isn't about me. What's important here is to make sure he doesn't make it out alive. However that happens, and by whoever's hand, doesn't matter to me."

Greg's eyes flickered to her own and she realized he had made that decision for her. She knew how badly he wanted to kill Zachariah, but he was willing to risk that opportunity, all in an effort to keep her prophecy from coming true.

He directed his attention to the speaker system. "Michael, Cara, and Isaac, have you positioned your teams at the victims' addresses?"

"Yes," they answered, one after another.

"Good, there's one last thing I need to address," Greg said. "We have reason to believe that Zachariah has the power to copy another's ability if he drinks their blood."

A wave of shock and fury flew through the room. Several of the warriors' eyes widened, and some gasped and cursed, while others sat silent, their lips drawn in a tight line.

"We also have reason to believe that there will be several traps waiting for us which we are not used to. I have two priorities: the safety of all of my people, and ending this war. I leave the decision of adding someone to the circle to each of you." Greg indicated his team with a wave of his hand. "If you believe we can convert a vampire from Zachariah's ways to ours, bring them with you and we will discuss after this is over. But if you do not, kill them."

The command hung in the air, making it heavy as each officer shouldered its weight.

Merida spoke, breaking through the silence. "When do we leave?"

"Forty-five minutes and in groups of three. Provide area reports in fifteen-minute increments," Greg said. "Merida, Mya, and Dom, you go first. Scout and radio back if you see anything."

ONCE THE MEETING ENDED, THE TEAM SHIFTED AND BROKE INTO smaller groups. They wandered the house, visited Greg's armory—which Daniella had yet to see herself—or congregated in the kitchen to feast on the refreshments.

Greg brought her around to meet each member of his team. They were pleasant and most were happy for the two of them. Some even shared stories of how Greg had saved their lives, making him blush. He tried to drag her away, but she'd dug in her heels until he squirmed from the praise. It was nice. Familial.

Luke's arm wrapped around her shoulder and Daniella laughed, giving him a hug. "Hey you!"

"Hey." He smiled. "I still can't believe you're coming with us tonight."

She wagged a finger at him. "Before you start with your big brother protective crap, I have a reason to."

He raised his hands in surrender. "You'll hear none of that from me."

"You're not going to argue?" Daniella raised an eyebrow.

Luke cocked his head to the side. "No?"

"What is wrong with you?"

Luke laughed, but the sound seemed forced to her. "I'm just happy for the two of you, Dani. If Greg says it's okay and you can help him somehow, I'm all for it."

"Luke what's going—"

"Hey," Mya interrupted, "we're about to head out, but I left a bag on the bed for you in that room." She pointed to the left. "Go through it before you meet up with us, okay?"

Daniella nodded and the two shared a hug. "Stay safe, please," she whispered to her friend.

Mya laughed. "Don't worry, I'll be just fine."

When Daniella turned back to address Luke, he was gone. She searched the first floor for him but couldn't find him anywhere. What was going on with him, and why was he hiding it from her?

With a sigh, she gave up and went to investigate Mya's gift. Searching through the bag, she pulled out a small note with jagged, curved writing.

"Thank you for listening and still deciding to come. Wear these. They'll help you stay as fluid as possible. -Mya."

The bag contained a black tank top, leather jacket, pants, and combat boots. She chuckled and changed into the apparel. Flipping her hair from under the top, Daniella stared at herself in the floor-length mirror. She looked strong, dangerous. *Fierce.*

A tingle rippled over her body and in the mirror she saw Greg, his gaze dark and wicked. "Don't," she whispered.

He chuckled. "As if that was ever a possibility." With each step towards her, he rolled his hips. A memory of just how skillful those hips were flashed through her mind and she moaned.

Greg's nostrils flared as he breathed her in and then his hands were everywhere, sliding up her shirt, under her bra to squeeze her breast while his fingers came to cup her through the leather pants.

"Greg, please," she panted as he undid the button and lowered the zipper. "Do you know how hard it was to get these on?"

"I'll help you after," he huffed in her ear, "but I need you, *now.*"

Her head lolled back as he rubbed her nipple. She pushed her hips against his when Greg slipped his fingers under her thong and over her labia, teasing her lips. Then he rubbed her clit and his fingers slipped down, spreading her lips. He moaned. "Fuck, you're so wet, Ella."

She ground against him, trapped between his heady strokes and hard cock. He moaned and glided his fingers inside her. She twisted, and Greg took her lips in a passionate kiss. He swallowed her fervent moans, his tongue tangling with hers.

Daniella shoved her pants down, widening her legs to give him more access. He rewarded her by sliding his fingers deeper while he fucked her mouth, sending another pool of wetness to her core.

She gripped his hair with one hand while she fought to unbutton his pants.

Greg lifted his mouth from hers and smacked her ass hard, making her whimper and moan. "Stay quiet for me," he commanded, and then he dropped to his knees, replacing his fingers with his mouth. He sucked her pussy, then licked between her lips before delving into her core.

Daniella covered her mouth, resting her forehead against the mirror to quiet her moans while he ravaged her. Greg ate her like a starving man, and when he stood, she was barely holding herself together. She turned her head in time to see his cock spring free before he filled her with one solid thrust.

He clamped his hand over her mouth as she cried. Squeezing her hips, Greg pulled her back against him with each thrust. Daniella grabbed a hold of his nape, her nails scratching his skin as he pounded harder inside her.

Greg traced her ear with his tongue. "Look at us in the mirror," he moaned. "Watch me as I fuck you."

She watched his cock glide in and out of her, watched as her pussy swallowed every inch of him. He guided her hand down to where they were joined and pulled out of her until only the tip of his shaft was left inside. Wrapping their hands around his cock, he gasped in her ear.

"Do you feel how drenched I am? That's all you, baby, all you," he growled as he slid into her again, inch by glorious inch. "That's it, take it. Take all of me."

And she did. Fuck, she did. Daniella wanted to swallow him whole.

He ruined her against that mirror. Greg squeezed her breasts while his lips latched on to hers to drink every cry he tore from her. When he lifted his head from hers again, he moved to her neck and bit her. She closed her eyes, pressing her hand against her mouth as she tried to smother her scream. Still he moved, and still she took him.

She grabbed hold of him anywhere, everywhere, holding on for dear life as he fucked her, *possessed* her. He forced her hand to the edge of the mirror, holding it in his own, adding the sound of the mirror rocking against the wall to the passionate slap of his hips against her ass. Daniella came so hard that she saw stars, and with one last maddening thrust, Greg followed her into the abyss.

When she exited the bathroom, Greg was sitting on the bed with a dagger on each side of him.

"What's this?" she asked.

"They're for you. We're too fast for guns or most modern weapons." He shuddered as he breathed. "I thought these would work well for you."

Standing in front of him, she rested her hands on his shoulders while he wrapped his arms around her. "Thank you."

Greg nuzzled her stomach as she ran her fingers through his hair.

"Are you scared?" she whispered.

He nodded against her stomach and then met her eyes. "I trust you and I believe in you. But yes, I'm still scared. It's something I'll need to work on."

Daniella rubbed his cheek. "Will you let me help you?"

"You already are," he replied, bringing her hand to his lips for a gentle kiss.

The soft beep of an alarm started from his watch, and with a sigh he turned it off and stood. "It's time. Daniella," he began, saying her name as if he savored it, cherished it, "I love you so much. Be safe for me, please."

"I will." She grabbed onto his shirt as he bent to kiss her. "Promise me you will be too."

"I promise."

CHAPTER 20

The forest felt like death. Whatever animals had come to this place had died brutally and left a stain on the land. The dirt was tainted with it. There were no chirps of birds, no rustle in the trees, not even a single insect. The entire forest was eerily silent.

A part of her wanted to reach out, to heal the land and bring it back to its previous glory, but now wasn't the time.

"Are you all right?" Greg asked.

Daniella shuddered but nodded. "They're here and they have been for a very long time."

He squeezed her hand, and for just a moment she leaned into his strength. Then they joined the group and entered the dark cavern.

As they ventured deeper, Daniella called upon the spirit of light to allow her to see, setting her eyes aglow. She didn't feel the spirit of darkness or any warning cultivate within her body.

Perhaps it was a sign that the outcome of this battle would be in their favor.

Daniella paused at the entrance of another passageway and used her connection with the spirits to sense. She felt nothing. Merida stood beside her, using her ability to look through items, and also confirmed there to be no threats in the passageway. The group advanced forward, pausing and searching each junction they found this way, only to come up empty. But then they came upon a large opening, and when they exited, they were greeted by Zachariah and his vast army.

"Well, if this isn't a surprise!" Zachariah clapped, while Johanna stood by his side. "I was expecting you, Greg, but bringing Daniella? What an interesting turn of events! I take it you got my message." Zachariah fixed his gaze on Daniella. "Thank you for that friend of yours. Stacy, was it? She was absolutely delicious. I enjoyed her, really, although you were a much better play toy." His smirk deepened. "You didn't scream as much."

Energy flew out from Daniella, so strong it shook the cavern walls, rippling through the space, creating fissures in the ground. She let the full force of the water spirit take her over, a beautiful wave of destruction winding through her body, infusing her with strength and blending with her desire to kill.

Daniella pushed that intent to every vampire that stood between her and her enemy. They groaned and staggered, but they weren't who she wanted. No, she wanted Zachariah. She wanted to feel his blood boil, for him to become so delirious he couldn't move, couldn't speak, couldn't even scream. She wanted him to know what death felt like, and she wanted it to be at her hand.

In an instant, their group moved as one. Greg launched

forward, the others coming in waves as they worked to slay their adversaries.

Zachariah's eyes widened at Daniella's attack. He staggered, but his enhanced strength fought her. She pushed harder, satisfied when he fell back against the wall. But then he grabbed Johanna's wrist and fled down another passageway.

Daniella dashed after him, but the darkness screamed at her. She spun away just in time to avoid a vampire launching himself from the ceiling. With a crazed stare, he ran his tongue over teeth that were much too large for his mouth, like he could *taste* her.

In your dreams.

He swung at her. Daniella dodged his attack, and his next two. His size was a weakness she exploited. When he tried to hit her again, she spun, infusing her kick with a force of air as it hit his gut. He doubled over. Knowing he'd recover quickly, she called on the earth to create vines to tie around his throat. He struggled and ripped them off, but not before she plunged her dagger deep into his skull.

Instinctively, Daniella pulled it out and his lifeless body dropped to the floor in a pool of blood. Her hand shook when the realization hit her. She'd *killed* someone. It was different when she used her abilities. They could consume her, block out what she'd done in the heat of the moment so her emotions weren't involved. But this? No, this had been done by her hand. But that was what she'd agreed to, wasn't it?

He can't hurt anyone else. None of the people lying here can, and that's what's important. That's why you came here today.

Daniella gripped her dagger tighter and turned away. A blur caught her eye as another vampire sped toward her. She focused on him, tracking his movements. He reached for her.

She grabbed his arm, ducked, and flipped him onto his back. Her dagger was in his head the moment he hit the ground. Taking his life hurt her, but she reminded herself why she was there and moved forward with her mission.

Daniella stepped over his body and sprinted to catch up with her team. She froze in front of the field of dead vampires, ones that she helped kill with her abilities, and shuddered.

That pause became her downfall as four vampires surrounded her. Her adrenaline spiked as fear coated her skin, but she shook it off.

Stay calm. Think.

One vampire lurched toward her. Daniella called on her connection with light, blinding the group. She impaled the nearest vampire with her dagger. His body dropped and she used the new path to escape. Daniella jumped over him, but another vampire yanked her back by her hair. Flipping her other dagger, she stabbed him in the gut and twisted. He howled, throwing her to the ground. She scrambled to get up, but wasn't fast enough.

The third vampire pounced on her, his hands around her throat. She squirmed, tried to kick him off, but he was too strong. Daniella released a surge of electricity, sending it through his body. He screamed as she crawled out from underneath him, but then the fourth grabbed her from behind. She tried to electrocute him as well, but he slammed her head into the cavern wall. Pain erupted behind her eyes.

No!

She called upon fire, sending flames to burn his skin, but he hit her again. Her vision clouded as his hot breath huffed against her face.

He's going to bite me. No...

Using her darkness, she called for Greg, begging the connection to reach him. The vampire snarled, but the bite never came. Suddenly, she was free. She turned in time to see Greg rip the man's throat apart. He broke the neck of the gutted vampire before using his sword to behead the one she'd electrocuted.

His red eyes met hers as he stalked toward her.

"Greg—"

He pulled her into his arms, burying his head in her neck.

She clung to him, and after a few deep breaths she whispered, "I'm okay."

His shirt was covered in something sticky, and when she finally lifted her head, Daniella realized it was blood. "Greg!" She pushed at his chest, running her hands over his shirt. "Where are you hurt?"

"It's not my blood," he bit out. Greg swiped at her temple, a look of pure rage coming over him. He growled.

She gasped as she realized he wasn't the only one covered in blood. Her hands, arms, even her chest were coated in the horrible red spray, and now she was bleeding from her forehead.

He pressed a gentle kiss to the gash and then traced it with his tongue. She sighed at his touch. The heaviness in her head cleared as he healed her, bringing her back to the present. Daniella moved to pull away from him, but he held her still.

"We don't have time—" she began.

"We do. They're all dead or will be soon." Greg ran his fingers through her hair. "We'd cleared this area of vampires. The ones that attacked you came from outside. Marcus and Antoine are making sure that area is clear as well."

"And Zachariah? Did you kill him?"

He shook his head. "I came for you first."

"Then let's go." She took his hand, but he pulled her back.

"Ella—"

"I'm okay, I promise. We have to kill him. Let's go."

Marcus and Antoine appeared beside them.

"We've dispatched the vampires outside," Marcus said.

"Good. Guard the entrance. The team will explore any channels they find for five minutes and then work their way back to you."

While the others paired off to carry out Greg's orders, Mya, Luke, Merida, Dominick, Darius, Jason, and Anna stayed with them. Their group set off to find Zachariah and Johanna and put an end to this war.

They made it to an opening with two different passageways. Before they could take another step forward, Luke took off, taking the passage to the right.

"Luke!" they yelled out in unison, but he was already gone.

"What the fuck is his problem?" Mya hissed.

"I don't know," Greg growled in reply. "Mya, go get him. Dom, Merida, and Anna go with her. Drag his ass back to the entrance if you have to."

They nodded and took off behind him. Daniella stared after them, trying to make sense of Luke's actions. While nothing had warned her of that path, the sudden separation filled her with unease.

Greg squeezed her hand. "They'll be fine, I promise."

She met his gaze and allowed his words to reassure her. Then together, they took the path to the left.

"That wasn't the only explosion," Greg said, his eyes fixed on the trees.

"What?" she gasped.

Greg lifted her in his arms, carrying her as he followed down the path. "The entire cave system collapsed. Everyone returned to the main entrance except for Mya, Merida, Dom, and Luke. But if they found them, that means they're okay—"

He stopped dead in his tracks and Daniella gaped at the sight. They were there, standing, moving about just fine, but the surprise was the multiple groups of women in various states of undress who sat around them. Their skin was covered in blood, dirt, and filth. Countless wounds marred their flesh, alongside bruises from what looked like weeks of torture.

"Put me down," Daniella ordered. When Greg didn't move immediately, she smacked his arm to get his attention. "Put me down!"

He did, and then he helped her toward the women.

She took off her jacket, wrapping it around the nearest woman as Merida approached. "What can we do?" Daniella asked.

"They need food, water." Merida shook her head, her expression strained as she fought to keep herself from losing control. "I don't even think half of them realize they're alive."

"Okay." Daniella opened her heart to the spirits. She asked for rain, and it came as a gentle sprinkle over the area. She wanted to do more, to ask the earth to bring them food, but she couldn't. This act alone took everything she had.

Many of the women didn't move at first, didn't even seem to register they were outside. But slowly, one shifted, then another. Tears fell down their faces, mixing in with the rainwater as they tilted their heads back. Finally, they drank deep gulps. Some were so thirsty that they choked on the liquid, but even then they tried to swallow more, as if they hadn't drunk anything for days.

It broke her heart.

"What happened? Where did you find them?" Greg asked, his voice thick.

"When we ran after Luke, I saw another chamber inside," Merida said. "At first I thought it was a group of vampires that were planning to ambush us, but then we found them." Her gaze flickered to the women and she spoke in a hushed tone. "They were used for blood and anything else he wanted. Some of them aren't even human, and judging by their conditions, they've been down there for a long time."

"How did you get out?" Daniella asked.

"Luke. I'm not sure how, but he led us out. Greg, something happened to him in that cave. I've never seen him like this. We can take care of the girls, but please, go help him. He's over there." Merida tilted her head to the left.

When Daniella and Greg approached Luke, he was looking over the women but his eyes were glazed, unfocused, like he didn't really see them. He seemed to be searching for something, or someone.

"Luke?" Greg called to him, getting his attention.

"Johanna. Have you seen Johanna?" Luke's eyes were red, wild. He looked over another woman before shaking his head and moving to the next. "I have to find her."

"Luke," Greg said carefully, "the last time we saw her, she was with Zachariah."

"I know!" he shouted, but then his voice dropped to a whisper. "But she could be here. She could be here. I have to find her."

"Luke," Daniella tried, "I don't think she's here."

"Then where is she?" Luke's voice boomed, making the women around them jump. He ran up to Greg and clutched his shirt. "Tell me we killed him. Tell me he's dead, at least. Please!"

Greg shook his head.

"Someone has to have seen something! What direction did they go off to? Where are they, Greg?" His voice wavered as he choked back tears.

Greg squeezed his wrists. "Luke, they escaped in the explosions. We don't know where they've gone. We're looking, but we have to take care of the people here first," he explained gently, like a parent speaking to a child.

Luke hung his head. "No!" he screamed, falling to his knees. "No, no, no."

Daniella wrapped her arms around Luke's shaking and sobbing form, as did Greg.

"Luke," she tried again. He lifted his head to her voice, but instead of her best friend, she saw a broken shell of a man. "Can you tell us why you're looking for Johanna?"

Luke's eyes were drowning in despair as he met her own. "She's my mate, Dani."

At his words, Daniella and Greg drew back. Her eyes widened and she gasped. She turned to Greg to see a mixture of fury, regret, and horror blanket his face.

Luke wept and wailed, his anguish seeping into her soul as he splintered and fell apart. "She's my mate, and he took her."

NIGHT FURY

CHAPTER 1

THE DAY OF THE BATTLE

Something called to Luke, playing with the fringes of his mind, teasing him with answers to questions he'd never dared to speak out loud. But he needed those answers desperately. He needed them to help make sense of everything he'd felt over the last few months, and they were worth everything, even Greg's wrath.

Luke ran away from the group, ignoring Greg's shout. He followed the call as it pulled him further down the passage. It turned, narrowed, and then opened to a full room. The moment Luke entered, he was forced to duck, missing a punch aimed at his head.

"You weren't who I was hoping for." Zachariah smirked, his brown eyes gleaming. "But you'll do."

Luke rushed him. He landed a punch to Zachariah's face and another to his gut before jumping back in time to miss Zachariah's counterattack. Ducking under a kick, Luke delivered a punch to the underside of Zachariah's knee, satisfied when the bone splintered.

It wasn't enough.

Zachariah caught him with an elbow to the chest. He kneed Luke in his ribs before punching the side of his head. When Zachariah's kick connected, Luke flew back, rolling until he hit the cavern wall.

Luke stood slowly, faking weakness. The healing agent in his blood was already working through his system and renewing his strength, but he needed to be smart about this. Zachariah's enhanced strength would make him difficult to take down directly, and there was still speculation that Zachariah could copy another immortal's ability. Without knowing how that ability worked, being impulsive could land Luke in a very dangerous situation.

And then there was Johanna. She stood in the middle of the room, her face blank, emotionless. She was still under Zachariah's control. Luke had strategically pulled Zachariah away from Johanna during the fight, but he was still too close to her. Luke knew that if pushed, Zachariah would use Johanna as a hostage, and Luke would never risk her life. The best strategy was to tire Zachariah out without using his abilities. If Luke made him believe that he was weaker, Zachariah would grow cocky, ensuring Luke's victory.

As Luke went to step forward, his body froze. An unseen pressure knocked him to his knees. He struggled against it, but the bone-crushing weight held him down, pushing his stomach flat against the dirt.

"Luke?" a soft voice whispered in his head.

His eyes darted around the room, but no one else had entered. Zachariah stood unmoving, entirely too still, and Luke wondered if he felt the same pressure. Luke's eyes darted to Johanna. While she hadn't moved, something seemed different about her—electric.

Confused, he responded mentally, *"Johanna?"*

"Good." Her sigh of relief flitted through him. *"You can hear me."*

"How are you doing this? What are you—"

"That doesn't matter now. Please, stay down and lie still. Don't fight me."

Something akin to panic squeezed at his chest. Was it hers or was it his? *"Johanna, whatever this is, stop it. Let me go."*

"No!" The force of her shout was so strong it made his ears ring. *"You don't understand. You can't kill him!"*

"Yes, I can!" Luke tried to will his body to move but it wasn't responding to him.

"No, you can't!" Johanna's voice softened. *"Please, stop. Zachariah isn't the leader you've believed him to be. It's someone else, and she is far more powerful than you or I. If you kill him, she will come after you, and she won't stop until she breaks you. I don't ... I don't want to see you hurt. I don't want anyone to ever experience that again. Now please, stop—"*

"Johanna—"

"We don't have any more time! You'll be able to move when I'm gone. As soon as you can, take the passage to the left. It'll lead you outside."

Zachariah suddenly twitched and shook his head, as if coming out of a daze. He stared down at Luke and then *tsked*. "I thought he would have lasted longer. Oh well." He turned toward Johanna. "Since he left me so unsatisfied, you'll have to make up for it. Now, let's go." Zachariah grabbed her by the arm and dragged her behind him.

Johanna followed him meekly, but Luke heard her quiet sob in his mind, and recognition pierced his heart. He fought against the pressure holding him down like a wild man.

Move! Move damn it! Move! he urged himself.

"I'm sorry," she hiccuped. *"At least you'll be safe. Goodbye, Luke."*

"Johanna!" he screamed, fighting against her power until she disappeared around a corridor.

And just like that, she was gone.

Luke was still screaming when he woke up.

Every night for the last two months Luke had awoken drenched in sweat, his mouth open, screaming at the horrible memory. It never changed, never stopped, never got better, never distorted. It was always the same. It was the day he finally got the answer to one of his questions, the moment he realized Johanna was his mate.

The four walls of his bedroom felt like they were closing in, and the air was too hot, too humid to breathe. He kicked off the covers and goosebumps raced over his skin as a brush of cool air flitted over him. He was the problem—not this room, not this house, not anything else. He was the one who was broken, the one who had failed.

He'd failed Johanna. Occasionally, Luke would relive his nightmare as a specter. His corporal form would float just above the unfolding scene, and in those moments he'd revisit everything. If he had taken more risks instead of being concerned about Zachariah stealing his power, if he had moved closer to Johanna instead of away, would she have felt safe enough to reach out to him then? Would she be in his arms right now?

Those weren't the only times he should have fought harder for her. Luke would give anything to go back to the times he'd tried to speak to Johanna at work and she'd run away from him. If he had followed her, pressed her to explain why she kept avoiding him, would she be here right now? If nothing else, he would have finally known why she was able to combat the connection between them, the mate bond that had finally snapped into place in that cavern.

Luke would even have been at peace if she had outright rejected him. It would have devastated and destroyed him, but this? Not knowing if she was even ... He couldn't go there, not again, because if she wasn't alive, he'd lose it. He'd lose every single piece of himself and spend the last remaining minutes of his life killing Zachariah and anyone else he could get his hands on before they took him down.

The only thing that gave him hope was that after being on the receiving end of Johanna's powers, he knew Zachariah would never give her up easily. She was extraordinarily power-ful. A feeling of pride for his mate flashed through his heart before it was crushed under the heavy weight of despair. If it weren't for those powers, would she even be in that position?

No, she'd be dead.

That thought had him reaching out before his arm froze in mid-air, shaking so badly with the need to hurt, to break, to destroy with his rage. Luke took a deep breath, then another, and another, trying to settle his mind.

The simple fact was that if Johanna wasn't powerful and Zachariah discovered she was Luke's mate, he would have killed her, much like he had tried to kill Daniella. At least this way Johanna was alive, and Luke was sure she would stay that way.

But that still didn't answer how Johanna had hidden their mate bond, and Luke was sure she had. Even if she were able to hide it from everyone else, he should have been able to feel it immediately. And why was it that he finally felt their mate bond in that cavern when she had seemed so ... different? So real? When her voice seemed softer yet stronger than he had ever heard it, and she had become so determined, so protective over him? Why then and not before?

Luke rested his head back against the headboard and ran a shaky hand through his brown hair, swiping the stuck strands from his forehead. No matter how hard he tried to figure it out, he couldn't. Every time one mystery resolved itself, another one unfurled. It was endless, and it would stay that way until he found her—and he *would* find her. But rage still barred its fangs and tore at him, peeling back more and more layers until it reached his soul and covered it in something dark and sadistic.

Luke sighed. He couldn't keep doing this. He couldn't keep being this way. It wouldn't be good for the battle tonight, yet another attempt at finding her.

You'll find her. You'll find her, he chanted in his head, hoping that thinking the words would somehow make them come true.

Luke needed to move, to do something to keep his mind busy. Checking his phone, he saw he'd only slept for two hours and had another two before he'd have to drive to Greg and Daniella's home for the strategy meeting. He cracked his knuckles and left his room, heading toward his gym where he beat and kicked the punching bag, unleashing a fraction of his wrath until the bag itself exploded. But even then he didn't stop, not until he'd ripped it to shreds.

CHAPTER 2

The wind picked up, tousling Luke's hair as he sped down the back roads to Greg and Daniella's house. He'd be a little early for the strategy meeting, but he needed the escape.

Breaking that punching bag felt good, too good, and he would have moved on to something else if he'd stayed home. His emotions had always been a little too intense—passionate was the word Luke liked to use—but while he was known for being a loose cannon, for the first time in his life he felt like one.

Luke took another deep breath, like Dani kept telling him he should do, and let the fresh air carry away his thoughts. He wasn't alone here, even if he felt like it in his rage and anguish. He was surrounded by people who loved him, people who were willing to fight to help him get Johanna back. And even though that was more than most could ask for, it wasn't enough. It would never be enough, not until she was by his side.

Luke's somber mood engulfed him as he approached the

house. He swiped his badge and froze at the entrance when he heard Dani laugh, knowing he'd intruded on something. The sound was cut short, and Luke sighed before shutting the door.

Greg and Daniella were sympathetic to Luke's grief and tried not to do anything that would remind him of his pain, including being affectionate in front of him. It hurt Luke to be grateful for that. He wanted them to be happy and had always pushed for them to be together, but if he was being honest, he couldn't stand seeing it now. And for that, he was a bastard. He loathed and cursed the part of him that couldn't witness two people he loved be happy, not when he knew that his person wasn't next to him.

But she will be, he reminded himself again.

As he entered the kitchen, Dani greeted him with a soft smile and met him for a hug. "Hey, you."

"Hey," Luke said as he feigned a small smile, but she was on to him. Dani squeezed his arm as they separated and her dark brown eyes met his, full of concern, worry, and something else.

Luke averted his gaze, not wanting her to see how close he was to drowning in the weight of his emotions, and instead looked over her head to Greg. "Sorry I'm a little early."

"No, you're actually right on time," Greg said, exchanging a hug with Luke next.

Confused, Luke moved to join them at the breakfast nook, taking a seat on the barstool across from them. "Is something going on?"

Dani gave him a tiny smile, her voice soft as she passed him a manilla folder. "You should know before everyone else. I hope ... I hope it helps."

Luke looked between her and Greg, but their faces gave nothing away. Suddenly the folder seemed too heavy, as if it held the weight of his damnation, salvation, or both. Fear swam through Luke's veins. He was terrified that if he opened the envelope, the small bit of hope he held onto would be ruined, that the ground would break open under him to swallow him whole.

"Go on, open it." Dani squeezed his hand. "It's okay."

Luke looked at the comparison of their skin on top of one another—Dani's dark brown, to his olive—and used it as a visual aid, an anchor to remind him that she and Greg were right there. He would not drown. They would keep him afloat.

With more care than Luke had ever taken with anything in his whole life, he opened the folder. In it was a pack of pages with faces of people who worked for their company. Luke tilted his head as he recognized the data from their HRIS system, and then he saw it. An extra number on the first page circled, another on the next, two on the next, five after that. Every page he flipped through had a circled set of numbers.

"I don't understand. What is this?" Luke asked, squeezing the folder too tight as his nerves began to furrow and bundle under his skin, making his heart beat faster.

"It will make sense with this." Greg handed him another folder, his hazel eyes gleaming.

Luke snatched it from him. Opening the folder, he first saw a header containing a key with numbers and corresponding page counts, which seemed familiar though out of place, and several sets of coordinates. On the other side were pictures of mapped areas.

The question of the key picked at Luke's mind, and he studied it until he realized what it meant. His eyes darted from one folder to another, comparing the numbers and flipping through the mapped areas and overview points of each location. The pieces fell together like that of a giant puzzle, and he realized that the key referenced the HRIS data folder, and the coordinates were made from the circled numbers within it. Luke finally looked up at Greg and Dani, and jabbed a finger at the paperwork. "Where did these come from? What's here?"

Greg slid his arm around Daniella's waist as he leaned forward to tap on the first set of coordinates. "This is where we're going today."

"And as for where we got them from"—Dani's eyes shone as they stared into his own—"they came from Johanna."

"What?" Luke gasped, drawing back. "That's impossible, she's not ... We didn't—"

Find her, he finished internally, unable to say the words aloud.

"I asked Mya to look into what Johanna was doing before she was taken," Greg began.

Luke's throat constricted at the word 'taken,' and his shoulders tensed. Dani squeezed his hand again and he gave her a small nod, trying to convince them both that he was okay.

Greg tapped on one of the circled numbers. "Mya noticed that some of the employees' ID numbers were too long, some by one number, others by several." Greg tapped on the roster of locations next. "Once she figured out their pattern, Mya made the key and put together whatever coordinates she could. She was able to find seventeen locations. There's more to work through, but Mya can't make sense of them until we find Johanna."

Luke shook. He didn't know whether it was from excitement, hope or fear, but it was uncontrollable. It was only when Dani gave his hand another hard squeeze that his gaze flickered to hers and he realized he hadn't been breathing.

Breathe. You can't have a panic attack. You need to pay attention to what's going on here.

"It's okay," Dani said, as if she were reading his mind. "Just breathe, it's okay."

Luke nodded like a child and followed her advice: One breath, in, hold, out, second breath, in, hold, out, and another, and another.

Greg leaned forward, and Luke's wide eyes moved to his. Greg's presence reminded him that he was safe, that if Greg was in control, Luke could also be in control. Luke nodded again, and then once more, not trusting himself to speak.

"Luke, you know that I am going to do everything in my power to get her back to you, don't you?" Greg said.

Luke nodded again. He felt calmer, surer, and yet somehow still as if he were floating, as if he'd taken some sort of drug, maybe speed and acid mixed together, that had him flying through the clouds with a sputtering engine, constantly high but scared of the drop he knew would come.

"And you know that I wouldn't lie to you, right?" Greg said, his voice calm but strong.

Luke's hand balled into a tight fist under Dani's, and he watched as her gaze slid to Greg's and then back to his own. That drop, the free fall, the flipping of his stomach as gravity pulled him down, it was coming so fast, so soon, he could taste it. Still, Luke answered, "Yes."

Greg gave a short, stiff nod and then sighed. "We don't have any way to survey these areas before we attack them."

Luke understood immediately. They had no way to confirm if Johanna was there, if his mate would be found in this location or any of the ones on this roster.

Greg continued. "We're going to hit them hard and fast. But

by doing this we're running a risk. If Johanna is at any of these locations, we'll grab her, but if she isn't then they might move her ... or worse."

Blame her.

Luke swallowed. As far as they knew, she was the only one who had come into contact with the inner workings of both their group and Zachariah's. It would be easy for Zachariah to suspect her of slipping them information at some point, especially if they didn't find more information at the location they planned to raid in a few short hours.

"What's important to remember," Dani said, snapping Luke out of his thoughts, "is that somehow she found out about these locations. She could have found them on a computer or some sort of paperwork, but I don't think that's the case. There's simply too many for someone to remember unless they saw them several times."

"Or had been at those locations multiple times," Luke said.

"Exactly." Greg smiled. "And if she's been at these locations multiple times—"

"Then we might find her there." Luke breathed out heavily. The tightness in his chest floated out, and with it his eyes watered. He didn't even know tears had begun to slide down his cheeks until a droplet fell on the folder, quickly followed by another.

"We will find her," Greg said, his voice stern and sure. "There's plenty to worry about, Luke, but of that I can assure you."

"Th-thank you." Luke's voice cracked before he fully dissolved into tears, and his family wrapped him in their arms.

LUKE TOOK HIS SEAT AT THE TABLE NEXT TO HIS COUSIN, MYA. They exchanged a small smile before he said, "Thank you."

Something in her eyes flickered, her face falling into a sad sort of kindness that echoed his own pain. Luke's heart broke for her. She was trying to help him fix his pain, when hers would never be resolved. Her mate, Erik, was dead.

"I'll always do anything I can to help you, you know that," Mya said.

Greg and Daniella entered the room, cutting their conversation short. Greg sat first, Daniella perching on the arm of the chair, as had become a custom for them. For the first time, Luke imagined Johanna there with him, her blonde hair flowing over her shoulders and down to her waist, her blue eyes scanning the room, studying everyone. He knew she'd be welcomed here, and not just because he was family and original to this circle. No, she would be welcomed because of the information Greg and Daniella had shared in the kitchen. In the history of their circle, no one had ever provided such important information about an enemy, and no one had ever risked their life to do so. When Luke found Johanna, he'd make sure to share with her exactly what he thought about her little contribution.

Mya kicked his leg under the table, calling attention to its restless bouncing. He immediately stopped, turning back to Greg and Daniella.

"We'll attack this location at 10:00 a.m., then these three locations at 3:00 p.m.," Greg said, using his pointer to identify each set of coordinates. "For the half of you that are here, we work like normal, three teams leaving in fifteen-minute increments to scope the location before we attack. However, when we return we will not have another strategy meeting. Instead, we will assign A, B, and C teams and hit the three locations at the same time. I will be in charge of team A. We've handpicked a team for Luke who will be in charge of team B—"

Luke blinked, his eyes widening at the statement. Never had Greg given him such a level of responsibility. Luke's abilities were best in sneak attacks, but he never expected to be trusted to fight on his own away from Greg and Mya. He was impulsive, quick to anger, and his patience only lasted for as long as he had to use it to outsmart his enemy.

Luke's mouth fell open, words coming to the surface, but it closed when he caught the look in Dani's gaze, a simple smile that spoke volumes to him. *We trust you.*

Mya said something beside him, answered some question, and Luke snapped back to the present.

Greg gave her a single nod before turning back to the other members at the table. "We leave in fifteen."

CHAPTER 3

Luke met with his team.

Merida and Dominick were both people Luke admired and trusted. They understood his predicament; they were mated, and if there was anyone who could understand almost losing their mate and the trials to get them back, it was the two of them. Jason, Cara, and Anna completed their group, and he knew that their fighting styles and combined abilities strengthened an already incredible lineup that Luke couldn't believe he'd been assigned to lead. Yet not a single member looked at him the way he expected them to, as someone who wouldn't be able to guide them, whose irresponsibility would get them killed. Instead, they treated him with respect. Something about it made him feel proud, until the walls caved in and he realized this must be some sort of big mistake.

Luke excused himself and went to find Greg. He needed to tell him this was wrong, that Greg should not entrust him with the lives of others. After all, look how well that had gone for Johanna.

He spotted Greg with his arm wrapped around Daniella, speaking to another battle officer. Dani caught his approach and a mischievous look crossed her face. Then she tilted her head up and whispered something into Greg's ear, causing him to turn to look at Luke as well.

Dani approached Luke, giving him a light pat on the shoulder. "Just accept it," she whispered before she sauntered away.

Luke blinked for a moment and then glared daggers into the back of her head. He knew she could feel his stare, just like she knew why he'd come to speak to Greg. Dani was his best friend, and she understood him in a way most people didn't. It also meant she was well versed on calling him out on his bullshit before he'd even opened his mouth, and she enjoyed doing it on a regular basis. But this wasn't about him, not really. It wasn't about pride, confidence, or his lack thereof. This was about the others and how they deserved someone who would lead them. Someone who could be cautious, level-headed, and would not snap at a moment's notice. Someone who was not him.

Luke followed Greg into another room, all the while grinding his teeth at Greg's nonchalance. He barely waited for the door to close before he started.

"What the hell were you thinking?" Luke shouted. "I'm not fit to run a team. I'm not reliable or responsible enough for this, and those people, *your* people, are going to be at risk!"

Greg cocked an eyebrow, his tone even as he spoke. "What are you talking about, Luke?"

"You know exactly what I'm talking about." Luke huffed, burning a path into the carpet as he paced. "Greg, I'm not a leader like you are. Do I need to remind you that I ran off on not just you, someone who has practically raised me, but Mya, Dani, and the rest of your team, just because I thought I could rescue my mate? And I couldn't even do that right. I even had Zachariah in the palm of my hand!" Luke hands balled into fists as he shook them. "I wasn't able to kill him, and you think it's a smart idea to have me lead a team?"

"Luke—" Greg began, but Luke interrupted him, his shoulders drooping as he went on.

"Greg, let's just cut to the chase and be honest here. There's a reason why people think of me the way they do, and they're not wrong. I shouldn't be trusted with other people's lives. If we weren't related, I wouldn't even be this high in the circle. I've already failed enough for one lifetime, so please don't make me ruin someone else's life just because you're trying to be supportive or give me a distraction. This isn't the right way."

"Lucas," Greg bit out, his tone laced with anger. "Has anyone ever said any of those things to you?"

Luke rolled his eyes. "Of course not, but—"

"Then why the fuck are you saying them?" Greg shouted.

"Because they're the truth!" Luke shouted back. "And you know they are too!"

Greg tensed. "The only negative things I've ever called you are crazy and a pain in my ass."

"Greg—"

"Let me finish."

Luke ground his teeth but kept silent.

"Do you know what circle members have to agree to before we allow them to become battle officers?"

"No." Luke crossed his arms, narrowing his eyes. "It's another one of the many things I don't know."

Greg glared at him but continued. "They agree to take direction and action from us, to acknowledge that we are capable of leading. If any of them, *any* of them, ever said those things to you or disrespected you in *any* way, they wouldn't have a seat at our table."

Luke's eyes widened. "But—"

"Furthermore, every single person who joined your team volunteered."

"What?" Luke's mouth fell open.

"Yeah, they volunteered." Greg pushed a hand through his russet-colored hair. "Luke, have you always felt this way? That we ... that I don't value you?"

Luke averted his gaze from Greg's form. "It's not that, I just ... No, I don't think I felt that way before..."

"Johanna?"

Luke flinched at her name. "Yes. But still, I can be honest enough to say I haven't always made the right decisions. I haven't lived my life the way you've lived yours, being cautious and responsible. I've lived to have fun, to enjoy life. Then we lost Erik, and everything was just numb." He smiled slightly. "Until Daniella."

Greg's lips tilted upward, just briefly. "Until Daniella."

"It was so good to see that you had found your mate, especially with it being such a rare thing for us, and with Dani and I being so close it made me feel better, like I had some sort of purpose. But then Johanna came into the picture and everything has been upside down for me ever since. I handled everything wrong, Greg, everything, and I guess it's just made me reflect on the other choices I've made in my life." It was Luke's turn to run a hand through his own brown hair, ruffling the strands, fraying them to match the state of his nerves.

Greg tapped the desk, then nodded to a chair. "Sit please, we need to work this out."

Luke obliged and waited for him to speak.

"You said you weren't like me, and that's true, you're not." Greg's eyes bore into Luke's own. "But you don't need to be. You're just you, and that's exactly who you should be. Yes, you've made brash decisions, but so have I. Yes, you can be more impulsive than I am, more impatient, and to some that makes you irresponsible."

Luke's gaze shifted away from Greg's as shame filled him.

"But," Greg said, his tone sharp enough to pull Luke's attention back to him, "that doesn't mean you're less than anyone else here, including myself. The same people who would call you any of those things are the same people who may not like the decisions I make to keep this circle running. Do you really think everyone agrees with me all the time?"

Luke shook his head. "Of course not, but—"

"But *nothing*. If you can see that, then you should also be able to see that no one would believe you're any of those things all the time. Yes, you ran after Johanna on your own, but did you know we all wanted to run after you, to abandon everything and make sure you were safe? The only reason anyone hesitated was because they rely on me, and I had to force myself to walk away from you. I had to trust and believe you knew how to keep yourself safe, and if you needed help, the others would do right by you." Greg breathed. "Was I pissed? Of course, but not just at you. I was upset at myself for not being able to do what I wanted to, which was take care of my little cousin." He smiled.

If Luke had felt like himself, he would have rolled his eyes at the sentiment, but he didn't. Luke held onto Greg's words with a vice grip, finally understanding just how much he needed them. Luke had thought his heart had grown cold, surrounded by the ice he believed he needed to keep his distance from everyone else, because if that ice cracked, he would hurt everyone and they would see just how weak he had become. But the look on Greg's face, so soft, filled with a kindness that shone in his eyes and in his smile, made Luke realize that maybe the ice wasn't his ally. Maybe it was keeping him trapped instead of keeping him safe.

"Luke," Greg began, "I need you. I need you here and in the circle. You know me well enough to know I don't say that lightly. It hurts me to know I made you think you were replaceable or not enough, even for a moment."

Greg sighed. "I've always hated what happened during our childhood, so I wanted to take care of you. I didn't want you to ever feel alone again. But I pushed too hard." He slumped forward, clasping onto the desk with his palms to support his torso. "I wanted you to live your life as a child should, and then as a vampire should be able to. If you wanted money, women, fun, entertainment, whatever, I wanted you to have that. I wanted you to be able to enjoy your life with no attachments or responsibility, with nothing but support from me while not needing to concern yourself with me. That's the reason I haven't given you circle responsibilities, like Mya or Merida and Dom. But that doesn't mean I could ever replace you. You are irreplaceable to me."

Luke swallowed down the ball of emotions in his throat and watched as Greg did the same.

"You keep me honest, don't you know that? You're the only one who walks in here like he owns the place and has the balls to call me out. I trust you in that way. You argue with me, you fight with me to make sure I always do what's right. Luke, you're not only just as much of a part of this circle as I am, you run it with me. I may be the figurehead, the person who attends the meetings, puts things in place, and issues the orders, but it is not without your counsel."

Luke was breaking apart, physically and emotionally. He had to use his arms to support his head, as his elbows dug into his knees to keep from sliding to the ground.

How could I be so stupid? No, stop. You're doing it again. You are not stupid, you were just … blind.

"I envy you sometimes," Greg whispered, making Luke's head snap up. "You don't know how many times I've had to stop my reactions and contain my emotions because the people around me needed me to be their sense of calm. But you don't have to do that. Why would I ever want to chain you down and reduce you to what I go through on a daily basis? Look at myself and Ella. Look how long we waited. Do you think I would ever want you to go through something like that? You even helped keep me sane with her."

Luke's eyes widened. "What are you talking about?"

"I trusted you to look out for her, Luke. That's why when I went out of town or overseas, I never asked anyone to look out for her. I knew you would. I trusted you with the safety of my mate. If nothing else can explain to you how I think of you, how much I value you, that should tell you everything."

Luke grasped the bridge of his nose and took a long, deep breath. "I can't … I didn't even think of that."

"Well, now you are, so late is better than never." Greg smiled.

Luke glared at him before they chuckled, the laugh clearing the tension in the room. "I'm sorry for all of this. I guess … I just didn't realize how much this had messed me up." He sighed. "I never stopped to see things from your perspective, and that was wrong of me."

"No, it was wrong of me to never tell you. We all have faults, right? I'm learning one of mine is that I tend to not share things. I would rather carry the burden alone so that it won't hurt others."

Luke chuckled. "Sounds like Dani is keeping you in line."

Greg laughed with him. "She's definitely trying. Listen, whatever it is you're going through now, however you're feeling, you need to know it's okay. Luke, you're worried about the safety of your mate. You're in despair and that will fuck with you in the absolute worst ways. In those moments, everything you do feels like it's not enough, like it's caving in and you can't breathe."

Luke breathed for a moment before he settled, and a little more of the ice around his heart cracked. "You're right, it does. I feel that way all the time. It makes me feel so ... useless, and then I just become so angry. Angry at myself, angry at everyone, the world, fate. Do you know how many things I've broken at my house? It's getting expensive."

Greg's eyebrow rose. "You have over a billion dollars in dividends from company stocks."

"And if we don't find Johanna soon, they'll be finished by the end of the week." He sighed. "It's pitiful. I've never felt so weak."

Greg nodded. "I've felt like that many times, especially recently."

Luke didn't need to ask. He knew what Greg was talking about. When Daniella had been attacked by Zachariah, Greg seemed broken. In that moment, Luke hadn't known what Greg was feeling, but now he did, and watching him here, standing tall, seeming so strong, Luke could only ask, "How did you get through it?"

"With you guys. I may be resilient, but I can't carry the weight of the world on my shoulders, and when I'm falling, you all help me up." Greg's gaze met Luke's own. "Will you let us do the same for you?"

He nodded. "Please, I-I can't do this on my own."

Greg walked over to him and squeezed his shoulder. "And you will never have to."

CHAPTER 4

Luke desperately wanted to rush into the warehouses in front of him, rip everyone apart, and find his mate. The hope in his chest promised him that Johanna would be here and the constant, endless, gnawing grief in his soul would ease, even if just a fraction.

But that was him speaking emotionally, and his emotions had done a number on his head.

He looked at Greg. One conversation wasn't going to change everything, but it did help. It had reminded Luke that he was better than this, and he would need to remember that in today's battle and the next. He needed to be logical here.

There was a big possibility that Johanna wouldn't be at this location, and from the poor state of the exteriors and broken windows which couldn't keep out the cold wind, he hoped she wouldn't be inside. The warehouses looked abandoned. Those with wood seemed rotted, warped, and filled with the elements of the nearby sea. The surrounding buildings seemed just as bad, their once silver metal now turned to rust.

But Luke and the rest of the battle officers believed these appearances to be a façade. This location had nine buildings from what they'd seen, and each was equipped with high quality cameras. While they hadn't heard anything or seen any vehicles or movement from outside the warehouse buildings, none of the buildings they'd scoped had dust in front of the door, which meant someone, somewhere, was indeed home.

Greg nodded to them, and Luke knew the game was on. He squeezed his hands, rotating his arms and rolling his shoulders back. Daniella moved beside him and caught his gaze. If anyone had told Luke a couple of months ago that his best friend would be on the front lines with them, he wouldn't have believed it. But Daniella's life had changed greatly in a short amount of time, and she'd been forced to change with it or become buried by it. Daniella had taken the existence of vampires and immortals, her new relationship, and dedication to their circle the same way she did everything else, with committed determination.

Dani gave him a soft, reassuring smile, but as she turned to the building closest to them, her smile changed into a vengeful grimace that sent a chill down Luke's spine. She wasn't bloodthirsty. She didn't enjoy killing others or being involved in this war—Luke knew that like he knew his own hand—but Daniella was an advocate for justice. Her wrath was prevalent in her abilities as she pulled the cold air toward her, creating a whipping gust that cut and sucked the warmth out of his body. That gust built into a mini tornado before it flew forward in the direction of each building. As it hit, the windows concaved to her power, sending shards of glass everywhere and slamming the doors open.

A click sounded from Luke's right, and he watched as the door exploded, flying off the building while a fire raged inside. They were far enough away that the blast wouldn't harm them, but the shockwaves and sound were jarring. Suddenly, the fire stalled its normal expansion, then shriveled and died.

Dani's doing.

She used her powers to build the wind again, and then sent it flying once more to each building to trigger the opening of any secret doors.

The second blast roused their adversaries, and at least twenty men appeared. Luke called his power to him. A fog rolled in from the sea, blanketing the area in shrouded mist. But there was a sound, metal singing through the air, and Greg surged forward, catching the knife that was meant for Daniella's head. At Greg's roar, they charged forward. Snarls and screams ripped through the air around him as Luke weaved through the enemy. The fog hid the bodies of those that fell, but he knew where each of his team members were.

As Luke cut the head off another vampire, ten more appeared. He vanished, dissipating into shadow. Luke slithered along the ground, jumping from place to place until he found Greg's shadow. His darkness curled around Greg, curving into his power, a signal they'd long forged between them to alert to disturbances. Greg gave a small nod. As soon as he reached out with his own energetic ability to alert the others, Luke was off, jumping and sprinting from one shadow to the next until he was behind the vampires. His blood sang with the need to kill them, but he had other duties to follow.

Luke found their exit, a cellar beneath one of the buildings that seemed to connect to the others. That meant that the other buildings were either decoys, traps, or escape routes. Luke kept to his shadowed form as he slipped inside, the fighting continuing in the open air. He raced along the walls, only pausing to inspect doorways for more traps.

Deeper down the tunnels he found two vampires. He killed one of them within seconds, but the other one's death he purposefully prolonged, cutting his arm off when he could have severed his head. The vampire screamed, giving Luke what he wanted. The sound would alert others that may be waiting.

When no one came, Luke cut off his other arm. The vampire fell to the ground, his cries of pain echoing so loudly they hurt Luke's own ears. Still, no one appeared. Satisfied, Luke gave the man mercy by cutting off his head.

Even though Luke had proved that the nearby area was clear, or that any lingering vampires were otherwise preoccupied, he knew he couldn't let down his guard. Zachariah loved to set traps. He got a sick satisfaction by trying to prove he was smarter than everyone else, and Luke was not about to give it to him. Doing the next best thing he could think of, Luke took the dead vampire's arms and carried them on his shoulder as he sunk back into his shadowed form. When he neared the next entrance, he threw one of the arms toward the top, spiraling it so that it would clear the doorway vertically, like a body. When no explosion or threat appeared, Luke reclaimed the arm from the floor and continued along.

Nearing another passageway, Luke threw the arm again and was surprised when someone caught it.

Merida stepped through the door frame and cringed at the limb in her hand. "Really?"

"Don't judge," Luke said as he rematerialized from his shadows. "It's a good way to test for traps. Your head didn't get blown off now, did it?"

Merida handed the appendage back to Luke and dusted her hands off, although he didn't know why—they were already covered in blood. "Yes, but you killed him. It's a little weird to use his limbs this way. It's kind of like violating the body."

Luke side-eyed her. "You're just mad that's the appendage I cut off. If it would have been his dick, you would have been happy."

Merida covered her mouth with the back of her hand, smothering her laughter. "You know what? You're right. But please don't ever do that. I can take a lot of things seriously, but dicks flying through doorways is not one of them."

Luke laughed deep from his gut. His eyes watered and he wiped them with the shirt's sleeves. "Duly noted."

Recovering, he straightened his back and took in Merida's appearance and the lack of Dom or any of his animal forms hanging off her. She noticed and nodded to the right. "Dom's checking out that passage. We've got four more minutes before Greg wants us topside."

Luke resumed navigating the passage with Merida in tow, and then she called out to him. He paused and turned toward her. "What is it?"

"There's something at the top of the opening. Probably an explosive."

Luke nodded. Taking a step back, he threw one of the deceased vampire's arms at the opening. The moment it passed through, the mechanism ticked and then exploded, causing the passage to shake as the vibrations bounced and pulsed through the air. Compacted dirt and boulders rained down, effectively closing the earlier opening.

Behind them a whistle sounded through the air, making Luke tilt his head to the side. But when he glanced at Merida and saw her small smile, he knew what, or rather who, had made the noise.

The sound of a bird's wings grew closer to them, and then feather turned to skin and bone as Dom's figure appeared in front of Merida. He wrapped his arm around her shoulders, pulling her close to his side while her own arm found its way around his waist. Their heads tilted toward one another as they kissed.

Luke turned his head from the display of affection to give them some semblance of privacy and to keep his thoughts of envy at bay. But even though they spoke quietly, Luke heard Dom's concern for his mate and Merida's reassurance that she was fine loud and clear. Luke's eyes closed, fingers tightening into fists as he fought against his racing, aching heart. He took deep breaths, not wanting them to see that he had such a clear weakness. That he was so...

Stop it! You're not weak. You didn't fail. The only way you do that is if you never get her back, and that's exactly what will happen if you continue to think this way. Enough! Enough...

Luke swallowed hard and plastered a neutral expression on his face as he addressed Dom. "How was your passage?"

"Riddled with explosives. It seems they split half of the passages into safe routes and the other half into traps. While I was in animal form, I heard Greg and Daniella closest to the passage you went down, Meri. Seems like they're waiting for us." Dom gave Merida's shoulder a squeeze before letting her go.

Luke nodded. "Then let's go."

He tossed the last remnant of the vampire he killed onto the ground and followed the couple out, hoping that the investigation at the other warehouse buildings had provided more information than they'd found down there.

Greg and Daniella's house was buzzing with activity. The rest of the battle officers had arrived, anxious and excited to meet their new teams. Normally, whoever was called to a fight fought with the rest of the unit as one team. It was a good plan, one which allowed for more people to be available should an issue or surprise arise, but assigning and working with teams in this new way was the dawn of a new era. It was a signal of trust, trust that each member knew what they were doing and would work to support the others within their groups.

It was also a sign that Greg was letting go of his tight grip on the reins. While everyone rested their weight upon Greg's shoulders, each battle officer had proven themselves to be capable of fighting, surviving, and saving those they thought were worth the cause over the countless years. It was a celebratory moment for everyone there, especially Greg, and no matter the sadness in his heart, Luke could feel the joy too. He smiled as he watched their members from the bar, and for the first time in several lonely months he felt the comradery and familial bonds that had woven between each person. Those bonds spread as the hours passed by. Normally, Luke would have partaken in them, but he had other, bigger things on his mind.

He flipped through the paperwork they'd retrieved from the warehouse raid. Most of it was from the building that had exploded prior to the fight. Thanks to Daniella's powers, several of the documents had been saved. Luke didn't know what he would find in them, so he did his best to curve any hope that it would lead to Johanna. Hope had begun to feel just as much of a vice as fear and doubt, so instead he let himself get lost in the details, information, coordinates, and connections. He recorded, filed, and sorted the paperwork into what made sense to him. His creative mind painted a picture, one that continued to grow and expand into something he was sure would lead to an answer.

"There's a lot of things I thought I would find you doing, but paperwork wasn't one of them," Dani said as she entered the room with a drink in her hand. She offered it to him, and he took it with a nod of thanks.

"Hey, just trying to make myself useful." Luke smiled, but at the look on her face it turned to a grimace.

Her eyes narrowed. "Say that one more time and see what's going to happen to you. You might be a vampire, but I can and will be more than happy to kick your ass."

Luke couldn't help but smile, even as she huffed. "You're right, I'm sorry." He sighed, leaning back in the chair. "On the plus side, Greg already chewed me out for being negative. Will that make you take pity on me?"

Dani pulled up a chair, turning the back of it to face him before she sat down, crossing her arms on the top. "Technically speaking, I have been taking pity on you, even though you've been ignoring me."

"I have not—" He stopped at her glare and squeezed the bridge of his nose before softening more into the chair. "I'm sorry."

Dani looked him over before sighing as well. "It's okay. I

understand, I do, and I know this isn't something I can fix for you. I also know Mya was worse. With Erik, I mean."

Luke gulped at the reminder of his cousin broken by the death of her mate. He had to clear his throat before he could speak. "I guess she was, but it's hard to see a difference between her and I right now." His gaze moved to the ceiling, studying the mosaic of lines and curves within the woodwork to try to silence his self-deprecating thoughts.

"There are differences," she said, and he met her eyes. "You still have hope, and you haven't given up. You're angry. You have every right to be, and I know how easy it is to turn that anger onto yourself, but you still have hope. You might think that's a weakness, but that's the hardest part of it all. That hope is your strength, Luke."

Luke stared at her, really stared at her for a moment. Then he stopped and thought about her circumstances. Daniella lost her mother when she was young, which had caused her to go into the foster system. That trauma was why she'd worked her ass off and hadn't made time for the small things that made her happy. While a parental bond was not a mate bond, the grief felt was the same, and even though Daniella was hundreds of years younger than himself and his family, at times she seemed to be wiser than all of them put together.

Dani squeezed his wrist with her hand. "I know you'll find Johanna and that the two of you will be a wonderful, beautiful couple. I don't need anyone to tell me that. I know because I believe in you. You helped me turn my life around, Luke, and I wouldn't have found the joy and love I have now without you."

Her eyes began to water, and Luke bit his lip to stop from succumbing to tears as well.

"You will get her back, Luke. I swear it. I'll help you get your mate, and once you have her, I'll help you keep her. I promise. Even if I have to scream your praises from the top of every rooftop to convince her. You're not alone. If you can't believe in yourself, believe in me. I won't let you down."

Luke wrapped his arms around her, and they sunk into the embrace as he tilted his head back to keep his tears at bay. Finally, when he could speak, he whispered to her, "I believe in you. Even if I can't believe in myself, I'll always believe in you."

CHAPTER 5

It hurt. Everything hurt. Every single piece of her felt as though it was both on fire and numb at the same time. Her legs barely moved on their own.

That she had made it this far was purely due to her will power. Johanna couldn't open her eyes to navigate. The only thing guiding her was the touch of the rough cavern wall. She'd lost the strength to stand away from it, and now allowed it to cut into her skin as she dragged herself forward, inch by inch. The protection of her clothing was gone, either from when Zachariah had torn it from her, her fight to break free, or taken by the wall itself. Each jagged curve of rock pressed into her skin, and the more she fought against the blackness calling to her, the more she allowed the wall to cut into her. The pain kept her awake, kept her alive, for now. But for how long was the question.

Zachariah knew. Somehow, he had found out that she had leaked information. Johanna didn't think he was one hundred percent certain, but he suspected her, and that was enough to damage her body beyond repair. After all, how many times had he done it before?

A rock pressed against her wrist, causing her to hiss. She bit her lip, forgetting it too was busted, and winced as pain shot through her again. Still, she continued to move, but how much longer could she go on?

Why was she moving again?

Why wasn't she giving up?

She paused for a moment as a face came into her mind. Ah, him. That's why. Luke. *Her* Luke.

Some deity probably laughed at her claim over her mate. A man who deserved and could do much better than her. He wouldn't have wanted her even back when she was whole, back when her skin was not covered in cuts and stab wounds, serrated and hanging away from her body, back when she had not been tainted by Luke's very own enemy, when her mind, her very body, had not been stolen from her.

But still, Luke was hers, and in her dreams he wanted her. He was who she pictured when Zachariah abused her. It was Luke's arms she'd grown accustomed to as her safe place. It was him she envisioned when she entered the sanctuary of her mind, the one place that Zachariah couldn't reach, the place that her consciousness escaped to when he poisoned her. In Johanna's mind she could run her fingers through Luke's soft ash brown hair and she could stare into his green-gray eyes, the same eyes that made the whole world melt away until there was nothing left. If Luke saw her now, her once golden hair matted in blood, dirt, mud, and shit, her skin covered in the same suet, those eyes would harden. He'd be disgusted, as disgusted as she was with herself. Still, even though it would hurt, she wanted to gaze into those eyes one more time.

Johanna had done everything she could to help him, to protect him. She had even masked their mating bond until she'd seen him in the cave, until she had to feel him, had to connect with him just for a moment, even if it was the first and last time. She'd given up on being saved from Zachariah and had thought she'd accepted her fate to die at his hands. But even though that may be her destiny, she refused to let anyone else follow the same path. She'd saved people when she could, helped them escape, and controlled Zachariah's own vampire allies to allow their departure, so when he condemned someone, it would be them.

Perhaps that's why she never blamed the gods. Johanna was just like the villains who held her captive. She judged them and decided their lives were worth nothing. They were just as responsible for every injury, every scream she and the others endured. If those bastards died, Johanna's heart hurt for the lives they could have had, but the warrior in her soul—the one she had grown to be, the one who promised to outsmart her enemy at every turn— said "Good riddance." That's how far she'd fallen.

She had to stop herself from laughing at the irony of her circumstances. Johanna had been willing to die until the moment Zachariah tried to kill her. Then she wanted to live. Now, at this very moment, she wanted to breathe, to be free. But that wouldn't come for her. No. She was just as evil as they were, taking another's life and finding joy in their deaths.

She had become the very monster she strove to protect against.

Johanna sunk to her knees, her legs no longer working.

Blood seeped out of her scrapes and cuts, but poured from the stab wound to her side, the one that she knew would kill her.

She rested her head back against the wall and cried silently, until finally she couldn't hear, couldn't feel, couldn't taste. She simply was. And in that moment, just one more time, she saw his face.

Goodbye, Luke. I'm sorry I never got to truly know you. I'm sorry I couldn't be the mate you deserved. But I hope, at least, with my death, you'll be free.

And then she slipped away into nothing but the cold, dark black.

SOMETHING FELT OFF TO LUKE. IT WAS A STRANGE FEELING UNDER his skin, digging into his heart, which kept causing him to pause. It was as if something was calling to him, tugging him somewhere.

It gnawed at him as he left with his team for their battle. At first, he thought it might be a warning that something bad would happen during their raid, or that someone would get hurt or worse, and he warned his team because of it. But everything went off without a hitch. Every member played their part. They defeated the few vampires there and gathered all the intel they could, but still the feeling continued.

Luke and his team returned to Greg and Daniella's home, as expected. He set the files and a USB they had collected from the raid down on a table, alongside an SD card of pictures they had taken. His intent was to review them while they waited for the others, but then a lightning-like surge flew through his body, constricting around his muscles before fleeing, only to be replaced by the gnawing feeling clawing at him. It tugged him along until he mindlessly walked out the door and got in his car. Only then did he regain control.

Luke knew he should wait for the others, but this, whatever it was, felt as if he were running out of time. He had to go. He didn't know why, but he had to. Shifting his car into gear, he pulled down the driveway and then he was off, but that didn't make the feeling any better. Instead the feeling grew, spreading out from his heart through his torso until he clenched the steering wheel hard.

Something's wrong. What is this?

Luke did the only thing he could. He called Greg.

"Hey," Greg said, and Luke could hear him shuffling around. "We just got back. Where are you?"

"Something—" Luke coughed, trying to clear his throat as it suddenly felt hoarse and tight.

"Luke? What's wrong?"

"I don't know," he choked out, swerving around the bend of another curve as he followed the tug. "Something's leading me somewhere."

Luke coughed again, his eyes watering against the tightness in his chest. He heard Greg shout, starting a conversation in the background that Luke couldn't focus on.

"Mya just checked your GPS. You're heading home." Greg said.

"Home?"

"Yes." Another conversation carried on in the background before Greg spoke to him. "Can you try to take a deep breath, then try to describe the feeling."

Luke inhaled and exhaled, but it hurt. It was as if someone was breaking through his ribcage, trying to tear out his heart.

"It feels like someone's ripping me apart." He cursed as another whip of pain went through him, another lash that squeezed. "Like a fucking snake is wrapped around my body and it's crushing me. It started in my heart and—"

He groaned, biting back a scream.

There was a murmur in the background, and then Greg shouted before coming back to him. "Luke, it's Johanna…"

"What?" Luke took a curve too fast, almost hitting the guard rail.

"We're coming." Another pause. "Try to push reassurance through the line. Push as hard as you can, okay? But we're coming."

At Johanna's name, panic mixed in with the feeling. "I don't understand—"

Greg's voice was steady and calm, but his words froze every cell in Luke's body, "Luke, she's dying. What you're feeling is the death of your mate."

Luke's eyes widened. His hands shook but he righted himself as he raced down the road faster than before, his body reacting quicker than his mind could process.

"Get home," Greg bit out. "We're coming. We're right behind you, but she needs to know you're going to be there, so push into whatever connection you feel with her, so she knows not to give up."

The roar of an engine ended the call, and the silence was louder than Luke's disbelief. It did feel like he was dying, like pieces of him were being hammered away, like he was fighting fate itself. But he would fight fate, the universe, the gods themselves if it meant he could save his mate, so he did. With every breath, he pushed against the tightness. Luke remembered the last time he had seen Johanna, how she had spoken to him telepathically, and he tried that. He'd try anything to get her to keep going.

"Johanna? Can you hear me?"

Nothing.

He tried again. *"Johanna?"*

Luke was met with silence, and he restrained himself from punching the steering wheel. He took another turn too quickly, his whole car shifting to one side as it lifted around a curve and then slammed back down, but he didn't care.

"I'm coming, baby. I'm coming. Please, whatever you're feeling, hold on for me, please."

Five minutes later, he pulled into the circular driveway of his home, and then he was out, dashing over the gravel and grass. He ran, using every ounce of his speed until he reached the back of his property where the pull was the strongest.

Luke's panicked state had him looking around for a standing human being, and then lower, scanning. The still air suddenly moved, and beneath the smell of flowers from his garden he finally scented her blood, and then he saw her.

Luke rushed to her, a gasp leaving his lips at the sight of his mate. In all his years, he had never seen someone so sullied and broken. He cradled Johanna in his arms, scanning her skin and taking in her injuries. Strands of her long, blonde, wavy hair were stuck to her face, covered in blood and other matter he could smell and feel beneath his fingertips. Her lips and nails were blue. There were finger marks, bite wounds, gashes and rope burns around her neck. Her clothes were tattered and shredded, and beneath them her skin hung drastically from starvation, caked in the same substances as her face and hair, making it difficult for him to take in all her wounds. Each breath she took was too shallow, too fast.

Looking down, Luke watched as blood poured from the stab wound in her side.

He didn't want to move her in case her spinal cord or organs had been punctured, but he had to get her inside and laid down for Mya to assess and heal her body properly. As gently as he could, Luke picked Johanna up, cradling her head to his chest. He lifted his foot to kick in the door, not wanting to spare any time, but then he paused. Only the inner circle knew where he lived, and each of those members had met earlier to raid Zachariah's locations. How exactly had Johanna found her way to his home?

Luke turned back to scan the distance, but he didn't see anything. He took a long, deep breath, trying to see if he could smell another being, but it was only them. The only other living scent was a family of deer beyond the tree line, and they were no more interested in him than Luke was in them.

Despite that, he did have to agree that this would be the perfect trap. Johanna's state and the pain he fought against through their bond, even now, had blinded him from checking his surroundings or even his home. He decided that it didn't matter. Even if this were a trap, he had to save Johanna. Greg, Daniella, and Mya would be here soon, and even if he lost his life in the process, he refused to lose hers. He would need to be cautious though, to force his mind into overdrive even though his body and heart were breaking apart.

Luke shifted Johanna slightly to pull his keys out from his pocket and put them in the heavy, wooden back door. He turned the knob and twisted his body so he would get hurt in place of Johanna if someone were waiting for them or had planted a trap. When he slowly opened the door, nothing happened, and when Luke took another whiff of his space, searching for any being's scents that did not belong, he couldn't find any.

Satisfied, he moved to the nearest flat surface—his dining room table—and shoved everything off so he could lay Johanna down as gently as possible. She didn't groan, didn't make a sound as he adjusted her, and that scared him even more. He fixed her legs onto the table, being mindful of their gashes and split open flesh, then he looked her over. Her state of nakedness dawned on him, but he pushed the thoughts away as his eyes landed on her wound. He knew he would need to get clean blankets and a towel to hold against her side. He didn't want to leave his mate defenseless when she needed him the most, but he knew he had to while he still could. The pain in his body was growing, causing his muscles to clench and spasm, and he was worried that it may incapacitate him entirely.

Luke shrunk to his shadowed form, finding the fluidity easier to move in. He raced, slithering under baseboards and across rooms to grab blankets and towels before rematerializing beside Johanna. He pressed a towel to the wound at her side. With his other hand, he covered her. Even in this state, even with pain and fogginess marring his brain, Johanna was still beautiful to him, and he wanted to be the only one to see her body.

His fingers shook as he picked up his cellphone and called Greg. He waited for him to answer before saying, "Kitchen."

Greg grunted in response, his focus clearly on the road. "We'll be there in three minutes."

"Hurry, please." Luke swallowed, his voice sounding weak even to his own ears. "She's bleeding out."

Tires screeched in the background. "We're coming, hold on for me."

"Stay on the phone, Luke. We need to make sure you stay with us too," Dani said.

"Okay," Luke responded, but he wasn't really speaking to them. He couldn't seem to focus. Instead, he leaned down, his forehead touching Johanna's as he rubbed her cheek softly. Luke closed his eyes, breathing her in, not the blood, the sweat, the shit, or the other scents, but the essence of her that was hidden underneath it all.

"Johanna?" he called to her through their bond. *"You spoke to me like this once, and I'd give anything to hear your voice again."*

Luke paused in his stroking of her skin, grimacing as another lash of pain went through him. *"Was that you? Are you mad at me for not rescuing you, sunflower? Although it seems you didn't need me in the end."*

Another slice of pain, this one harder, sharper. *"Would you forgive me if I told you I'd give my life for yours? That I'd switch places with you if I could?"*

A lightning bolt of pain followed, so strong it left him gasping. His hand clenched the table as he breathed through the feeling, a broken smile forming at his lips. *"So it is you. Remind me not to make you mad in the future."*

The pain was still present and debilitating, but less intense.

"I know we didn't have the greatest beginning, Johanna. There are so many things I wish I could go back and do differently, but I don't believe this is our end. Please, give me a chance to show you what we could have together. Don't give up on me before we've even started."

The door to his house slammed open followed by a stampede of footsteps. *"The calvary is here, sunflower. I know this all must hurt so, so much, but please, just a little longer. I've been searching for you for such a long time. I can't lose you, not yet. Stay with me, please."*

Luke pulled back from her just as Greg, Daniella, and Mya came into the room. They paused for a split second, Daniella gasping while Greg and Mya cursed at Johanna's state, and then they flew into action. Mya and Daniella took turns at the table while Greg searched Luke's cabinets. Luke moved to help Greg, but he stopped him.

"Stay there, she needs you." Greg pulled out a bowl and cup, then began to fill one of them with water.

Luke nodded. "Okay. Mya, she has a stab wound on her right side." He lifted the blanket to show his cousin, who cursed again.

Daniella fished around in the drawer before handing Mya a sharp knife. Mya nodded in thanks and then slit a deep gash into her palm. She clenched her fist once, twice, before sliding her hand into the wound to speed its recovery.

"Would you do my other hand for me, please?" Mya asked Daniella.

Dani hummed in response, cutting into Mya's other hand. Greg brought the cup to her and laid in on the table. Mya put her hand on top of it, letting the blood drip into it while Greg and Daniella went around washing whatever cuts they could without raising the blanket further than was necessary. Once enough blood was in the cup, Mya handed it to Greg.

"Put it on whatever wounds you find so we can heal as many areas as possible at the same time," Greg instructed Daniella, and they set off working together.

Luke continued to run his fingers over Johanna's cheek, taking in her appearance and looking for changes. Her lips were still blue, her skin still pale and clammy. "Is she accepting your blood?"

"Yes, but it's going to take a while. We were really close to losing her, but I think she stayed around for you." Mya flexed her fingers again, sending more blood into Johanna. "You did well, Luke, but you're going to need some of my blood too."

He frowned at that. "I do? Why?"

"Because you look like you were on death's door with her. Your skin is pale, your eyes are glazed over, and I can hear your heart beating a mile a minute." Mya lifted her free hand to his mouth. "Drink."

Luke looked at her for a moment to judge if she was sure. When she narrowed her eyes, he clasped onto her arm and bit into her wrist. Blood squirted into his mouth, and he slurped it down. He squeezed her wrist as her healing magic hit him like a sucker punch, flowing through his veins and into the pathways that fed his organs. Every part of him felt revitalized, his vision clearer, hearing sharper, senses stronger.

Slowly Luke released Mya's wrist and found that the pain he felt before had vanished. Luke turned his gaze back to his mate. Johanna's skin seemed rosier, and his soul sung in praise. "Thank you."

"Where did you find her?" Greg asked as he continued to coat Johanna's wounds in Mya's blood.

"At my back door." Luke stroked his fingers over Johanna's hair. "I don't understand how she got here. I didn't sense anyone."

The mood in the room shifted as each of his family members went on high alert. Greg turned to Daniella. "Baby, could you check the environment while I make sure the house is clear?"

She nodded. "Of course."

Luke took the cup of blood from Dani's hands, and she closed her eyes, calling on her magic. Static electricity sizzled the air, making Luke's hairs stand on end as he tended to his mate. He kept his mind on Johanna, trusting Dani and Greg to be the supportive shield he needed right now.

"The house is clear," Greg said.

A few moments later, Dani said, "There's no one outside or in the surrounding land either."

"I don't know how she got here"—Luke looked over Johanna again—"but I'm happy she's here."

Beside him, Mya nodded and retracted her hand from Johanna's wound, healing the gash on her hand in the blink of an eye. "That's all that matters. She's here, safe, and she's healing."

Luke released the breath he didn't realize he was holding. "How long will it take her to recover?"

"Give her a few hours." Mya handed the cup to Greg who took it to the sink and began to clean up the items they'd used.

"Can I move her? I don't want her to wake up to ... this." Luke swallowed, gesturing to the evidence of Johanna's injuries.

Mya shook her head. "No, I wouldn't just yet. But if you have a loose shirt or jacket, we could put that on her."

"I'll change her." Luke brushed his fingers over Johanna's head, a gentle, light caress. "Dani, can you—"

"I've got it," she said, walking off in the direction of his bedroom.

Mya continued to gather the towels around Johanna before setting off to the laundry room. Luke called out to her, stopping her in her tracks. "Thank you for saving her."

Mya gave a stiff nod before she left.

Thank you for saving me.

CHAPTER 6

Five hours had passed. Johanna's breathing was mostly normal, which settled some of the fear in Luke's chest, but she was still unconscious. Sometimes her pulse raced under his fingertips, but it didn't seem to be from any type of external stimulus. She didn't respond to his voice, to him trying to initiate a telepathic connection with her, his touch, nothing.

Mya gave him the okay to get her cleaned up, knowing Johanna had enough of her blood in her system that any major damage would have been repaired. But even Mya was at a loss as to why Johanna wouldn't stir.

It's fine. Everything will be okay. Everything is okay.

His mate was under his roof, at his side, in his very arms. It was simply not possible that anything could be wrong, but if something was then he would fix it. For now, Luke would start with what he could control.

He carried Johanna into his bedroom, and didn't stop until he reached bathroom and shut the door behind them. Luke rested her in a corner and drew them a bath before removing the blanket he'd wrapped her in. Then he began gently peeling away the stuck remnants of her clothing. He kept glancing at her face, just in case she opened her eyes in the middle of him undressing her, but she did not.

Luke removed his own clothes, gathered the garments together and tossed them into the trash. Even if they could be salvaged and the blood removed, he did not want the reminder of how he'd found his mate.

With the tub quickly filling, he added soap and brought an array of devices over to the side of the tub for his task before lifting his mate and easing them both into the hot water. Johanna's relaxed body melted against his and he had to blow out a harsh breath at her nearness. Months of emotions bubbled to the surface and for just one moment, he hugged her to him. Tears slid down his face as he buried his head in her neck to breathe her in.

For so long he'd looked for her, searched for her, thought about her, dreamt about the last time he'd seen her, fantasized about her and about what life could possibly be like with her at his side. Even his body, traitor that it was, reacted to her. Even though they were both filthy, he still wanted her *desperately.* Having her in his arms stirred the need to bite her, to take her and make her his, but that wasn't right, not like this. He would not touch her, ever, until she was awake, had consented to their bond, and wanted him in the same way he wanted her. Until then, no matter how long it took or how long he had to wait for her to awaken, he would stay by her side, watch over her, protect her, spoil her, treasure her, and cherish her. He knew it like he knew his own name. And if he was lucky, during that time he'd get to know her and the bond between them would go from being something that marked her as his mate to her being the woman he loved fiercely.

Luke swallowed his emotions back, devoting himself to the task at hand. He picked up the scrub brush and went to work, dipping it into the hot water before pouring soap onto it and scrubbing Johanna's back. The strands of her hair were stuck there at first, but the hot water loosened them enough to allow him to slide them over her shoulder. He scrubbed her, cleaning away the filth that marred her flesh until her light skin was rosy pink.

Luke moved thoroughly from place to place, sometimes having to go over one section of her back multiple times before getting it clean. Finally, when he could no longer see beneath the water to clean the top of her ass, he shifted her and drained the tub before filling it and starting the process over again.

Five washes later, he had cleaned the majority of her body while doing his best not to focus on her creamy skin and luscious curves. Mya's blood had not only healed her wounds but filled the spaces of her body that had concaved from starvation. She wasn't back to the weight he'd seen her at before, one that made her hips full, thighs thick, ass abundant, and stomach curved in a way that made him want to gather it into his hands and squeeze its softness, but at least she was on her way.

Luke stood with her, carrying her to the shower to wash her hair. The waist length tresses were at least a little cleaner from the bath, but her scalp needed a good scrub to lift away the last of the debris. Gently he scrubbed her scalp with shampoo several times, then conditioned and detangled her hair while still in the shower. Only after he was done with her did he finally wash himself as well, a reprieve that had his hardened cock settling down a little.

After drying off his mate and himself, he dressed Johanna in one of his shirts and a pair of his boxers, making a mental note to get her comfortable clothes to wear around the house. Then he dressed himself before making the tough decision to lay her down in a spare room instead of his own bed. One day she would willingly lie there, but until then he wanted her to be comfortable and feel safe with him.

Johanna still hadn't awoken, and if she didn't soon they'd need to get more medical supplies to give her liquid nutrients. Luke setup the IV for vitamins and nutrients and added a naso-gastric tube for Johanna, just in case.

Settling the sheets and comforter around her, he sighed heavily. "I don't know what you're going through," he said softly, "but I'm here. You're safe here and I promise to take care of you."

Luke kissed her head before stepping out of the room to find his family. As he approached Mya, Dani, and Greg, he took in the tenseness of their shoulders and realized something else had occurred.

"What happened?" Luke asked.

Dani's hand slid away as Mya's posture grew straighter, her lips thinning. "Nothing," Mya said. "How's Johanna? Is she awake yet?"

"No." Luke took a seat at the table, his eyes touching Greg's own. Luke could sense sympathy and anger in them, but it didn't feel as though either emotion was just for him. "What's going on?" Luke asked again.

"Nothing," Mya bit out.

"Mya—" Dani started.

Luke cut her off, his hand clenching into a fist. "I'm not going to sit here and act like I believe whatever lie you're trying to tell yourself." He paused, thinking back to earlier when he'd thanked her. Mya always had a difficult time accepting thanks, and he thought the fact that his mate had been saved while hers hadn't might have been the cause for her gruff behavior, but now he knew better.

"Luke," Greg said carefully, "why don't we go into another room to talk?"

Mya's head snapped up as she bared her teeth. "Just say it here! Let him know! Don't try and fucking coddle me!"

"Then don't give me a reason to!" Greg shouted, causing Mya to jerk back into her seat at his explosion.

Dani's hand squeezed Mya's shoulder, and that was all it took for Mya to break down, tears streaming over her bronze skin.

"Let's go, okay?" Dani said softly.

She nodded and Dani helped her out of her chair, leaving Greg and Luke to listen to Mya's sobs and Dani's placating words echoing down the hall. It had been a long time since Luke had seen Mya so distraught, so broken.

"Greg, what the fuck happened?"

Greg clasped his hands together, then brought them up to his lips. He took a deep breath before locking his eyes on Luke. "When you told us what you were feeling earlier, Darius was the one who recognized it as the loss of your mate."

Luke shook his head. "Okay?"

"We thought a mate could only physically feel that loss if they had consummated their relationship and satisfied the mate bond, something you never got the chance to do."

"Where are you going with this?" Luke asked.

"Mya has never felt what you did, Luke. Ever. If Erik was her mate, which we know he was, and he died, she should have felt that even without their bond being consummated."

Greg sat back in his chair with a sigh, squeezing the bridge of his nose before fixing his eyes back on Luke.

"For three hundred years she's been mourning a death that never happened. He's alive, Luke. Erik is alive."

CHAPTER 7

He was running out of options. A week had passed and Johanna was still unconscious. Luke stayed by her side nearly every minute of the day, not wanting to miss the moment she opened her pretty blue eyes, but it never happened. Johanna was still responding to some sort of mental stimulus, twitching her face every so often, scrunching her cute pert nose, wrinkling her forehead, and even breaking out into a cold sweat, but she just wouldn't open her eyes. It wasn't truly a coma as her body seemed to be functioning, but it was as if she was under some sort of spell.

While Luke had watched over her and taken care of her, he browsed the books and articles he had on magic, lore, witches, and witchcraft. When they gave him no answers, he reached out to anyone he could think of from their inner circle with an ability that might be able to help.

Greg had the ability to look into past memories, but both he and Luke knew they could not use his power on Johanna. When Greg used that ability without permission, it ripped the person apart, locking them into a type of mental paralysis while he forced the scenes to play for the both of them. As Johanna was not fully catatonic and she at least had the ability for telepathy, there was a small chance she may be able to give Greg mental permission, but it wasn't a risk they were willing to take.

Dani was much the same. While she'd been learning how to use her powers on a scientific level, she explained to Luke that working with someone's memory was complex. Still, when she came over to check on him and make sure he was taking care of himself, or fill in the gaps where he wasn't, she tried using her magic on him. Thus far she'd been able to look into some of his short-term memories, but Dani had no control over what she saw and had a hard time pulling herself out without affecting him as well.

Luke couldn't get a hold of Mya. She wasn't returning his calls or answering his texts or emails. According to Dani and Greg, she'd gone off the deep end in her search to find Erik, tearing through their archives, hacking agencies, and setting off on solo missions only to come back empty-handed and covered in blood.

Jason had seen Johanna. He'd cautioned Luke against getting his hopes up as his specialty was to hurt, not heal, but still Luke appreciated the effort. And for that effort, Jason had been flung back against a wall the moment he tried to look inside Johanna's head. When he'd recovered, Jason told Luke that there was a large mental barrier around her that he couldn't break through. Jason also guessed Johanna was cognizant enough to know Luke was beside her and not someone else, or else she would have lashed out at him too.

That news should have made Luke feel some sort of elation, but it only confused him more. What was she protecting herself from if she knew he was here with her? Was she trying to figure out if he would hurt her as well? If so, why would she leave her body open to him but not her mind? And there was still the lingering question of how she ended up on his property.

Astrid was finally able to see Johanna toward the end of the week. Luke was happy when Dani arrived at his house before her. He needed the support, and Astrid was his last hope. If she couldn't figure out what was going on, he wasn't sure what his next steps would be.

"Thank you for being here," Luke said as Dani pulled up a chair beside him.

She smiled. "Where else would I be?" Her gaze left his and moved to Johanna's form. "Has anything changed?"

Luke shook his head. "No. Her pulse is the same, heartbeat the same, breathing patterns all the same. Her hand fidgeted for the first time today though."

"Well, that's something." Dani's tone was light, hopeful, but Luke struggled to put stock in it.

The chime of his doorbell interrupted their conversation. Dani gave his hand a hard squeeze, then headed to the door to let Astrid in.

Luke stood, plastered a smile on his face, and gave her a tight hug once she entered the room. "Hi, Astrid."

"Hello, Luke," Astrid said. Then she recoiled, shuddering as if something disgusting had touched her.

Luke moved to ask her what was wrong, but then he realized her gaze wasn't on him, it was on Johanna's form.

"You don't have to be so feisty," Astrid huffed, coming to stand beside the bed.

Luke shared a look with Dani, but she shook her head and shrugged. "Astrid, who are you talking to?" he asked.

"Your mate. She's quite protective over you."

Luke's eyes widened. "What?"

Astrid didn't turn to him. Instead she looked at Dani, her head cocked to the side in question. "I'm surprised you don't feel it too."

Dani's gaze shifted between Astrid and Luke. "Feel what?"

Astrid made a soft humming sound before she slowly twiddled her fingers a few inches above Johanna's body as if she was plucking the strings of an instrument. Astrid paused around Johanna's waist, near the wound that had almost killed her. "Ah I see. You were there when Luke brought her in. You helped save her."

"Yes, I did," Dani confirmed, her tone full of questions.

Instead of taking his earlier spot, Luke sat on the corner of the bed. He knew he was crowding Astrid, but for some reason he felt compelled to be as close to Johanna as possible. There was an electricity in the air, a call that made the hairs on his arms stand straight, and it called for him to protect his mate, even though he knew she was perfectly safe.

Astrid gave him a knowing smile but didn't say a word. When she reached the crown of Johanna's head, Astrid pulled back and considered her. She hummed again before taking Luke's seat, her face practically beaming. "Your mate, while unconscious, has very strong cumental abilities, and she is protecting you and everyone you come in contact with."

"How?" Luke didn't even realize he had reached for Johanna's hand until it was clasped in his. The sudden feeling of her skin on his surprised him, but he couldn't fathom pulling away.

"Johanna is watching over this room, even this house. When I walked in, I felt as though I was being watched, and then I felt pressure when we hugged, as if someone was trying to push me back and away from you." Astrid made a circle with her hand. "All of that, was your sweet—although possessive and jealous—mate."

Luke studied Johanna. She seemed so still, even relaxed, except for her chest. Her breathing had changed, grown faster as if her adrenaline was rising.

"What does that all mean, Astrid?" Dani asked.

Astrid sighed, settling back in the chair. "It means that the magic that is keeping her unconscious is her own."

"How do I get her out of it?" Luke asked.

"You don't," Astrid replied, her voice sharp. "You cannot force her out of the magic. She has to feel safe enough to break it all on her own."

Luke turned in Astrid's direction, ready to speak, but she stopped him with the stillness in her normally swirling silver eyes. "Johanna has ... she's gone through a lot, Luke. And I think throughout that time, even though the two of you were not together, she relied on any memory or thought of you to ... separate herself from her trauma. She used you as her saving grace. But something tells me she also spent a lot of time protecting you, which is why she's like this now. She's stuck at a crossroads between those two thoughts. I don't think she realizes that she's not in hell anymore."

Luke clenched his jaw, grinding his teeth to keep from shouting his rage. He was so incredibly tired of it being this way for them. Johanna deserved more and Luke wanted to give it to her, but yet again she was somewhere he couldn't reach her.

He took a deep breath. "What can I do?"

"I think you're already doing a good job," Astrid said carefully. "She just needs a little more time. Has she responded to you in any way?"

Luke shook his head. "She moves a little sometimes. Small things. Expressions, mostly. I thought they were signs she was coming out of it, but they don't seem to be, and they don't seem to be responses to me either."

"What about the day you found her?" Astrid asked.

Luke paused, thinking back. "Not really. I felt where she was." He twirled a piece of Johanna's hair around his finger. "And at some point I spoke to her, and the pain of losing her would either get stronger or weaker as if she was responding to me. But I haven't felt, heard, or seen anything that seems like a response since."

"Maybe ..." Dani began, meeting Astrid's eyes. At her nod she continued. "Maybe you're wrong, Luke. Maybe when she moves, she is responding to you in her own way, and when she can't, she sends the thoughts through you."

"What do you mean, Dani?" Luke asked.

"What you're doing right now, the way you're touching her. In all the time I've been here, you've never done that. You tend to sit beside her"—Dani nodded to the chair—"not this. Maybe, you're responding to her mental abilities. Since she can't touch you, she's asking you to touch her."

Astrid nodded. "That's exactly what I think is happening. Johanna clearly acknowledges you as her mate. She's protected you for a long time, and I think it's ingrained in her to continue to do so. Because Daniella, Greg, and Mya were here when you found her and helped to save her, Johanna has decided they're safe. She can sense they provide you comfort as well, and because of that she trusts them. But other people will not feel welcomed the same way you all do, not until she deems them safe as well."

Astrid crossed her legs, resting her head on her palm. "What you're doing right now is responding to her pull. Your bond works like a conduit. The same magnetic system but on a mental and emotional level, most likely due to Johanna's powers. And I'm sure that when she does wake up it will be even stronger."

Luke bit his lip but nodded. It made sense, and if he were honest, he liked it. He liked knowing there was a secret connection between them, that Johanna knew and accepted him as her mate and trusted him to look out for her when she needed time to rest. He supposed, in a way, maybe that's all this was. That was the mindset change he needed, the swing toward the positive.

Johanna would need time to heal from everything that happened to her, just like she would need time to see that they could work together. This was the beginning of that, her time to rest and recover her strength. If she was cognizant enough to orchestrate all of this, then she was aware enough to awaken on her own. He just needed to give her time, and that was something he could do.

A smile graced his lips as he turned to Astrid. "Thank you. I feel like you've given me the answers I needed." Luke's gaze shifted to the floor with a sigh. "I've been drowning for a while with all of this, and sometimes it felt like I couldn't reach the surface no matter how hard I tried to swim."

"That's understandable," Dani said, and he met her dark

brown eyes. "You have every reason to feel that way. Just try to remember that no matter how dark it gets in those moments, you're not alone. We're right there with you. We're reaching out to you, and we will always make sure you're safe. You can breathe, Luke. You can breathe."

CHAPTER 8

Luke's heart felt lighter as he said goodbye to Dani and Astrid and walked back into Johanna's room. For a moment he just stood there, observing her. He tried to see if he could feel the energy or presence Astrid had when she first arrived. He knew it was probably stupid to try, but he had to, because feeling Johanna in any way was better than not feeling her at all.

Luke approached the bed hesitantly. He had vowed to keep a respectable distance away from her until she was awake and able to consent to his touch, but even without feeling the pull from her again, he knew he needed this, *they* needed this. He sat on the bed instead of the chair. His hip pressed against her own as he captured her hand in his and leaned over her.

She was still, breathing normally, her golden hair spread around her shoulders and beautiful body like an angel. Angelic though she might be, Luke now knew that his little angel had fire in her. Luke breathed in her scent before brushing his fingertips through her mane, following the long tresses until they ended and curled around her waist. He traced back up the path until he reached her face, then caressed the softness of her full cheeks. He slid down her jaw, her throat, and stroked her pulse, feeling it thump against the pad of his thumb. He ended at her shoulder, and drew back just slightly, so he could take in more of her with his gaze.

"I wasn't sure if I wanted a mate," Luke began, then paused, shaking his head. "That's not true. I didn't want to find my mate. I was terrified to."

He rested his foot on the tufted frame of the bed and continued. "When I was a kid, I thought my whole world had ended. I'd lost my mother to the plague, my aunt and uncle had fallen ill, and Greg was forced to leave us and join the army. Even though I had no concept of death at the time, I fully expected to contract the plague and end up like my mother."

Luke stroked the back of Johanna's hand. "But then Greg came back as a vampire. He saved us, and I was grateful. I was grateful to him and Erik for letting me be a child, and I kept that mentality far into my twenties as a vampire."

He sighed. "I was restless, jumping from one thing to the next, gathering all the knowledge I could. I needed experiences to feel alive because I never imagined being able to live forever. I think," his voice quieted, "no, I know that for a while there, I thought I was invincible."

Luke took a deep breath, his shoulders sinking forward as he continued with his story. "I still thought I was invincible when the wars started. I bathed myself in the blood of others without batting an eye, because they were trying to take the one thing that mattered to me: my way of life. Greg, Mya, Erik, they were all part of that. Being a vampire has its perks, yes, but the biggest drawback is watching the faces of people you grow to care for die. I couldn't, I *wouldn't,* let anyone take another person from me, and I used every ounce of my false invincibility to do so. And then we started saving people."

Luke's eyes met Johanna's face, and even though her own eyes were closed, he still stared at them as if he could will them to open, as if he could connect to her, to make her understand him. "Do you know what it's like to save someone's life, to see them believe they're going to die and then give them another chance to live? That ... that did something to me."

"I started to change. I learned everything I could from doctors and surgeons who risked their lives on the front lines to heal their armies. I learned how to build shelters, houses, even hospitals, so that others could have somewhere to turn to. That's when I became terrified of having a mate, because I learned that I couldn't save everyone. Immortal didn't mean invincible, and it didn't mean I was an omniscient god. I couldn't always be there, and there was a possibility that one day my mate would need me and I couldn't be there to save her, to save *you.*"

Luke ran a frustrated hand through his hair and sighed again. "I kept myself busy in every possible way I could. I do that a lot. When I'm stressed, I need to keep my hands busy, keep my mind elsewhere. It worked for a while, until Mya lost Erik."

He turned her hand in his, rubbing the space between her thumb and index finger, feeling a sense of comfort that logically he knew he must have imagined, but nonetheless wanted to believe was real.

"Erik was a father figure to all of us and losing him changed something in us. For me, it was the chaotic way I went after things, the way I obsessed when I didn't know what else to do. But it damn near killed Mya. For once, someone needed me and I didn't want to let her down. We were like that for a long time, until Dani, and now you. Mates are very rare for us immortals, and whether we meet our mates is entirely up to chance. We never know where, or why, or how."

Luke smiled. "But you, sweet little sunflower, walked into my life, infected my mind, and you haven't left it since, even when I didn't know you were my mate. So, while I find it incredibly adorable that you're chasing women out of my—and what I hope you'll accept to be your—house, you should know they never stood a chance." He brushed her cheek with his thumb. "Because I am yours, Johanna, just as much as you are mine, and when you come back to me, I will spend my days reminding you of that in every way I can."

"THANK YOU FOR PICKING UP THE WALLPAPER," LUKE SAID TO Dani as he joined her at her green SUV.

Dani smiled, unlocking the trunk for him. "You're welcome."

While Luke began to grab the rolls and other supplies, Dani picked up several large bags from the backseat. Luke tilted his head to look inside them, but she swerved around him before he could ask.

Luke rolled his eyes and huffed as he followed her into his house, where she was already busy unloading the bags in Johanna's room.

"Are you going to tell me what else you got?" Luke asked as he set the wallpaper rolls down on the floor.

"A little bit of this, a little bit of that," Dani said in a sing-song voice as she bobbed her head, sending her dark brown curls swaying left to right. She blew him a kiss when he eyed her suspiciously. Then Luke saw her pull out a bundle of clothes.

"Are those for Johanna?" he asked.

"Yes. While I'm sure you get some weird, sick sort of alpha male satisfaction from having her in your clothes, she should have some of her own."

He was, in fact, satisfied every time he changed Johanna into his clothes, but that was beside the point. "How did you figure out her size?"

When Luke had casually mentioned to Dani that he wanted to hire a seamstress to measure Johanna so he could purchase clothing for her, Dani had nearly cut his head off. According to her, there were some things a woman had to volunteer on her own, and her clothing size was one of them. Luke thought it was ridiculous, especially since he was only asking to make his mate more comfortable, but Dani told him she'd take care of it.

"There's a reason why those high-end expensive stores have personal shoppers," she said as she put away another set of clothes, something pink catching his eye. As Dani headed back outside, she stopped and looked over her shoulder at Luke. "I like the new furniture by the way. It's very warm ... cozy."

To keep his mind off when Johanna might regain consciousness, Luke had kept himself busy. At first, he sketched Johanna, mixing her form with outfits and small details he remembered from when she would flit in and out of the office. It had been months since he'd felt that type of inspiration, and he was grateful that having her with him, even in this state, helped him find it again.

He'd also finished all his creative projects at work, setting the firm three weeks ahead. Then he pruned his garden and even designed a new plot on his property for future vegetables. He was regularly cooking again, sending Daniella and Greg home with dinners and desserts, or eating with them on the occasions they joined him in his home to catch up.

But now he had turned his attention to making this space into something he hoped Johanna would like. He didn't really know her tastes, so he focused all his choices around one picture. On her first day at The Novak Firm, IT had taken a picture of her for her badge. In it, her hair had been in a low ponytail, the curls slung over her shoulder. She wore a yellow cardigan and knee length black dress covered in daisies. Her lips had a subtle tint, making them seem pinker, and she may have worn some makeup around her eyes, but nothing else. In the picture, she was smiling. It was the only time in the four months she'd worked at The Novak Firm that Luke could remember her genuinely smiling. Something about that photo stuck with Luke, and he wondered if that was the last time she'd been free from all of this. If it was, then Luke would use that knowledge to help her feel not only safe here, but welcomed.

He had added beadboard halfway up the wall. While he'd waited for the wallpaper to come back in stock, Luke purchased furniture that he'd repurposed in a soft pale green color. He chose pale yellow and white curtains, which matched the other accent pieces—a chair, pillows, and comforter set—that he'd ordered. According to his research, the aesthetic was called 'bohemian farmhouse,' but it just reminded him of his nickname for Johanna: sunflower.

Luke thumbed one of the bags Dani brought in before she

walked back into the room with several more. "How much did you buy?"

She waved her hand dismissively at him, then pulled out a few bottles of shampoo and conditioner, followed by some new brushes.

Luke crossed his arms. "I already have those."

"No, what you have is shampoo and conditioner for straight hair, like yours. Johanna's hair is curlier and a closer texture to mine, so she needs different products."

Luke pouted, and Dani laughed. "You're doing a great job, Luke, I'm not saying you're not. I'm just going to teach you how to do a better one. Curly hair, even a texture not as tight as mine, needs a whole different routine. Think of it this way—if nothing else, you'll know how to do your children's hair if it's curly like Jo's."

Luke fumbled, dropping the bottle he was handing to Dani. She caught it, took one look at him, and burst out laughing. "You're blushing!"

"Shut up!" He threw a loofah at her when she laughed even more. "You're the one who brought up children. Where did that come from?"

"Oh, I don't know, probably the little birdie who told me how much of a horn dog you used to be. I knew you were a freak, but damn, Luke! What were you trying to test the theory of, use it or lose it?"

"I swear I fucking hate you." Luke rolled his eyes, but there was a grin on his face that grew until he finally laughed right alongside Dani. It felt good. He wasn't sure if it was the laugh, finishing this project for Johanna, or what, but there was a glee in the air, and for the first time Luke let himself feel it.

IT HAD BEEN A GOOD NIGHT. DANI AND GREG HAD STAYED FOR dinner, beef Wellington with scalloped potatoes, carrots, and garlic butter biscuits. They'd talked for a while before Dani promised to come over tomorrow with Greg following later in the afternoon.

Luke pushed them out the door when they tried to help him clean up. He didn't want them to see what had become his nightly routine of saving a plate for Johanna, just in case today was the day she woke up. He always packed a sealed container and stored it in his refrigerator. If she didn't wake by the next morning, he would freeze whatever he could or eat the serving for lunch. To others it might be pathetic, but to Luke it was all a part of taking care of his mate. Hopeful delusions still involved hope, and he liked that a lot more than he liked being angry.

Nothing had changed when Luke entered Johanna's room, so he kissed her head and settled into the chair beside her bed for a little while, sketching her again. This time she was a spirit, a beautiful muse whispering in her lover's ear, inspiring his thoughts at all hours of the day, which wasn't far from the truth.

Eventually, his lines became sloppy as his eyes grew tired. With a sigh and one more look at Johanna, he picked up his sketching materials and deposited them in his studio. After taking a shower and changing his clothes, Luke grabbed his pillow and blanket from his bedroom and carried them through to Johanna's room, laying them out on the couch.

A small shuffle made him turn to look at the bed. Johanna's eyes were still closed, but he came over to her anyway. He stood by her side for a few moments before sitting down on the bed and taking her hand in his. Then he tucked a piece of her golden hair behind her ear and whispered, "You're safe. I'm right here, and I'm not going anywhere. You're not alone anymore, I promise."

Luke leaned down to kiss her forehead goodnight, but when he pulled back ocean blue eyes stared up at him. For a solid minute he didn't move, didn't speak, didn't breathe.

Please don't be a dream, please don't be a dream. That's too cruel. Please be real.

"Johanna?" He said her name softly, scared that if he spoke louder all of this would somehow be whisked away.

She blinked, opened her mouth, closed it, then opened it again.

"Luke?" she managed quietly.

His heart skipped a beat, his muscles tensed and every cell in his body came alive. He had to close his fist around her pillow to keep from yanking her into his arms. "You're awake!"

CHAPTER 9

"A-Awake?" Johanna asked.

Her throat was dry. Each time she swallowed, her saliva felt thick, sticky, but the feeling worsened when she looked into Luke's gray-green eyes. She couldn't look away from them. They captivated her. Every second that passed they broke through some unknown barrier, sinking deeper and deeper into her soul. He was leaning above her, supported by the arm beside her head. His stomach lightly rubbed against hers every time he took a breath, every time *she* took a shaky breath.

He was undeniable.

While having a mate wasn't something typical between a witch or psychic pair, Johanna knew all about mate bonds. She knew what they felt like, what they pushed for, and it was clear to her that not only were they mates, but their bond was incredibly strong. It flowed through her, lighting her body aflame. Every piece of her felt as if it had been dormant for weeks, months, *decades,* but was now shocked awake.

His lips twitched, drawing her gaze as they spread into a slow smile. She had to bite her lip to keep from doing something stupid, like moaning. Then she parted her own lips and he inhaled, as if stealing the very air that left her. When she licked her lips, he bent forward, closer, and she wanted a taste just as badly as he seemed to. Beside her, the pillow tilted as Luke gripped it tight, but the hand near her hip that covered her own caressed her skin so softly, so featherlight yet achingly familiar.

Why did this feel familiar? When have we done this before?

The thought died in her mind as he neared her. Johanna lifted her hand, fingers aching to touch his face, to pull him closer and align with him, but the action made her hiss as something jabbed the inside of her arm. That single sound cut through the overwhelming chemistry between them, and Luke pulled away, leaving Johanna somewhere between gratefulness and disappointment. She moved to sit up, and Luke inched toward her. At the widening of her eyes, he grinned.

"Let me help you."

A shy smile spread across her lips before she nodded. Being mindful of what she now recognized were IVs in her arms, she placed her hands on Luke's broad shoulders, feeling his muscles tense under her touch. A blush spread across her skin, and she tilted her head away.

Luke wrapped his arm around her to support her as she slowly sat up. He fluffed her pillow before sliding to the side of her. Then his arms were under her body, and Johanna squeaked as he picked her up with ease. This was the first time in her adult life someone had moved her without a second thought, but Luke carefully placed her down against the headboard as if she weighed nothing. She wiggled, settling into the mattress. He still had a gleeful smile on his face, almost like he held a secret, something she'd forgotten. Whatever it was, she could tell it meant the world to him.

Johanna took a moment to look at him then, really look at him. His hair was wet, slightly wavy, while the ends held a curl. The dark strands fell to his eyes. He had high cheekbones, like a regal king, and she liked how the flesh around them changed when he smiled. She liked his lips too, liked how full and wide they were. His beard was a shadow around his face, connecting all the pieces together in a map Johanna wanted to follow with her fingers.

Her gaze traveled lower, taking in the span of his neck, his corded muscles big enough to show strength, but not overdone. They were muscles with a purpose. Johanna could tell Luke was a protector. He wouldn't hesitate to run into a burning building for someone he loved.

Suddenly, Johanna wanted to be that person. She wanted to be protected by him, wrapped in his strong arms, pressed against the width of his chest. She wanted to trail her fingers down his cut abs ... No, she wanted to taste them, to follow the panes of his body with her tongue until she reached—

"See something you like?"

Johanna jumped. Her eyes met Luke's and found them swimming with a mixture of amusement and something darker, more intense. She turned away, knowing she was blushing again, and heard his soft laugh. He took hold of her wrist, drawing her attention back to him, and motioned to the IV in her arm. "Let me take these out for you to help you feel a little more comfortable."

She nodded as he removed the tape.

"This will only hurt for a moment, okay?" Luke pulled the

needle out and Johanna let out a soft hiss. But then he bent forward, and she watched in shock and fascination as he closed his mouth over the growing drop of blood. He swiped his tongue over it and her toes curled under the blanket. A second and third swipe had her clenching her thighs together, but then he pulled away.

Luke wouldn't look at her, and his movements were stiff as he began to remove the patches and equipment that had been monitoring her. Their disconnection triggered a loud beep, and with a sigh Luke got up to unplug the machine. Only then, with distance between them, did his eyes touch hers, so dark in the low light, and Johanna realized that he could smell her desire.

"Do you need anything?" Luke asked, his voice low, seductive.

The implication behind his words had Johanna fisting the comforter in her hands. Taking a deep breath was a mistake because she could smell him everywhere, including on her. As she swallowed, she was reminded of how dry her throat was and that it needed *actual* liquid. "Could I get a glass of water, please?"

"Of course. Would you like something to eat too?"

Johanna had to put a hand over her heart to stop it from pounding out of her chest. That question might have been simple to anyone else, but a man had never looked at her and asked if she wanted to eat. It was always that she should eat less, that she was 'so pretty' with her blonde hair, blue eyes, and pale skin, that if she just lost a little weight she could be anything she wanted to be, that she would be taken seriously if she put effort into the way she looked.

Even though Johanna promptly cut off anyone who said that to her, it didn't mean their words didn't hurt. The world had eaten her self-esteem and spit out the woman she was now, the one who couldn't fathom why anyone would look at her the way Luke had, not once, not twice, but three times in the ten minutes they'd been alone together. It could have been the mate bond—a rational explanation—but when she saw his concerned gaze, she knew that wasn't fully the case. The mate bond only pushed the two people connected by it to consummate the bond. It didn't create feelings. It didn't force someone to care.

That realization softened her, and she smiled at Luke. He seemed awestruck by that, which made her laugh. Finally she said, "I'm not hungry yet, but thank you."

He seemed speechless for a moment, making her giggle again. Then he shuffled toward the door. "I'll be right back."

Johanna was still smiling when he left, until her eyes connected with the door frame and the decoration around it. The floral wallpaper was her style, and the same could be said for the furniture in its green hues. It reminded her of a garden, but while it was beautiful, it wasn't a room she was familiar with. She also hadn't heard any other voices or movement so far in the house. Johanna closed her eyes and tried to connect with anyone who may be on the premises, but the only person she found was Luke. This had to be his house, so why was she here?

Again it felt like she was missing something. She tried to remember, but it all seemed to be hidden from her, stuck behind some imaginary boulder that she couldn't move or pass through. She tried harder, closing her eyes again, her eyebrows furrowing as she focused inward, advancing, pressing on the mental block. When she did, she cried out, flying forward in the bed and into Luke's sudden arms.

"Johanna? What's wrong?"

She wailed, sobs tearing from her body and spilling into his. Johanna felt like she had been struck by lightning; her nerve endings were on fire, burning away until they shriveled and died.

Luke pulled her closer, rocking her in his arms while she burrowed her head into the crook of his neck. He stroked her hair as he gently shushed her. "It's okay, sunflower, you're safe. It's okay. I promise it's all going to be okay."

Sunflower?

The single world delivered a second shock to Johanna's system, causing her to freeze. He had been the one who saved her. His voice had led her out of her own personal hell. Every step that she took as she tried to find her way out had been heavy, and she continued to sink lower and lower into the abysmal sea of fear, guilt, anger, misery, and, above all, pain. The pain was unbearable. But then she heard his stories. The voice that spoke to her became her own guiding light, but it was muddled, like sounds underwater. Its cadence and tone were all wrong, and she couldn't place who was speaking to her, not even if the voice was male or female. She just knew that it meant the world to her. It had soothed her to know she wasn't alone, and though she couldn't remember who it belonged to, she needed to get back to it.

I couldn't remember. I can't remember.

"Why can't I remember?"

Luke's rhythmic stroking stopped, and she realized then that she'd spoken out loud. He tilted his head back, and when she lifted her own, he wiped the tears from her eyes. "What's the last thing you remember?"

Johanna shook her head, but Luke cupped her cheeks. His

touch was soft yet constant, reminding her that she wasn't alone. She just had to reach out, to try.

"It hurts. There's something affecting my memories, and when I try to remove it, it hurts."

His hand went into her hair again, smoothing it away from her face. "Then leave it. It might be there for a reason."

"But what reason—"

The grimace on his face silenced her. He knew something, and whatever it was, it was terrible.

"Luke did someone—"

His face grew tense as a haunted look invaded his eyes. Johanna squeezed his shoulders, hoping to ease whatever news he was about to share. He looked over her again before he said in a tight whisper, "You were almost dead when I found you."

Johanna gasped, her eyes growing wide.

"And you've been here, at my house, unconscious for the last two weeks." He took a deep breath, his face stoic. "During that time, we've only interacted through your abilities. You've gone from protecting this house and me, for a variety of reasons, to communicating with me on mental and energetic levels. So whatever is happening, you did it to protect yourself."

She shook her head rapidly. "No, no. I don't have the ability to create mental blocks. Those are higher level skills in my family —" Johanna yelped as another bolt of pain flew through her body, causing her to squeeze Luke's shoulders in a death grip.

"Johanna!" He gripped her arms, pulling her closer, holding her tighter.

She took a deep breath. As her grip eased, he instructed her to take another one, going so far as to take one with her. Slowly, ever so slowly, the pain went away. Only then did she look up at him, confused and shocked. "Is there some way to be sure that no one else did this to me?"

Luke nodded. "I called a witch that we've known for centuries. She can trace magic, and the only source she felt came from you." He rubbed the length of her spine as she fell against him, her body needing his for strength and support. They stayed like that for precious minutes before he asked, "What triggers the pain?"

Johanna's fingers slid down his sides, coming to rest at his back as she held onto him. She was scared that even the mention of what happened would trigger the pain, but she knew she had to share the information for him to help.

"When I try to remember what happened, or when I think of my ancestors." She braced herself but felt nothing. She sighed in relief, then cautiously turned over her next words in her head to pick ones that would hopefully not trigger the pain again. "My mental abilities are hereditary, like most witches, but I still don't know how I could have made this mental block."

Luke's arms tightened around her as she settled into his warmth. "Can you tell me what your powers are?"

"Telepathy, mind control, telekinesis, and teleportation."

"Teleportation?" Luke asked.

She nodded. "That's the hardest one to learn, but it is entirely possible." Johanna bit her lip, making a noise of disgust.

"What is it?" Luke continued to rub her back, the soothing motion making her feel safe enough to be honest.

"Those abilities were used to kill people in the past, even vampires. Because of that, I wasn't taught to master them," Johanna whispered.

Luke made a soft humming sound. "They probably

deserved it. That may cause some complications with The Council later, but it doesn't cause any with me. How do you create a mental block?"

"It's extremely complicated. It needs a lot of practice and focus, but essentially an item is determined and a restriction is placed upon it. Whenever that person violates that restriction, a punishment occurs."

"Like your pain?"

"Yes. But I can't think of a reason why I would block out so much. The larger the block, the more energy it takes and the harder it is to break it."

Luke continued to rub her back, his fingers caressing her skin as she snuggled closer into his embrace. She knew it was strange, but thus far all their interactions had been, and she didn't have the strength to fight against the comfort he made her feel.

Luke's voice was quiet, gentle, as he asked again, "What's the last thing you remember?"

Johanna closed her eyes, letting the lull of his heartbeat give her confidence as she tried to remember something, anything. "I was leaving the hospital after visiting ... my grandmother!" She pulled back, beaming with excitement. "She'll know what to do if I just—"

Luke's face went from confusion, to horror, and then a blank sadness that infected her, squeezing her heart.

"Luke, what is it?" she asked shakily.

"Johanna," he said with a swallow, "your grandmother passed away six months ago."

And just like that, Johanna shattered all over again.

CHAPTER 10

Luke sighed and looked down at the golden angel pressed against his chest.

Last night had been a whirlwind. Johanna had been distraught at the news of her grandmother's death. The grief, the realization that she had lost six months of time and couldn't even try to remember anything about her family without feeling the backlash of her own abilities, and the information that she had been unconscious for weeks was too much for her to bear. She'd cried herself to sleep, and Luke didn't blame her. In his opinion, she was taking the news well. He couldn't imagine how it would feel to not have the support of people he loved and trusted around him, especially when he woke up in a strange place with someone he didn't know.

Then there was their mate bond. In the span of the few minutes she'd been awake, he'd nearly kissed her three times, and he was deeply aware that it wouldn't have stopped there. What was worse was he knew she wanted him as well. Mate bonds had different intensities and theirs was incredible, but he'd resist it or die trying. Luke wanted Johanna to feel comfortable with him, and while in her moment of grief she'd turned toward him and had desired him, he knew a lot of that may have been from the mate bond itself. He wanted her care, her love, and he was willing to fight through anything for her, even the need to take her and make her his. This wasn't the time for that. No, his mate needed someone to be there for her right now, and that's what he wanted to be: her confidant. He wanted her to trust him completely, and while fucking her into oblivion would be enjoyable, her possible regret afterwards would kill him.

And then there was his own fear and insecurity. Johanna had to rely on him until she got her memories back, and while he was sure that would foster some sort of feelings for him, would she choose him in the long run, especially after she remembered what happened to her? Luke wasn't sure of the torture she'd been through, but he had several concerning ideas—after all, she had blocked herself from remembering six months of trauma. But one day she would remember every-thing, and she might blame him in the same ways he blamed himself.

He looked down at her, his fingers sliding through her hair carefully, not wanting to wake her. Her chest rose and fell peacefully, her breathing long and deep. Her hand curled over his chest where she had been holding onto him, while her head rest on his shoulder. Her long legs bowed over one of his under-neath the blanket they shared.

The sight of her in his arms restored a piece of his soul, but he still couldn't sleep. Instead, Luke remained her faithful protector, staying awake to watch over her. He didn't want to miss when she woke up, didn't want her to feel alone. An irrational piece of him was also scared that she wouldn't wake up, that somehow she might have locked herself in another mental battle that would keep her away for days, maybe months.

While vampires didn't need sleep, they did function better with it. Maybe once he closed his eyes and finally rested, he'd be able to make some sense out of this mess. But until then he'd wait, and wonder, and worry, and try to tell himself everything was fine. Because it would be fine, it had to be.

Hours later, after the sun began to filter through the pale curtains and slowly bathe the room in light, Johanna stirred. It was a mesmerizing thing to Luke. She flexed first, wiggling her toes ever so slightly. The hand over his heart clenched. Her heartbeat quickened as it breathed energy into her gorgeous body. She shifted again, ever so slightly, but this time it was her hips that moved, and Luke had to bite his lip to keep from moaning. Then she did it again, but a frown appeared on her face as if she was confused.

"Good morning to you too, sunflower," Luke said, his voice teasing and slightly husky.

Her eyes flew open so wide he laughed, and then her mouth flew into a little "O" shape that was far too tempting. Luke mourned when it fell into a frown and a sad expression took over her face. He pulled her closer and his heart beat a little faster, satisfaction coursing through his veins when she snuggled into his warmth.

"Hey, it's going to be okay," he murmured.

Gently, because he couldn't resist, he kissed her forehead while his fingers softly massaged the knots starting to form in her shoulders. "I was thinking, maybe I could call Greg and Dani. They might be able to help you with your amnesia."

Johanna sighed softly. "I don't know if that would help, plus..." She trailed off, stiffening in his embrace.

Luke tilted her chin up to make her meet his eyes. "You don't have to guard yourself ever again, especially not around me. Whatever you're feeling or thinking, I want to know. I'm not going to judge you."

She averted her eyes, a small blush tinting her cheeks before she settled back down, tucking her head under his chin. She didn't speak for a few moments, but then a soft whisper left her lips. "I'm scared of remembering. I don't know what happened to me to get me here, but I know there are some things I wouldn't want to relive again. To block out my grandmother's death and force myself through this grief all over again, means that whatever is tied to it is worse than what I'm feeling right now." Johanna shivered, so Luke pulled her closer. "I don't know if the people I ... love are safe, or if I'm missing other important details. I realize that b-but..."

"It's okay," Luke whispered back. "It's okay to be scared. What you're feeling is completely normal. Anyone would feel that way. No one's going to force you to remember anything. If I ask Greg and Dani for their help, the most they could do is try to track down your ... loved ones and at least make sure they're safe while you're healing." His hand slipped under her hair to rub the back of her neck until she melted into him. "You don't have to save everyone, sunflower, and you especially can't if you don't heal."

She was quiet for a while, and Luke's mind spun with ways to help her feel better about the situation. He was so deep into his thoughts that he almost missed her say, "Okay."

"Okay?" he repeated.

Johanna nodded against his chest. "Please call them. I'd like to try."

Luke leaned against the door frame with his arms crossed as he waited for Johanna to get ready. He was worried about her. It hurt him to see her in so much pain, and he hoped that his family would be able to help her.

She stepped out of the bathroom in one of his shirts tucked into a pair of shorts. Her hair was brushed over one shoulder, spiraling down the length of her body, and he had to take a deep breath when her eyes met his.

"I'm ready," she said with a small attempt at a smile, but the slight tremble to her wrist, the way her shoulders rose closer to the top of her head as she tensed her back, and each stiff step she took told Luke otherwise.

He stepped closer to her, and she tilted her head up to meet his gaze. Her eyes widened ever so slightly as he stepped into her space, but she didn't shy away from him.

"Can you trust me, just for a second?" Luke asked.

She nodded softly, so Luke cupped her cheek. As he did so, Johanna's eyes fluttered closed. Soft as a wisp, he trailed his fingers down over her jaw to her neck, until he fit the back of it in his hand and drew her to him. His other arm slid around her waist, and he held her. She was tall, Luke guessed somewhere around 5'10", but even so her head only came to his chest, right over his heart and exactly where it was supposed to be.

In no time at all the tenseness flew away from her body. He took it until she too held him in the embrace.

"Better?" he whispered into her hair.

She nodded again before taking a step away from him. "I'm sorry."

Luke captured her face in his hands, making her meet his gaze. "Don't be sorry. Don't ever be sorry for needing a shoulder to lean on. I know"—his voice grew softer—"I know that all of this is strange and new for you. I know that you don't know me, but that isn't going to stop me from being here for you. I want to be here for you, and I will be, anytime you need me. There's no shame in having someone you can lean on, is there?"

Tears gathered in Johanna's eyes, but she didn't let them fall. Instead she shook her head and cupped his hands, giving them a soft squeeze. "Thank you."

They stepped away from each other. Johanna wiped her eyes and tilted her head toward the door. "They'll be here in a couple of minutes. We should go."

"They can wait as long as we need them to," Luke huffed.

Johanna looked at him for a moment, and then she laughed. It was a small hiccup of a thing that seemed to surprise her as much as it did him. Then it grew louder. Her hands went to her eyes again as she wiped at them with the backs of her fingers. Luke cautiously wondered if she'd crossed over into hysteria, but then she asked through a fit of giggles, "Are you always this argumentative?"

His eyes widened and he snorted. "I am not argumentative," he said, looking away.

Johanna laughed again, and even though he was embarrassed, it made him smile. "We will have to work on that. Come on." She held her hand out to him, and for a moment Luke stood dumbstruck at the action.

We.

The simple word shot through his heart like lightning.

A worried look came over Johanna's face and she began to draw back her hand.

No!

Luke reached out and took her fingers in his, interlacing them with his own. She visibly relaxed and together they walked out of the bedroom.

The front door opened as they entered the living room, and in walked Greg and Dani, followed by Mya. Luke had to school his face to not show the surprise he felt at Mya's appearance. Luke wanted to rip her a new one for ignoring him, but he knew now wasn't the time. At least she was here, and that was all he could ask for.

Johanna said hello to each of them. Luke noticed that she called them by name, which only served to further his suspicions that Zachariah had started torturing Johanna after she had begun working for the firm. The group made small talk for a few minutes, but then the conversation grew quiet and the silence awkward.

Luke broke it first. "Can you explain what it is you want to do to Johanna?"

Dani nodded. "I communicate with elemental spirits, and they in turn let me utilize their powers for my needs. I believe that by using the elemental spirit of water, I will be able to look into your memories without forcing you to see them as well. That way I'll be able to see if your—"

"Loved ones," Luke interjected.

Dani nodded. "Loved ones are safe."

"It may also help us see what happened to you and maybe help you get an idea of how to retrieve your memories," Greg added.

"And you?" Johanna asked Mya.

"I'm here for moral support." Mya swallowed. "It's also possible you may have information I'm searching for." Her gaze moved to Luke. "But I also wanted to make sure the both of you were ... well."

"We'll talk after," Luke said, and Mya nodded in response.

"Do you have any questions?" Dani asked.

Johanna shook her head. "No. Just ... thank you all for doing this."

"Of course, and thank you for letting me try." Dani smiled, then turned to Greg. "Could you get me a bowl of water, honey?"

Greg walked into the kitchen and Dani turned her gaze to Luke as she approached the couch he and Johanna were sitting on. "Sorry, bud, but for this I'll need you to not touch Johanna, or else I might end up seeing your memories as well."

Luke hesitated, not wanting to move away from Johanna. While outwardly she seemed fine, her spine was so straight and tense that he was concerned it would break in half. He was beginning to realize this was something she did when she thought she needed to hide. She froze her expression and did everything she could to make herself invisible, to make those around her believe she wasn't a concern. Luke was familiar with the action because he'd been doing the same thing for the last six months, and he didn't like that his mate felt she needed to hide here, when she was safe with him. Whatever had made this a normal response for her had happened before Zachariah, before Johanna had ever come into Luke's life. Luke wanted to erase it, and while he knew he couldn't get rid of it in an instant, he could at least take the first step in trying.

Luke leaned forward, shocking Johanna into looking up at him. "I see you, Johanna. You don't have to be scared. I'm right here, and I will never let anything happen to you again," he whispered into her ear, low and quiet enough that even she would have to strain to hear him.

When he pulled away, her eyes were warmer. He squeezed her hand and she squeezed back before he scooted away.

While he knew Dani had not heard what he'd said to Johanna, he saw the smile that touched her face before she sat down. Greg carefully placed the bowl of water in Dani's outstretched hands, and she turned to Johanna, her voice soft, coaxing, as she spoke.

"We'll need to both take a sip of this, then run our hands through the water, and lay them on top of one another. I believe that will allow your power to accept my intrusion into your mind, and then I will look at your memories. You shouldn't feel anything while I do this, but if you do I want you to say something right away and I will pull out, okay?"

Johanna nodded. She took a deep breath and took the first sip of water, and then Dani followed. They both slipped their hands into the water, coating their skin with the liquid, and then sat cross legged on the couch, facing one another. Dani placed her hands on Johanna's lap, palms up, and instructed Johanna to clasp them with her own. Once she did, Dani said, "Close your eyes. My magic tends to feel like electricity, and since I'm working on you internally, you may feel small charges under your skin. But I promise I won't hurt you."

"I know," Johanna said softly.

A pressure released into the room, weighted enough to feel as if the humidity in their environment had changed, but of a soft quality, like steam hitting the skin. When Johanna spoke again, her voice had a strength to it that it had lacked before. "I allow you in, Daniella."

Dani smiled and closed her eyes. A static electricity blended into the humid pressure in the air, connecting with the surrounding moisture and firing small bolts around them. Luke watched the spectacle, as amazing as it was terrifying. Neither Dani nor Johanna seemed to move beyond a small tense here and there. Sometimes Dani's face fell into a frown, or Johanna's and Dani's arms twitched, but otherwise they were soundless, motionless.

Then Dani screamed.

Greg, Mya, and Luke were on their feet in an instant. The three watched as she yanked Johanna into her arms and cried, her sobs reverberating off the walls. Luke looked at Johanna, taking in the tears rolling down her cheeks that were at odds with the look in her eyes. She seemed confused, her brow in a frown even as the tears continued to pour from her.

Greg approached Dani, but the look she gave him, gave everyone in turn, was fierce. She pulled Johanna closer as if she was protecting her *from* them. Dani's message was clear and heartbreaking, and it told Luke everything he needed to know: Whatever had happened to Johanna was worse than he could have imagined, and it was possible that one day his mate would look at him with just as rage and damnation as Daniella did.

WHEN THEY WERE FINALLY ABLE TO PRY DANI AWAY FROM Johanna, Greg and Mya ushered her into the kitchen while Luke knelt at Johanna's feet.

"Sunflower," he murmured into her hair as he hugged her, "do you remember—"

"No! No, but I feel ... everything." Johanna clung to him as he gently rubbed her back. "I don't remember anything, but I feel *so* much!"

Luke stayed quiet, waiting for Johanna to continue. He didn't understand what had just happened or what she was feeling, and because of that he didn't know how to fix it for her.

"Everything hurts," she mumbled into his neck. "All I feel is guilt. Every time I look at all of you, I feel so guilty and I don't know why. I don't know what I did, but I'm so sorry. I'm so, so sorry."

She pulled back, shaking her head. "I shouldn't be here, I should—"

"Don't *ever* say that again," Luke hissed, making Johanna's eyes widen. He squeezed her sides. "I want you here. I *need* you here. Whatever it is you're feeling, it's not from us."

"But—"

"You haven't done anything wrong, sunflower. I swear to you, you haven't." Gently, so very gently so that Johanna could pull away if she was uncomfortable, Luke cupped her cheeks. He wiped away her tears and leaned his forehead against her own. "Breathe with me."

Her eyes shut, and she took one slow, shuddering breath, then another. Little by little she relaxed against him. Luke pulled back, wiping at her eyes and cheeks once more until she looked up at him with eyes filled with sorrow.

"I do feel guilt," he said softly, and she bit her bottom lip, "but I don't feel guilty *because* of you. I feel guilty *for* you. I hate that you're here right now, feeling this way. I hate how much you've cried since you regained consciousness. I hate that you felt the need to protect yourself so much that you locked away your memories. You are the one person I should have been strong enough to protect and keep safe, and I didn't. And I'm not the only one who feels that way. We, everyone under this roof right now, feel that way about you. You deserved better than that, sunflower, and you still do."

Johanna made an indescribable noise, something between a groan and a whimper.

He wiped more of the wetness away from her skin. "You may have had to make choices that you didn't like, that under normal circumstances you would never have made. But your circumstances weren't normal, and no one here will ever blame you for whatever you did."

Johanna squeezed his hand. "Just because you won't blame me for it, doesn't mean I shouldn't be blamed."

"Well then, if we're going by that logic, do you blame me?"

"What?" She drew back, a snarl on her lips.

Luke had to fight back a smile at her reaction. "Do you blame me for not saving you?"

"Of course not," she huffed. "And you did save me. You're the reason I'm here today."

"Well then, if you can manage to not blame me when the whole reason you ended up in this mess is because you're my mate, then I think you can cut yourself a little slack, don't you?"

She shuddered in his arms, so Luke took hold of her chin, making her meet his eyes. He gazed into them, trying to convey the awe he felt for her and her strength, the pride he had in her. "You made choices to survive, Johanna, and I for one am happy you made those choices, because if you didn't survive, I would have gone with you."

Johanna gasped and tried to draw back, but he wouldn't let her. Fire raged in her blue orbs as she clasped onto his shirt and tried to shake him, but he wouldn't budge. His resistance only seemed to make her angrier.

"You can't say that," she hissed. "You can't say things like that. That's not right. You didn't even know me. You didn't even *love* me. You can't just up and toss away your life like that for me. I would've never allowed that."

Luke smiled and clasped her hands as he leaned into her, pushing them both back against the couch, but when he spoke his voice was a low growl. "Interesting you say that, little sunflower. Would you like to know how I found out you were my mate? The *exact* way you let me find out?"

"How?" she said between rapid breaths.

"You masked our mate bond for months. Months!" he bit out. "Every time I tried to talk to you, you ran away from me. Every time I showed an ounce of interest in you, you rejected me. For *months*. And then in the middle of a battle with my enemy you used your powers to hold me down while claiming it was to protect me. Then you left. You made me watch you leave with *him!* You made me watch him drag you away from me, all because you wanted to save me. So do not tell me what I would and wouldn't do for you. Do not tell me that I have to love you to offer to save your life, to beg someone to take mine in place of yours, when you did it so easily. Love had nothing to do with it. Our mate bond and what could be between us one day was enough for you to make that choice, and it is enough for me every day, every fucking *second*, to decide to make that choice for *you!*"

"Luke, I'm sorry," she whimpered, and the sound made his blood boil hotter. She made a low, soft whine, and he watched as the fight left her. Her anger and righteousness morphed with his to form a single, sudden emotion: desire.

Johanna pulled at his shirt, dragging him closer, and he pinned her down against the back of the couch until there was no room between them. Her silky thighs hugged his waist as he grabbed her hips. She was so close, so fucking close, and he had hoped, dreamed, fucking prayed for this moment more times than he could count.

Her lips parted as his descended, coming achingly close, and then he heard a noise in the other room and everything came rushing back.

Luke sighed, clasping onto the back of the couch as he tried to remind himself that he couldn't act on the very real temptation in front of him.

Johanna's eyes opened and she whined. She rolled her hips, but he held her still, and when she couldn't pull him to her, she huffed.

Luke had initially thought there was nothing sexier than having Johanna against him, but he was wrong. Seeing her want him just as much as he wanted her was a whole new high, and it was killing him to fight against it.

"Why?" she murmured.

Against his better judgment, he rested his head in the crook of her neck, felt her pulse pounding under her skin, and groaned.

She clawed at his back, trying to get him to satisfy the need rushing through her, but he resisted.

"I can't. Not yet, sunflower," he whispered against her skin.

"Why?" she demanded again.

"Because I would rather not traumatize my family with the sight of me thrusting into you, and I'd prefer to keep your screams to myself."

"Luke," she moaned, squirming in the chair, a blush falling over her pale skin all the way down to the tops of her breasts.

The scent of her desire grew heavier in the air. He took a

deep breath, inhaling it. He could almost taste it on his tongue. And the sight of her, with her legs spread around him, hands on his chest, and her beautiful full breasts rising and falling with every short, rapid breath she took had him begging the gods for patience and strength. Luke had to force himself away from her *right now*, or else he would go back on everything he'd said and find out exactly how good her pussy would feel when it was milking his cock.

Finally he shifted, and Johanna's hands fell away as he stood. His voice was still thick and husky as he said, "I'm going to go find out what Dani saw. I'll be right back."

Johanna blinked sharply, as if he'd dumped cold water on her. Then she nodded, and Luke left while he still could.

CHAPTER 11

Luke entered his kitchen to see Dani huddled between Greg and Mya. Her red eyes met his and he sighed as he crossed the space to stand at the island in front of her.

Her eyes darted around and behind him before coming back to his face. "Where is she?"

"In the living room," Luke said.

Dani's voice cracked as she spoke. "How is she?"

"Confused." Luke reached across the table to squeeze Dani's hands. That they had stood so many times in this same position while she comforted him wasn't lost on Luke. In fact, it terrified him. It had been months since he'd seen Dani so shaken.

"Johanna is ... struggling," he said finally. "Whatever the two of you did has forced her to feel things from the last few months. She still doesn't remember anything, but she's experiencing the emotions of those lost memories. Right now, the primary one is guilt. I've explained to her that there's no reason for her to feel that way, but I don't know what I'm fighting yet, Dani. What did you see?"

Dani looked to Greg, who nodded. She sniffled and rubbed her eyes before taking a deep breath and letting it out. "I could only see the surface level, there's ... a lot under there that I can't access. I don't think it's safe to say his name around her right now." Her gaze touched each of them and Luke knew she meant Zachariah. "But we don't have to worry about him coming after her. That's the good news. I don't quite understand how, but I think she teleported to you."

Luke jerked back. "To me?"

"Yes. I don't know how her magic works—she's the only one who can answer that—but her desire was to see you. This house has the biggest concentration of your energy, so she came here. He doesn't know where she is. He doesn't know your address. At least, he never learned it from her, so she's safe here." Dani's eyes narrowed and she balled her hands into a fist. "But he will come after her, Luke. He enjoyed using her powers as a weapon, and he won't be willing to lose them."

A deep, animalistic growl came out of Luke. "Over my dead fucking body."

Dani took a deep breath. Greg squeezed her arm and Mya rubbed her back in comfort while Dani leveled him with a heartbreaking stare. "That's not the worst of the news. H-He raped her. Brutally. For sport. Every time we won, he took it out on her. Every single time. He *butchered* her. Those marks that were on her body when you found her were just from one day. He figured out how to use something similar to Mya's power to heal her so that we wouldn't see her wounds when she came to work. But he took his hatred of us out on her every chance he got."

Luke couldn't see, couldn't hear, couldn't feel anything besides rage. Insurmountable, undeniable, soul-binding rage that made him want to scream. He wanted to wage war, to tear the city apart until he found Zachariah and killed him and everyone that stood in between them with his bare hands.

Luke turned, looking for something, anything, to use as a weapon as he prepared for the fight of his life.

In an instant Mya was in front of him. "Luke! Stop!"

He went to push past her, but she refused to move. "Stop! Stop it, Luke. Don't do anything to scare her right now, please!"

But it wasn't Mya's voice that reached him, or Dani's or Greg's presence that shocked him still. It was Johanna's form standing in the kitchen. He took in her wide eyes and the sudden paleness of her skin, and he knew that she had heard everything. Instantaneously everything fled him and all he saw, all that mattered, was her.

Luke stalked over to her, but she put up a hand. He watched her erect that shield of hers, the one he had hoped she would never feel the need to use again.

"Sunflower—"

"It's okay, Luke," Johanna said in a level tone.

"It is *not* okay," he growled, grabbing hold of her arm and pulling her close to him.

She let him, but she didn't warm to his embrace or the nearness of his body like she had before. Instead she looked into his eyes, and he was chilled by the coldness in hers.

"It's okay for right now, then. I need to know what happened to me. I need those answers and I don't have time to react to them." Her gaze flickered and just a small bit of something warmer came through. Johanna whispered, soft enough so that even he could barely hear, "If you still want me after all of this, protect me then. But I need this now."

She pulled away from him and approached the island. "Please tell me everything you know, Daniella."

Johanna took a seat at the island. Her abilities as a mind witch allowed her to turn on and off different portions of her body, and to survive this she shut off her emotional epicenter: her heart. She could deal with her emotions later, but they had no place here.

Daniella, Greg, and Mya stood as a unit, carrying a pain that didn't belong to them. It belonged to Johanna and her alone. Seeing them like this was yet another reminder of why she couldn't stand to feel right now. They had one another to lean on, and it was evident that they loved each other dearly. She was the outcast here and this situation was all her own. No matter how welcoming they were, that was the truth. They could remember their pasts. They had not blocked out months of time and were not forcing themselves to play catch up. Not even twenty-four hours had passed since Johanna discovered how drastically her life had changed, and yet again she was forced to learn something so intimate, so horribly tragic and personal from a stranger.

Life had taught Johanna that respect was given to those who appeared to be strong and dependable, not weak and vulnerable. The world ate those souls up for breakfast. She believed more of the people in this room, even hoped one day she might be able to trust them with the pieces of her that she buried, but right now, in this very moment? No, now was not the time.

Johanna closed the last fissure of her heart just as Luke came up behind her, his warmth radiating into her skin. With one arm he leaned onto the counter, grasping the edge of it in his hand while he cupped her waist with the other. Even with her heart closed off, her body eased against his. Johanna squeezed his hand at her waist gently, a silent message of thanks before she focused back on Daniella.

"I heard everything you said to Luke," Johanna began, her voice unwavering. "Were you able to see anything else? Anything about my loved ones?"

Daniella sat up straighter at her tone. Her eyes were still red and watery, but not a single tear fell down her cheeks. "Not your immediate family, no. But I did see your grandmother." She took a deep breath as Johanna waited for her to continue. "He killed her in front of you."

Gasps and curses echoed around the room. Luke's hand clasped the countertop so tight Johanna thought she heard it crack.

Johanna gave a curt nod, and when she spoke again her voice was robotic, even to her. "Thank you for telling me. Did you see anything else?"

Daniella watched her for a moment, a question in her eyes, but then she shook her head. "No, that was all."

"Would you mind if we spoke alone?" Johanna said to Daniella.

Luke stiffened at her back, and she turned to look up at him. "It'll just be for a moment."

"I don't want to leave you," he said.

The look he gave her did something to her psyche. One of the bolts opened, the chain slipped out, and Johanna had to swallow hard as she was hit by a tidal wave of emotions. She breathed, squeezed his wrist, and said, "I'm fine."

His eyes narrowed at her words.

"I'll be fine. *Please.*"

"Luke, let's give them a second, alright? It's been a long day, and they both have some things they need to get off their chests," Greg said.

Mya nodded and made her way out of the room, but Luke looked like he wanted to argue and Johanna knew he had so much more left to say. He stared into her eyes, and something there must have gotten through to him because he finally took a step away from her, and then another, and another.

As Luke left, he took something of hers. Her safety. Luke was the only semblance of comfort she had and without it, without *him*, there was something missing. Now she was left with this woman, someone who had seen so much more of her than she had ever wanted to show someone. It was terrifying.

Daniella's hands tentatively touched Johanna's, and she drew back at once, shock etched onto her face. Her chest felt tight and the air in the room seemed too thin. Daniella reached forward again, and this time Johanna had nowhere to go except to let Daniella touch her.

Daniella's fingers were soft and soothing on Johanna's own, and at the center of her palms Johanna's muscles began to relax. Slowly the feeling moved up her skin. With a gasp, Johanna realized that for the second time Daniella was doing something to help her, even when Johanna already owed her so much.

"T-Thank you," Johanna said.

Daniella gave her a small smile, then nodded to her side. "Why don't you come sit over here so we can talk privately.

Vampires can hear ridiculously well, and I'm sure they're probably listening right now!"

There was scurrying in the background that would have made Johanna laugh in any other circumstance. She moved to sit beside Daniella, and they turned to face one another, knees touching while their elbows rested on the island.

Once they'd settled, Daniella spoke. "'I'm sorry' doesn't even begin to describe how I feel for you, but I am. I am so incredibly sorry for what you went through."

"And I'm sorry you saw it," Johanna said softly.

"I'm not," Daniella replied, her voice stern. "We should have done better. We should have known *something.*"

Johanna pressed her nails into her skin. "You can't blame yourself for that. Luke said I hid our mate bond. Between that and not being able to remember things about those I love the most, I don't think I would have let you."

Daniella touched her hand. "But why would you do that? You understand you're important, don't you?"

Johanna's smile was twisted and cruel, cut by misery and pain as she replied, "I'd say I'm not if this went on for six months and no one batted an eye."

Daniella winced.

"I don't blame you. I don't blame Greg or Mya, and I certainly don't blame Luke. But the fact is I'm one person in a crowd of a million people. If he did that to me, he did it to others too. The reason why it matters right now is because I'm Luke's mate."

"That's not true," Daniella hissed.

"Isn't it? If I was in such bad shape, weren't there others who were worse? Did they make it out alive? Where are their heroes?

Who misses them? Who comforts them? I got lucky," she said, spitting the bitter word from her tongue, "that's all."

The air grew hot between them. Daniella's spine lengthened as she sat up to her full height, and even though she was shorter than Johanna, she suddenly seemed so much taller, so much wiser. "They made it out alive," she said cuttingly.

"What?" Johanna said, her jaw falling open in shock.

"They made it out alive because you helped us save them."

Johanna shook her head rapidly. "I ... But ... I-I couldn't—"

"You shouldn't have, but you most certainly *did!* The last time Luke saw you, you saved his life. And when you saved his life and told him how to get to safety, you saved the lives of over eighty other enslaved immortals. If that wasn't enough, you also gave us the coordinates to several other locations where we've been able to rescue even more people and drive our enemy into a corner. So if you want to know who their hero is, it's *you.*"

Even though Daniella's voice was quiet, her words flayed Johanna all the way down to her bones. She was torn apart and reconstructed into something else all at once.

Daniella's eyes grew soft as she gathered Johanna in her arms and held her. Her tears were silent but heavy with the weight of her sorrow, but Daniella never said a word to her. Instead, she rocked Johanna from side to side as she hummed a soft melody.

Slowly Johanna's tears stopped and Daniella, feeling the shift, released her. Johanna wiped at her eyes before Daniella handed her a box of tissues. Both of them looked at the box, then at one another, and laughed a laugh of those with a bond forged by indescribable trauma.

"I'm sorry for that," Johanna said.

"Don't be." Daniella sighed. "Honestly, I'm just happy I could be there for you."

"I can see why Luke likes you," Johanna said softly. Daniella was a beautiful woman, with springy dark brown curls that framed a heart-shaped face, kind brown eyes, and a stubborn tilt to her jaw. And yet her beauty went so much deeper than that. Johanna was in awe of her, and suddenly she felt so very shy and stupid in front of her.

Daniella hummed. "I wasn't always this way. Luke changes the people around him, whether you want to change or not. But it's always for the better."

Johanna nodded but averted her gaze.

"He likes you too, you know," Daniella said softly.

Johanna could feel her cheeks heat. While guilt had been the first emotion Johanna felt when it came to the missing six months of her life, there was another emotion she felt when it came to Daniella: envy.

She took a deep breath, wanting to clear the air while she still had the chance. "Did I ... do anything to you? Before, I mean, in the last couple of months."

Daniella cocked her head to the side. "No, why?"

This is ridiculous. You were being ridiculous back then and you still are right now.

Johanna sighed. "I saw you and Luke together before all of this. The two of you were in an embrace. I know it was just a hug but ... I was jealous of your relationship with him. That you could be that close to him. I think our enemy..." She gulped, swallowing back the emotions in her throat. "I think our enemy took me not too long after that, so I was worried that I had gone after you somehow."

Daniella bit her lip, and once Johanna finished, she

laughed. A true, wholehearted, full belly-clenching laugh so alive, so infectious, that Johanna cracked a smile too.

"I'm sorry, I'm sorry just ... Oh boy. Listen, I love Luke with all my heart, but like a brother. He's a great guy, one of the best I know, but he drives me way too crazy for that to ever happen." Daniella squeezed her arm. "Believe me, he's all yours, and I think the both of you know it too."

Johanna fidgeted but Daniella's smile only grew wider.

"Luke is my best friend, and I would really, *really* love to get to know the woman he's crazy about, if she doesn't mind."

A shy smile touched Johanna's lips, and she squeezed Daniella's hand. "I'd really love that."

"Good. Now, do you want to go see him?" Daniella asked.

Johanna tensed. "I-I don't know how he's going to see me after all of this. I'm worried he'll think I'm damaged goods," she whispered.

"He most certainly will not. Luke saw you. He's the one who brought you into his house and did what he could to make sure you held on until we got here. He's also the one who cleaned you up afterward."

"What?" Johanna said, covering her mouth.

"He wouldn't let anyone take care of you. Luke's been the only one watching over you the whole time you've been uncon-scious. While we didn't know where all your wounds were, he did, and I'm sure he had his suspicions about what caused them. But being suspicious is different to having the truth laid out in front of you. That's why he got so upset."

Johanna's hand fell to her lap. She opened her mouth to speak but found that she couldn't form the words.

"My point is that never changed how he treated you. If it didn't then, it wouldn't now. I know Luke well. I watched him, especially while we looked for you. You've been the only thing on his mind for a while now. That isn't going to go away because of the abuse you went through. If anything, Luke's going to be even more up your ass than he was before." Daniella squeezed her arm again. "Do you see yourself as damaged goods?"

Johanna thought over her question and then sighed. "It's hard not to. All of this is a lot, and it's going to take some time to process it."

"Then take that time. You're allowed to feel whatever you feel and have whatever thoughts you have. But feeling those things and having those thoughts doesn't make them true." Daniella sighed. "A few months ago, the monster that took you killed my friend."

Johanna gasped but Daniella continued. "He killed her because he couldn't get to me. In that moment I felt so guilty for being safe and alive and with a wonderful man who wanted me by his side. I felt like I robbed her of everything she could have had. And you know what Greg told me? That I shouldn't feel guilty for being alive. I could affect so many people's lives. In fact, I already had. He told me that I could do a lot of good by being here, and so can you. I'm not going to ask you to give Luke a chance, but I am going to ask you to give yourself a chance. Have you ever done that before?"

The answer was automatic, and a weight left her chest as Johanna whispered, "No."

"Well, maybe now's a good time to start."

CHAPTER 12

The room fell silent when Johanna and Daniella entered. Johanna's eyes found Luke's immediately. She froze as everything else fell away. For a moment they just stared at one another, until Johanna noticed the little frown lines that stood out at the corner of his eyes and his now ruffled hair. Even his stance was different—tense and seemingly unmovable.

Is he even breathing? Am I?

She took a deep breath and watched his shoulders relax a fraction. Then it hit her all at once: he was worried about her.

Her heart softened. A second beat picked up under her skin, but it shattered at the clearing of a throat. When she came back to her senses, she realized she had been moving unconsciously toward Luke. Johanna looked away from him quickly, but not fast enough to miss the small, relieved smile on his face.

"We're going to head out for the day. Everyone needs their rest," Greg said.

"Thank you, everyone, for helping me," Johanna said.

Daniella nodded and then slipped her arms around Johanna in a hug. "I'll check on you in a bit, okay? Maybe we could get together later in the week and go shopping."

Greg groaned and Daniella shot him a glare. "Hush you."

Johanna smiled at their teasing. "I'd like that."

Before they left, Johanna pulled Mya aside. "I'm sorry I couldn't help you. But the second I remember something, I'll let you know. I promise. You'll find…"

Him.

Johanna drew back, unsure of why that word had come to her mind when Mya had never said what she was looking for.

At her hesitation, Mya stood straighter, hope warming her face. It was the first time she hadn't appeared devastated since the moment she'd entered Luke's home, and it made Johanna hesitate. But she couldn't give her false hope. Even if a part of her did know something, it, much like everything else, was locked away in her memories.

She cleared her throat and tried again. "You'll find what you're looking for."

Mya's shoulders dropped and she bobbed her head in a nod before filing out behind Dani and Greg.

Johanna was once again alone with Luke, but nothing felt the same. She was off balance, unsure of what to do, and to his credit he seemed to be in the same boat. Luke rested his head against the door, hand still on the knob, his body hunched over on the frame as if it was the only thing keeping him up.

She opened her mouth to speak, but words failed her and the fear that the ground had fallen out from underneath them was too thick for her to ignore.

Luke turned and marched toward her like a man ready for

battle, only to stop a foot away. His eyes were so intense, full of a thousand different emotions, that they took Johanna's breath away. She realized then that he was afraid too, but not for the same reasons she was. His fear was out of respect. She could see it in his eyes, in the tenseness of his jaw as he ground his teeth together, in how his hand was frozen in mid-air as he resisted touching her. But Johanna's fear was out of self-loathing. That fear was rapidly forming a chasm between them, and if she didn't try to move past that feeling, it would only get wider.

Daniella's words repeated in her head. *Give yourself a chance.*

She took a step forward, closing the space between them. Their bodies swayed together, caught in each other's magnetism, but neither reached for one another.

Finally, Luke sighed, and the hand that had been hovering in the air caressed her cheek.

Johanna's eyes closed as she fought against the tears that threatened to spill out. One simple touch from Luke was all it took to decimate her heart. She wanted to tell him everything, every single horrible thought she had in that moment so he could see how messed up she was. She wanted to be vulnerable, to lay herself at his feet and show him all her broken pieces so he could decide if this was really the road he wanted to walk down, if she was really enough.

But the fact that he didn't pull her closer, didn't initiate any further contact except the whispering caress of his fingertips along her skin, told her that he knew. Somehow, he knew. He *noticed* her. Luke saw more than she willingly let on, and no matter how much she tried, she couldn't escape his gaze. And there was something so harrowing, so heartbreakingly glorious within that knowledge, that it sparked a tiny speck of courage which grew inside of her, urging her to open her eyes to meet his.

His breath hitched as he searched her gaze for something. Then, ever so softly, Luke whispered, "Stay with me."

She stared at him, confused. "How did you know?"

"Because I know what it's like to blame yourself for something and to wish things were different. I know what it's like to think you aren't enough and that you'll drag everyone else down if you let them in." His thumb grazed along her jaw as he said again, "Stay with me."

"And what if you change your mind?" Johanna said, averting her gaze.

"I won't," he replied without any hesitation.

"What if you do?"

Luke tilted her chin up, drawing her eyes back to his. "I would never do such a thing, but in the event there was ever something that affected the possibility of there being an 'us,' I would talk to you about it. That's what one does when they want to keep someone in their life. They fight for them."

His arm slid around her back, pushing her against his body, and even though his hold was light enough that she could leave, she didn't. Then he silenced every thought, every question she could have asked him.

"I still want you, sunflower. In fact, I'm beginning to think I've never wanted you more."

She crumbled. The floor fell out from under her, her knees buckled, and she fell into a heaping, sobbing mess. But Luke caught her, and she was starting to hope he always would.

JOHANNA LEANED HER HEAD AGAINST THE WINDOW, STARING OUT into the backyard. The full moon shone, casting a blue light over every blade of grass and flower in Luke's garden. It was beautiful, but it could not pull her out of her thoughts. She was here, but not here. Seeing, but not focusing.

The rest of the day with Luke had been quiet. He comforted her while she remained silent. It wasn't that she didn't want to talk about what she was feeling—she did, but she'd been stuck on where to begin, what she could say that wouldn't scare him away but would help Luke to understand why she was like this now.

He'd given her time and taken care of her. She'd found out about the food he'd kept for her, but it had only reminded her of how much he had done for her, how much he cared. It both helped and hurt her, leaving her feeling that he had drawn the short end of the stick. But she couldn't tell him that, because she knew if she did, he'd convince her otherwise. Even in the short time since she'd awoken, she knew that's what he would do. Much like he'd said earlier, he'd fight for her. The question was, did she deserve to be fought for? And who fought on Luke's behalf? She wanted to fight for him, and that added a new level of depth and confusion to her already endless feelings.

She'd taken the feelings to bed with her and woken up shortly after, choking on a scream, so here she sat, procrastinating what she knew she'd have to do. She couldn't keep going like this. Even she knew that forcing herself to do a deep dive into her emotions wasn't healthy, but the alternative was worse. She couldn't keep crying. She couldn't move on from her thoughts, she couldn't sleep, she barely wanted to eat, and she couldn't possibly make a good, conscious decision when she was so utterly terrified of *everything* she did.

Johanna took a deep breath. As she released it, she fastened back on her emotional chains, secured the locks, turned everything off, and then approached things one by one: shame, guilt, the expectations she had laid upon herself, sadness, anger, hatred.

Johanna heard a noise and turned her head just as the door creeped open. In it stood Luke. Everything about him made her feel safe. He was tall, probably 6'5" or 6'6", his shoulders were broad, and he was a solid wall of muscle. His presence, his *persistence*, shook her. It made her feel lucky, honored, feelings she wasn't used to. Now, though, she felt like running both toward and away from him.

He seemed to know that. She really didn't understand how, but once again he understood her.

Luke entered the room slowly, watching her every move. Finally, he said. "Couldn't sleep?"

Johanna shook her head and curled herself more into a ball against the wall.

"May I?" He gestured to the other end of the window seat, and she nodded again.

Luke moved toward Johanna like a lion whose cage had been opened—wary if what he could see was real, but courageous enough to find out. He sat down, his back against the wall, mirroring her stance while he propped one foot on the cushion and left the other on the floor. Then he held out his hand to her.

She was startled at first, but then she looked from his hand up into his eyes. There were no questions there, no doubt or fear, nothing but absolute certainty. And that certainty, that assurance that he had in not only her but in them had her closing her fingers around his and allowing herself to be drawn into his lap.

Johanna rested her head against his chest, peering out of the window while he wrapped his arms around her. She clasped onto his arm with both of hers. With a simple embrace he had separated her from the scared scrap of a being she had been. Now she felt at peace. Treasured. At home.

Luke didn't say anything, and neither did she for a while. They simply were. Then something in her changed, and she realized this was how she wanted them to be. She desired this, *craved* this, but she couldn't keep it if she didn't let go of the ugly monster in her heart.

"I wish we would have been like this before," Johanna said, eyes fixed on the moon-bathed garden.

"So do I," Luke said, and they both sighed.

"Luke, I..." Johanna took a deep breath and fitted herself closer, snuggling into his warmth. "I'm scared to tell you about what I've gone through before, but I know I have to if I want you to understand me and why I'm like this. Can I?"

He kissed her head. "You can always talk to me about anything you want. I want to get to know you, sunflower, and it means a lot to me that you're willing to let me."

A retort started to form in Johanna mind, telling her that he wouldn't want to hear this story, but she bit it back. Taking another deep breath, she began.

"I lived in a small town as a child. I was a big girl, even at that age, and that made me the butt of every joke and bullied by everyone: boys and girls, even their parents."

Luke tightened his arms around her.

"It hurt. They weren't just cruel to me, but also to my loved ones. They assumed that they were neglectful of me and my health since I was the only one like this." Johanna waved her hand over her body. "I never fought them. I never said anything. I remember some people stood up for me at first, but as time went on and we all grew up it became just me on my own."

Luke's hand moved along her back, trying to erase the tension in her spine.

"I let in anyone who wanted to be a part of my life. I dedicated myself to them. I thought having someone was better than having no one, and it didn't matter if they only kept me around because I fulfilled a need for them, or that I was a second option. I just ... I didn't want to feel alone anymore. That continued through college. There, I..."

She swallowed hard, trying to fight back the anxiety clawing at her throat. Luke's arms tightened around her, reminding her that she wasn't alone, that she didn't need to drown in her memories.

She breathed, then whispered, "I was ... sexually assaulted by the man I was dating."

"What?" Luke said, his arms tightening even more.

"Luke—"

"Who was it, Johanna?"

She could feel him shaking around her, and when she looked into his eyes, they were red, furious. "Luke, you can't hurt him," she said gently, squeezing his arm.

"Like hell I can't. Give me his name, Johanna, right now."

She smiled despite the memory and his murderous intent. "Luke, as a vampire you're forbidden from killing humans, remember?"

"He hurt *you*," Luke hissed.

Johanna brushed her fingers over his cheek. "He did, but I took care of it."

"What?"

"If you let me finish my story, I'll tell you how."

Johanna watched him weigh his options. His muscles were still tense and his eyes still bright red, so she knew she hadn't convinced him to let this go.

"I wouldn't want anything to happen to you, especially not because of me," Johanna whispered as she caressed his skin. "Please."

Luke rested his head back against the wall and blew out a harsh breath. With it, some of the tension left his body and when he looked at her again, his eyes were almost back to normal.

"Thank you."

Luke grunted in response. Johanna rested her head under his, but this time she wrapped her arms around his back. He sighed and hugged her. It was a little too tight, but she wouldn't complain.

"I left college after that. I was too ashamed to tell my loved ones what happened. Soon after, my grandmother got sick. The closest hospital was in New York so I decided to move here to spend as much time with her as I could. Everyone thought it was a horrible idea. You need to be tough to make it out here, you need to have a backbone. You need to be a fighter, and I'd never shown any promise in those areas."

Luke huffed but otherwise stayed silent.

"At first, they were right. It was hard being here essentially on my own. But this was my chance at a fresh start away from all the horrible experiences I'd had back home. No one knew me here, and so I could be anything, anyone, I wanted to be. My grandmother was also a formidable woman. She was a child during one of our wars, and she believed if you were backed into a corner, you should always fight to get yourself out."

"She sounds like a wonderful woman," Luke said, relaxing a little more under her.

"She was. You would have loved her. She was good for me, and the city was good for me too. But then I found out the man from college had taken pictures and a video of me the night he'd assaulted me."

Luke tensed again and she could tell he was going to say something, so she cut him off before he could. "I took him to court. When the case seemed like it wasn't going in my favor, I forced it to. I manipulated the judge with my powers, and I took revenge on the man who assaulted me. He's in a mental hospital right now, and he will never, *ever* get out."

"Good," Luke said firmly.

"That's not *good*, Luke!" She tried to draw back from him but he wouldn't let her. "That's not something someone should do. That's not something a *good* person would do. I broke him, and I enjoyed it. I was *proud* of it! I went on with my life. I had no remorse back then, but now I find out that it happened all over again and I dragged my grandmother into it. She died because of *me!* What if that's my penance? What if all of that was just karmic justice for what I'd done? What happens if I do it again and I draw someone else into it, like you? I'm not ... I'm not worth it, Luke. I'm just not."

Luke brushed her hair back from her face. "So that's what you're scared of?"

A little part of Johanna shriveled and died as she nodded.

"Sunflower, no one deserves what happened to you."

She shook her head.

"Do you think I'm a good person?" he asked.

She sighed. "Of course you are."

Luke's lips tipped up at her response. "I've killed people. A lot of people."

"And I'm sure you did it for a reason."

"So what's the difference between me and you?"

Johanna threw her arms in the air. "I was selfish, Luke! I did it because I was angry and I wanted justice."

"The difference between being called the hero or the villain is the person telling the story," Luke said.

"I don't understand what you mean."

"It's simple. You think you're the villain because you took revenge, but you're not. Against all the odds, you took what happened to you and let it go. You moved on with your life until it escalated, and when you tried to get justice for yourself and thought you wouldn't, you made sure you did. You call that being selfish, but you don't know who else that person assaulted. By getting away with it once, they could have done it a hundred other times. They could have been planning to do it again the night they won the case. You don't know what could have happened, but you stopped whatever it was from happening. That makes you good, Johanna."

She shook her head, but he cupped her cheeks to make her focus on him.

"You're good, sunflower. And as for what happened to you and your grandmother, I don't think karma had anything to do with that. I think..." He paused seeming to search for the words.

Johanna gripped his wrists in desperation. "Please, tell me."

"I think the reason you went through all of this is because you had the strength to."

Johanna's eyes widened.

"I need you understand that doesn't mean I think you deserved *any* of what happened to you. You don't, and the fact that you thought you did breaks my heart." Luke's fingertips rubbed over her cheek. "He took you because of who you are, and he kept you because of what you can do. But you beat him, sunflower. You saved people. You've continued to save people, and that's just from what we know now. Imagine what else we'll find out once you get your memories back. You took a horrible situation and did something good with it. Most people wouldn't be able to do that. Most people would have sacrificed everyone else over themselves. You did the complete opposite. You're a hero to those people, and every time you treat yourself like the villain you are trivializing what they went through. I know you don't want to do that."

She shook her head. "I don't, but I don't know how—"

"I understand how you were treated, and I understand why you think so poorly of yourself, but are those people around you right now?"

"No."

"Then why the fuck should their opinions matter?"

Johanna stared at him in shock.

"Every time you undervalue yourself, you let them win. Every. Single. Time. Meanwhile those people are off living their poor excuses of lives. Do you think they ever think of you, that you ever cross their minds? No. They've probably done that to a hundred other people by now. Does it seem fair to you that you're stuck while they're moving on?"

"N-No." She gulped. "But how can I change that?"

"Focus on you," he said quietly. "Think about what you want, every single day. I'm going to ask you and I want you to answer me as honestly as you possibly can. You need to learn how to put yourself first and that you don't need to sacrifice yourself for anyone else." His fingers brushed through her hair, squeezing her back. "You're allowed to do that, sunflower. Your words, thoughts and opinions have value. *You* have value."

She was shaking, bits of her heart exploding at his words. Logically she knew he was right, and if the roles had been reversed then she would have said the same things to him. Yet she never imagined she'd ever hear them come out of another person's mouth.

Johanna clung to him. She wrapped her arms around him and buried her head in his neck where she breathed in his scent.

"Would you do something for me?" Luke asked suddenly.

Johanna lifted her head. "Anything. What is it?"

"You spoke to me telepathically once. When you do that, can you only hear someone's communicative thoughts, or can you interact with all their thoughts?"

"Either or." She tilted her head to the side. "Why are you asking?"

"I want you to do that with me. I want you to see all my thoughts about you."

She drew back. "What are you talking about? Why would you want that?"

"Because I don't want you to ever doubt the way I see you."

"Luke..."

He squeezed her waist. "Please?"

"I ... Okay."

He pulled her as close as he could, until she had no choice but to straddle his lap to accommodate them. Luke widened his legs, forcing her to spread her knees further and settle more onto his lap. She gasped, and goosebumps broke out across her skin when he chuckled slowly.

She took a breath, trying to slow her racing heart. "You know we don't have to be this close."

He smiled and tilted his head to hers. For a moment Johanna thought he was going to kiss her, but he rested his forehead against her own and stared into her eyes. "The last time we did this I couldn't reach you, so I don't want any space between us now."

She gulped and licked her suddenly dry lips. Then she closed her eyes in the hope of blocking out the intensity of his stare, but she could still feel him watching her. She blushed. "Close your eyes."

He laughed, the rumble of the sound making his chest brush against hers just as each puff of air tickled her lips.

Taking a deep breath, she gently pushed into his mind, feeling him resist her for all of a second. Then she was in.

The mind reflected a person's behaviors, so every mind was different. While Johanna was typically respectful of entering a person's mind, she enjoyed being able to see them for what they were. But Luke's mind had to be one of the most glorious she'd ever come across.

It was like a gallery, with blotches of paint and short form notes spilled along the marble walls and floors. Golden columns lined every archway, and when Johanna looked up, she could see an open sky-like field filled with countless shapes. Then she saw him. He looked into her eyes and everything changed.

The hall shifted, flying away until it was fully replaced with suns, the large, gleaming balls of light surrounding them. A giant bird flew in and out of focus before settling on the top of a cage covered in flames.

"This is how I see you," Luke said. *"To me, you are the sun. But you're also this bird, learning how to fly in a world that tried to tear you apart."* He reached his hand out and pointed at the bird. *"You'll learn how to fly, sunflower. This world could never keep you down. I won't let it."*

"Luke…" she said out loud, swimming in the mess he was making of her.

"Do you know why I call you sunflower?"

"No," she whimpered, opening her eyes.

"Because you are resilient. You persevere. You're strong, courageous, a beacon of hope." His hand slid from her waist up her side, tracing along her body. His fingertips lightly grazed the side of her breast, causing her to bite back a moan.

Johanna gripped his shoulders, her voice breathless as she said, "Luke, what are you doing to me?"

"Letting you know how beautiful I think you are, how utterly *desirable* you are to me." He released a sharp breath as he grabbed a hold of her hips and pulled her forward. She rocked against him, and they both moaned.

"I am over seven hundred years old, Johanna, from a time when women who looked like you would have been treated correctly, like a fucking blessing. Society is only obsessed with being thin now because of food scarcity and a million other things my brain can't focus on because I'm near you. But I can tell you that not a single one of them is true. The word 'fat' has a negative connotation to it, but that's not what it means, and it damn sure doesn't mean you're ugly, unintelligent, unhealthy, nor anything else anyone has ever called you. If you ever doubt that, feel free to look through my thoughts and I'll show you everything I've dreamt of doing to you since I first laid eyes on you."

She grew wetter with every word. Her nipples had turned into hard peaks, so sensitive that even the light rubbing of her nightgown as she panted was too much. Her body shook with need and want, but there was more than just desire coursing through her veins. Johanna felt vulnerable. Luke had turned her into fragmented chaos. Her soul begged for him to pluck her strings like an instrument and play her to whatever tune he wanted, just as long as he played her, as long as he touched her. Luke's honesty had flayed her open in such a way that she didn't want to ever be closed again. No, she wanted him to fill her empty spaces until every breath, every cell of her body had tasted his. And just as he had assured her, she wanted to assure him of where she stood, of what she wanted from him.

"I..." She took a deep breath to steady her nerves. "It's not only my loved ones that I don't remember."

He tilted his head, confused.

"It's you. I don't remember you. I protected the people I love ... and the person I knew I could fall in love with." She stared into his eyes, and a pop of satisfaction settled into her heart at his shock. "When I was unconscious, I heard you. I didn't know it was you at the time, but you're the reason I woke up. You made me feel safe. You made me feel comfortable, like I could trust you, like I ... had a home in you."

Johanna rubbed his chest, right over his pounding heart. "I want that home, Luke. I want you, and I'm willing to do whatever it is I need to do to be that for you. I want to be someone you can trust and confide in, someone that one day you can love."

His breath rushed out of him with a hiss, then grew shallow

as he panted. Luke closed his eyes and tilted his head back, appearing tortured. A low, rumbling growl spilled out of his throat as he gripped the window seat hard enough to break it.

"Luke?" She reached out for him, gently caressing the side of his neck. His pulse thundered against her fingers so strongly she was concerned he was going to have a heart attack.

"I should have picked a different name for you, something wicked and dangerous," he murmured.

"What?"

His eyes opened, the darkness within them making her gasp. "You cannot say that to a man and then expect him not to struggle with losing control."

She blinked, then her mouth formed an "O" as she realized what he meant. His confession made her feel powerful, and with a soft giggle she started to get off his lap, but he pulled her back down.

"Absolutely not." His fingers flexed around her hips and a shiver traveled along her spine. "Stay, I just need a second to calm down."

She was still smiling as she nodded and rested her head in the crook of his neck. Every breath he took pushed at her chest and she took one with him, needing to settle herself as well.

Then he whispered, "I don't think you're going to have to wait very long."

"Hmm?"

"For me to fall in love with you."

CHAPTER 13

Johanna and Luke had spent most of every day of the last month together. She couldn't remember ever laughing as much as she had in her time with him, nor feeling as warm and cared for as he made her feel. They ate together, and no matter how busy Luke got, he always stopped to cuddle and sleep with her. When Luke wasn't with her, he was off being a busybody, flitting around doing something to what he liked to call "their" house, or working for the firm. Then Daniella announced she was pregnant, and he added worrying over her to that list. It was adorable.

There was really only one problem with all of this. Multiple times a day he asked her what she wanted, as a way to remind her to check in with herself. As the days went on and he kept asking her that question, she kept having to stop herself from saying "you."

Sometimes she thought he knew. The side of his lip would curl into a smirk, and she swore he almost dared her with her eyes to say it, but she never did. She didn't know how to yet. Yes, she felt like she was healing quickly—due to having such a positive and caring environment around her with someone who treated her well, and her growing friendship with Daniella—but at the end of the day she still didn't feel as worthy as she now knew she should.

So, much like Luke, she kept herself busy when he worked. Johanna had started looking the roster of employee IDs, hoping to find more coordinates, but it was difficult. While she had clearly been the one to come up with the code, it was like looking at someone else's handiwork. The her that had made these had been in an entirely different mental space. She had been efficient, powerful, *desperate*. She wanted to save as many people as she could, and it was hard to be forced to see herself the same way Luke and the others saw her.

What she had done was incredible and compared to the way she saw herself now, it felt like she'd taken ten steps back in time. Every time she thought she might have figured out part of her code, doubt crept over her and caused her to second-guess herself. It was important that when she determined a new location, it was correct. If not, she could very well be sending everyone on a wild goose chase or, if she wasn't careful, into a trap. She was playing with people's lives, so she had to do this correctly. Luke, Daniella, Greg, and even Mya were counting on her and she didn't want to let them down.

She sighed, raking her fingers through her hair as she leaned her elbows on the table. She stayed like that as she heard Luke step into the room.

"Hey," he said, dropping a kiss on her forehead. "Having a tough time?"

She looked up at him. "Yes. I just have no idea what I was

thinking when I made these. I can't get into that headspace to figure any of this out."

He frowned as he sat down next to her. "I wouldn't want you to get into that headspace. You were being held captive and I don't think you believed you were going to make it out alive. I'd rather you feel comfortable now and never figure these out than feel that way again."

She slumped in the chair. "I swear, did you write the book on smooth talking and how to be a Casanova? I can never win with you."

He laughed so deeply it brought a smile to her face. "What can I say? You bring out the best in me."

"Charmer."

Luke pulled her into his lap and she came easily, wrapping her arms around him. "How would you feel about taking a break?"

"A break?" She tilted her head to the side. "What do you mean?"

"I would like to take you out on a date. I thought we could take my bike down to the beach, have a nice dinner, maybe dance a little. It would be good for us."

She sighed as the warmth of his gesture ran through her. "But can we really go out? What about—"

"We'll be fine." He kissed her head again. "I know the area well. It would be odd for him, or anyone against us, for that matter, to be out there. Plus, there's also a couple of immortals I know who like to frequent the restaurant. They'll help us if we need it."

Johanna released a breath, letting it carry the tension out of her body before she looked up at him and smiled. "Then I'd really love to go with you. I'll go get ready."

She kissed his cheek and caught the wide grin on his face before she wriggled off his lap and went to get dressed.

JOHANNA HAD NEVER BEEN ON THE BACK OF A BIKE BEFORE AND wasn't quite sure what to expect, but the moment Luke took off she knew she'd never be the same. The feeling of the wind blowing around her as they sped off was exhilarating. She felt free, as if nothing and no one could hold her back. The purr of the machine between her legs was exciting, and the intimacy of holding on to Luke's back while he sat in between her legs, guiding the bike down the road, wasn't lost on her.

Johanna knew motorcycle riding could be dangerous, but she trusted Luke. Her body naturally understood what to do every time he took a turn, and he was careful with her, never going too fast, stopping too short, or cutting any corners. Like with everything else he'd done since she'd woken up in his house, Luke kept her care in mind, and it was making her libido jump off the charts.

By the time they got to the beach her legs were so wobbly she'd nearly fallen when she tried to get off the bike. Luke caught her with an arm around her waist and asked her if she was okay. She said yes, but she wanted to pummel him when she saw that damn smirk on his face. He knew! He freaking knew *and* he was amused by her reaction to him. The jerk!

Still, as they walked down the beach, listening to the waves crash against the shore and the soft laughter of children surrounding them, she felt at peace. Looking up at Luke, she smiled. "Thank you for bringing me here. It's really nice."

His features softened with his own smile, and he wrapped

his arm around her shoulders, falling into step beside her. "The smile on your face is thanks enough."

She laughed at him. "You're such a sap."

"You love it."

"I do," she agreed, the words slipping out of her mouth. For a second, she thought to backtrack, until she turned and saw that Luke was frozen in shock like a giant, handsome statue. Laughter spilled from her at the sight, and before she knew what was happening, he picked her up and threw her over his shoulder. Johanna laughed even harder, wiggling and yelling at him to put her down.

"Not a chance in hell. I cannot believe you, teasing me like that," he said gruffly.

"Oh my god! Are you *blushing?*"

Luke made a noise in his throat that set her into a whole new fit of giggles, and then his hand landed on her ass with a loud *whack!*

"Luke! No you did not!"

"I did, and, actually, I'll do it again." He smacked her ass again, and then he gripped her flesh, kneading it in his large palms.

"Luke, people can see!" she hissed.

He shrugged his shoulders under her, making her bounce. "Sounds like a them problem."

"You're impossible!"

"Yes, but now that I know you love it, why would I try to be anything else?"

JOHANNA HEARD THE RESTAURANT BEFORE SHE SAW IT, BUT THEN the two-story establishment covered in chipped blue paint came into view. It felt homey, with its waves of patrons, clinks of utensils, and laughter bouncing off the walls.

The staff smiled at her and Luke and welcomed them both warmly, but none more so than two of Luke's friends. Tommy, a werewolf, and Loe, a faerie, slid into their booth with them. Luke kept Johanna by his side and slung an arm over her shoulders while he introduced her as his mate. There was no hesitation in his voice, no hint of question. Even she caught the pride in his words, and she noticed his friends saw it too.

After hearing her darkest secrets, living with her for over a month, taking care of her, providing for her, and spending time with her, Luke seemed overjoyed about her being his mate. He'd said as much so many times she'd lost count, but it was one thing to say it behind closed doors and another to show it publicly. The weight of his conviction shocked her. It forced Johanna to finally question why she couldn't let go of her own self-doubt, and the answer was because she feared what would happen when she did.

But now, in this moment, she didn't want to be scared. She didn't want to have any of the fear, doubt, shame, or self-criticism she fought with daily. No, now she just wanted to be Johanna, Luke's mate. She wanted to listen to the way his friends made fun of him and the stories they told. She wanted to hear him laugh, let the warmth of his body seep into her pores ... so she did.

Eventually Tommy and Loe left to give Johanna and Luke privacy, and the evening gave way to eating, talking, laughing and teasing. Later, when she was full of good food and company, Luke twirled her in his arms in a darkened corner of the room and danced with her. Johanna couldn't remember the last time she danced, and she was grateful that Luke had made sure to keep the moment private between them. Like normal, he seemed to just sense her, to know her without her saying a word or sharing her thoughts with him. It felt so good to be so in tune with someone.

Luke's eyes flickered away from hers for a moment before he said, "The sun's setting. Why don't we go out to the pier and watch it together before we head home?"

Johanna nodded. The sun had been a long way from setting when they had stepped into the bar, but it was easy to lose track of time when she was with him.

"Let me go use the restroom," she said, squeezing his hand before separating from him.

"I'll wait for you at the entrance."

Johanna stared at herself in the bathroom mirror, taking in the person she saw. Her cheeks were rounder and fuller than she remembered, but high. Smile lines had started to form around her mouth, and her eyes twinkled back at her with joy and mirth. She looked younger, more at ease, as if life had been good to her.

It hadn't, she knew that, but when she tried, she couldn't recall all the moments she used to hold on to with a vice grip because *some* life was better than *none.* Now she felt grateful, because the person staring back at her was someone she'd always hoped she could be but had lost faith would ever appear. For the first time in her life, Johanna was starting to love herself, to care more about who she was and to believe she could do anything she put her mind to.

She awoke each day with an open heart, and at the core of it were the feelings she kept for Luke. Maybe tonight she'd be honest and tell him. He deserved to know, after not only helping her to start the chain reaction that was guiding her down the path of who she wanted to be, but for also nurturing and protecting her while she traveled it.

With new resolve, she dried her hands and opened the bathroom door. She was on her way to the entrance when a rowdy man tumbled into her path, causing her to jump backward to avoid running into him.

"Fuck off, all of ya!" he said, his voice slurring as he mumbled.

"Excuse me," Johanna said as he blocked her own path to the outside.

"Ah, look what we have here." He tried to smile but it came out crooked. "Come on, pretty lady, dance with me."

"No, thank you. Excuse me, I'd like to leave."

His laughter was interrupted by a hiccup. He stepped closer to her, so Johanna stepped away.

"Like to leave with me, huh?" he said with a drunken wink.

Johanna had to restrain her temper. She was utterly disgusted by his words, but this man was clearly an angry drunk and she didn't want to make him more upset or cause an issue, so she forced herself to be polite. "No. Please get out of my way."

"Oh!" he said in a sing-song voice. "She thinks she's too good for me, huh? Now listen here, you fat bitch—"

"Is there a reason," a voice started behind her, low and deadly, "that you're harassing my wife?"

Luke's arm wrapped around her, and Johanna's back straightened against his chest.

"Hey, m-man," he stuttered, slurring his words as he held up his hands. "I'm n-not causing any trouble. But this broad here—"

"My wife, you mean?" Luke snarled, the rumble in his chest vibrating against her back.

"Yeah, yeah, your girl or whatever—"

"Luke," Johanna said to him telepathically, but he didn't answer her. She wanted to turn to look at him, to see if that would make him refocus onto her, but something in her told her not to. Luke wasn't thinking with the mind of a human right now; he was solely a predator protecting what was his.

"Luke," she tried again, ignoring the man's voice.

When Luke still didn't respond, Johanna ran her palm down the arm around her waist. She clasped his fingers, and he squeezed her stomach, hard. It was a warning, but she didn't care. If she didn't stop him, he'd do something that would get him in trouble with The Council. There were too many humans here for him to become violent, and as she looked around the restaurant, she could see people on their cell phones. If Luke did *anything* supernatural, those devices would turn on them in a heartbeat.

"Luke! You can't. Please, let it go!"

The only answer she received back was a growl.

"—yeah, you know man, bitches can't be trusted," the man, clearly unaware of how close he was to his own death, said with a shrug and a sly grin, as if he was winning a game.

Behind her, Luke buried his lips in her hair, parting the strands. He kissed her head but then she felt the sharpness of his fangs as he grinned against her scalp.

Fuck.

"I'm sorry, Luke, but I can't let you get in trouble for me."

Johanna used her power to freeze his body in place. The

ease and speed of which her ability worked surprised her, but she didn't have time for the shock. She refocused, making sure not to put Luke under full paralysis. He could still hear and experience his surroundings, but he would not be able to move.

She closed their telepathic connection. Johanna didn't want to hear what she assumed would be curses and demands for her to let him go, but even with that closure she felt his anger, and it was now directed at her.

So be it.

She took his anger and let it meld with her own. Together they created a dark explosion that flew through her veins and ignited her resolve. She looked at the man. "Shut up—"

He balled his hands into fists. "Now you listen here—"

"No, *you* listen!" Johanna hissed. "When a woman says no, she means no! How many times does someone have to say that for you to get it through your fucking head? What do you think you are, God's gift to the female race?"

He laughed in her face. "Oh you've got a mouth on you. Has your man never taught you how to use it right? I'm sure you could keep him a lot longer if you learned how to shut up."

Her eyes narrowed and she smirked. "And I'm sure if you knew what to do with your mouth you wouldn't be here drunk, alone, and stumbling over your own two feet."

"You bitch—"

Johanna was tired. For just one night, one *fucking* night, she didn't want anything to get in the way. Not her endless list of issues and criticisms, not her past experiences, nothing. And it had worked, she had *made* it work, and they were having a great night! But now this incredibly self-entitled piece of shit had ruined everything, and she fucking refused to let this continue.

It was easy to get into his mind. He had zero defenses, and

with the liquor coursing through his veins he was a fucking mess. Still, she wasn't gentle about it, making it hurt as she slipped herself in. The mind was a map of chaos to someone not familiar with it, but Johanna *lived* here. The mind, even if it belonged to another person, was her home, so it was simple to find the place she was looking for: the faculties for relieving the bowels and bladder. All it took was a gentle push, and then she was out just as quickly as she'd slipped in.

Her grin grew into a small laugh. "Never mind. Even if you knew what to do with your mouth, no one would ever, *ever* want a man who smells like shit and can't even hold his own piss."

Horror dawned his face. He looked down, watching the wetness spreading over his pants. His eyes widened, and then he was running past Johanna and Luke and into the male stalls.

Johanna laughed again, a full body laugh that had her bending forward and then back as she rocked on her heels. But when she brushed against Luke's still frozen form, she paused. The victory that pumped through her died, because while she'd saved the man's life, Luke definitely wasn't going to be happy.

Instead of being timid, Johanna tilted her head up to his and pulled her magic back slowly. He glared at her, and she glared right back.

"It was for your own good," she said as soon as he began to move.

"Don't *ever* do that again," he hissed.

"Then don't *make* me do that again," she snarled back. "Now are we going to go, or do I need to use my power to drag you out of here too?"

He withdrew his arm from around her stomach, and she let his hand go. He mockingly waved in front of her. "After you, sunflower."

She rolled her eyes at him and flicked her hair behind her shoulder, making sure to hit him with it. He made a lighter rumbling sound in his chest, and even though she knew he was upset with her, she smiled. Oddly enough, she found that she liked the feeling of pushing his buttons more than she liked how her normal apologizing attitude made her feel. Johanna filed that away and allowed him to lead them both toward the door and out of the restaurant.

CHAPTER 14

He was pissed. No, he was absolutely fucking *livid*. They were having a wonderful day, and then this fucking asshole had to come and harass *his* mate! Luke wanted to rip into his neck with his bare hands, to watch the fear gather in his eyes right before the life drained out of them. He wanted to bathe in his blood and offer his head to Johanna on a fucking platter.

Logically, he realized that might have been taking it a little too far and that Johanna hadn't asked him for any of those items, but emotionally he didn't give a damn. The moment, the fucking *second* that dipshit had looked at his mate, even had the balls to speak to her, much less in the demeaning manner he had, the best thing he could be was a skinned rug for Johanna to walk over. She deserved so much better, and Luke was tired of hearing—and now having firsthand experience of—her not getting it. If it was that bad when he was there, how bad had it been when he wasn't? No, he didn't need to ask that question. He already knew, and that made everything worse.

He also couldn't believe Johanna had used her powers on him, even if on some core level he knew that she had been right to. Johanna was more important to him than anything, including The Council. He just wanted his mate to be happy and treated fairly. Luke wanted to protect her, and she'd hurt his pride by stopping him from doing as he pleased.

And then she'd had the *audacity* to fucking tease him! He was used to meek and timid Johanna, the side of her that called him to temper himself down, to hold his passions at bay. Did he want to fuck her into oblivion when she was like that? Yes, but that wasn't what she needed from him. She needed his patience, so he gave it to her. She needed him to support her while she worked through everything, to be there for her, and it was easier to remind himself of that when she wasn't tempting the absolute fuck out of him.

She hadn't apologized, and it was clear by the way she was walking in front of him, her back rigid like she was gearing up for a fight either against or for him, that she wasn't going to. It was driving him crazy, as was the way that she walked when she was frustrated, swinging her hips with every step. She was killing him, fucking destroying him, and he was ten seconds away from pulling her behind something and finally sating them both.

It didn't take long for the battle to explode between them. The moment they found a private space on the pier, Johanna rounded on him.

"What the *fuck* were you thinking?" she hissed.

"What was *I* thinking? What were *you* thinking?" he growled back, caging her in.

"*I* was thinking about how much I don't want you to end up dying or whatever type of shit it is that The Council would do to you for harming a human in public. That place was packed, Luke! We wouldn't have been able to make it out of that!" She slapped her hands against his chest as if it would put any space between them.

"I don't fucking care about that!" he shouted, refusing to budge from against her.

"Well, I fucking care about you!"

Luke staggered, taking a step away from her. His chest heaved as if she was stealing the very breath from his soul.

"Luke," she said, reaching out to him and gripping onto his shirt. "I don't want to lose you. I will fight whatever and whoever to make sure that doesn't happen, even if it means fighting you."

His heart skipped a beat, and then it pounded so hard under her hand that he was sure she could feel it. He took her in, the way her hair shone and picked up the radiance of the sun's last rays around them, how her blue eyes were so open, so vulnerable to him that he could see the depths of courage and care in them. She was everything, *everything* he could ever want or dream of. She was his *all*.

Luke stepped forward. His arms slid around her waist as he pulled her to him. She made a sound, a ruptured sigh as if he'd stolen the noise from her, then buried her head in his neck. Luke bent forward until he could rest his own head in her neck, listening to the rapid pounding of her pulse under her skin. Her fingers buried into his hair, twisting around the strands. He groaned, his shoulders sagging as his anger left him and fled away into the wind.

"You're killing me, sunflower," he murmured into her skin.

He felt her lips curve against his shoulder, but then her smile fell. Johanna's arms tightened around him as she whispered, "I'd fight and maim and kill everything on this planet before I ever let anything happen to you."

Luke groaned again as fire raged through his veins. He was caught between the swell of pride that his mate would fight for him, the weight of her care, and the knowledge that he would never, *ever* let her put herself in harm's way. His fingers brushed back her hair and he kissed her neck. A soft hum left her mouth as she tilted her head to the side to give him access. He smiled at her trust before traveling upward with soft kisses until he reached her jaw. Then he lifted his head to stare into her eyes while he cupped her cheeks.

"Don't go that far for me, sunflower," he said.

Her eyes burned with conviction as she stared back at him, but her voice was level and stern when she spoke. "I will if I have to. I'll always do whatever I have to for you, Luke. You're worth it."

He couldn't speak. She was dragging him under. Luke kissed her head and cradled it to his chest. He kept her there, pressed against him, because he couldn't bear the thought of a single shred of space between them. Her fingers twirled strands of his hair, her nails grazing his neck, raising goosebumps over his skin.

Luke closed his eyes and just allowed himself to revel in everything he felt for her: the deep love, the fear and concern that raced through him every time he thought about the dangers she'd been through, the guilt and shame over the moments he hadn't been there to protect her, everything. Telling her was on the tip of his tongue, but he held back, just as he always did, because he didn't want to add more onto her shoulders. He didn't want Johanna to feel as though she owed him anything, or that she needed to rush to meet him somewhere she wasn't ready to be. But this, the quiet times spent in one another's arms? It was in those moments he believed she knew. Even if he didn't say it, she knew everything that was in his heart for her, just like he knew everything that was in hers for him.

The waves lapped at the shore around them. Luke used his hearing to listen to their surroundings and ensure their safety, but he still kept one ear focused on her breathing, her heartbeat, the way her blood flowed through her veins. A little jump started in her heart before she pulled her head back, and he looked down at her. She searched his gaze for something but then her face turned rosy. He grinned. He liked where this was going already.

"Yes, sunflower?"

She licked her lips and his gaze flickered there, capturing the motion before returning to her eyes.

"Back at the bar, you ... you called me your wife."

He smiled and answered unashamed, "I did."

Her breathing hitched in her throat, making his grin grow.

"B-but that means things," she murmured.

"Things?" he said, teasing her. "What things?"

She narrowed her eyes and smacked his arm. "You know what things. Love. Marriage."

"It does? I had no idea."

"Luke!" she said, exasperated, but it only made him laugh harder.

He bent down, his face level with hers, and whispered, "Is there something you're trying to ask me, sunflower?"

She bit her lip and her gaze heated before it slid away from his. He brought it back with a gentle squeeze of her chin.

"I called you my wife because that's how I think of you. You are my mate, the other half of my soul. You delight me, you drive me crazy, and I know now that the reason fate made me immortal was to meet you. I may have called you that word in the heat of the moment, but that's because it's how I feel. My intentions are to marry you one day, my vicious little sunflower, and if you're asking my feelings for you, well..." He smirked. "Yes, I love you."

She gasped, her eyes growing wide at the confession, but it was him who was shocked when her mouth, seconds before in a perfect little "O", pressed against his.

Luke had imagined kissing Johanna more times than he could count. He fantasized about how soft and warm her lips would be, how delicious she would taste, the soft noise she would make when he parted her lips with his tongue. He craved the way she'd sigh into his arms and moan in her pleasure. What he had never imagined, though, was that she would kiss *him* first.

He was so shocked that he hadn't moved, and it wasn't until she pulled back from him, her nervousness visibly morphing into horror, that he sprang into action. Luke cupped the back of her neck and pulled her in for another kiss. His name left her lips in a sigh before their mouths fused together.

There was a moment, just one, where everything felt new. Luke felt as if he was flying, high on the elation coursing through his veins. He'd waited for this single moment for so long, but one kiss wasn't enough. He was greedy, hungry, fucking *starving* for her.

Luke growled low in his throat and Johanna answered with

a torn whine that unlocked something in him. His blood heated, raged, and then they turned chaotic. Her hands snaked into his hair, pressing and tugging to keep him close, drawing a groan from him. Luke squeezed her waist, tugging her closer, desperate to eliminate even a tiny breath of air from between them. Then he pushed them back as one, pinning Johanna against the pier. She moaned, the sound going straight to his aching cock.

His fingers slid down her body, reaching her ass. He cupped it and squeezed her flesh, eliciting another moan that set his body aflame. Luke pushed her up, leaning back from the pier to give her just enough room to latch onto him. Johanna wrapped her legs around his back, crossing her ankles behind him. She clung to him, just as mindless and demanding as he was.

He couldn't get enough of her. She tasted like dinner—the slight tang of cheese and seafood, hints of parsley, garlic, and basil mixing with the sweetness of the strawberry daiquiri she'd tried. She was decadent. It was too much, but it was not enough.

Cupping her ass, Luke moved, and when he found the back of a nearby building, he slammed his sunflower against the metal structure. Johanna tugged on his shirt, trying to pull him closer as if she wanted to climb inside his skin.

Luke hid them with his shadow magic, knowing he'd kill anyone who interrupted them. If the world were ending right now, the chaos would have to wait until he was done with her, if he would *ever* be done with her.

He gripped the outside of her thigh, adjusting her against his body, then he pushed up, tilted his hips, and ground against her core. The sensation was overwhelming even with the barrier of clothes between them, and they both moaned into each other's mouths. Luke did it again and again, showing her all the ways he wished he could be inside her, how he *would* be inside her.

His lips broke away from hers for a torturous second before they found her chin, her jaw, her throat. She tasted divine. He felt her swallow, and the predator in him roared as she tilted her head back against the metal structure and offered him her neck. He almost bit her right then and there, but instead he brushed the back of his hand over her chest, felt the goosebumps that broke out over her skin, and smirked against her collarbone. Then he yanked the tank top and the bra she wore underneath until her breasts popped free. He reveled in how they overflowed from his palms as he licked a path up her neck to her ear.

"Look at you," he purred.

His fingers pulled and squeezed her hard nipples, and she arched her back, pushing more into his hands as she moaned.

"So beautiful, so perfect," he said, his breathing ragged as he devoured her with his gaze. "You would let me do anything I wanted to you."

"Yes," she hissed, tightening her grip on his hair.

"Even out here in the public?" He kissed down to her chest. "Are you into exhibitionism, sunflower?"

"No, I..." She moaned as he kissed her breast softly, slowly. "It's y-you, Luke!"

He looked up at her as his mouth closed around her nipple and he sucked hard. She squeezed his shoulders and wrapped her arms around him as he took more of her breast into his mouth. He bathed her skin with his tongue, marveling at her taste while his fingers trailed lower, down to her jeans. Luke undid their closure. He paused for a moment, breathing in the scent of her desire, and then he slid his fingers under her underwear, running a digit through the slit of her lips.

She gasped, and when he slid two fingers inside of her wet heat, she covered her mouth to muffle her cry.

Luke let go of her nipple and stared into her eyes. They were so dark, so dilated, that they appeared to be jet black, and he was sure they matched his own.

"No one can see you," he said, sliding his fingers out until the tips brushed her entrance. "No one can hear you." He thrust them inside of her again as he ripped her hand away from her lips. "I will *never* let anyone hear you like this. Every sound you make is *mine*. They, just like you, belong to *me*."

She bit her lip and he thrust his fingers harder until she cried out.

"Good girl," he murmured. "That's my good girl."

Luke circled her clit with his thumb, and her whole body shuddered. Her breath caught and she rocked her hips against his hand. He was blown away by the sight. "That's it, baby, take your pleasure. Show me what you want."

Her hands fisted his shirt as she tried to speak around the moans he tore from her. "I-*Fuck,* I want you, please. I want *you!*"

Luke groaned. "I love the sound of you begging." He brought his lips down to the breast he had yet to taste, making her moan another curse. He licked her nipple and used the opportunity to speak while he continued to thumb her clit. "But you don't need to do that. You have me, sunflower. What more could you want?"

He bit her nipple and Johanna cried out. Her legs tightened around him, thighs flexing as they shook, even as she fought off her orgasm and tried to shove off his leather jacket. When he refused to let her, she huffed, so he curled his fingers, making her cry out once more, "You! I want you! Inside me! Luke, *please!*"

Luke moaned. She was driving him crazy. With a *pop* he released the nipple he was sucking. He could feel his pre-cum leak from his cock as she writhed against him, his fingers pounding in and out of her wet heat. "You want me to fuck you, Johanna? You want me to take you, to fill you with my come?"

"Yes! Yes! Please!" she begged. Her fingers inched lower, and Luke knew he'd be lost if she got anywhere near his dick.

He grabbed both of her wrists with one hand and pinned them above her head. The position made her arch her back slightly, and her eyes opened wide at the change, but he didn't give her a moment to adjust. Instead he moved his fingers faster and increased the pressure on her clit until she was shaking.

"Oh, sunflower, I have dreamed nearly every damn day of fucking you. But I'm not going to right now."

"Why?" The word left her mouth as half a plea and half a demand.

Luke curled his fingers again and witnessed her orgasm for the first time. Johanna squeezed her eyes shut as her mouth fell open and she cried out for him. Her legs tightened around his body like he was the only thing keeping her on this planet, while her pussy spasmed around his fingers, gripping them for dear life as if it could somehow take them deeper.

He groaned, his eyes rolling back in his head as he imagined how fucking good it would feel to be inside that hungry little thing, how it would feel to own her, to drown in her wetness and taste every inch of her skin. Luke was famished for her. She was his every wish, every fantasy, every desire, and as Johanna came down from her high, he withdrew his fingers and sucked them clean. He moaned at the taste of her. Saliva pooled in his mouth at the thought of more before she broke him from his train of thought.

"Why?" she asked again, her voice softer, breathless.

Luke ran his fingers up and down the inside of her thighs, wishing he could rip her pants off and enjoy her fully. Her breath hitched as he drew a digit over her flesh, teasing from her pussy up to her clit and back down. She shuddered, and when he slowly slid it inside of her, she let out a hum of pleasure.

"When I fuck you, sunflower, I will take everything from you." He slid his thumb up and down her clit, rubbing the nub as she gasped. "I will take every noise you make, every look you give me, every breath you breathe, every sensation of your skin, every emotion you have, every thought, your blood, even your very soul. I will take *all* that you are in the same way you have consumed *everything* that I am."

He slid two fingers into her, drawing another moan from her lips. "And even after I've taken all of you, I won't stop. I won't stop until we're so tied together that I'm in your veins, Johanna, until you couldn't get me out of you if you tried."

"Luke!" she moaned.

He kissed her until her lips were red, even with his healing magic. He sucked, and nipped, and teased them until they parted, and then he explored her mouth with his tongue, drinking in her taste while he fucked her with his fingers. Luke showed her exactly how he would be with her, and even when Johanna came, he didn't stop rubbing his tongue against hers, nor pressing, rubbing, even pinching her clit, not until she came once more. Only then did this hunger for her begin to calm.

CHAPTER 15

One week. That's how much time had passed since what Johanna now called 'The Incident' at the beach. She still couldn't formulate what happened into proper words. She never expected Luke to tell her that he loved her, nor to let things get so out of hand. His lips, his touch, being pressed up against him the way she had been, had all felt so incredible, but she never would have expected what came after that glorious experience.

Nothing.

Absolutely nothing.

Luke hadn't touched her, at least not in the way she desired to be touched. Sure, he rubbed her back, passed his fingers through her hair, and they still cuddled when they fell asleep, but that was it. Nothing else. He hadn't touched her intimately. He hadn't kissed her either, and it was driving her mad. It felt like they were constantly playing a game where one of them stood in the middle and the other circled them. Round and round they'd go, getting closer and closer until eventually they switched spots, then the cycle would start all over again. They never seemed to be in the same space. Instead, they were constantly teasing, thinking, or working around one another without being on the same page.

It was *infuriating.*

Johanna understood there were several reasons for this. After all, she was still healing from everything. Even she could see how Luke constantly put her care first, so it made her wonder what it was that he saw in her that made him hold back, and how did she make it stop?

She'd tried to figure it out for the first couple of days, to no avail. Then she thought about what he'd demanded if he was going to fuck her. Every time she thought of those words, her blood turned molten, liquid pooled in her belly, and she could barely breathe, much less speak. But she remembered them, every single word, and she'd give it all to Luke, give him everything he wanted ... but he wouldn't take it.

No matter what she did or how many times she told him she was his, he didn't seem to believe she meant it. Running out of options, she finally decided to ask Dani for advice. According to her, both of them were incredibly dense, stubborn, and really two peas in the same pod. It was an annoying observation, but one that Johanna did have to agree with—if only slightly.

Johanna had gotten better at voicing what she wanted, at believing she was allowed to want things and to demand nothing less. Yet, until Luke had admitted his feelings for her, she didn't fully believe it could be possible for someone to love her in the way she'd always craved. It made sense that perhaps Luke felt something of that too. Dani even thought that Luke still blamed himself for what had happened to Johanna and couldn't believe her feelings because he didn't think he was worthy of them. That, more than anything else, had spurred her into action, which was the exact reason why Johanna had pushed herself out of her comfort zone and was now lying naked under the covers, waiting for her mate.

An hour had passed by the time Luke's body crossed the threshold into their room. It was a new game he'd started to play with her—waiting until she'd fallen asleep to join her in bed. That was something else Johanna would fix ... later.

She watched as Luke opened a drawer and grabbed a pair of black pants to sleep in.

"What are you still doing up?" he asked as he shut the drawer and turned to face her.

"I was waiting for you."

Luke moved toward her, causing her heartbeat to quicken. Leaning down, he kissed her forehead and then took a deep breath. When his lips parted, she wished they were on her skin again, somewhere lower.

"You didn't have to wait up for me."

"I know, but I wanted to." The beat in her heart fluttered as she admitted, "I missed you."

He sighed, brushing his fingers through her hair at her temple. "I've missed you too. I'll be right there, okay?"

Johanna nodded, turned on her side and watched him disappear into the bathroom. It seemed as if he were gone for an eternity, each second stretching her nerves. When he appeared again, he shut off the light, settling the room into complete darkness. Then he slipped under the covers.

She knew the exact moment he realized she was naked. Luke's breath hitched in his throat, and her heart was beating so fast she thought she might have a stroke.

"You're..."

"Yes," she whispered.

Luke didn't move closer or further away from her. Johanna turned her head to meet his gaze, and even though she couldn't see it in the dark, she could feel it. He was completely focused on her, the intensity of his stare like a tangible force.

When he spoke next, his voice was strained, and a little part of her reveled in it. "Why?"

"Because..." She swallowed hard and tried again. "I want to be your mate, Luke. Make me your mate."

The sheets ruffled behind her, but she didn't move, barely breathed, so scared that something would snap them both out of this moment. Then his chest pressed against her back as he spooned her. She was so relieved that a soft sigh left her lips, but Luke's fingers suddenly slid under her chin, making her tilt her head to meet his eyes. Once her eyes adjusted to the darkness, she saw the fire raging in his.

Luke's mouth moved, but no words came out. His lips parted as he ran his tongue across them and she followed the movement, hyper aware of every little thing he did. Johanna committed to memory every breath he took, the warmth of his body behind her, the feel of the hairs on his arm as they tickled her neck and throat. She wanted it all, because she couldn't stand not having a single piece of him any longer.

Finally he spoke, his voice gravely and low. "Sunflower, are you sure? I need to hear it. I need to know—"

"Yes. *Yes,*" she said again, hoping he believed her. Tilting slightly, she cupped his cheek, trying to communicate by touch everything she wished she knew how to say.

He groaned, released a harsh breath, and whispered, "Remember, you asked for this."

Then his lips crushed against hers.

Luke's kisses were all-consuming. He enraptured all her senses and threw her off balance by his gravitational pull, and she loved it. She loved him.

His fingers slid down her throat as he deepened his kiss. Luke moved slowly, deliberately, owning her flesh. His hand cupped her neck, fingers at the sides as he squeezed, choking her. Johanna moaned deep in her throat. Wet heat flooded her core and she squeezed her thighs to ease the ache. She was so sensitive to his touch, so filled with longing that if she wasn't careful, she wouldn't last.

Unconsciously, Johanna rocked her hips back against Luke's, searching for the pleasure only he could provide, and he moaned. He pushed against her, pressing the outline of his erection against her ass as they moaned together. Luke's hand squeezed around her throat again, wringing another moan from her, and she felt like putty in his hands. She was so crazy for him and he hadn't even touched her yet.

Johanna tilted her head back against the pillow, lining her lips with Luke's to deepen the kiss. He groaned as she licked the seam of his lips, and then he opened for her, his tongue pushing into her mouth, licking, flicking, and teasing her own. She buried her hand in his hair to keep his mouth fused with hers. Her other hand was trapped under her body by him, as if he knew how much she ached to touch him.

Luke brushed the back of his fingers from her shoulder down her chest, so slowly it was as if he was completely unaffected in their passionate dance, as if he had all the time in the world. But his rapid breathing and the pounding of his heart against her back told her the truth: he needed this just as much as she did.

Johanna pulled back from him, taking in his face, the soft glow starting in his eyes as she whispered, "Please."

He looked down at her as if he worshipped the ground she walked on, as if her saying the simple word was somehow the most treasured gift she'd ever given him. Then he said, "I've got you, sunflower. I'll give you anything you want."

She shook her head. "Take," she urged, her breath catching in her lungs as he kissed her ear, traced its pathways with his tongue. "Take what you wanted from me."

She felt him smile against her flesh, then his hand grasped her breast, cupping and squeezing it while he ground into her ass. His other hand groped her stomach as he whispered into her ear, "What do you want me to take, sunflower?"

She moaned, arching and pressing into his body, searching more for his touch. "Everything."

"That's so broad, my love." He kissed her neck, and she could feel the sharp points of his teeth press against her skin as the hand on her stomach slid lower. "Tell me what you want me to take," he whispered, trailing a path from her neck to her shoulder. He moaned, as if the simple taste of her gave him pleasure. "Tell me what's mine."

Johanna squeezed the hand that cupped her breast. "My body," she breathed, and he rewarded her with another squeeze. Then he rolled her nipple with his thumb before pinching the small bud, making her cry out.

"Yes," he moaned. "What else?"

"My heart." It was beating so hard for him, and as his fingers walked along her skin, sliding lower, closer to the place she needed him most, she thought she would lose her mind.

"What else?" he growled, biting her shoulder, grinding harder into her body.

She gasped as his finger finally reached her clit, sliding up and down the bud. "Breath."

"Yes."

She moaned. "Sounds."

"Yes." He circled her clit, tearing another whimper from her lips.

Her head fell back against his shoulder as every nerve ending in her body came alive. "My mind, my soul."

"Yes," he hissed, increasing the pressure on her clit, drawing a tortured cry from her.

"My blood."

He squeezed her breast hard, pinching her nipple, causing her to cry out at the delicious mix of pain and pleasure.

"Good girl," he whispered, rubbing her faster. He was working her closer to an orgasm, an explosion that would send her flying off this planet to the moon in bliss, but she didn't want to go there alone.

Johanna reached behind her with her free hand. She pulled at his pants, pleased that he let her. She was even more pleased when she found his dick free, readily thrusting into her hand. She grasped it, pumped, and he moaned a curse that made her smile.

The speed of his fingers increased and she moaned his name. Johanna spread her thighs. She needed him inside of her *right* now. He grasped the inside of her thigh and moved until his dick was against the lips of her pussy. Then he pushed her thigh down, trapping his cock there, and thrust. Her thighs were soaked in her wetness, making him glide easily. Luke did it again and again. Johanna pushed her hips back, clenching around him and he moaned louder. His fingers pinched her clit, causing her to cry out as more of her wetness pooled between her thighs.

Johanna slid her hand down and rubbed the head of his cock in sync with his thrusts, making him go faster, wilder. Her body jerked against his. She loved the feel of him, loved the thickness between her legs, but she wanted him inside her, and nothing, not even this, not even his fingers on her clit, his lips on her own, or the way he stroked and squeezed her skin would fill that ache. It was a craving. He was the drug, and this was her new addiction, and she wouldn't stop until she got what she wanted, what they *both* wanted.

Luke was close. She could tell in the way he moved, how he squeezed her hips and pushed her closer to her own orgasm, but she refused to have him come anywhere but inside of her. She *needed* it in a way she couldn't express. The next time his hips jerked back, she grasped his dick, and when he pushed forward, she tilted just enough to get the head of his cock inside of her.

Even though she wanted this, even though she wouldn't go back on this decision, for a split second she wondered what Luke would think of her. But then he was pushing inside of her and every thought, worry, and concern melted from her mind. There was just him, just this.

He pushed, and pushed, and pushed until she curled her fingers in the sheets, holding on for dear life.

"Luke!" she cried.

"I know baby, I know." He groaned, pushing deeper. "You're taking it so well, sunflower."

She moaned his name again, throwing her head back as her pussy throbbed around him.

"There's my good girl. Look at you taking me so deep." He

bit her ear and a shudder passed between them. "So good, so perfect," he moaned. "Made for me."

"Yes!"

And then he was seated in her fully. She had never felt so utterly filled and stretched by anything in her whole life. Luke pulled out to the tip before he rammed back inside, making her scream his name. It was one thrust, just one, before she was suddenly in the air. Then her back was against his chest and she was on top of him.

There was the sound of clothing ripping, and when he spread his legs, now free from the constraints of his pants, he used his knees to spread hers too.

"Luke?" she said breathlessly.

"I wanted to be gentle," he began, "but I can't do that now."

He eased her back down on his cock, spearing her, the position forced her to take him in a whole new way. When he thrust into her to the hilt, she knew she was done for. He gripped her hips and rammed into her, over and over. She shook, spasming against his body, but he kept going. He rested his hand on her stomach and pushed lightly on her belly. A new sensation filled her as she cried out, arching her back, both wanting to escape the pleasure and take more of it at the same time. He wouldn't let her go, she knew that now like she knew the back of her hand. Luke would *never* let her go, never let her get away from him. This was what it meant for him to take her, and she would give everything for him to never stop.

Each thrust was a new shock to her system. Luke rubbed her clit, making her soar to new heights of pleasure. She cried for him, screamed, tears gathering in her eyes, but he kept fucking her in a dirty, thorough claiming of her skin. Her head fell back, and when she linked herself with Luke's thoughts she moaned loudly, knowing he was just as lost as she was. Then she tilted her head to offer him the last thing she could.

His fangs pierced her skin. The mixture of pain and pleasure as he drank her blood made her release a full body scream that started from her toes and coasted up her body at the speed of a freight train before her cries filled the room and she came. She came so hard she saw stars behind her eyes, and then Luke followed her and she cried out again in joy that finally, *finally* they were one.

LUKE COULDN'T HELP THE SMILE THAT GHOSTED HIS LIPS AS Johanna lay on top of him. Her sweat was mixed with his, her blood flowing through his system. He was still inside of her, and even with all of that, he was still hungry for her. No matter how many times he had her, it would never be enough. But now that he knew he *could* have her, he was willing to try to take his fill.

Her heartbeat was rapidly thumping against his body as he lifted her. He eased out of her slowly, gently, but she was so sensitive she moaned, and the sound went straight to his cock. It twitched for her, already standing at attention to nestle itself back inside her, but Luke had other plans.

He laid Johanna down beside him, and then he rolled on top of her. Her eyes fluttered open to stare up at him. He enjoyed watching the wheels in her head turn as she took in his smirk. He knew the moment the realization hit her because her eyes widened. She cast her gaze down his body, her breath hitching as she saw his erection.

"How?" she asked, and he chuckled at the question as if her

pussy hadn't just grown wet at the thought of him inside her again.

"Did you really think once would be enough for me?" He hummed as he nestled between her thighs, making her spread her legs wider for him.

"No," she said, breathless. Then she moaned as his cock slid between her folds. "But so soon?"

"Yes, so soon," he chuckled, the sound cutting into a moan as he slid the tip of his cock between her lips again. "Have you seen yourself? I get an erection every time you walk into a room. It's created a lot of uncomfortable situations."

She laughed, the husky sound traveling over his body.

"And that too," he said, nipping her neck and making her purr.

"My laugh?" Johanna wrapped her arms around his back. She tried to pull him to her, and he chuckled, laving the crook of her neck with his tongue as he settled his weight fully on top of her. The sigh of contentment she gave him made a low growl rumble in his throat.

"Yes. I've wanted you for so long."

Luke pushed up slightly, his fingertips running through her hair as it fanned around her head. He met her eyes, and another course of satisfaction ran through him as she leveled her gaze at him. She could see in the dark now, better than a normal human. It was a small reminder of what they'd just shared, that she was now immortal, their bond consummated.

"I'm going to spend days inside of your pussy," he whispered gravelly.

"Impossible."

He smiled, accepting her words as a challenge as he kissed down her neck. "Definitely possible and going to happen."

"Luke," she moaned, tilting her head back even as she tried to argue with him. "That is *not* possible." Her breath hitched as he sucked on the base of her throat. "I'll need to eat, and so will you."

"Absolutely," he murmured on her skin as he bit her chest, earning another moan from her. "You'll eat, and I'll eat you. Problem solved."

"Luke—"

"Stop arguing with me."

He cupped her breasts, pinching her hard nipples. Then he ran his tongue between her breasts, along the underside of one mound, and then over her nipple. "It makes me want to ram inside of you and fuck you until the only thing you can do with your mouth is yell my name."

"Oh fuck," she gasped and arched her back.

"Much better."

He sucked one nipple into his mouth, teasing the other with his fingers. He ran his free hand over her stomach, squeezing her flesh and making her moan. A pretty, little blush ran over her skin, but he didn't have to ask why.

"You're beautiful, just like this. Exquisite. I've spent a lot of my life looking at beautiful things, but you? All of them combined could never amount to your beauty." He squeezed and cupped the flesh of her stomach with both of her hands and met her gaze. "This world is stupid."

Luke's fingers reached down to her pussy, no, *his* pussy, and stroked her folds. "One hundred years ago women would have died to look like you. This was healthy." He rubbed over her stomach, then her clit. She bucked, so Luke grabbed her hips and continued his ministrations while holding her gaze. "Your body meant that you could eat well, that you could survive a winter, that you could give birth to healthy children. The rules may have changed, but that doesn't mean a single fucking thing to me, and it shouldn't to you."

He rammed two fingers inside of her and shuddered at her wetness, at the feeling of it tangled with his own come.

"You were beautiful," he said.

He thrust his fingers harder, watched her back arch as she threw her head back and cried out.

"You are beautiful."

He moved faster, curled his fingers, and watched as she started to shake.

"You will always be beautiful."

Then he rubbed her clit, and she yelled his name.

"Say it," he demanded.

She whimpered and he moved faster, pulling another cry from her lips.

"Say it," he repeated. "Say it or I'll stop."

"Yes! Yes!" she cried out.

"Yes, *what*?" he growled, adding a third finger and she damn near came off the bed.

"Luke!"

"Say. It." He commanded, pride and satisfaction pumping through his veins as he watched his mate come undone.

"I'm beautiful," she cried. "I'm beautiful!"

"Good girl," he purred. "Now come on my fingers, I have a meal to enjoy."

Her pussy clenched around his fingers. With three more thrusts, she came, gripping the sheets and crying out in her pleasure. The sound undid him. It unlocked something in his soul that turned him ravenous, and instead of letting her catch her breath, his mouth claimed her core. He kept rubbing her clit in circles, felt the shivers in her spine as she tried to come down from her high, but he wouldn't let her. He pulled his fingers to the tips of her lips, spreading her, and before she could formulate a question he licked between her folds.

She mewed. Her back arched again as he started his feast, keeping his tongue flat as he slid up and down her pussy lips, tasting them both. She was fucking delicious, like cherries and sugared peaches, and it made him lose all control. He spread her legs further, lifted them over his shoulders and grasped her hips, then he slid his tongue inside of her. She jerked underneath him, and her cries filled the air as he ate her like a starved man.

Luke wasn't satisfied when she came on his lips for the third time in a row, nor when he sucked her clit, slid his fingers back inside of her, and then pierced the flesh of her thigh to drink her blood. Nothing filled him or satisfied his hunger until he knelt between her legs, lined his cock up with her entrance, and thrust home. Only then did he feel complete. Everything before was just the appetizer, but this, here, being inside of his mate where he could take her over and over again was the only thing that sated the beast within him. Here, with his mate's arms around him, her heart beating just as fast as his own, her pussy milking his cock, he felt whole.

Words bubbled out of his throat, things he'd longed to say to her. "Marry me," he moaned against her neck as he thrust harder inside of her.

"Yes!" she shouted without even a moment's hesitation, and it only served to heighten his own pleasure.

He moaned her name. His hands gripped her thighs, spreading and raising them higher as he fit himself deeper inside of her, wishing he could become one with her. "Baby, I'm going to fill you."

Her nails dug into her skin as she moaned, as she fucking begged for it. *"Please!"*

Luke groaned. He didn't stop until he was so deep he was pushing against her cervix. His hand fell to her stomach as he said again, "I'm going to fill you up. I'm going to breed you. I want you pregnant with my child. I want you ... I want *everything* with you."

"Yes!" she moaned, and nodded as if she was trying to make him understand. "Yes, Luke!" She gasped as he hit a new spot in her that had her quivering underneath him, so he did it again. "Luke, yes! Everything. I w-want everything. Oh God! I love you!"

Her confession spurred him. Luke was going so hard, so deep, losing himself so thoroughly in her that he didn't trust himself not to break her. He took her hands and pinned them to the headboard with his own as he kept moving inside her. In time with his thrusts, the headboard slammed against the wall so hard that it creaked. Then the wood splintered and part of the bed broke, tilting them to the side.

He kept going, and the new position drove Johanna fucking wild. Her eyes rolled back in her head, and he was lost, just like her. His fangs broke into the skin of her neck as he drank her blood. It flowed into his mouth, the taste like ambrosia, and when she came around him he swore he'd been blessed. The walls of her pussy tightened around his cock, dragging him under, and he roared out his release. Streams of come shot into her and he kept thrusting, his movements jerky and uneven but enough to draw another orgasm out of his mate. The feeling had him emptying his balls inside of her until he collapsed, broken apart like a shattered vase and put back together with her as the glue.

And just like that, he knew he would never be the same, and he never wanted to be again. Life before her had been a lie. Now there was only Johanna—his sunflower, his stars, his moon, the center of his universe—and the future they would make together, a future that he would spend the rest of his long days cherishing just as much as he cherished her.

CHAPTER 16

Luke hugged Johanna to his side and the smile she gave him blew his heart apart. The venue Dani and Greg had picked for their engagement party was beautiful, as was the love that was so clearly shared between not only the two of them, but everyone in attendance.

But none of it held a candle to his mate.

She looked gorgeous in her black halter top gown that had quickly become his favorite, due to the slit that ran up to her thigh. The opening gave him easy access—which he'd already taken advantage of before they left the house—and based on the way Johanna was looking at him, he'd be taking advantage of it again before they got home.

They approached Dani and Greg and exchanged hugs with them.

"Congratulations, you two!" Johanna said, nodding to Dani's slightly rounded belly and the diamond glittering on her finger.

Dani looked from her to Luke and smirked. "I'd say congratulations are in store for the two of you too. It's about damn time."

"Dani!" Johanna said with a laugh.

Luke wrapped his arm around her waist and pulled Johanna to his side. "Don't bother, love. She gets a kick out of this."

"Of course I do, especially when I'm right," Dani said and they all shared a laugh.

Luke bent down to Dani's stomach and gently patted her belly. "How's my niece or nephew?"

"Keeping the both of us up all night," Dani said, curling into Greg's side.

"Already?" Johanna asked.

"Well, our little one is already telling me what they prefer to eat, and if I try anything else I have a horrible case of nausea."

Luke frowned. "Is our healing magic not working?"

Greg shook his head. "I think it's because Ella's human, and since we're still in the first trimester it's too early to change her into a vampire."

Luke coughed into his hand to keep from laughing at the look Dani gave Greg when he said 'we,' as if he was also carrying the baby. But then it cleared, and Dani smoothed Greg's furrowed brows. "You worry too much."

They shared a look which Johanna caught. "Is everything okay?" she asked.

Dani and Greg shared another look and then they both stared at Luke. He understood immediately: Zachariah.

Johanna shifted by his side, drawing his gaze. "Go ahead and talk, I'll just—"

"No," Luke said.

"Stay, really," said Dani.

"We just don't want to make you uncomfortable," Greg added.

Johanna lips turned upward, but the action didn't match her blank eyes.

"I want you to stay, but only if talking about this won't hurt you," Luke said to her telepathically as he squeezed her hip.

She nodded to him. "I'll be fine. Please, go ahead."

Dani sighed. "We still haven't found him."

Greg ran his fingers through her hair. "And he's been entirely too quiet for my liking."

"How many of the coordinates have you been able to visit?" Johanna asked.

"Almost all of them. At first, we'd at least find some of his people," Dani said.

"But lately the locations have either been vacant or full of traps." Greg's tone softened as he addressed Johanna. "I think he knows that you're with us, and we're concerned he's just biding his time. Ella and I actually discussed canceling this event."

"I'm happy you didn't. You both deserve this. He shouldn't get to ruin it," Johanna said, her voice so stern that Luke knew she wasn't just talking about what Greg and Dani deserved, but what she deserved as well.

"Johanna's right," Luke said. "This is a celebratory event, and an important one. We all need tonight." He patted Greg's shoulder. "I'm happy you didn't cancel."

Greg nodded, yet the frown on his face didn't disappear.

"I..." Johanna began, then she rolled her shoulders back and met their eyes. "I'm sorry I still can't remember anything. I can't be of more help in that regard, but I can at least help you to ease your mind now if you're concerned about security."

Greg's eyebrows rose. "Really? How?"

"A psychic net. I can connect to each person's mind here and create a net. If someone sees any type of suspicious activity, it's immediately reported back to all of us at the same time. That way we can make sure Dani and the baby are safe while also investigating the issue," Johanna explained.

Luke rubbed her hip. "Doesn't that use a lot of magic?"

Johanna shook her head. "No, it's rudimentary for me. It's more of a dormant thing that will only be activated when the criteria is met."

Dani squeezed her hand. "That would be amazing. Thank you, Jo."

Johanna looked pleased with herself, but Luke still wasn't sure. He leaned down and dropped a kiss on her temple while he spoke to her again telepathically.

"If you push it, sunflower, I will take you into the nearest room and spank that gorgeous ass of yours. This is your only warning."

She blushed before replying, *"That isn't much of a warning when you were already planning on getting me alone."*

He smirked into her hair. *"Keep being a cheeky brat and I'll make sure everyone at this party hears you scream when I fuck you."*

Her blush darkened. *"Shut up! I can't concentrate when you do that."*

Luke chuckled but did as she said. He held her closer while he felt the pressure of her magic. It flitted, dancing around them like a ballerina for several seconds. Then the pressure eased to something of a tingle at the back of his mind, and he knew that was her net.

A few moments later Johanna's face lit up in delight. "There, it's done. It isn't much, but hopefully it will be enough to help the two of you have a good time tonight."

Dani and Johanna shared a hug. "Thank you so much."

"Of course!" Johanna smiled.

Luke wrapped his arm around her shoulder. "Now if you excuse us, I need to have a word with my mate."

Johanna's eyes widened and she blushed again, making Dani and Greg laugh before Luke led her away and made good on his promise.

"Luke!" Johanna yelled, laughing as he closed the door to their house behind them. "Put me down!"

He smacked her ass, making her yelp. He did it again, then squeezed and caressed her flesh. The sting coupled with his touch made her moan. She tried to shift off his shoulder once more, but he held her steady.

"What was it you were saying, sunflower?" Luke stepped into the kitchen, "Ah, that's right. Something about putting you down." He jumped, making her stomach free fall as she screamed from the movement, then he set her onto the counter.

"Luke!" She laughed, bracing his shoulders. "Would you stop tossing me around like a rag doll?"

"It's about time you get used to it, sunflower. Now open up and feed me that pussy, baby." He tapped her knees. "I'm hungry."

A shudder ran through her. There was nothing she could do but obey him when he spoke to her like that. She spread her legs wide to accommodate him. Luke cupped the back of her knees and pulled her to the edge of the counter as he pressed his body against hers.

They attacked each other in an instant. His mouth

descended on hers and she pulled at him, wrapping her legs around his waist, keeping him where she wanted him. A low rumble left his throat as he pressed his hips into hers and ground against her already wet core.

Johanna moaned into his mouth and shoved his jacket off him, elated that she was one step closer to having his flesh against hers, but frantic and needy to have more.

Luke broke the kiss. He licked and nipped down her neck, sucking on her skin as his hands roamed up her back. "I like this dress on you," he said in a gravely whisper, "but if you don't tell me how to get it off, I'll rip it to shreds."

"Neanderthal," she gasped.

Luke aligned his erection, pressing hard against her core as he rocked their hips. "Five seconds," he warned.

"It's on the side!"

Luke hiked her dress up and she lifted her hips, jerking against him as her bare bottom hit the cold counter.

"Good girl," he growled, and her thighs clenched around him.

Luke found the closure and opened it, helping Johanna to pull the material over her head. He paused as she sat nearly naked on the counter, the same glorious, adoring gaze filling his eyes. He took her in, looking over every bit of her skin as if he were memorizing her body. "I will never get enough of you."

Then he was on her.

Her bra was tossed away and his lips replaced the fabric, licking, sucking, and biting her flesh. She arched into his embrace. Her hands slid down his chest, pulling up at his tucked shirt until it was free. Then she reached for his belt and unbuckled it. Undoing the button underneath, she carefully unzipped his pants around his engorged cock.

He hissed, then yanked her hands away and pinned them behind her. She moaned, jerking and struggling to get free.

Luke raked his teeth over her nipple, causing her to gasp and her toes to curl in her heels. "I need to taste you first."

She pushed her hips against his. "Luke, I need you."

He smiled and stood, reaching his full height. "And you'll have me. But this hungry little thing right here?" He slid his fingers down to her pussy, cupping her lips before he spread them and teased her entrance, drawing a moan from her. "She'll take anything I offer her, won't she?"

She moaned his name and her head fell back.

"Won't she?" He bit her lip, drawing it into his mouth.

"Y-Yes! Yes!"

Luke kissed her but refused to let go of her wrists. Instead, he delved deeper inside of her, his fingers strumming her like a guitar, guiding her like the conductor of an orchestra. He knew all the chords, all the ways to make her reach new highs she didn't know she could. He pursued her, corned her, trapped her, until all she could see, feel, taste, smell, even think of was him. And she let him, and she would let him for the rest of fucking eternity.

She came with his fingers thrusting into her, his taste on her lips, trapped against his body. She came so fucking hard, and then he angled her in a way that she had no choice but to lay back while he made her come over and over again. He licked, sucked, bit, nipped, touched, rubbed, thrust, and fucked her with his fingers so many times she lost count, and she took it all. Johanna kept her legs over his shoulders, tangled her fingers in his hair. She rode him every time he entered her, her hips jerking and moving of their own accord until she reached her completion.

Luke was right; she was hungry for him, and it was a hunger that would never be filled.

Finally he lifted his mouth from her, and her legs fell away. A small smile graced her lips as she knew that soon they would be joined. Johanna was frantic for it, for his cock, for the feeling of having him so deep inside of her that it felt like he was part of her.

He pushed his pants and boxer briefs down, and she sat up to take his length in her hands. Luke groaned, his head falling back as she pumped up and down his shaft. He was hot, like magma in her palms. Johanna was so far gone that when a bead of pre-cum appeared at the tip, she swiped it with her finger and sucked the taste of him into her mouth.

Luke lost control. In one fell swoop he entered her, but it wasn't enough for either of them. His hands found her ass as he pushed and she pulled, wanting the entirety of her body plastered against his. He knew, understood without her even saying a word or sending the thought to him, and in another second she was pressed against the cold refrigerator. The temperature difference sent chills up her body, but she was too crazed by Luke to notice.

His scent was all over her, something warm and spicy, a mixture of mint, oranges, and vanilla. It made the flames between them burn even higher, and every single one of his thrusts had her crying out his name. But still she wanted more, and more, and more. She wanted him inside her in a way no one else could ever be. She wanted to be full of him, constantly, *always.*

"Luke!" she moaned, her heels digging into his ass, her nails pushing into his back.

"I know baby," he moaned. "I know. I feel it too."

She groaned and her eyes fell to his neck. He swallowed and she wanted to taste … to drink.

"Wait!" Johanna said and Luke immediately froze.

Even in his breathless voice, his concern was evident. "Are you okay? Did I hurt you?"

"No." She cleared her throat, trying to regain her voice, her breath. "No, but I … I want…"

She licked her lips. She didn't know where this was coming from. Maybe it was connecting with so many vampires earlier, or the pleasure she felt when Luke drank from her, or maybe it was her desire to be stronger, to protect him. Maybe it was everything, but she needed this so much that she would get on her hands and knees and beg if that's what it took to get his blood inside of her.

"I want to drink your blood."

He shook his head. "What did you say?"

"I want to drink your blood."

Luke swallowed, and even though she didn't feel his hips move, she swore that somehow he grew inside of her. Her pussy tightened around him in response and they both moaned.

"Sunflower," Luke groaned. "You can't do that."

"Please. Please, I-I need it."

Luke cupped her face. "Baby, if you drink my blood like that, you'll become a vampire."

She met his darkened eyes. "I know."

He groaned her name, squeezing his eyes shut as if she were torturing him.

"I know I'll become a vampire. I want to be one."

His arm came to rest on the fridge, followed by his head as he mumbled incoherently.

"Please," she said again.

Luke was quiet for a moment before he whispered. "Why?"

"Because I want to be as strong as you. I want to be able to protect you, and I-I *need* it." She rocked her hips, drawing a moan from both of them.

His lips latched onto her ear as he slowly rolled his hips, thrusting inside of her. "Tell me why you need it, sunflower."

"Because I *crave* you!" She hissed as he bit her ear, the words tumbling out of her. "I need to be full of you, I need to always have you in me. I need you, *please!*"

"Oh fuck," he said moaned as he held her hips and rammed inside of her hard.

She let out a cry, but frustration built in her when he didn't do it again.

"Grab the knife to your right," he said, his lips brushing her skin with every word.

Even in her shock she found herself listening, reaching for the blade, excitement coursing through her veins.

"You'll have to cut me here," he said, tracing the artery of his neck.

"Will it hurt you?"

"No, I'll be fine. But you have to understand that this will change you. You'll be faster, stronger, *hungrier* for years until you learn how to control yourself."

"I understand. Can I now, please?" Johanna asked, scared that he'd change his mind if she asked any more questions.

"Yes, whenever you'd like—Ah!"

And then she was sucking at his skin, drinking his blood. The first gulp was acidic, fatty, but as she gulped down more she began to notice something else, flavors that she shouldn't be able to taste. Then Luke started ramming into her uncontrollably and she couldn't stop. She held him, grasping him to her as close as possible while he made her mindless in her pleasure against the refrigerator.

Johanna lifted her head and cried out as he claimed the very essence of who she was. Her veins felt as though they'd expanded, shooting fire and lightning through her body. She wanted more. Her lips found Luke's neck again and her teeth, now pointed, dug into his skin, ready to feast. She didn't have time for shock or confusion, she was too desperate, too *crazed* for him.

He cried out, bucking inside of her like a wild beast, and she took him and drank from him, her moans muffled against his skin. Luke buckled, sliding down to the floor, then his hand weaved into her hair and he pulled her back. His lips found her neck, teeth sliding in as he fed on her blood. She screamed, writhing, jerking, pushing, and pulling against him as her orgasm coasted through her veins.

And then she *felt* his, felt each trail of come as it shot inside of her, felt the way her pussy spasmed around him in both her pleasure and his. Testing the new sensation, she scratched her nails down his back and felt as if he'd done the same thing to her. Immediately, Luke was hard, and just as quickly he pounded into her, pushing her into the floor with his body. Their linked pleasure was too much, and they came together soon after, and again, and again, and again, losing track of time, their surroundings, everything except one another.

CHAPTER 17

Luke ran his fingers though her hair and they both let out a soft sigh.

Johanna snuggled more into his chest, her fingertips gently stroking his shoulder. "Remind me why you have to go again," she murmured, tickling his skin with her lips.

He chuckled. "Because, my dear, sweet sunflower, you're a vampire now, and The Council likes to keep track of newly turned vampires."

She hummed. "That sounds like something that could be easily taken care of with a phone call."

Luke let out a bark of laughter and held her closer to him. "Is this your way of saying you'll miss me?"

Johanna's lips curved into a smile against his neck before she lifted her head and kissed him sweetly. "No, that's my way of saying I'll miss you." She ran her fingers through his hair, tousling it. "Why do you have to go, really?"

"Greg already petitioned for our mate bond with The Council. By going, I'll be reinforcing that by letting them know that you've been turned, while also taking care of a couple of other things."

She hummed again. "Why did he have to petition for us?"

Luke sighed. "The Council cannot interfere with a mate bond pair, if that's what you're asking. But if a vampire loses their mate, it can be catastrophic for the rest of our species. It's the same for the other immortals. There have been cases of immortals going on killing sprees, abusing their powers, turning people against their will. The loss utterly destroys them, and at that stage they have nothing to lose.

"When Greg goes to petition for a mate bond or mated couple, he agrees to be held responsible for any incidents their mate bond may cause. If one of the mated pair is in danger, Greg will help to get them out. If one of the mated pair dies, Greg will be there to assist and take care of the surviving mate. But if one of the mated pair decided tomorrow to wage war on the world, Greg will be the person who cleans up the mess, and also who The Council will blame."

Johanna gasped. "That's horrible! That shouldn't be completely on him."

Luke nodded. "I agree with you, but unfortunately that's the pressure they put on him. When I go to The Council today, I will re-petition them to share the responsibility of our mate bond and of anything that happens now that you're a vampire."

He kissed her head. "I trust you. You're doing well with your cravings, strength, and speed, but it's just something that must be done. It will also be a way to prove to them that I am taking more responsibility with our circle, like we talked about, and help Greg to not worry as much while Dani is pregnant."

Johanna's hand slid from his shoulder up to the back of his neck as she massaged his skin. "It'll be good for him. And for you too, I think."

He kissed her head. "Yeah, it will be."

LUKE HAD A HUGE SMILE ON HIS FACE AS HE DROVE BACK TO THEIR house. The meeting had gone well. He had believed it would, but as this was his first time implementing himself in The Council's dealings, he had been nervous.

But much like Johanna had suspected, that wasn't the real reason he'd gone. Luke needed to access The Council's archives. According to Johanna, her family had participated in past vampire wars and killed their fair share of them. The Council had files on every war and the participants, whether they won or lost, and Luke wanted to use that to find Johanna's family.

Something in his blood sang when he opened their folder. If that wasn't enough, Johanna had told him she looked the most like her grandmother, and she was right. They had been nearly identical in their twenties.

He only hoped that when he showed his sunflower, it would make her happy. She hadn't spoken about her family in quite some time, but every so often he'd catch a sad expression on her face, as if she were missing something or someone. While Johanna hadn't said anything negative about her family and it was clear she loved them very much, he didn't know them and wasn't sure if he was doing the right thing. Still, Luke reasoned it was only right to at least try. After all, Luke planned to ask them for their blessing to marry Johanna, and he couldn't do that if he never found them.

But as Luke pulled up to his and Johanna's house, his joy faded away. Something was wrong. There was a heavy weight in the air, so stifling that as he exited the garage, he crumpled to the floor.

He realized immediately that it was Johanna. This was the same pressure she had used when she held him down in the cave, only now it was ten times worse, wide and crushing. Luke didn't understand what had happened, but he knew he had to get to her. He had to keep her safe.

He couldn't walk or even crawl to find her, so he dematerialized into shadow. Even then he could still feel her power. He searched for the shadow of other items and used them to propel himself forward and throughout the house until he found her floating above the couch, dangling by her waist as if held by an invisible string.

His senses told him no one had entered the house, nor was there anyone in the surrounding area. So what had triggered her to use her power like this?

Luke blended into Johanna's shadow. He reached for her but was only met with pain. His arm felt as if it had been crushed under a steamroller, but he didn't care or acknowledge the agony he felt. He would heal, but his mate was in danger and nothing would be right in the world again until she was safe.

"Johanna!" he screamed out to her.

The unbearable weight that held him down dissipated, pulled back into Johanna so fast that it created a vacuum effect, knocking objects and tossing pieces of furniture as if they were nothing. Her power hit her like an internal combustion, and she began to fall through the air.

Luke materialized and caught her, cradling her in his arms as he settled her on the couch.

"Johanna?" he called, but she still didn't open her eyes. "Come on, sunflower, don't do this to me again."

Still, no response.

"Baby, *please,*" he begged, cupping her cheek. "Please, I need you."

Her eyelids fluttered and she looked up at him, but it wasn't the stare he was used to. She looked at him like it was the first time she was seeing him, truly seeing him, and he realized then what was different. In her eyes he saw pain, agony, and heartbreak. Darkness roamed there freely, only clearing when a small ray of hope rushed to the surface as she finally focused on him.

"Luke?"

"Baby, I'm right here. I'm *right* here," he said, trying to convince them both that everything was alright, that there was no reason for the sudden, frantic beating of his heart.

Then her eyes watered, and she sobbed. Her arms wrapped around his neck so tight that she would have choked him if he were human. She cried his name over and over, the only word among her screams and heartbreaking wails.

Luke held her to his chest, his heart breaking just as much as hers seemed to be, because it suddenly all made sense. This wasn't because he'd been gone for a few hours. She clung to him as if he'd been gone for days, for months, and there was only one realization that he could come to from her reaction.

She finally remembered everything.

THE NEXT FEW DAYS WERE DIFFICULT FOR THEM. JOHANNA HAD regained her memories, and they had wrecked her. The first day she had allowed him to hold her while she cried. She barely ate unless he forced a cup of blood into her hands, and she wouldn't sleep unless he held her so close that she could barely breathe. Only then did she seem to feel any sort of peace.

The next day she was trying to conquer the world. She asked him to call his family so she could relay the information she had about Zachariah and his inner workings. Johanna never once brought up what happened to her while she had been held captive, but he knew she remembered. She'd closed her mind to him. He felt robbed of their connection, but Luke knew it wasn't for her benefit. It was for his. It was obvious in how she recounted her story, in the pauses, deep breaths, the small shudders and flinches she unconsciously made even while he stood behind her and held her.

His presence didn't seem to be enough to take away the pain she felt. Luke knew it was irrational to hope it would be, but it stung nonetheless. The only thing that counteracted his shattered pride was watching Johanna's perseverance, and he hated that as much as he was honored by it. Even while she was hurting, even while she seemed to be dying inside, she put all of that aside. Her sole purpose was to help them win this war and save as many tortured immortals as she could.

Her information was invaluable. Johanna explained that Zachariah was a pseudo-leader, nothing more than a puppet. The real leader was a woman who went by the name of

Constance. Johanna didn't believe she was a vampire, although she did seem to have some vampiric abilities. Instead, her real talent was the magic to possess someone. That was the magic Johanna had been under for six months.

Johanna was kidnapped by Zachariah after visiting her grandmother in the hospital. He moved her to another location and forced her to drink a bowl of Constance's blood, which contained trace levels of magic. After that, she was no longer herself. Everything she said and did was under Constance's command. Constance and Zachariah planned to use her to gain information on Greg and the inner workings of The Novak Firm and their circle.

Because Johanna's abilities dealt with the mind, she was able to block part of herself away. Whenever Constance or Zachariah asked her to report back to them, Johanna told them she wasn't high enough in the company to learn anything. During that time she had tried to get help, and for that they killed her grandmother. They would have killed her too, but in her rage Johanna came out of her possession and used her abilities on Zachariah. That was how he found out she could control another's mind, and after he and his allies subdued her, he began to feed on her and use her as his aid.

She also told them that she knew Erik. In fact, he had been her friend and had helped to keep her sane while she was stuck in that hellhole. Then she delivered the final blow: If they had gone fifty feet further down the same passage in the caves where they'd found the women, they would have found him too.

That broke Mya, but Johanna quickly assured them that he was still alive. Erik was the reason Constance and Zachariah had enhanced healing abilities. Constance needed him as she routinely siphoned his blood to try to enhance the strength of the rest of the vampires that served her. As far as Johanna knew, her attempts had failed, but Constance could have succeeded in the time Johanna had been with Luke.

The information Johanna had given was beyond beneficial but had also left everyone drained. Everyone but her. The moment Dani, Greg, and Mya left, Johanna set to work. She grabbed the paperwork containing her coordinates and tore them apart. Luke tried to get her to rest, but she explained that she knew of a few more locations and she wanted to make sure she noted them down. She believed that while Zachariah may have abandoned some of the places they'd raided, these were his acting home bases and he wouldn't leave them willingly.

Luke sighed and agreed with her, but he'd noticed a pattern. Every time he came to check on her, she did a double take when she saw him, as if she expected someone else. If he stood in the doorway and called her name, she almost jumped out of her skin. Each time she told him she was fine, and each time he suggested she rest and come back to her work tomorrow, she shook her head and ignored him.

Finally, Luke had had enough. He approached her, saying her name as softly as he could, but it had the same effect. He couldn't take it anymore.

"Sunflower, you've done enough now. Why don't you—"

"No," she said, not looking up from the papers strewn around her. "I'm not done yet."

"Baby, you've been at this for hours."

"It's fine. I'm fine. Just let me finish."

"Johanna—"

She whirled around to face him. "No!"

Luke took a step toward her, his arms held out to take her in his embrace, but she flinched.

He froze entirely. Slowly her face changed from one of fear to horror. His throat felt like sandpaper as the realization fell from his lips. "Are you scared of me? Do you see *him* when you look at me?"

"No!"

Luke took a step back.

"No! No, *please*," Johanna said again. She reached for him, her fingers grasping onto his shirt. The warmth of her body seeped into his, but he didn't know how to react, how to move, or if moving at all would frighten her more.

"Luke, I swear I don't see him. I don't see him when I look at you."

She was manic now, shaking her head, and when he finally closed his arms around her, he felt the visceral shudder through her system. Then she began to tremble.

"I'm not scared of you," she said, her eyes swimming in tears. "I'm scared *for* you."

"Sunflower," he began, but the single tear that rolled down her cheek made him pause. Hesitantly, he cupped her face, and she choked back a sob as he wiped the tear away.

"He threatened you every day," she whispered. "Every single day. Every time I thought about running away, every time I thought about trying to get help. I even..." She paused, biting her lip hard, as if that pain was better than the one pouring out of her and into him. "I threatened to kill myself if he went after you."

Luke gasped. He could never imagine a world without her in it, and that she was willing to kill herself for *him* ... He shook his head, speechless.

"He told me that if I did that, he'd kill you. I don't doubt you, Luke. I swear I don't. But…" She looked away from him for a moment so he rubbed her cheeks, bringing her gaze back to his. "I know what he did to me. I know everything he did to me. I don't want, no, I can't *stand* the idea of him ever doing that to you. I need to find him."

Johanna reached back, extracting herself from his arms to gather the papers in her hands. She shook as she held them, presenting them to him as if they were the secret key she had spent her life searching for. "If I can find him, if I can kill him, he can't hurt you. I just need to figure this out."

She slammed the papers back on the table and stormed back to him. He met her halfway, pulling her into his arms with an angry sigh.

"I can do this," Johanna said as she rested her head over his chest. "I have to do this for you, for Mya and Erik, for whoever else he's holding captive right now. I can do this. I *have* to do this."

Luke held her as he tried to steady the rage building within him. Johanna didn't need his rage. She needed his empathy, and he would give her all that he was.

"Do you love me?" he asked her.

She clutched onto his back, pressing her body into his as if she could swallow him whole, as if she could merge their bodies in some way. "More than life itself."

"And I love you just as much. Tell me, sunflower, if I was the one going through all of this, what would you say to me? What would you want me to do?"

Her head snapped up as her wide eyes met his, and he knew he had her. Johanna struggled doing things for herself, Luke knew that, but he realized that if he made himself the example then her love, her need to protect him, would outweigh anything else and she wouldn't be able to argue. Instead, she would be forced to see reason.

Johanna tilted her head down and away from his, but he gently grasped her chin and made her meet his eyes. "Tell me."

"I'd..."

"You'd make me rest. You'd take care of me, support me, do anything and give me anything I needed to renew my strength." Luke ran his fingers over her skin. "You'd wipe away all my fears and fight all of my battles with a smile on your face, wouldn't you, my sweet sunflower?"

"Y-Yes," she hiccuped, fighting back tears.

"Then let me do this for you. You are my love, my everything. What hurts you, hurts me. What frightens you, frightens me. If there is something you want to fight or kill, *I* will be your weapon and your shield. Let me fight with you, please. Aren't we better together?"

She nodded, more tears falling down her face that he kissed away. "But I-I don't know how."

"First, come rest with me. Then we'll attack your internal battles full on, whether you want to fight them together, or if you'd be willing to consider getting an outside perspective, such as therapy. I'll even go with you."

"B-But the coordinates—"

He shushed her softly, tucking her hair behind her ears. "They'll still be there. You've gone through so much, sunflower. It's time to rest. It's okay to rest. We'll look at them tomorrow."

Johanna bit her lip, clearly battling a war inside herself.

Luke slowly let his hands slide down her neck, over her shoulders, and down her arms until he reached her hands. He squeezed her hands in his and held them as he brought them to his lips and kissed them both. "Come with me, sunflower. I don't want to sleep without you."

She bit her lip again but nodded.

Hope flared to life inside of Luke, and as they left the room together, he knew they would get through this. It may be a long, turbulent road, but they would see the other side, and he felt grateful to have someone who would fight just as hard for him as he would for her.

CHAPTER 18

Agreeing to therapy was a difficult thing for Johanna. It hurt her pride to have something wrong with her. It hurt to have to reach out to someone else. She was a mental witch, having trained her mind for years to be able to deal with her powers, to go inside other's heads and come out unscathed. And yet, here she was.

Her appointment with Estelle had lasted an additional hour over what they'd scheduled. Estelle had worked with several of the women Greg, Dani, Luke, and Mya had saved from the caves, which is why she believed she would also be able to help Johanna.

At first, Johanna was nervous. Estelle began with rudimentary questions which Johanna answered honestly. Then Estelle simply said, "Have you always felt like you needed to be the hero?"

"The hero?" Johanna asked.

"Yes, that the only time you have worth and value is when

you're rescuing someone else from their perils. That if you've sacrificed yourself for the greater good, then it was all worth it because you've served your purpose."

Johanna's mouth fell open. She didn't even know she was crying until she felt the wetness roll down her cheeks. In just a few moments, Estelle had ripped into Johanna's psyche and unveiled a truth so close to her heart she thought she could hide it forever. The façade fell apart, just as Johanna did at the seams, and she cried. She cried as she told her story to Estelle, she cried as she talked about her childhood, she cried as she talked about the abuse she'd gone through and how robbed she felt of everything—another truth she kept to herself for fear that it was selfish.

Estelle listened and handed her tissues while Johanna opened her entire heart. She never rushed her, never quieted her, didn't even take notes. She just listened, and Johanna didn't realize how much she'd needed that.

When she finished, Estelle told her that she believed Johanna had PTSD. She explained there were different types of PTSD, and that war had many different faces. Because she wanted to know, Estelle walked Johanna through what she thought was the best course of action. First, journaling. Johanna needed to get in touch with her emotions and make time for them instead of blocking them off to try to function throughout her day. Between that, talk therapy, and mindfulness practices, she believed Johanna would be just fine.

Luke took her to get an actual notebook, as she figured she'd procrastinate journaling if she used something electronic, and the next day she tried it. She sat in the sunroom, pulled out her notebook, opened to the first page, and wrote: *This is stupid.*

The dismissive words shocked her. She froze with her pen

in her hand, her heart beating a mile a minute as if she were not allowed to voice her innermost feelings and thoughts this way. Then she took a deep breath and reminded herself that she was. She had to do this to get better, and she could judge herself for what she wrote later. Now she could just be free.

This feels like a waste of time. I feel like I should be doing twenty million other things. We still haven't found Zachariah; I'm still having a hard time correcting the last few coordinates and remembering exactly when I switched from one coding system to another because it all just takes me back. I remember how everything felt, how hopeless I felt. I truly believed there would be no way out. I truly believed I was going to die.

Her hand shook at the revelation, but she couldn't stop now.

I wanted to die. I didn't want to feel guilty anymore. I didn't want to be hurt anymore. Death would have been so much easier.

Johanna broke down, crumbling over the table. Luke was at her side in an instant and she turned into his embrace. He picked her up and carried her, sitting with her on one of the couches while she cried into his shirt. He rubbed her hair and stroked her back, but otherwise said nothing. He never asked what happened to make her cry, or what she'd written. He was just there throughout it all.

By her next session, Johanna was excited to start meditation, to do *anything* else but fucking cry. She had never cried so much in her entire life, and she was tired of it. Estelle, on the other hand, thought she was making progress, but Johanna couldn't see it herself.

Estelle says I need to cut myself some slack. It's not that I don't believe her, I just don't know how to. That's the problem, isn't it?

Johanna sighed.

I feel as though I have more problems than solutions, and sometimes it doesn't seem worth it at all. I feel weak. I feel pitiful. I feel like the world is just moving around me while I'm stuck standing still. Every time I try to move with it, I fall into a pothole, or a sewage drain, or something. But even all of that feels ridiculous.

I'm here. I'm alive right now. I'm living and breathing and safe. I'm safe, and yet I've never felt more afraid. I remember feeling like this when I regained consciousness, that if I reached out too far, if I hoped just a little too much, that everything would come crumbling down and it would all be my fault. It would serve me right for trying.

But I want to try. I wish I didn't, but I want to.

Johanna sat up straighter in her chair as her resolve burst through her.

Dani's wedding is in less than three months, and by then I will be better. That's a promise to me and to everyone I love.

I won't give up.

As excited as Johanna had been for her meditation practices, it wasn't going well. She couldn't seem to sit in the quiet and train her mind to turn off. Each time she closed her eyes, another thought, another feeling, another longing emerged and buzzed around her head until with a frustrated sigh she opened her eyes.

The moment she did, Luke appeared in the doorway with what looked like a yoga mat.

"What are you doing?"

"You've been having a hard time with meditation, so I thought I'd come try it with you."

A small smile graced her face as he lined the mat up in front of her own. "You don't have to do that."

"I know, but I want to," he said, sitting down to face her.

Johanna tilted her head to the side as he settled in. "I know you want to help, and I appreciate it more than I can ever tell you, but having you in front of me is only going to distract me more."

He smirked, and she realized just how much she'd missed that little knowing curl of his lips.

"Glad to see you're still interested, but no. This is couples' meditation. I found a guided meditation app and figured that might help you since it will be something to listen to. Afterward we can do the couples' breathwork session, if you'd like to give it a try," he said softly.

Johanna reached out and squeezed his hand. "Yes, I would. Thank you for doing all of this for me."

Luke cupped her cheek. She closed her eyes, feeling the warmth of his palm on her skin.

"I will always do anything I can for you. Remember, we're in this together."

He started the app and Johanna followed its instructions. It guided her to breathe in and take in the scents around her, so she focused on Luke's unique fragrance. It filled her nostrils just as his heartbeat and breathing filled her ears, and she sighed. The tension in her body settled down as Johanna fell into a rhythm with him, and then the guided meditation ended and she wondered where the time had gone.

Luke opened his eyes and seemed to be just as lost as she was. He held out his hand to her and she took it. Then he spread his legs, picked her up, and deposited her on his lap. She squeaked and he laughed.

Johanna wrapped her legs around him. He pulled her close and they just held one another. She could feel the beating of his heart, so strong it felt like it was her own. She felt the rumble of his chest as each breath filled and left his lungs. The tickle of his body hair awakened her every nerve ending, and yet she'd never felt so peaceful in her entire life.

They stayed like that for minutes, maybe even hours. All she knew was that in that moment she felt as though they were one, and it was the most beautiful thing she'd ever experienced.

After a while, Luke slipped his arms from her back and she did the same, believing he meant to pull away entirely, instead he took her hand and laid it over his heart. Then he did the same with his hand over hers. He rested his forehead against her own, and they shared their breaths.

Then he whispered to her, "Together."

She whispered the word back, meaning it with every ounce of her heart, and a little more of her anguish slipped away.

SHE WAS PISSED.

Johanna had finished putting together all the coordinates and was overjoyed at the prospect of Zachariah finally being dealt with, but he wasn't at any of the locations. Johanna checked her work again and again, thinking maybe she'd messed up a set of numbers and had thrown everything else off, but that wasn't the case. He truly had up and abandoned every place she knew of, which confirmed several things for her.

Zachariah knew where she was. He knew who she was with

and what she had done, but the most terrifying of all the conclusions was that his army was growing. If he had retreated, it meant that he was either kidnapping more people or turning more vampires against their will.

She knew how it happened. The trauma broke their minds and Zachariah used that to imprint on them the same way a mother did to her ducklings. He offered them food and a home if they did his bidding, and they almost always agreed. She'd seen it more than enough times to count, and it wasn't fucking fair!

And this anger, this fucking wrath, settled into her bones. She couldn't get it out no matter what she tried.

Estelle suggested adding physical activity to her routine, and Luke took her to the gym Mya used to train vampires and teach the women they'd rescued self-defense. The moment Johanna saw Mya fight, she knew this was where she needed to be. Mya agreed to train her, and she was brutal. She didn't hold back punches, she went for the jugular. She was more like a wild tiger than a vampire as she fought, but it was good for Johanna. It fulfilled her need to be useful, to feel strong and capable, while also giving her a place to direct her anger. Over time, Johanna realized that was what Mya used it for as well.

But the anger was still there. It may not have been as loud or as prevalent, but it was there, under everything, in her sinews and bones. It sat in wait until she could use it, and Johanna knew the moment she did she would never be the same.

"SHOW ME WHAT MYA'S BEEN TEACHING YOU," LUKE SAID AS HE stepped out of their house and into the backyard.

Johanna rotated her elbows and took in his appearance, letting her gaze roam over him. It had been two months since the last time they had been intimate with one another, and even though she knew it was out of consideration for what she'd been through, her desire for him was driving her crazy.

She missed him, and seeing him like this—shirtless, glistening in sweat, his hair pushed back from his forehead from the amount of times he'd raked his gloved hands through it—didn't help. In fact, she wanted to follow the droplets of sweat over his body until—

Johanna ducked as his hand shot out to hit her. She blocked his next strike, then parried with a kick toward his abdomen. He jumped away from her and she planted her hands on her hips.

"What in the hell do you think you're doing?"

"Training ... or trying to. You were too busy staring." He smirked.

"Fine, have it your way."

Johanna launched herself at him. She punched at his chest, and he spun away from her. Luke kicked at her feet, so she jumped away from him. On and on they moved, blocking and countering each other's attacks. As she ducked under another punch, she realized that she was smiling. For the first time in what felt like several grueling weeks, she was having fun.

But then something ran across her body, like a featherlight touch had caressed every inch of her skin all at once, stimulating all of her. She froze, her back arched as a gasp left her, and then Luke swept her feet out from under her and she toppled to the ground.

Johanna tried to get her feet around him in a defensive maneuver, but he seemed to know what she was thinking. He pinned her leg beneath him while pulling the other one over his shoulder. Then he pinned her hands to the sides of her head.

She was breathless, panting from the exertion and from the effect he had on her.

Luke's gaze traveled down her body, then back up. He leaned close to her lips, holding her gaze as he whispered, "I win."

She tried to pull her arms out from his grasp, but he only tightened his grip and held her still. "That was a dirty trick," she said.

"Dirty or not, it got me exactly what I wanted." Luke leaned down to her neck and breathed in. The sigh he released was euphoric as it flitted over her skin, raising goosebumps over her flesh.

"And what is it that you want?"

"Just a kiss," Luke said as he lowered her thigh, fitting himself between her legs.

"Just one?" Johanna whimpered.

Luke smiled. "Unless you're feeling generous."

Johanna licked her lips as she focused on his mouth. She could nearly taste him as she whispered, "Yes. *Always.*"

Luke's lips descended upon hers, but it wasn't the kind of kiss she was used to from him. Her fierce protector had turned soft, gentle, kind, and somehow this simple kiss cut her more than anything else. It opened her to an entirely new universe, where she was the sun and the stars and he was the space that kept her afloat. Without him, without his grasp on her wrists and his gentle fingers on her cheek, his lips would have carried her away. They were so soothing, his kiss so tender, that they unleashed a deep yearning within her soul.

But then he pulled away, just barely. His breath fanned her face, and when she looked into his eyes all she saw was adoration, a love that renewed the strings of her heart and tied her back into him in an infinite loop.

"I love you," he whispered, the words stealing away her breath before he claimed her lips once more.

His fingers tangled with hers as he kept her pinned to the ground with his body. He was overwhelming her senses and yet she couldn't get enough. She couldn't go a second without him knowing, *feeling* what was in her heart for him.

Johanna reopened the telepathic connection between them. She felt his warmth and his love swim through her mind, and she sent hers out to him. She knew the moment he felt it. He shuddered and his lips broke away from hers on a sigh, so she took the chance to whisper back to him, "I love you too. I always will."

The smile he gave her could light up cities, could rival the sun, and in that moment she knew that she would have gone through every second of her life, every horror, again, as long as it lead her to him.

It had only become worse. Every moment she spent around Luke was torturous. Johanna couldn't focus during their meditations or when he pulled her onto his lap while they talked. She'd started taking painting lessons from him, yet even those quiet moments where she was supposed to be focusing on her feelings and her art were ruined, all because he wasn't inside her.

Their training sessions—if she could even call them that

anymore—were a mess. The amount of times she'd lost now was honestly embarrassing, but it truly wasn't her fault. Luke started teaching her jujutsu, specifically the holds, throws, and various stretches to increase her flexibility. This also meant she spent the majority of her time pressed against him in some way, shape, or form, or on her back with him on top of her.

Perhaps the worst thing of all was how he didn't seem to be affected in the same way she was. He just smiled, or otherwise seemed indifferent when they touched. His mind didn't reveal anything to her either. In fact, he seemed to be distracted, thinking of twenty million things when she was around.

She couldn't make sense of it at all. Did he not feel drawn to her anymore? Did he not desire her, crave her in the same way she did him? Had their connection somehow dulled for him over time? He loved her, but he wouldn't touch her. He was there for her, but he was also miles away. It was maddening. It was heartbreaking. It *hurt*.

Johanna tried to put it behind her. She was just overreacting. If it wasn't that, then she was sure Luke was somehow doing this for her. He loved her, she knew that. There was not a doubt in her mind when it came to his heart, which meant there had to be an answer somewhere else.

She spoke to Estelle about it, and the therapist's advice was two-fold: To finally be honest with Luke about her desires, something they had been discussing for the last two weeks, and to just ask him. But Johanna couldn't. She tried to tell herself it was because she valued Luke's wishes and trusted his choices. And she did. Johanna believed in Luke, truly, but a small seed of doubt was beginning to grow in her, and without any reassurance it was taking root. The roots steadied, grew, and then one day bore fruit.

Johanna heard the shower running with her enhanced senses, but after a while she picked up on another sound. It was small, muffled by the water, but it was there. She stepped closer to the room, then past the bed, and she realized what it was.

A moan.

Luke was in there. It was his voice, his moans that filled the room. Johanna was shocked, broken as she stood there listening to the man she loved get off on something that wasn't her. Her feet moved unconsciously, heart crumbling with every step she took and with every note of his pleasure. She didn't realize what she was doing until she slammed the bathroom door open.

Luke whirled around, wide eyed, his hand still around his cock, and betrayal surged through her that he would rather do this than be inside of her.

"Sunflower—"

She shook her head, backing away as he began to exit the shower. He took a step toward her, so she ran. Johanna didn't know what she was doing or where she was going, but hearing his footsteps behind her made her legs move faster. Johanna used every bit of her vampire speed to get away from him, because she couldn't be around him right now. She couldn't bear to see the evidence that she had tried to fight against. He didn't desire her, not anymore. But could she blame him after she'd been ruined by his enemy, after the last few months of her healing and trauma? It was too much for him.

That was the last thought she had before she went flying through the air.

Luke turned, cradling her as they landed and taking the force of the impact. She tried to sit up to get off and away from him, but he rolled them over and pinned her down. Johanna struggled against him, trying to push, pull, buck him off her until—

"Stop!"

His voice quelled her fight. The dark growl commanded her to listen, to obey, and she hated her treacherous body for it. Tears of frustration clouded her eyes, but she shook her head to clear them. She was ready to give him a piece of her mind, but she froze the moment she saw the bright red glow in his eyes.

"Johanna, why the fuck did you run from me?"

"You know why!" She tried to pull out of his grip again, but he only tightened his clasp on her wrists, squeezing until she whimpered.

"No. If I knew why, I wouldn't be asking. Why were you running? What triggered your blood lust? Tell me, right now."

Her eyes widened as she realized they must be just as red as his were. She tilted her head away, shame flowing through her, but he grasped her chin hard and pulled her back to meet his gaze.

"*Now*," he growled.

"You!" Tears pooled in her eyes. She blinked them away, but her voice still quivered as she spoke. "You don't want me anymore."

"Why would you—" Luke ran a hand through his hair and let out a frustrated sigh. "For the love of the gods. Baby, *of course* I want you."

"Then why won't you take me?" she yelled.

"That's what this is about?" He breathed, and then his lips twitched into that damn frustrating smirk and she saw red.

"Yes!" Johanna swore that somehow his eyes burned brighter at her outburst, but that didn't stop her. "We haven't been intimate in months! You sit here and do these training sessions with me, where you do nothing but tease me every damn second, but you're not affected by them, by *me*. Being close to me does nothing to you! Instead, you wear the same fucking smile you have on your face right now! And then, to make matters worse, I find you jerking off in the shower. You'd rather do that than be inside of me, and it *hurts!*"

"Sunflower—"

"Don't fucking call me that!"

Suddenly Luke's fingers wrapped around her throat. He squeezed and the sensation went straight to her core. Her lips parted and he loosened his grip enough to let her pull in a breath.

"Now are you going to be a good girl and let me speak, or do I need to find other ways to keep you quiet?"

She moaned. Gods help her, she moaned. "Luke—"

He growled in response and lowered his head to hers until he was all she could see, all she could feel, until he overwhelmed her senses in just the way she longed for him to. "You don't speak. You don't say a single word until I finish. Do you understand?"

Goosebumps broke out over her skin from the danger in his voice, the very threat of punishment if she didn't comply. She licked her lips and his eyes fell there for a moment before he shuddered, his fingers flexing around her throat, choking her once more. The look in his eyes, his wildness, his pleasure, had her spreading her legs wider for him. He pushed against her pelvis and it was only then that she realized he was fully naked and still incredibly hard.

He took her silence as her answer, and his fingers ran over her skin. "Everything you said was wrong."

She opened her mouth to argue but his sharp look practically *dared* her to disobey him. She promptly pressed her lips back together.

"I started those training sessions for two reasons. One was to help you. Really, it was, but the other reason was much more selfish."

His hand ran down her shirt and he ripped it away from her. His aggression made her cry out as the walls of her pussy clenched, already wet and begging for him to fill her.

Luke's eyes ran over her breasts, still in her bra, and then he ripped it away from her too. He tore it into shreds as if the material had offended him somehow. "You drive me crazy, sunflower. Absolutely crazy, and I needed another way to get my hands on you while still understanding you may need time to heal."

His hands drifted lower over her stomach. She arched her back, her skin heated by his touch. He groaned as he ripped away the closure of her pants, tore at them until there was nothing left.

"You said my teasing hurt you, well it fucking *killed* me, but I hoped it would help to make you comfortable with me, and that eventually you'd desire my touch again. What I didn't know was that somehow I'd make you lose your damn mind and think I didn't want you." Luke brushed the tip of his dick in between her folds and they both moaned. "Does that feel like I don't want you?"

She whimpered, wanting to answer but not wanting to break his rule.

A dark chuckle rumbled through him. "You can answer that," he said, leaning down and sucking her neck, making her moan again.

Johanna arched against him, lifted her hips, and tried to get him inside of her, but he moved so slowly, so calculated and controlled that she wanted to scream. She was so far gone she whimpered, barely able to speak. "N-no. But the shower."

Luke gripped her hips, keeping her still. "I love you. I love you enough to try to be gentle with you, to be vulnerable with you. All those times you were underneath me I wanted to rut you like a damn dog in heat. I imagined I could damn near feel your pussy swallowing me whole. But you needed time. I needed you. I still need you and I still want you. I want you so much it hurts."

He brushed her hair away from her face, the action completely at odds with the crazed look in his eyes. "What you saw in the shower was that. I needed to be inside of you so badly that it fucking hurt, and I thought, stupidly, that maybe I could take care of it, and that once I did it would be better for the both of us. I was barely hanging on, and while I knew you'd let me fuck you, I didn't want you to regret it." His grip on her wrists tightened. "But I couldn't come."

Her eyes widened but he continued.

"That's right, I can't come if I'm not inside of you. I can't come if the scent of you isn't on me, if your pussy isn't sucking me dry."

Johanna moaned his name. She writhed underneath him, so close to coming from his words alone that she knew she'd explode the moment he entered her.

"It's the same thing for you too, isn't it, sunflower?" His fingertips grazed her clit and she arched under him as if struck by lightning. "You can't come if it isn't with me. Say it."

"Yes!" she cried.

"Good girl," he purred as he pinched her clit. "Now tell me you want it. Tell me you want my cock inside your drenched pussy. I need to hear it before I take you."

The words were on the tip of her lips, but she swallowed them back, needing to say something else instead. "Luke, let go of my wrists, please."

"Are you going to try to hit me?"

She shook her head and he let them go. Johanna brought her hands to his face, cupping her cheeks. "I've been practicing how to say this to you."

His eyes widened. "Practicing?"

She nodded, then she licked her lips, took a deep breath, and gazed into his blood red eyes. "I want you to come inside of me, Luke. Please, be rough with me."

Luke cursed, his whole body shuddering against hers. Then with a groan he thrust inside of her, filling her to the brim.

Johanna wrapped her arms and legs around him as her orgasm rolled through her. Luke's hands went into her hair, pulling her head back as he sunk his fangs into her neck, tilted her hips, then reached his own climax inside of her. But they both needed more.

Luke's cock never softened. Instead, Johanna swore it grew harder as he rammed inside of her. Her moans filled the air, carried off by the wind as she went wild beneath him. Johanna scored his back with her nails, digging them into his flesh as he pounded inside of her.

Luke lifted his head and offered his neck to her. When her fangs slid into his skin, she swore she reached a new level of euphoria. He moaned her name, squeezed her hips and fucked the ever-loving shit out of her. He never stopped, never slowed, not even when they both came again.

Before Johanna knew what was happening, she was on her stomach. "Knees up," was all Luke said, and she instantly did as she was told.

His fingers slid through her pussy lips, and she looked back in time to see the utter look of pleasure on his face, even as she felt it radiate through her body.

"This is how I like to see you, fucking dripping in my come."

"Yes!" she cried as he slid two fingers inside of her, making them both moan.

He took his fingers out and she clenched around him, trying to keep them inside of her. The action made him chuckle, even as he lined himself up with her. "You want me that bad, hmm?"

"Yes," she purred.

Luke cursed and held the fingers that were just inside of her to her lips.

"Suck," he said.

She obeyed, making him curse again. Then he slipped his fingers out of her mouth and rammed his cock inside her pussy in one full thrust. They both gasped. Luke leaned down over her body, pushing her further into the dirt. He gathered her hair in his hand, twisting it around his fist.

"This is for you telling me not to call you my sunflower. That is *my* name for you, and if you ever tell me not to call you that again I will make sure my handprint stays on your ass *permanently.*"

She looked back at him with a smirk of her very own and said, "Yes, sir."

Luke's eyes fell shut. He trembled against her, and she felt every bit of the pleasure that word had caused him. Then he pulled out of her and rammed back inside so hard she nearly lost her balance. "Fucking brat."

"Yours," she said in a moan as he moved again.

"Yes, always mine" he hissed. There was no more room for

words as he took her, his hand on her shoulder and her hair wrapped in his fist.

He fucked her as if he was a starved, crazed man, and Johanna was right there with him. Then Luke used his powers. Shadows wrapped around her, and she felt as if a thousand fingertips were caressing her body, squeezing her breasts, clamping down on her nipples, teasing her clit, grabbing her ass. Unable to take the stimulation, she shouted his name into the forest just as he roared hers as he came. Then he pulled her back onto her knees, his hand wrapped around her throat as he bucked inside of her. She laid her hand over his and squeezed. He groaned, tilted his head to the side and sank his fangs back into her skin.

Johanna's hips moved of their own accord. He fucked her and she rode him as they both worked themselves in a frenzy, nearing another explosive orgasm. Luke offered her his arm, so she bit into it, drinking his blood, letting it fill her and take her over completely just as the rest of him had. She was his and he was hers, and as they mated in the forest she swore they both screamed loud enough that the whole world heard it.

CHAPTER 19

Johanna smiled as the sunlight caught on the teardrop diamond engagement ring on her finger. She spread her fingers around the steering wheel, admiring how the light hit the gem at different angles.

Luke and Johanna were doing well. They'd learned to stop keeping secrets from one another, no matter how embarrassing or insecure it might make them, and it made a world of a difference. The night of Greg and Dani's wedding, Luke pulled her aside and finally told her that he'd searched for and found her family. She was overjoyed that he'd done this for her, but even more so when he explained that he wanted ask them for her hand in marriage. Johanna said yes, even though he refused to accept her answer until he received their blessing.

Their first meeting hadn't exactly been ideal. Her family was wary of Luke after they found out everything that happened to her, even though their connection and mate bond were obvious. Still, he wore them down until he got their blessing, and now they were discussing dates for their own wedding.

Johanna caught her reflection in the window. Her blue eyes shone, her skin glowed and she knew it was all because of him. Her Luke. She was so happy, so at peace in the serenity that he'd wrapped her in. He'd taught her so much about love, about life, and he made her excited for every day she saw, all because she knew he would be right there beside her. She never knew things could be so good, never imagined her life could be so filled with joy, and she was grateful for it all. In fact, she couldn't wait to get home and show that gratefulness to him.

Johanna turned down the road to their house, but instead of bliss, she only felt dread. She wasn't sure why. She knew Luke was home and waiting for her, yet something just felt off. Johanna tried to reach him telepathically, but she couldn't. There was only static, as if their connection had been severed.

That was impossible. While Johanna had taught Luke ways to shield his mind, he didn't have the ability to shield her, nor would he want to. This wasn't like him. Something was wrong.

Johanna threw the car in park and bounded up the stairs. She went to grab the handle of the front door but paused. Luke and Mya had trained her for things like this. She couldn't just go barging in. She needed to be logical first and push her emotions to the side.

She took a deep breath. Johanna couldn't smell anyone else outside, nor could she see anyone, but she could feel something or someone trying to mask their energy, and it wasn't Luke.

Johanna opened the door to their house. She let the mate bond pull her to Luke, but as she got closer, she heard a laugh, a voice that chilled her to the bone.

No.

Her eyes locked on Luke when she stepped inside the room, but his expression was blank as he stared at her. Beside him she saw the one man she hoped to never see alive again.

Zachariah.

"Hello, pet."

That word triggered such an adverse reaction in her that she nearly vomited on the spot. Instead, Johanna swallowed back the bile and stood taller. She would not let him get to her. She would not be a pawn in his games ever again. "What do you want, Zachariah?"

"That answer should be obvious. You."

Johanna laughed, cackled at the fucking audacity of this godforsaken creature. "I'm not sure what level of delusion you're on that makes you believe that's ever going to happen, but the answer is no."

"Aw, pet." He held his hands out to her, an evil grin on his face. "Didn't you miss me? We did such great things together. You were a beautiful weapon, and since you had such a hard time staying away from your mate, I even brought him over to our side just for you. You're welcome," he spat.

Johanna didn't have to ask what he'd done to Luke. It was obvious in the blood that marred his skin, in the way he didn't move, barely even blinked when his nemesis stood beside him.

"Cat got your tongue? That's alright. Today's a celebration day for me so I'm willing to let impudence slide. But here's the thing, either you come with me, or I'll just find someone else." He grinned. "Like your little sister, Tamara, or maybe your mother, Corrine."

Her eyes widened at their names.

"That's right. Luke tried not to give me the information, but in the end he was just too weak." Zachariah shrugged. "Your choice of mate was honestly abysmal, Johanna."

"Fine, I'll go," she said with a nod, a plan forming in her mind.

Zachariah smiled. "I knew I could count on you to make the right choice."

She smiled back, feeling her grin grow. The rage that had been dormant within her came to the surface, and with it her powers. Johanna pushed past the magic Constance used to guard Zachariah, and dove into his mind. It was a place of nightmares and terror, covered in so much tar and darkness that she doubted anyone could stay unscathed for long. But that didn't matter, because now that she had wormed her way inside, she could read him like a book.

Luke moved under Zachariah's silent command. He lunged at her clumsily, a by-product of Constance's possession, but Luke had trained her how to protect herself from anyone, including him. She grabbed hold of his arm and ducked, spinning underneath him. The momentum made him flip over her and crash to the floor. Instantaneously, she pulled out of Zachariah's mind and into Luke's, issuing a command to force him to sleep.

Zachariah appeared in front of her in a flash, a smile on his face as if he'd won his prize. She wasn't surprised to find him crowding her space, nor was she fearful when he grabbed her. Instead, she let him.

"It's cute that you thought that would work," he said with a sneer.

She smirked. "Oh, I didn't. I just needed to separate the two of you."

"And what did you think that would achieve?"

"This."

She spun. Using her momentum, she turned her hand to the side and struck his neck, directly on his carotid artery. His eyes grew wide as he staggered back from her, and it only served to make her smile larger.

"You see, I know your powers enhance your body, but that enhancement is triggered by your mind. Without that trigger, well, you're just an old, weak sack of shit."

"What did you do?" he screeched.

"Simply switched your power off. I'm giving you a dose of your own medicine, Zachariah. It hurts, doesn't it, to feel less than."

She kicked him in the ribs.

"To feel powerless."

She kicked him again.

"To have your abilities, the very essence of who you are, taken from you."

Zachariah reared back to punch her, but she spun, dodging the attack only to kick him in the face and smile triumphantly as he went down.

"This is impossible," he bit out. "There's no way you could be stronger than me."

She smiled and let him get up before she looked him dead in his eyes. "I've always been stronger than you. A fucking ant is stronger than you. You just had opportunity and a sick, perverse agenda funded by an absolute bitch. Your only strengths were your powers and your ability to hold things over another person's head. Without those you're *nothing*. And the moment, the fucking *second* you touched my mate, you were never going to make it out of here alive."

He roared and moved to attack her, but Johanna was quicker, freezing his body in place.

The windows shattered and the doors slammed open as twenty of Zachariah's men invaded the house.

"Am I supposed to be scared?" Johanna said. They tried to move, but she froze them in place as well. "When you started losing, you stopped focusing on whatever magic it was that let you mask your group. But now that the gangs all here, I think it's time to say goodbye."

Johanna dug deep inside of herself, pouring everything she could into her attack, every ounce of rage, betrayal, and hurt fueled her power. She raised her hands to the ceiling as the men struggled to break free of her magic, but she wouldn't let them. She looked at Luke's sleeping form one more time before she slammed her hands down to her sides.

Her power surged through the house, and then the building caved in on itself. Every inch of the roof and every section of every floor imploded and crashed down upon Zachariah and the men he'd brought with him.

Johanna staggered under her magic, but she refused to fall. Her job wasn't done yet.

She reached for the dagger Luke forced her to carry, and went to the last place she'd seen Zachariah. Using her magic, she lifted the heavy stone and concrete to reveal his crushed form. Even though she believed he was dead, she had to make sure. She pushed the knife through his flesh, skull, and into his brain, but only when she pulled it out was she satisfied.

Then she fell. Weak and tired, she crawled over to Luke and pulled him into her arms. The battle may have been over, but the one inside of him was still raging strong. Johanna was sure that when he came to, he would still be under the effects of

Constance's possession magic, and there was only one thing she thought could break it.

Using the last ounces of her strength, Johanna teleported them both to Dani and Greg's house. She struggled to breathe, the exertion of her powers taking over, but still she fought her unconsciousness. She had to take care of Luke. He had to be okay.

They crash-landed in the kitchen.

"What the fuck?" Dani yelled as she sprung up from her seat, cradling her bump.

"Johanna, what happened?" Greg asked.

"It was Zachariah." Johanna looked around. "Where's Mya?"

"Mya? Wait. What do you mean Zachariah? Johanna, what the fuck happened?" Dani said.

"We don't have time! Please, I think Mya can help me get him back to normal. Where is she?"

Greg already had her on the line. "She's getting here as fast as she can."

"How long?" Johanna asked, running her hand over Luke's cheek.

"Twenty minutes," Greg said.

"Tell her to hurry, please. I don't know how much longer I can stay conscious." Johanna groaned. The feedback from the amount of power she used hit her all at once and she screamed as pain flew through her.

Dani held onto her as she swayed. "Johanna!"

"I'm fine. I'll be fine. I just used too much power."

Greg came to her side. "What can we do to help you?"

"Nothing." She looked up at him. "Zachariah must have ambushed Luke at our house. They gave him Constance's blood and he's under her possession magic. I forced him to sleep, but the last command Zachariah gave him was to hurt me. If I fall unconscious, it's the first thing he'll do."

"How do we get him out of it?" Dani asked.

"Blood. I'm going to try to force my powers into him through my blood. I think if we mix that with Mya's then it will sever the magic."

Dani immediately grabbed a bowl and knife to collect Johanna's blood.

"Johanna, where is Zachariah?" Greg asked.

"Dead."

Dani whirled back around to her as Greg's eyes widened.

"I killed him. Him and twenty of his men," she said through the pain. She ran her hand through Luke's hair. "He won't be able to hurt anyone else."

"Are you sure he's dead?" Greg asked.

Johanna pulled out the dagger she'd used to stab Zachariah. "I stabbed his brain with this. You'll find his body, as well as the others, underneath the rubble of our house." She swayed again, almost falling to the side, but Greg caught her. "I won't be able to stay conscious for much longer. Take care of him, please."

"Of course," he said.

As her consciousness faded, Johanna whispered, "Tell him … I love … him—"

Then she screamed as pain flooded her body and the world went black.

SHE WAS WARM, SO INCREDIBLY WARM AND COMFORTABLE. THE arm around her waist tightened, and Johanna snuggled further into Luke's chest.

Luke.

Her eyes snapped open. She lifted her head from his neck and stared down at him.

"Luke?"

Please don't be a dream, please don't be a dream.

"Good morning, sunflower," he said with a small smile.

"Luke!" She threw her arms around him, laughing even as she cried.

Luke clung to her, kissing her head and every bit of skin he could find. She joined him, kissing his beard, his jaw, his chin, his lips. She laughed until she felt the wetness from his own eyes on his cheeks. Johanna had never seen him cry, and it broke her heart to do so.

"Baby," she whispered, wiping away the moisture.

He shook his head. "I saw you. The whole time, I saw you standing there with Zachariah next to you and I couldn't reach out to you. I couldn't get to you. I'm so sorry. I'm so, so sorry."

She shook her head as her tears fell and mixed with his own. "No, please no. I know what you went through and I know what it feels like. Please don't blame yourself."

"I have to. I let you down, I was supposed to protect you—"

"You did!" Johanna kissed his hands. "You did. If it wasn't for you, I wouldn't have known how to fight. I wouldn't have found the courage."

He smiled, brushing away her tears. "You were amazing, but you used so much power. You've been asleep for days, sunflower. I was so scared."

"I'm sorry, but I had to make sure you were safe. I didn't want him to ever hurt you, me, or anyone ever again."

He kissed her head as he cradled her to his chest, his grip hard and sure on her body. "You made sure of that."

She nodded, breathing in his scent, but then she pulled back in shock. "What happened when I passed out? Was anyone hurt? Were we able to clear Constance's magic? Did it hurt you?"

"No," he said, but his smile was pained. "Greg tied me down after you lost consciousness. Mixing your blood with Mya's worked to clear the possession. I was back to normal within a few minutes." Luke ran his fingers through her hair. "You saved me, sunflower, my little warrior."

"I swore I would do anything for you, even—"

"Fight, maim, or kill. I remember."

They shared a small smile before Johanna rested her head back in the crook of his neck. "About our house..."

He laughed, the sound vibrating through him so hard it shook her. "Yeah, that's not getting fixed for a while."

She frowned. "I'm sorry."

"Don't be. A house can be repaired or fixed, or a new one bought, but there is nothing in this world that matters more than you."

She kissed his neck, and he ran his palms over her back, kneading her muscles.

"Where do we go from here?" she asked.

"Well, we should probably find another house to buy, and there are a million other things that we'll have to fix to win this war and protect the people we love." His hands slid down to her ass and he squeezed her cheeks. "But for right now, I was thinking that we happen to be safe, alone, and already in bed. It would be a shame to waste such a wonderful opportunity."

She laughed as he rolled them over and settled between her thighs.

"I've missed you," he whispered, kissing her shoulder and sliding down the strap of her nightgown.

She cupped his face and stared deeply into the most beautiful mix of green and gray. "I love you."

Luke's eyes softened, filled with adoration and passion. He cupped her hands and whispered against her lips, "I love you too, and I will for the rest of time."

NIGHT FALL

PROLOGUE

The first time she met him, she was dying.

The plague had taken over villages, entire continents. So many lives had been lost and now that tally included her mother, father, and aunt. Mya tried to take care of them, tried to hope that if she could just do something, that if she was fast enough, worked hard enough, they would survive. And if not, at least she could help them hold on until her brother, Gregori, came back with a cure. He would come back; she was sure of it. They all just had to stay strong and have faith until then.

But hours turned into days, days into weeks, and still Gregori was gone. And now she, and her cousin, Lucas, had fallen ill.

Waiting for a cure changed to waiting for death. Mya could feel the Black Plague eating away at her flesh, fogging her mind, ruining her, turning her into something other than the young, healthy, vibrant girl she once was.

At the end, there was no one left to watch over them. No one to feed them, wash them, or ease their suffering. Mya and Lucas had tried so hard not to succumb to the illness, but eventually they collapsed on the floor, and soon they were covered in their own boils, piss, vomit, and fecal matter, too weak to move. If the plague did not kill them, starvation would.

It was difficult to know she was dying and could not do a single thing about it. Mya did not want to die, but what was the alternative? Even if Gregori came back with a cure, it would never revive the limbs she lost to gangrene, or the delirium that had set in at her high fever. And who was to say that Gregori was still alive? He may be just as dead as she was bound to be.

That was the state Gregori had found them in. She could not see clearly by the time Gregori and his companion entered their small family home. She half thought she had imagined his return. But then she heard his companion's voice, and it stole her entire focus. Mya did not know what it was about that voice. She had heard men speak before, and while she and Lucas had been alone for some time, she still remembered the voices of the other inhabitants of their village ... back when they were still alive, that was. Still, the slightly accented voice— so deep and rich, patient and controlled, yet strained, as if he cared about her survival—touched her, deeply. That there was anyone left to care when she was so close to death warmed her heart, made her suffering ease just slightly.

It was a mixture of that feeling and the panic in Gregori's voice that made tears spill from her eyes. It was too late. She was too far gone, and she wished her brother had been saved from seeing her like this so that he could remember her the way she was before the plague, before he left. Yet her single string of happiness came from the notion that he would be by her side when she died.

Her wish to have him near her was a selfish one. She looked up to him, respected him, wanted more for him, but also needed him. He gave her the courage she needed to accept her death without bitterness or resentment.

But then she felt his presence next to her. He was far too close. And what about Lucas? Why was Gregori not going to Lucas? Had he already died? Was she the only one left, deliriously waiting for hope when there was none?

No, there may not be hope for her, and perhaps there was no hope for her cousin, but Gregori should survive. He *needed* to survive, which meant he needed to leave this plague infested house and save himself.

Gregori moved to cradle her, but she pushed him away. He leaned over her once more, and she fought with all her might to shove him once again. That bought her a few inches, but she was too weak for anything more.

Gregori warned her not to fight him, but still she thrashed. She sobbed in their native tongue, warning him, *begging* him to save Lucas, and if he could not, to at least save himself.

Then a hand, heavy but gentle, grasped her shoulder, surging warmth through her body. Mya's blurry eyes shifted to Gregori's companion's as the man spoke for the first time, "Be still. Gregori has brought you a cure. Listen to your brother and take it."

The last of her energy fled from her as if it had been washed away by a great tide, and she fell back onto the hard floor, so tired that she could do nothing more but obey. The stranger touched her again, his hand shifting to her jaw where he squeezed until he forced her to open her cracked and bleeding lips.

Liquid dripped into her mouth and slid to the back of her throat. She swallowed, and the first wave of heat hit her, pleasurable and shocking. Mya could suddenly taste a fury of flavors—acidic, meaty, savory, salty, iron, and something almost close to smoke. Every part of her being came alive as fire burst through her body, setting her aflame. She felt renewed, energized, capable, stronger than she had ever been in her entire life. She wanted more of the delicious drink; she *craved* it.

Unable to control her fervor and now free from the stranger's touch, she grasped her brother's hand to her lips and sunk her teeth—no, no longer teeth ... *fangs*—into Gregori's wrist, drinking his blood in mouthfuls. She should have been disgusted by the notion, concerned by her illness, but she was too lost to the power he had given her through his blood. It was only when the stranger pulled her away, did she settle calmly onto her back, high on something she could not name.

She felt her brother leave her and move to the side where she had last seen her cousin. After several moments, her eyes focused and she glanced at the unknown being in front of her. A gasp left her lips at his beauty, and she blushed at the twitch of a smile on his lips, embarrassed by her state of undress and filth.

That was the first time she met Erik Devereux, and he looked like an angel.

1

THE 14TH CENTURY

Mya hated England. She hated its up-and-coming center, preferring the old, rocky, dirt roads of Spain. She missed playing on them, getting her feet dirty, her clothing soiled. She missed the simplicity of it all. There was something natural about the Spanish landscape, something England could not grasp no matter how many times it attempted to with its perfectly spaced, manicured trees. It was not wild, not like her. But England was her home now.

Erik had become her family's guardian. Due to his status as lord of the region, Erik was able to keep Gregori out of England's upcoming wars. He took on the task of tutoring both Gregori and Lucas in a variety of subjects, from education to creative skills, and, lastly, battle.

He had hired a female tutor for Mya, hoping to give her someone to relate to. But that was an impossible task. Mya did not care for the woman and only agreed to attend her lessons so she could play outside afterward. That was the only time she felt free. She climbed the tall oak trees, chased insects, and tore through the garden beds on her adventures to "help" their chef. She would flee to the stables, sneaking around the stablemen to slip fruit and vegetables to the horses, but it was that last forbidden adventure that had her crying on the back stairs that afternoon.

She heard the crunching of rock under boots in front of her. Then she heard them pause. She knew by the sound of the steps that it was Erik, but she refused to meet his gaze. She did not want him to see her cry. He did so much for them, for her. He spoiled her and she knew he gave her far too much attention. Even unhappy, Mya did not want to seem ungrateful or make things harder on Erik or her family. But Erik knew her intrinsically. She did not know how, but he knew what she needed, and no matter how determined she was to handle her issues on her own, Erik would not let her. And he always got his way.

Erik slipped his hands under her arms, lifting her. Then he turned and took her place on the seat, setting her in his lap, a habit he had continued from when she was a child. He held her with her back to his chest and let her sit there in silence as more tears rolled down her cheeks, turning into full sobs of sorrow.

When she quieted, Erik asked, "Why are you crying, *fagr skjaldmær min*?"

Mya shook her head. "I am not crying."

He laughed, the sound as comforting as the warm rays of the sun. "Then what is the reason for the waterfalls pouring from your eyes?"

She shook her head with a small grunt.

Erik ran his fingers through her long dark tresses, bunching the curled strands between his fingers. "Tell me, *fagr skjaldmær min.*"

"When will you tell me what that means?" Mya asked, attempting to distract him as she sniffled and leaned more into his body, letting his strength run through her.

"When you are older."

When she pouted, and turned her head to face him, he said. "Now, Mya."

She sighed. "One of the stablemen..." She paused, glancing at Erik to see how much trouble she would be in for wandering around the horses.

"I already know where you go, *fagr skjaldmær min.*"

She gasped. "You do?"

"Of course I do. Why do you think I hired extra men? Their job is to watch over you, if I am otherwise engaged, and ensure none of the horses hurt you." Erik dropped a soft kiss to her temple. "There are not many places you could go that would escape my gaze. It is my job, my *duty*, to be there for you should you ever need me, and it is a role I take very seriously."

Mya blushed, but she did not know why. She was not sure what to call the level of affection and admiration that spiraled through her heart at his words. He made her feel safe, she realized, a feeling she had only felt before with her parents. Then the crawling feeling of misery tugged sharply at her heart once more and she had to stop herself from crying again.

"One of the stablemen asked if I was your daughter," she finally said. "I-I know he did not mean any harm, but it made me think about Papa and Mama." She trembled, and Erik drew her closer as if he wished to physically banish her grief. "I try not to think about them too often. It hurts so much when I do. I was not strong enough to protect them." She shook her head. "I should have been stronger."

"Mya–"

"What if it happens again?" she hiccupped.

Erik wiped the tears from her eyes. "We are vampires now. We do not have to worry about the plague—"

"But there are other things. You are always training Gregori and Lucas to fight because humans can kill us, yet you will not train me. Is it because I am too weak? Is it because you can only see me as a girl? Do you see me as nothing but a young woman, a child, too young to be useful? Your pseudo-daughter—"

"No," Erik said so sternly that it felt as if the world stopped. "You are not weak." He paused and stroked the soft skin of her cheek. "I remember the day Gregori brought me to you. I remember how hard you tried to fight to save Gregori from contracting the disease. Those are not the actions of a weakling. And I could never see you as a child, nor as my daughter."

Mya was too stunned to say anything, and he took advantage of her silence. "I see you as something so much more. Something more beautiful, more *fantastical* than I could ever explain to you. I cannot see you as I see Gregori and Lucas, nor can I treat you the same way I treat them. You hold my heart in a way that no one else ever will, and that love allows me to see you, to see through you into this thing here." He lightly poked at her chest, right above her heart. "You are strong, *fagr skjaldmær min*, and I am honored to be able to witness that strength every day."

She shattered, tossing her arms around Erik's neck hugging him as she cried into his body. His long, pale blonde hair tickled her face, neck, and shoulder as she stole into his warmth. He held her, gently rocking with her and rubbing her back until the grief of her parents' death left her.

The silence brought back his words, and Mya tried to analyze her own feelings for the man who had helped save her life. There was so much to Erik that she treasured, and yet so much she did not understand, including her feelings for him.

He was everywhere and everything to her. He was there when the memory of her near death kept her awake at night. He tucked her in and waited until she was asleep before he left. He was there to speak with her, to carry her, play with her, read to her. He fed her, clothed her, listened to her words, her thoughts. He valued her. Without him she would have nothing, she would *be* nothing.

But it was more than that.

She respected the man she found herself watching far too often. She respected how he treated those around him. He was stern but just, a merciful enforcer who both defended his lands and inspired his people. He was intelligent, courageous, brave. He gave so much and asked for so little back. To Mya, he was a symbol of perfection—something she should not be able to reach—that blessed her each day and night.

But what did all of that mean? She loved Erik in a way she did not love her brother or cousin. Mya did not have any companions, but she knew what she felt for Erik was more than that. If Erik asked her to lay down her life for him, she would do it with a smile.

It was not adoration or pure devotion. It was a simplistic need to bring him whatever level of joy she could, to give him something of what he gave to everyone else: A chance for survival. A chance for happiness. A second chance at life.

So there, in that moment, even though he had not asked

and even though she did not have a clear understanding of her feelings, she gave him what she could, something she had not given anyone outside of her family.

"You are in my heart too, Erik." Mya exhaled, and he shivered. "I do not know the love I feel for you. I have not felt it before, but it is there, nonetheless. It is all-consuming and never ending."

Erik's supple lips curled at her temple, then he inhaled as if he could breathe her in. "And for that, I am truly blessed."

MYA THOUGHT TO SKIP HER VISIT TO THE STABLES THE FOLLOWING day, not wanting to repeat what happened before, but she pushed through her fear. She enjoyed tending to the horses, and as a strong woman, she refused to be chased away from something that made her happy. So, with her basket of apples, carrots, and celery, Mya held her head high and entered the massive archway.

Every head snapped away from the sight of her, causing her confidence to drop. The stablemen normally did not pay attention to her, but this level of avoidance was unsettling. They seemed to cower with every step she took.

Mya knew that she did not inspire fear, and the only person she knew that did—Erik—was not in the stables. Mya would have known if he was behind her. He always smelled of pine, ash, smoke, and cinnamon, scents that brought her comfort and peace.

Still, she turned to check, but he was nowhere in sight. When she turned back to the men, they were already busying themselves with their normal day to day tasks, ensuring that their backs were to her.

Mya would have thought she had imagined the whole thing if it were not for the way the men scattered away from her every time she passed near them to feed one of the horses. They had never been overly friendly or conversational with her, above and beyond the watchful nature of their roles, but the way they veered away from her now, and the eyes that followed her back when she moved, did not feel like mere curiosity. Instead of apathy, they treated her as if she was a blight that could infect them.

She shrugged. Their actions made no matter to her. In all actuality she preferred to be left alone; speaking to people took too much energy from her, and she found their conversations not only tiring but uninspiring. Still, the sudden change was strange, but that was not the only thing that struck her as odd.

Mya had kept an eye out for the stableman who had spoken to her the day before, desperate to not run into him again, but as the morning wore on, she realized that she had not seen him at any of the usual posts in the stables or out on the field.

When Erik came to tuck her in later that night, she decided to give voice to the thoughts in her head.

"I went to the stables today," she said, studying him.

His entire body seemed to still, except for one small tic in his hand as he gripped the top of her comforter. His silver eyes met her own, and she noticed how hard they were. "I know. How were the horses?"

"Well, but—"

"Then I am overjoyed to hear you enjoyed your time."

His tone was clipped, angry, and it confused her as he

turned to walk away. Mya nearly let him, but she could not stop the words that tumbled from her mouth.

"Did you do something to that stableman?"

Again, Erik froze. His fists balled, clenched, then extended. She could see the tension in each movement, yet he did not answer her.

"Erik, did you do—"

"No one hurts you, Mya."

Her mouth dropped open, then closed quickly. She sat up, holding the comforter to her chest. "But he did not hurt me. It was my fault."

A rush of air hit her face as Erik appeared in front her, his nose mere centimeters from hers. His eyes were controlled, cold, *dangerous*, and it made something in her want something she could not name.

When he spoke, his voice was low, hoarse, drowning in some sort of emotion that made her heart pound and goosebumps snake up her skin.

"He did hurt you. Whether he meant to or not makes no difference to me. That is *inexcusable*," Erik hissed. "He dared to speak to you when he should not have, and by doing so he hurt you. No one hurts what is min—"

Erik took a deep breath and closed his eyes, attempting to settle his anger. His body shuddered as if he was forcing himself back from an invisible ledge. With another breath he centered himself, peered into her eyes, and said in a deep, controlled tone, "No one hurts what falls under my care."

"The men are not allowed to speak to me?" Mya whispered.

"Correct. They may not speak to you, touch you, or pay attention to you unless completely necessary."

She bit her lip and forced herself to swallow. His control

should have felt restrictive. She should have been angry with him, she should have told him she could take care of herself, but instead she felt her skin growing warm as a thrumming began between her thighs and her core grew damp. For a single moment Mya worried she may have gotten her cycle early, but this was not that. This feeling was pleasant, needy, something else that she had never felt before.

Erik's eyes grew darker, the black pupils bleeding over into his normal silver and making them appear gray at the edges. He inhaled as if he were smelling something, tasting the air. His breath grew labored, and a small part of his fang extended beyond his lips.

"Are you not mad at me?" he asked, his voice deeper than she had ever heard it.

Mya shook her head.

"Tell me why," he murmured as he leaned closer to her body, nearly eliminating the distance. He grabbed hold of her hair, twirling it between his fingers while his eyes roamed over her face, drinking in her every expression.

She bit her lip again, her eyes flickering away from his and falling back to his red lips. "I ... appreciate your protection, I suppose."

He hummed, then nodded. "Then I will tell you what I did to the stableman. I stalked him until he was running scared for his life. Then I tore off his head, drained his body of most of its blood, and fed his useless corpse to the pigs. His family will receive a large dowry for his reported accidental death, and none will be the wiser."

She gasped in shock, but the horror she should have felt was missing. Instead, a thrill of pleasure flew through her at how far Erik would go for her. His violence, his protection, made her feel treasured, cherished, reveled in.

"Tell me, Mya, does it scare you that I can be so callous? So cold and brutal?" he taunted.

Her heart felt as though it was going to pound out of her chest, and she grabbed onto his arm for support. His skin was warmer than usual, muscles bunched as he fisted her hair, drawing her head back slightly until she was staring straight into his eyes again. She answered him breathlessly, honestly.

"No."

"Why?" he crooned, and it was as if he was dragging the answer out of her, tearing it from the very depths of her soul.

She licked her suddenly dry lips, wrestling with the emotions he laid bare within her. Mya swallowed, paused, and on a shaky breath said, "Because I know you. I have watched you. I see you for who you are, and I love you and all that you are."

His fingers danced along her scalp sending tingles down her spine, and she whispered, "I am safe with you."

He smiled, his fangs fully protruding now. "Yes, you are, *fagr skjaldmær min.*"

With that Erik inhaled once more and clenched his jaw. Then he stood, and with each step he tugged something open in her, something raw and vicious. Then he paused, his hand on the doorknob, and without turning he said, "Should you face another issue with anyone, the staff, a stranger—"

"I will tell you," she said.

He nodded stiffly as he stood on the threshold. "Goodnight, Mya."

"Thank you," she whispered.

His answer was a curt nod before he left her room.

2

As the years passed, Mya's body had begun to change and mature. Her breasts grew heavier, fuller, and attracted more attention than she was used to from the town boys, ones who believed themselves to be men worthy of her affections.

According to many, her backside was just as distracting, and she was solely to blame for the males who drooled over her like a piece of meat every time she simply left the house to run an errand. It was her fault for being curvier, womanly, and not procuring clothing to defer their gaze. Some even snickered behind her back that she craved the attention. Ah, yes, because it was Mya's fault they could not stop themselves from staring at her. How she wished she could dig their eyeballs out of their heads—then they would really have something to blame her for.

To them, her silent indifference was her weakness, her admission of guilt. Their gossip soon turned cruel and painful, using her earth-toned skin to question her heritage, to spin the tale that she was a servant's child, that she only claimed to be related to Gregori and Lucas and was not actually their kin. But the worst rumor of all was that she had set her sights on Erik to keep his money for herself.

After all, Mya was eighteen now. According to the villagers she was much too old to still be unmarried. There had to be a reason she had waited so long, especially with her child-bearing hips. How it sounded like they wished her to be nothing more than a cow for a man to breed.

But Mya knew that even without her appearance, she still would have been pursued by mothers and sons alike, just as her family was. She was connected to Erik, lord of the land. Who would not want to court and marry her? She could have any man she wanted at the drop of the hat, except the actual man she wanted, it seemed.

It had gone so far, that Gregori and Lucas had offered to escort her on her adventures into town, all to curb the horrible behaviors Mya was subjugated to, but she refused them both. Their supervision would have made it all the more real, hurtful, and embarrassing.

She hated it all.

Mya hated how men ruled the world. Her parents had always taught her that there were things a man could do and things only a woman could do, but that both were in equal power. Her mother and aunt had lived together, taking care of their entire home from cooking and cleaning, to protecting their land from men who wished to steal it, men who believed there was no way women could take care of such a property.

When Mya's father, Henry, decided he wanted to marry her mother, Eleta, he had to fight to win her affection, but not just in the traditional sense. He had to better her mother's life. She did not need him, so Henry had to make Eleta want him. He had to show her that he would never hold her back, only lift her up. He had to make her love him.

To Mya, that was how a courtship worked. That was the example of love she held all relationships to, and none of the men who harassed, belittled, and accused her, who threw their fathers' dowries at her as if it was something for Mya to be impressed by, lived up to those standards.

No, her heart was reserved for Erik, and Mya did everything she could to be closer to him, to spend more time with him.

She left her wild hair long because she liked the way he played with it, twirling the strands around his fingertips as if he was searching for any reason to be close to her. She liked his scent and loved it even more when he came to her bedroom at night so she could drown herself in him before she went to sleep. She loved to watch Erik when he trained Gregori and Lucas, captivated by the way his muscles tensed and tendons squeezed when he threw a punch or kick, how his light blonde hair swayed around his shoulders as he ducked and rolled, parrying his opponents' attacks. She was jealous of the sweat that rolled down his chest when he was done, and she had taken to embracing him whenever they were alone just to claim a piece of him, even if it was just a simple touch. She understood it was foolish, just as she now understood the name for her body's reactions to him—*desire*.

Her attraction to him had grown into something she never knew she could feel. He was the only one she wanted to kiss her, to touch her, to do other things that she heard about from the married women in town. She wanted Erik to pleasure her, and she wanted to learn how to pleasure him, but the reality was it would never be. He was her guardian, and while she still did not understand the breadth of his feelings for her, she knew her thoughts were impure.

Mya respected Erik. She did her best to pretend that was all she felt, but she was tired of pretending. She did not care if it was wrong. She did not want to be pursued by anyone else, to possibly have to fake entertaining a suitor, or to continue to be on high alert every time she left their house just to fit into this time period.

There was something in her gut that told her it would only spell trouble if she continued, but for now that was the game she played as she donned the blue dress that had been carefully embroidered with golden filagree and small gems, coiled her hair and placed it into its typical net, picked her matching headdress and cloak, and went on her way, all while trying not to stomp her feet too hard while she walked.

Her tutor's general scolding flashed through her head, and she had to force herself to straighten her spine, roll her shoulders back, and keep her chin up. Eventually, as the wind blew against her and the sunshine warmed her skin, Mya's mood improved.

It lightened even more as she entered the local apothecary. Mya had taken up the study of medicine and anatomy privately, as she would never have been allowed to practice. The Black Plague still ran rampant among the poor. As a vampire, she did not need the medicine, but Mya wanted to protect those who had no way to receive the necessary medicine. The poor were subjugated to the filth at the hands of the rich, and it made Mya's stomach ill. She knew she could not change the world, and would not be able to save everyone, but she would do all that she could to make a difference.

She was also fascinated by what medicine could do to her

blood. Erik had supplied her with a space to practice her experiments, and he often assisted her in her thirst for knowledge by providing her herbs and the latest medical texts he could find. When he could not provide something she wanted, she stole it, and Erik supported her fully.

Mya took her time perusing the shelves before purchasing what she could without raising suspicion: a few herbs which held medicinal properties. She made a mental note of the herbs she would ask Erik to purchase for her, as well as a new rumored text based on the science of anatomy.

She was pleased when she left the apothecary, but the small skip in her step vanished when a door opened behind her and the Bennet twins stepped out, along with Richard Browne and Walter Godfrey. The Bennet twins were children of a noble who believed he and his family controlled the world and everything in it. They were brash. They stole, they lied, they harassed and assaulted women, and they viewed themselves above reproach. Their friends, Richard and Walter, believed the same.

Mya tried to scurry past them but was cut off by Walter. He attempted to grab her, but her vampire abilities made her faster than him. As she veered around one man, the next came from behind her. She turned, avoiding his grasp as well, and spun, but her basket of herbs unbalanced her and she found herself braced against the alley wall.

The breath rushed out of her as Randolph Bennet neared her, his brother, Gilbert, flanked to his side. She began to panic, not for her sake, but for theirs. It was imperative that no one find out she, her family, or Erik were vampires, and that meant Mya had to practice control in this situation. She had to monitor her emotions, not get too angry, too violent. Yet everything about these men told her that they were not going to let her go with a simple scare. They thought themselves to be powerful, but to her they were simply prey, and if they were not careful, she would catch them and eat them like the predator she was.

Mya stood straight against the wall, pressing back against it as much as possible to put space between herself and them. Before they could open their mouths, she said, "I am on my way home. Erik and the rest of my family are waiting for me. Please let me pass."

Richard snickered while Randolph braced his arm above her head. "I am sure they will not miss you for a couple of minutes."

"It will take longer than that to finish with her," Gilbert said with a smirk.

Mya ignored him and stared Randolph straight in his eyes. "Let me go, Randolph. I am not worth the trouble."

The boys behind him laughed, but Randolph's eyes gleamed as if she had said the exact words he needed to hear. "I would be inclined to agree with you, but you have avoided me at every turn, and for that you have to be punished."

"Randolph—"

"Enough, woman!" Randolph yelled, before he reared back and struck her.

The blow he dealt did not bruise her skin nor cause her any pain, but it shocked her. A feeling of injustice rose within her. How could they do this? Why had they done this? What harm had Mya ever caused them, or this world, to be forced to live such a life? Had she not been kind? Had she not kept to herself, done her best to not be a bother, to not bring trouble down upon others? Had she not tried to help others without asking for anything in return? Did she not deserve more?

You deserve more, a voice said to her.

Her voice. Her subconscious.

Pay attention now, it whispered. *Take your retribution.*

She blinked and the world came back into focus. Her face was against the timber panel of the alley while the men pushed and prodded her from behind. It took the four of them to shove her in place, their strength in numbers.

Air began to whip around her legs, and she gasped.

This was going to happen.

They were going to rape her.

Their laughs and hollers filled her ears, and her body turned numb.

What have I done to deserve this? Why is this happening to me?

Hands shoved her legs apart. She knew it, felt her body move, but reality seemed to distort itself. She was there and not there, just as they were there and not there. It was as if she was no longer in her body.

And yet their laughter remained. It grew louder, and their snide remarks followed as they argued about who would be the first to shove themselves inside of her and who would follow next, and after that, and after that.

Their laughter, their cheers as if they had won an honest victory, their *cruelty,* left a stain on her soul.

You are stronger than this, her subconscious growled.

Was she strong? No. She had always been weak. Had that not been why this world had been so barbaric toward her? Was that not why it had taken everything from her? It had taken her family, her way of life. Even something as simple as her studies and passions were unobtainable because she was a woman. And then there was her heart, so far locked away because she could never have the one person she wanted.

But at least she had herself. She had her body, her mind, her soul, and now these men, these insignificant little creatures, were trying to take them from her.

She hated it. She hated England. She hated the rules she had to follow. She hated the women whose words cut her so deeply. She hated the men that treated her as if she was nothing more than an object available to them whenever and however they wanted.

But most of all, perhaps, she hated herself. She hated that nothing would change no matter what she did or how she did it. She hated that as a woman, she would always be expected to sacrifice for someone else.

Mya knew what she was going to do.

She was going to let her anger rule her. She was going to turn into a vampire, a horrible monster to mankind. She was going to kill these men, and her family would be the ones to pay for it. And she hated herself the most because she could not —would not—stop.

Mya deserved more, and she would take her retribution with a smile.

She grasped the wrist of the nearest man and twisted until he screamed so loudly the sound punctured her ear drums. She healed almost instantly from the injury, but the small flinch of pain only strengthened her resolve.

Her eyes glazed over, her blood lust growing stronger and clouding her vision, until she could only feel the pop of his joints and hear the agonizing screams tearing from his body as she broke his bones. She could taste his blood and smell his sweat in the air—salty and sour, tinged with fear.

When the smell of urine flooded her senses, she threw the man away. His head landed with a loud, wet *whack* against the stones. Mya smiled at the sound and the now fresh scent of oozing blood. It sharpened her predatory senses, and while she still could not see the faces of the other men in front of her, she could make out their forms as they processed the shock of the last few seconds.

Then they pushed, hit, and beat her, but she felt no pain. Their blows did nothing but anger her more. They were still invading her space as if they had the right, as if they owned it, owned her, and their feeble attempts to hurt her were accompanied by berating claims that she had asked for this.

Time seemed to slow around her, every action the speed of a tortoise's next step. She parried each of their blows, moving so fast she could predict their next move from the rush of air that tickled the hair on her skin. It felt as if she was moving in the blink of an eye.

Why had she not done this sooner? This feeling, this freedom, was everything to her, and

Mya laughed loudly as she succumbed further. She lifted her arms, ready to push the men, already planning her next move. Maybe she would castrate them, make sure that they could never do this to another woman again. Perhaps she would just kill them outright, their lives payment for the atrocities she was sure they had forced upon other women. They should have never been brought into this world, and she, in her righteousness, would be their judge, jury, and executioner.

The sound of a door opening interrupted her thoughts, and she hissed at the intrusion.

"Aye! What are you boys doing?" a man shouted, before banging something against a metal pot. The sound stung her, so high pitched against her sensitive hearing that it made her head ring.

She looked up and could make out the face of the man, Tubert. He wobbled out of the door, using the frame to support himself on his wooden leg while he brandished the metal pot in an attempt to look intimidating.

Why had he inserted himself into this? Perhaps Tubert had nothing left to lose. Perhaps he wanted to be of importance to someone. Maybe he simply wanted to do something with his life, play at being the hero to raise his value in society. Perhaps he thought that saving her would garner him a reward.

Whatever was going through the man's mind did not matter. No one would get in the way of her justice, not even this man who played at defending her. If he tried to stop her, she would kill him just as surely as she would delight in killing these men. Until she peered down to Tubert's leg and saw Albin, Tubert's seven-year-old son, standing behind his father.

That was what brought Mya back from the edge and curbed her rage. She could never put a child through what she had gone through; she could never rob a child of their parent.

The blood lust cleared from her eyes, allowing her to see. The men's faces in front of her were white, their eyes wide and unblinking. Past them she saw Walter's body—whether dead or just unconscious she did not know—and her stomach turned under the sick satisfaction that sight gave her.

She needed to leave, now, before she succumbed to her blood lust again.

Mya turned and ran. Shouts rang out behind her, but she did not stop. Instead, she ran faster, scared of what she would do, who she would become, and how much she would like it if she turned back. She had put her family in danger, and she fully believed that Gilbert and his group would do everything in their power to use what had just happened to their advantage.

Many people had converted under the power of the church. Erik may be lord of these lands, but the church would be quick to investigate a claim of demonism. One rumor would be enough to qualify the investigation. Any demand for further proof would seem suspicious, and with so many of the townspeople converting, Erik would fall under scrutiny for not reporting her condition himself. There were already those who wanted to challenge his position, and this one action could finally give them the ability to do so.

Mya had caused this. She had brought this trouble into her home.

But what was the alternative?

Should she have stood there and let them rape her? Was that all she was good for? No. This was a situation where the circumstances would never have been in her favor, and her family would understand that. They would support her actions, she knew that deep in her soul, but she did not want them to endure her decisions as well.

If you kill the men who hurt you, they will not have to, the voice within her said.

Unconsciously, her pace slowed until she halted near a wooden wall.

Was that an option? Could that be her only option?

Yes, the voice hissed, begging her.

Mya could kill them. She could wait for them to be alone and then hunt them down one by one. She could easily find them. Walter's blood was still on her gown, and where he was the others would be sure to follow. She lifted the gown to her nose and inhaled. The blood was so sweet, so delectable, that her heart pounded in her chest.

Mya grasped onto the wall as her blood lust began to take her over once more. Could she do it? Could she take their lives to spare her family the consequences of her actions?

You will only kill those who deserve it. No one else.

It sounded too good to be true, but as she tossed the thought over in her mind, she knew it was the only way. If she killed them, no one else would know. Her family would be safe and she could leave, go somewhere else, perhaps back to Spain. That thought gave her so much warmth, satisfaction, and pleasure, that it sealed her fate.

Mya turned, a smirk tugging her lips. She gave into her blood lust and her vision faded to red. She took one step and pressed her toes to the path, ready to jump, to soar along the roofs of the buildings until she reached her prey. She lowered herself, feeling her energy build, and then—

An arm wrapped around her torso, the heavy weight keeping her still. Before she could even think to struggle, she was pulled back into the shadow of the alley.

The scent of pine, ash, smoke, and cinnamon hit her on her next inhale, and she froze.

Erik.

He cannot see me like this, she thought. *He cannot know.*

But he stood in front of her, plain as day, and his stare was as tangible as the fingers he ran over the torn areas of her gown.

She tried to speak to him, to tell him to leave her, to let her go, but she was not in control. The words came out garbled, incomprehensible, and it only shamed her more.

"Who touched you, *fagr skjaldmær min?*" he asked, his voice low, so calm and deadly that her skin broke out in chills.

Mya could not tell him. Not only because she could not voice the words, but because it pained her too. Erik's presence had always made her feel safe, as if he were her home. She trusted him to always come to her aid, but the thought of him doing so now threw her into a panic. If she told him, he would take on her battle. He would kill the men she was meant to kill, and therein lay the problem.

This was not for him to solve. This was not for him to do. She could not rely on him this time, and she refused to let him interfere. Too much could go wrong, and she would not let him implicate himself in his act of heroism. She wanted to prove to herself, to him, that she was just as much as a warrior as he, that she could be just as ruthless, calculating, and brave.

She would not miss this chance.

She would not let those men win.

Her blood lust pulsed under her emotions, twisting her desires into a desperate need for survival. The weight of her embarrassment, shame, guilt, anger, disappointment, hatred, and love merged into something ugly, and for the first time in her life she fought against Erik. She tried to push him away. When that did not work, she tried to hit and punch him, but he simply grabbed her hands by her wrists and shoved her back against the wall. The movement only made her fight more. Her consciousness ached because she could not break out of her blood lust.

She felt outside of her body again, and the sight she saw devastated her. She did not recognize the woman struggling against Erik. She was so lost, so chaotic, her jaw snapping at him as she tried to free her hands and claw at his skin. Mya would have never tried to hurt Erik. She did not want to rely on him, and she wanted him to let her go, but not like this.

This was not her, but she did not know how to regain her senses.

Tears dropped from her lashes as she realized that even with this power, she was weak. If she could not use her mind and be in control of her heart and body, what good was she to anyone?

She tried again to speak to Erik. The words were even more garbled now, coming out as feral, animalistic sounds and snarls, but somehow he knew. Erik used his body to keep her pinned against the wall. He grabbed hold of her neck, grasping it between his thumb and pointer finger. His hands were so large that his fingers reached under her ear, but his touch was gentle as he whispered, "I will not let you suffer this, *fagr skjaldmær min*. Forgive me."

His free hand slid into her hair, fisting the strands at her scalp. He tilted her face to his, holding her in place and then his lips came down against hers.

3

Everything in her stopped.

Her fight, her thoughts, her heart, her very breath all ground to a halt when he kissed her.

Sensations she had never known took her over. Erik's lips were soft, so warm and firm against her own. Gently he moved them against hers, and eventually she began to follow his movements. Mya did not feel the shift in her blood lust, did not even sense that it had started to die down, that the emotions that had once powered her change were now morphing into something else, something undeniable, incontrollable: *desire.*

Erik broke away from her, leaving her gasping both for breath and for his return. Mya tried to follow, but his hand was still in her hair, grasping the strands tighter, and she hoped, nearly prayed, that it meant he felt a shred of what she did.

Mya wished she could voice the words, that she was more experienced in this, but she was too breathless, too shocked and senseless to be able to speak. Then she peered into his silver eyes, and she saw it: the same desire was mirrored in them, an abundant hunger that was both dark and heavenly.

One moment, just one breath, passed, as if he was trying to win some internal battle, and then he was back on her again. She welcomed him. She knew better now, moving her lips against his, and as a reward Erik took her to new heights.

He licked the seam of her lips, triggering a breathless moan from her. She felt his tongue again, and when she parted her lips he slipped his tongue inside her mouth, coaxing a hum of satisfaction from her.

He teased her relentlessly, licking inside her mouth only to pull back and repeat the action all over again, as if this was some game, a source of amusement for him when it only left her wanting more.

She could not touch him, could not drag him closer. Her hands were still clasped behind her, and her body still pressed between his and the wall. Mya could not even pull her head away from the grasp he had on her hair, and every tug when she tried both frustrated and exhilarated her.

Erik was in control of this entire experience, and while she loved that she could surrender to him, she also wanted to give him something, to show him and herself she could bring him the same pleasure he brought her. So, when he left her mouth, a strand of saliva being the only thing that connected the two of them, and then returned, she opened her mouth, caught his lower lip, and sucked.

Erik's body tensed, straining against hers, so Mya did it again. This time her canines caught the skin of his lip. They were still sharp, sharper than she was used to, and without meaning to she cut his lip open. Two droplets of blood entered her mouth, dripping onto her tongue.

A tremor passed through her entire body, and although she knew it might be wrong— that she had never asked Erik's permission to drink his blood—she could not stop herself from tasting him, from sucking his blood into her mouth.

The moan that left her was loud and sinful, and Erik's own groan of pleasure turned what was once something of shocking passion into a turbulent chasm of war. His hands left the grip he had on her hair to wrap themselves around her. She took him, took his weight, his taste, and she craved every ounce of it more than air itself.

Mya's hands wound themselves in the tresses of his golden hair, twisting and pulling, gripping like he had done to her, to show him what she needed, what she desperately desired: for him not to stop. All she could feel was Erik—the way he sucked her lips, how his tongue felt when he ran it across hers, how he tasted like mint and honied pears.

Mya loved it. She loved the shivers that coursed through her body, the gooseflesh that puckered her skin, the way his lips seemed to transfer her whole body and soul to another dimension where only he resided.

Erik's hand slid up her back, and she moaned for him. He fisted her hair once more, bunching the strands and gripping them at her scalp as he kept her head tilted so he could kiss her deeper, more passionately, and she took every drop of what he gave.

Mya clung to him, her fingers digging into his shoulders and arms, feeling his muscles tense, tendons tighten and release, the way his chest shuddered each time she opened her mouth to his, each time he took another breath and breathed her in. She could feel how hard and fast his heart was beating, that it seemed to race just as quickly as hers. This was unforgiving, electrifying, and Mya could only succumb to the waves of pleasure that ignited her skin.

Her core grew wetter, her nipples so swollen and sensitive that every rub against her chemise was almost painful. Erik's erection pushed against her stomach, and the knowledge that he was so hard for her nearly made her weep. Mya knew he was large––she could tell that through his clothing––but the question of how he would fit inside her never crossed her mind. He would fit, and she would take him gladly. Mya expected the pain of having her virginity taken, but she would give it to him. She would take him with wild abandon, even if he split her in two, because this moment with him was worth everything.

Erik's teeth raked over her lip. There was a gentle sting, and then he tasted her, drank her blood like she had his. Euphoria filled her and she gasped at the heady feeling. Mya had drunk and exchanged blood plenty of times before, but this was different. It was as if her entire body was exploding cell by cell, molecule by molecule, shifting and changing, *accepting* Erik as a secret piece of her body that she had been missing all along. In her heart he had always been, and now her body demanded to be complete.

Erik heeded that call with a guttural groan. He lifted her, and she wrapped her arms tighter around him, grasping him. She refused to be separated from him even for a moment. With one hand he held her, bracing her against the wall, while the other slid down to her ankle, then up, taking her gown and chemise with it while the cold metal of his ring brushed her skin.

Mya shifted to help him raise her dress. When he tugged it to her waist, she wrapped her legs around him, crossing her ankles at his back. He groaned, guided her down just slightly and then pressed his clothed erection against her damp core.

She moaned so loudly into his mouth that someone was sure to have heard her, but it did not stop either of them. He did it again and again, guiding and pushing while he gripped and kneaded her behind. She circled her hips, brushing against him as he did her, and she delighted in the intensity of the shudders that racked his body. Erik's hand snaked up the back of her dress, and the cold air in contrast to the warmth of his large palm made her gasp.

He finally tore his mouth away from hers only to bring it lower. Erik kissed her jaw, then her neck, and Mya tilted her head back against the wall to give him access. She fisted his tunic, pulling at the material as she fought to feel his skin. She wanted to touch him, feel him bare against her, to leave her mark on him in the same way he was leaving his on her.

Erik kissed lower still, down to her breasts which heaved with every breath she took. He pulled at the material of her gown, but his finger slipped through a tear in the fabric.

The smell of blood that wafted from the shift of cloth hit them both, and they froze. That was where they had torn her gown that morning, a reminder of her assault. The memory hurt and angered her, but perhaps what was worse was the knowledge that she and Erik could not move past it, not like this, no matter how much she wanted to.

Mya reached to touch Erik's cheek, but he tilted his head away from her. The rejection stung, but she understood. Whatever the reason was this ... exchange had occurred, it was over and done with. Perhaps Erik had never meant for it to go this far in the first place.

Still, it crushed her heart when he said in a low voice, "Uncross your legs from me, Mya."

She blinked, embarrassed and disappointed that she clearly struggled to let him go, when he did not feel the same. Mya uncrossed her ankles from his back, but as she tried to lower her legs, he only pulled her closer, his grasp tight on her waist. Erik guided her to the ground, her descent a slow and blissful torture as Erik pressed into her. She brushed against his hips, thighs, calves, and ankles until her feet met the road. She was still so sensitive that she squeezed her eyes shut and bit her lip, trying to cover her moan.

"My apologies," Erik said, his voice gruff and hoarse. When Mya opened her eyes, he looked animalistic, feral. His cheekbones were sharper, the white of his skin now pink and flushed. His jaw was tight and his canines extended between his lips, but it was his eyes, the normal silver now red, that captivated her most of all.

Mya lifted her hand again to touch his face. This time he stilled so much that she could not even feel his chest move to breathe. She stopped, dropping her hand to his chest because the truth was right there in front of her. She may not know his feelings, but there was *something* there, and perhaps he struggled just as much as she did with letting go.

"No apology necessary," she whispered.

Erik released a harsh breath then braced his hand against the wooden wall. His fist tightened and extended several times and his entire body seemed to tremble before he said, "Who hurt you, *fagr skjaldmær min?* Tell me their names."

She tilted her head away from his, but he brought it back with a grasp of her chin.

"I do not want you to get involved," she said, her voice wavering under his intensity.

Erik's eyes narrowed, his face seeming to grow sharper as he bent down to her level. "I was bound to be involved the moment they came near you. They brought this fate upon themselves," he growled.

The deep predatory sound made her eyes widen, but it was the way Erik's hand stroked her chin, his fingers caressing her jaw gently as his eyes softened ever so slightly, that had her melting again.

"I will never hurt you, not you," he whispered as his eyes begged her to understand, to believe his words. "But I will kill whoever has done this to you."

"They are nobles," Mya hissed. "If they find out it was you—"

"I do not care."

"Erik!" she pleaded.

"I do not care!" he roared. "Nobles or not, they are a disgrace, a blight on this land. They do not deserve to breathe the same air as you. They should have never touched you. *No one* is allowed to touch you but me! You are *mine!*"

The words hung between them, suspended in the silence that was broken only by their rushed breathing.

Erik dropped his hand from her, and his face fell. "I—"

"I am yours, Erik"—Mya fiddled with the cloth of his tunic, unable to meet his eyes—"in every sense of the word."

When she finally gathered her courage to look up, the look of shock on his face caused her to laugh even as a tear slid down her cheek. Erik caught the droplet with his thumb, wiping away the wetness from her cheek, and yet the heartbreak in his gaze caused another one to fall.

"You are a gift, *fagr skjaldmær min*. One that I do not deserve, and one that I cannot accept no matter how much I want to."

The arrow of heartbreak buried itself deeper in Mya's chest, but she nodded. Mya bit her lip, using the pain to keep the weight of her sadness from spilling over, and whispered, "If you cannot accept me or take me, I will never allow another the chance."

"Mya," he began, but she shook her head. Erik took a breath and rubbed her cheek again, his touch bringing a warmth that only hurt her more because of how much she craved it. "Let me do what I can for you. Let me protect you. Let me be your shield, your guard. Please," he begged when she did not answer.

In all the years she had known Erik, he had never once begged her. Convinced her? Yes. Toyed with her? Yes. But begged her? No. Resisting him was hard enough, but once the plea had passed his lips, she knew that there was nothing she would not give him.

Taking a deep breath, she said, "Gilbert and Randolph Bennet. Richard Browne. Walter Godfrey."

Simply saying their names brought her so much anxiety and disgust that bile rose up her throat. She swallowed it down and continued, knowing she had no other choice.

"I hurt Walter, and the other three saw me turn. Tubert and Albin tried to defend me, and that is when I ran away. I do not think they saw what I-I am." She shook her head as fresh tears came to her eyes. "I am sorry. I am so sor—"

"Shh," Erik whispered as he hugged her tightly, his warmth chasing at the coldness in her bones. "You have done well, *fagr skjaldmær min*. So, so well," he murmured into her hair.

"But the nobles, they saw me," she cried into his chest.

"That was unavoidable, *fagr skjaldmær min.* You did the best you could, far better than I would have." He pulled back just slightly, enough to wipe the tears from her eyes. "I never doubted you for a moment. Your bravery knows no bounds."

She shook her head. "I am not brave. I am not like you."

"No, *fagr skjaldmær min*, you are *better.* Now, I need to call on your bravery once more."

Erik grasped her arms, leading her away from the wall. He checked her cloak and tightened it around her, hiding the rips in her gown. "Can you make it home safely for me?"

"Yes, but they may have told someone by now. If they did, the church—"

Erik stroked her cheek with his palm. "Mya, do not worry about me. I can handle this. Even if they told the church, I would happily kill the members and send them to their new god if it means I can keep you safe for one more day. Now go," he ordered.

She knew there would be no more trying, reasoning, or attempts at convincing; Erik had made up his mind and was now on his mission, and there would be nothing she could do to stop it.

She took a few steps, then paused and turned back to him. "Come home to me," she said.

She did not hear his reply, but she swore she saw him mouth the words, "I could never stay away."

4

E rik did not come home that night.

Mya waited for him in her room. When he did not come to her, she searched every room of the house. She even asked the staff if they had seen him, but everyone gave her the same story: Erik had left the grounds for an important meeting and would be back in due course.

That information should have made her feel more at ease, except Mya could not smell Erik's scent anywhere. His rooms were empty and his bed was made. There was not a single crinkle in the bed sheets or a curtain pulled back too far; nothing that would indicate someone had slept there. If he had not come home, who had given the household staff that message?

The only other people Erik trusted were Gregori and Lucas. But if he had spoken to them, how much had he told them? Mya did not believe Erik would have told them about yesterday's events, but it was possible they could have assumed what had happened. If they did not know and Mya went to ask them about Erik's whereabouts, they would pester her until she finally gave them the truth, and then both her brother and cousin would go on the same murderous rampage Erik was now on.

She did not want that. Mya wanted her family to live blissfully unaware of her troubles, and so she bit her tongue and held her curiosity. She would simply wait. While Erik often needed to go away for a week or two at a time, he always took staff with him and made ample preparations. This spontaneity was not like him, which meant it would only be a matter of time until the staff grew suspicious.

Another day came and went, and there was still no sign of Erik. Mya stayed awake the whole night awaiting his arrival, but he never entered their house. There was no creak of a floorboard, no whine of a door opening, no sudden breeze from a window. There was nothing.

The household staff gave Mya the same answer as the day before, and she was beginning to grow frustrated. She did not know where to turn. Not only was she worried about Erik, not sleeping had wreaked havoc on her metabolism. While a vampire did not need to eat or sleep, doing so allowed their body to enter a rested state where their metabolism would be better controlled. Without those, Mya needed to consume more blood, if she did not, it would be easier for her to lose control again.

That night she drank an extra cup of pig's blood and forced herself to settle down in bed, but her mind refused to calm, leaving her tossing and turning in a half-asleep state for hours. When she began to settle and finally drifted to sleep, she dreamed of warm arms wrapping around her.

"Shh, love," Erik said, his voice low and quiet. "Sleep now. I am with you."

A small smile graced her lips as he settled in behind her, the warmth of his chest seeping into her back and she further relaxed into his embrace.

The following morning, the sun shone brightly into her room, alerting her that she had slept well toward midday. She rolled over onto her back with a sigh. She knew the feeling of Erik sleeping beside her had simply been a dream, but it had felt so real, so deliciously perfect.

Tears rolled down her cheeks, the only release she could find for the weight of it all. Two days ago, her only concerns were unrequited love and a feeling of unbelonging. Now she was worried that the love of her life had fallen into chaos and possible ruin because of her, and beneath it all were the memories and emotions of that fateful day.

Rape was a common issue in England—and all over the world, Mya assumed—but as far as she was aware, nobles were normally spared from experiencing such a thing. It was more usual among the commoners, simply because the rich could afford justice and the poor could not.

It sickened her that this was an accepted normality of their society, but after having gone through it she realized it was so much worse. Mya had been spared by her vampire nature. Yes, Tubert and Albin had attempted to help her, but what could a crippled man and his young son do against four nobles? They, much like Erik, were willing to risk their lives to help her, but what about all the women who did not have someone to do that for them?

Mya was not sure if stopping her rape before it happened was better or worse for her psyche. Did she really deserve to feel as though she was a victim of a crime that she was lucky to not fully experience, when there were those that had it so much worse? Was it any better when she now knew the outside world was not safe for her, that at any time she could be made to go through the same thing again?

She shook her head, harshly wiping away the tears at her eyes.

No, comparing her trauma and pain to someone else's would never get her anywhere, yet it still hurt. It still cut at something inside her to have to go through all of this in silence. If Erik had not been there, she would never have told him. She would never have told *anyone*. Her secret would have died with those men, and now, once again, she wished she had killed them.

Perhaps she should not be so villainous. Perhaps that was not what a young woman of her stature should think of as a resolution. Perhaps her morals were skewed because she was more monster than human, and yet, humans could be the most monstrous of all.

Mya sniffed and wiped the snot from her nose. Those men may have not raped her, but they had stolen something from her: the last remaining strands of her naivety. Any innocence she once had was now gone. Mya could only see this world for the darkness that lay inside of it, and she, just like every being on this planet, held some of that darkness.

When Erik returned, and he *would* return to her, even if she had to hunt him down and bring him back kicking and scream-ing, she would ask him to help her understand that darkness. She would tame it, use it, morph it for the future, because she would never be a victim again. Her life, regardless of how much it made her ache inside, was still her own, and she was done living by the laws of others that did not serve her. She had the power to save herself from any fate she chose, but she needed to learn that power, learn how to use it and harness it in a way that worked best for her. And once she did, she would use it for others as well, and to hell with anyone who stood in her way.

Mya sat up and squared her shoulders with determination. She took a deep inhale, intent on calming her inner thoughts, but instead she choked on the scent on her skin: pine, ash, smoke, and cinnamon. She froze, then in a flurry of movement, she twisted her nightgown and lifted it to her nose. On her next inhale, she sobbed in realization. She had not dreamed of Erik; he had been there. She held her pillow up to her nose and smelled him all over it. A shaky laugh escaped her as she hugged it close. He had come home to her! He was safe.

He was in my bed.

The thought made her cheeks warm, but then a chirp drew her attention to her window. Pale red curtains were dusted in swirls of beige and bronze and held open by beige tassels at the corners, revealing a matching sheer curtain which allowed the light to filter in. Mya never liked to close her curtains, preferring to fall asleep to the sight of the moon and wake to the sun. As she watched the light filter through the thin fabric, she noticed a small red ribbon trapped under her window, keeping it cracked open just enough to let the typical call of the birds sound than normal.

Mya knew with absolute certainty she had left her window closed last night.

So that is how he entered my room.

She padded over and lifted the window with a small smile, plucking at the piece of red ribbon. When it did not come away in her hand, she realized it was tied to an object. Tugging on it led her to a bundle full of herbs.

Mya breathed in the fragrances of lavender, sage, mint, lungwort, and rose, all the herbs she had bought from the apothecary on her last outing. She fell to her seat beneath the window and hugged the herbs to her chest, basking in the aroma and thoughtfulness behind the gift. The fact that Erik would go to such lengths when he realized how much this meant to her was overwhelming. She was in awe of his care and attention, and she had to force herself to breathe through the tender feelings it invoked.

She needed to see him, to thank him and talk to him about her thoughts and desires. But if Erik was nearby, why would he have used her window to come in and out of her room? Why would he have left the herbs for her to find, instead of bringing it to her directly? Something was amiss.

Mya pulled on her indoor clothes and ran out of her room to find him, but much like before he was nowhere to be found. No one knew of his exact whereabouts, nor were they concerned. Erik had left a letter before heading out once again, stating that he would be busy for several more days but would return as soon as he could.

The news crushed her. Not because she expected his attention or a personal letter but because she knew it was a lie. Erik had never left her alone for so long without speaking to her directly and explaining where he was going. This had to do with her, with her assault. She knew that like she knew her own name. The worry came rushing back, crashing into her, and fresh tears spilled down her face, because she knew the truth. Whatever had happened, whatever Erik had done, had now grown increasingly more complicated, and it was all her fault.

THREE MORE DAYS HAD PASSED, AND WITH EACH ONE MYA FEARED she was losing her mind. More gifts had been left outside her window: a book she had been coveting regarding the study of physiology, more herbs—the kind that only doctors were allowed to purchase—and a letter.

She had read that letter more times than she could count, and yet she found herself sitting on the chair beside the window with it in her hand, reading his scrawled penmanship once again.

"Mya,

I hope these herbs will assist you in your experiments. I expect to hear about them when I return. Please do not worry. Make sure to eat and sleep regularly. I will be with you soon, fagr skjaldmœr min.

With all my love,

Erik."

Mya rested her head against the window and sighed, her breath fogging the glass as she tightened her grip on the letter.

Where are you? Are you hurt? Are you in danger? Why will you not let me see you, Erik? Why will you not tell me what has happened?

"Penny for your thoughts, little sister?"

Gregori's sudden presence made her jump in the chair. Mya clutched her racing heart, and while a smile appeared on her older brother's face, he did not laugh. That meant they were going to have a very serious and honest conversation, whether Mya wanted to or not. Still, she could at least try to speak half-truths.

"I am waiting for Erik to return home, that is all. Do you have any news on his arrival?"

"And who is to say he is not already here?" Gregori said with a smirk.

Mya's eyes grew wide. "He is? He has returned?"

Gregori stepped to the window, staring out into the distance. "How odd. Before Erik left, he gave me a series of instructions and messages to give the staff. But none were for you." He turned and his hazel eyes burned into her dark olive. "Why do you think that is?"

Mya's back straightened. Her eyes narrowed, but she continued to gaze out of the window. "I do not presume to know why Erik does or does not do something. Just as I do not know why he is not home. But you seem to, *brother*," she bit out.

Gregori took a chair and dragged it beside her, positioning the back toward her as he straddled the chair. The action was so at odds with their noble personas that it calmed her, even if she knew his seemingly relaxed posture was nothing but a facade.

Gregori crossed his arms on the top of the chair and rested his chin on them as he studied her. Mya refused to back down from the challenge and stared right back into his eyes. It was futile, though, as it always had been and likely always would be.

"I think you know exactly why Erik left, and if you do not want to tell me then that means it has to do with you." Gregori straightened and grasped the chair hard in his fists, his posture reminding her of Erik. "What happened to you?"

Mya opened her mouth to speak, but her body betrayed her and she shuddered before the lie could slip between her teeth. It was only for a moment, but her brother saw it. His eyes grew just a tad in realization before narrowing. His nostrils flared as he asked again, "What happened, Mya?"

She shook her head. "Gregori, I love you even if you are a royal pain in my side, but this does not concern you."

He glared at her, so she hurried to continue. "The only reason Erik knows is because he was there. I am not willing to tell you anything further. Please let this go."

Gregori tapped on the chair, his movements growing stronger with each beat until she worried the wood was snap under his ministrations. Then he simply let go. His shoulders tensed and released multiple times until eventually he lifted his hand and ran it through his short brown hair.

For a moment he simply stared at her, eyes flashing between annoyance and disappointment, then he sighed.

"I do not like when you keep secrets from me. But you are old enough to know what is best for you. However, I need to know this. Was Erik the one who hurt you?"

Mya could not stop her brow from furrowing. "No, Erik would never hurt me," she said without a moment of hesitation.

Gregori nodded then tapped on the chair again, his gaze turning to the window as he stood. In the silence Mya wondered if he believed that if he gave her time, she might tell him everything, but she would not. She turned to stare out the window too, curious as to whether Gregori had seen something, hopeful that perhaps Erik was just beyond her view.

"I see everything that happens here," Gregori began. He glanced her way once more, then back to the window. "It is my job to see everything that happens here. It is my job to fill Erik's role in its entirety when he's gone."

Mya looked up at him. She knew her brother took on the responsibilities of the house when Erik was away, but for the first time she wondered what all that entailed. Mya was so busy hating and questioning her place in this world that she had never stopped to question her family's. Was Gregori happy? Were the responsibilities placed on him too much?

Again, she realized how much he looked like Erik. It was in his stance, his form. She knew Erik was a mentor and friend to her brother, but did Gregori feel like she did, obligated to play a role he did not want? What were his dreams, and when was the last time she had asked?

Gregori's voice drew her out of her thoughts. "When Erik left, he gave me messages and instructions for the staff. He then asked me to make sure that you were well."

His eyes roamed over her features before he crossed his arms and gripped them, fingers clenching a tad too tightly. "He would not tell me what happened to you, and you will not tell me what happened to you. I have to say, as your older brother I am quite hurt that neither of you trust me. But I understand that there are some things that even I cannot resolve."

Mya opened her mouth to reassure him, but he silenced her with his next words.

"Erik and I have a pact when it comes to you."

Mya tilted her head to the side, frowning. "A pact? What do you mean?"

"The day after we arrived here, Erik asked me for my permission to watch over you, to take care of you."

Mya's breath caught in her throat and her eyes widened.

Gregori chuckled. "I would have responded the same way as you just did, except I saw how he looked at you. It is the same way that he has looked at you for years, and the same way that you have looked at him. I see the two of you, the way you are together. You are constantly drawn together like a moth to a flame, back and forth, to and from." He motioned with his fingers and sighed. "Although you never seem to act on that very apparent attraction, which saddens me. While I am incredibly protective of you, and perhaps slightly overbearing, I want you to be happy. It is for that reason that I gave Erik my approval, and it is the very same reason why I will give you the information I know you seek the most right now."

He turned to her, and she swallowed, hoping to wet her dry throat as her heart threatened to beat out of its cage.

"I hope that one day you will be able to trust me and tell me what happened to you."

Mya shook her head and grabbed her brother's arm. "It is not that I do not trust you. I just do not want—"

"I understand," he said, but Mya saw the hurt in his eyes, as if he had failed her in some way.

"Gregori, I trust you. I swear I do!"

"Perhaps you do in some things, but you do not trust me to take the correct actions. Maybe it is because you know me, and maybe you are correct. Maybe you are trying to protect me the same way I have tried to protect you. Still, without the knowledge of what you have suffered, I cannot attempt to assist you with your pain. I have created a space between us in which you do not feel that you can come to me."

He leveled her with his gaze. "I know that is why you did not ask me of Erik's whereabouts when you knew I would know the answer."

If it was possible Mya would have made herself as small as a mouse and scurried away from that gaze, because her brother was correct. She did not trust him, but it was not because he had done anything to her. She realized now that it was because she did not trust herself, and as such could not trust others completely.

"I hope that one day that will change," Gregori said. He

squeezed her hand and patted it gently before lowering it to her lap. Then his voice grew firmer, although tinged with a sliver of sadness. "At the southeast edge of the property lies a large oak tree wrapped in ivy. It is near a large field of clover. Do you know it?"

Mya knew by his voice that their conversation was coming to a close, so she nodded.

"Good. Cross the clover field into the woods. Continue through the woods until you hear a river. Make sure to keep it on your right. From there you will see a cabin. That is where Erik is staying."

Gregori watched her, waiting, and she gave a single nod of understanding.

"Settle whatever this is between the two of you. Once you have," he said, his voice softening, "come and talk to me. Can you do that for me, little sister?"

"Of course," she murmured.

Gregori dropped a kiss on her forehead and tucked a wiry strand of hair behind her ear. "Go at night. If I do not see that you have returned by the morning, I will go and find you. Please, whatever you do, return. I do not want to have to chase after you and find you both ... indecent."

"Gregori!" she objected, but he was already walking away, his laugh echoing down the hall at her blush.

5

The cabin was well hidden in the forest, under a deep canopy of trees and surrounded by brush. Ivy and vines grew along its sides, as if the forest was trying to reclaim it. If it were not for her enhanced senses and her brother's instructions, Mya would have missed it entirely.

When she had first set out for the cabin, Mya wondered what she might find, debating whether the cabin might be decrepit and cold. As soon as she saw it, she felt a rush of admiration for Erik's skill. The cabin might appear abandoned to others, but Mya knew better. It was lush and wild. It was *alive*. It was clear that Erik loved this place and took great care of it, and Mya felt a sense of honor in knowing its location.

She walked up the steps and paused at the door. Mya could not smell Erik in the cabin or the surrounding area, which meant there was a possibility he had laid a trap at the door to ensure no one entered while he was away. Still, she had to try. She was a vampire and could heal quickly should anything happen, and she was certain that he would come to her aid immediately if she triggered anything that could hurt her.

She tried the door and found it unlocked, so she opened it slowly. Relief washed over her when nothing exploded or hurled itself at her face. Surveying the room, Mya found a hearth, bed, basin, wooden storage chest, a small table, lantern, and a chair. Several of the furnishings appeared handmade. Had he built and furnished this place himself? How often did he use it as a quiet retreat? Was this why he always smelled of the forest?

Mya mulled over those questions, realizing she had far too many now, and decided to light the lantern while she sat and waited for Erik to return.

As time went by, her emotions grew, but none more so than the nervousness at Erik's reaction to seeing her. She was concerned that perhaps he had not only stayed away due to complications with protecting her, but that he may have been avoiding her as well. Yes, they had crossed a line neither of them could return from, but Erik had always sought her out in the past. Still, what if he regretted everything and that was why he had stayed away, because he did not know how to communicate that to her?

She shook her head. Something in her screamed that was not the reason. But then what else could be the cause? Mya was so inexperienced and unprepared for this situation, and it frustrated her. She gripped her gown, nails biting into the material, and decided it did not matter what the reason was. She would wait here for as long as it took to get the answers to her questions, and she would not give up until she did.

She had spent the past five days rationalizing Erik's actions and trying to understand everything that had happened, but it was all too much too soon. As she sat in the light of the lantern, Mya thought of her life and her choices. She analyzed what she was proud of and pictured what she hoped to achieve. She thought of her brother, of how much she loved and adored him and of the weight on his shoulders. She wondered if her cousin had the same weight or if he had been spared some of the responsibility by being the youngest between the three of them.

Then her thoughts turned to Erik, of how much he must have gone through to create the life he had. There was much she did not know about him, but that thought did not diminish her feelings toward him. In fact, it strengthened them. But just as she felt wonderment toward Erik, she felt guilty for not already having the answers to the secrets he kept.

She wanted to know those secrets, but had she ever truly asked? Mya reasoned that she could not ask what she did not know, but that was not entirely true. The truth was, as foolish as it may be, she was jealous of the years she had not known Erik. Those years had helped to make him into the man he was today, the man she loved completely, and yet she was jealous of the influences that had created that man, of the time other beings—both immortal and human—had spent with him, of those he may have cared for or even loved before her.

It was selfish and stupid, but it was how she felt nonetheless. She had to acknowledge those feelings honestly. She *wanted* to know Erik's secrets, his thoughts, his past, because she wanted to understand him and to know him in all ways.

As she looked around the cabin, taking in its simplicity, she wondered if Erik felt the same lack of balance she did. They lived in something akin to a castle, and yet he had a cabin hidden away from prying eyes. Did he crave the separation from the lies that embroidered their lives in the same way she did?

A soft click brought her focus back to the room. It was a sound no animal or insect could make, and her breath stalled in her chest. A moment later the door opened, and there Erik stood like a shadow, a creature of the night.

He did not move when he saw her, but she could feel his eyes on her even as he refused to meet her own. Then he entered the cabin, closed the door behind him and walked past her as if she did not exist.

"You should not be here, Mya."

It hurt that those were his first words to her. Her temper peaked but she swallowed it back, her need for answers more important than anything else. Instead, Mya observed and waited. She studied his back, took in his blond hair, now stained with flecks of red. She could smell the scent of blood rolling off him as he moved toward the basin, and when he turned, she saw that his tunic was covered in it. Seeing her staring, Erik ripped off the material as if it had offended him in some way and it on the floor.

His anger did not scare her. This was Erik, *her* Erik. He had the same wide shoulders and muscled back, the same nipped waist and long legs, thick and sturdy like tree trunks. Underneath the smell of blood and dirt was his same unique scent, and in that she found comfort and courage.

She stood. Erik tensed and she came near, but she paid him no mind. Standing beside him at the basin, she inspected the front of his body, finding more blood there than anywhere else. It was undeniably human and came from someone who she was certain was no longer with this world.

She ripped a piece of her gown. Erik's eyes fixed on her, but

Mya did not meet them. Instead, she wet the piece of cloth and held it to the back of his hand, wanting to help clean him. She needed to touch him, to connect with him and bridge the distance between them somehow.

"Do not," he warned, his voice exasperated, tired and longing, almost as if he felt the same way she did.

"Let me," she replied. Without waiting for his response, Mya placed her hand on his chest, and he allowed her to guide him to the side so that she could begin her task. She cleaned his fingers, then around his ring, his palm, his wrist, and the back of his hand. When all that was left was white skin, she asked, "Whose blood was this?"

"That is not of your concern."

While his words were curt, his tone lacked any force behind it.

"I did not wait five days and four nights for you, tossing and turning and wondering when you would come back home to me, and then walk all the way here for you to keep more secrets from me," she huffed.

Erik swallowed hard. Mya forced herself to take a shaky breath before she spoke again, trying once more to temper her anger. "In our ... companionship—"

"We are companions now?" Erik growled, the muscles in his arms clenching under her touch.

Mya's hackles rose. His stubbornness got under her skin and irritated her until she both wanted to kiss him and hit him. She forced herself to grip his wrist to stop from doing either.

"What else would you like me to call us? Do we have a relationship or are you going to continue to run away from me, to hide from me like a coward? I appreciate your gifts and your attempts at protecting me, but you were supposed to come home to me!"

He glowered at her. "Do not *ever* call me a coward again. I did come home to you! I simply—"

"Made sure to leave before I would see you."

He was quiet then, his arm limp in her grasp.

"Are you avoiding me?" she asked, her voice as soft as a whisper.

"I was..." he began, and then he grew silent.

She nodded, moving her attention to his other arm. "I have had a lot of time to think while you were away," she said, laughing coldly. "All I have been doing is thinking."

"Mya," he croaked. She knew he was pleading with her to understand something he refused to share, but it only angered her more.

"I have thought about what happened, about what it means. I have thought about how I feel about everything. I have thought about us and the times and history we share."

Erik was brimming, vibrating, and the tremors made her meet his silver eyes once more. They were shining so brightly, a startling, glowing silver that meant he was on the verge of falling into his vampire nature. Mya found it odd to think that it may be because of her, that she had that much power over him, that she could make him lose control simply with words, with breath, with her touch on his skin. It lit something in her, knowing his emotions may be so tied into her body that the connection they shared would start a war in his.

Then he asked, "Will you tell me what you have thought of?"

She nodded and lowered the cloth. Swallowing the thick ball of emotion in her throat, she gently placed her hands on his chest. Mya stared at the spot, relishing the warmth of his skin beneath her palms where his heartbeat strongly.

"Erik, I have been unhappy for a long time."

"I know," he whispered. His arms lifted as if to encircle her before falling to his sides again. She glanced at him and saw the look of defeat in his eyes. "I have tried to make you happy, but—"

"It was not for you to try. It was for me to try to understand everything in this world, to find my place in it. I have felt … jilted by life. I have lost my home, my family. I do not understand this society, and I am treated horribly for the crime of being a woman. I have no power. I cannot study or learn the things I wish to in order to create a career or name for myself."

Mya shook her head. "Everything we are is a lie, even down to your last name. Do you know how long I have wished I could call you Erik Haraldsen?"

Erik lifted his hand to her cheek and lightly caressed her. Then he tucked her hair behind her ear and followed the wild curled strands down her back, drawing her closer and whispering into her ear, "And do you know how often I wish I could call you so many things?"

His simple touch whisked her tension away so quickly, she had to bite her lip to keep it from quivering. Taking a shaky breath, she said, "I understand it is not only for human protection but for our own. I understand that myself, Gregori, and Lucas are not strong enough to defeat hordes of humans. We are too young as vampires, and while we could win against perhaps five or ten or fifteen humans together, we could not defend ourselves against the entire town. I understand, truly I do, but I wish at the very least that we could have been honest with one another."

Another tremor swept through him. Erik pulled her closer, as if he hoped to use his body to stave off her concerns. "I have seen you sad and angry. I have seen your hate, yet I have never known how to fix it. Tell me how I can fix it. Whatever it is, I swear I will do it."

Mya looked up at him, eyes blurry by tears she refused to let slip. "Be honest with me, for once. Let me see you, learn about you, understand you in all the ways I have yet to. I, in return, will be honest with you. Starting right now."

She took a deep breath and let it out, squared her shoulders, and fought to keep her voice steady. "When those four men attacked me, my hatred overtook me. That was why it was so easy for me to succumb to my vampire nature. I *wanted* to hurt them. Not only because I was a vampire, but because I hated them just as I hated this world. That startled me. It *scared* me. I have never felt that way before, or perhaps I have always felt that way and I simply stowed the feeling away."

Mya took another deep breath, and her hands grasped Erik's broad shoulders. "But I cannot live my life that way. If I do, something will eventually happen again."

Erik's eyes burned into hers. "That will never happen. I will *never* let that happen to you again."

"You do not know what the future holds. Rape occurs all the time, all across these countries. Women are raised to endure it, sold to their kings, to their emperors and their lords to pleasure them in whatever way they require *whenever* they require it. The only thing that has protected me from that fate has been your status. But after that happened..."

She trailed off and shook her head to clear her thoughts. "I understand that I can protect myself, but only if I know myself. I do not want to lose myself to hatred again. I have lost time,

Erik. I have lost time with my family, time enjoying my life, time with … you. I wanted to kill those boys, Erik. I should be upset or disgusted at myself for that, and yet I feel nothing but pride. In that moment I was finally able to have the power to complete an action that was entirely my own."

Erik pulled her head to his, bending to meet her midway and level his gaze with her own. His next words were said gently, carefully. "Those boys, their deaths were warranted. But it should have never been on you. It should have never gotten to this. You know that. Tell me you do."

Mya nodded. "I do, but I still want to learn what you did. I want to learn how to defend myself. I wanted to kill them, and I hate that you were able to take their lives when I could not. That truth, that knowledge, has left a stain on my soul. Erik, how many women hurt this way? How many children are stolen from their homes? How entitled are the rich of this world allowed to be?" She squeezed his shoulders tightly, begging him to see her, to understand. "My soul craves vengeance, Erik. I need this taste of independence. Please, teach me how to fight."

He shook his head, his voice tight as if pained. "Mya—"

She refused to hear him decline, instead deciding to push him harder. "I need you to teach me how to fight and how to work through this, because I will put all of us at risk if it ever happens again. I will lose control, Erik, we both know that. You have kept our vampire abilities and power a secret from me. I know you have done that for a good reason. I know I am not responsible. I know I am not reliable like my brother or a jovial entertainer like my cousin. I have far too much darkness in me for that. It is easy for me to be angry—"

"Because you have a reason to, *fagr skjaldmær min!* Do not belittle yourself." Erik squeezed her, clutching at her back.

"Your life is not as fair as ours. The life of a woman in these times is not easy. The troubles you face are terrible. You are allowed to feel the way you do, and I would be surprised if you did not. I wish you could see that. I wish you were not so hard on yourself."

Mya's arms flew through the air, then slapped down at her sides as her anger burst out of her. "I am hard on myself because I do not understand where I belong! I do not understand my strengths or my weaknesses. I do not understand any of it. You have given me preferential treatment for ... whatever reason you have, but that is no longer enough, Erik. Show me how to fight as you showed my brother and cousin, or I will learn how to do it myself, but I guarantee I will make a mistake without you."

A tic started in his jaw, and he averted his eyes from hers.

Mya lowered her voice, begging, pleading, all anger gone. "I want to be better than this. I am so tired of feeling weak and not good enough. I believe that if I can at least find a way to gather strength, to explore my anger in a healthy environment with someone that I trust"—she cupped his chin and his gaze met hers—"I will feel comfortable enough to be vulnerable, to be better, more alive, more appreciative. I do not just want to be angry like this world is angry, Erik."

He sighed and hugged her to him once more. "Mya, I will always do anything that you ask me, whether I should or not."

"Thank you," she murmured into his chest.

For a while they stayed that way, holding and swaying against one another until Erik whispered, "Tell me what else you thought of."

Mya felt Erik's body tighten against her own as if he was preparing himself for some sort of battle. She bit her lip. "Am I right to assume that you only kissed me as a distraction against my vampire nature?" she asked quietly.

Erik remained silent, and that silence ate away at Mya's heart. She could feel it pounding against her body, blood roaring and pumping furiously through her veins.

"Tell me, *please*," she begged. "I cannot continue to just stand here wondering—"

"It is not the only reason."

His confession was quiet, and yet it seemed to echo in her ears.

"Then why did you kiss me?"

"Do not make me have this conversation with you, Mya."

"We have to!"

"Mya."

His tone made her stop, the absolute dread and fear within it making her abandon everything, even breathing. In all the years she had known Erik, she had never once heard him sound afraid. He took a worried breath, one that she mimicked.

"I worry that if I tell you why, you will never look at me the same way again," he said finally.

A memory surfaced in Mya's mind, like the missing piece of a puzzle. "Is that why you told me you do not deserve me, even though I am yours?"

Erik nodded. When he met her eyes, she saw they were glazed over. In them was nothing more than a heartbroken man.

6

It was as if the words were torn from him so breathlessly, so regrettably.

"I kissed you because I want to, constantly. I want you, always. I want you in a way that is uncontrollable, irreversible, infinite. But I cannot have you, Mya."

Mya shook her head and placed her hands on his chest, hoping she could somehow grasp onto him and shake him from his reasoning. "Tell me why. I may be blind to many things, but I am not blind to the way you are with me. I think you feel the same way about me as I do about you, so—"

"I do," he admitted.

"Then why—"

"Because you do not know my past, Mya!" Erik roared, ripping himself away from her to pace the wooden floor. "I protected you from it, from me! You do not know." He shook his head and changed direction, pacing faster, his boots sounding like a stampede against the floorboards even as his voice grew softer. "You do not know."

His outburst did not shock her, because she felt his pain. "Erik," she said carefully, "the last person I need protection from is you."

He froze and turned to her. "That is where you are wrong."

Mya took a step toward him, but he turned away from her once more. Eyes fixed on the door, he said deeply, "Sit down. Sit down and I will tell you about my horrid past. Maybe then you will finally understand why I do not deserve your love or your heart, nor a single shred of your mind." Erik held his shaking hand to his face, then shoved it roughly through his hair. "Possibly not even your trust, no matter how much I long to be deserving of it."

Mya reached out for him, her hand wavering in the air, then stopped herself. She had fought so hard to get him to speak about this. He looked so broken and she knew this would be the only time he would ever give her these answers. She needed them, *they* needed them.

Mya ignored the voice within her that begged her to reach out for him, touch him, soothe him with her skin, and instead turned and sat on the edge of the bed. She positioned herself where she could track his movements if he continued to pace. Then she did her best to brace herself for whatever pain weighed so heavily on Erik's heart, because no matter what he thought, she would help heal that pain. She would always be there for him, and she was certain nothing could change her mind.

Erik was a desperate, frantic mass of energy that could not be released. Many times he stopped, looked at Mya, and opened his mouth, only to shake his head and resume battering the floorboard of the cabin. Just as Mya was about to break the electric silence, Erik grabbed the wooden chair and bowed his head. He closed his eyes and took several deep breaths. When he finally spoke, he did not raise his head.

"There are two things that are needed to turn someone: a want for survival or desire for vampirism, and the blood of a vampire."

He gripped the chair harder. "I was accidentally turned in the middle of a war that I had been honor-bound to fight in but knew I would not survive. Myself, my father and many of the males in our village set out for this battle, fully aware we may not return home. In the end, I had to watch them die."

Mya bit her lip hard to keep herself from interrupting, even as Erik's misery coated the cabin and the distance between them in an unwavering sea of darkness.

"No one was alive when I came back as ... this." He gestured to himself before returning his hands to the back of the chair. "No one taught me how to be a vampire. I ... made horrible, *unforgivable* mistakes."

Erik shuddered. "I did not know how to control my blood lust. I did not know how to feed properly. I did not know about animal blood. I was turned into a vampire in the middle of a raging war where blood *soaked* the ground, so I gorged myself on it. Then that battle ended, while my blood lust remained. After a while, I lost consciousness. I was closer to a village than I should have been for the inhabitants' safety."

He licked his lips nervously and his hands tightened on the chair, the wood creaking in his grip. "I hid out in the forest, terrified of what I was. I tried to kill myself, but nothing worked. Then I became hungry again. I did my best to keep away from people, I swear I did." His eyes met hers, filled with sorrow and damnation, before sliding away. "But the armies of our enemies, those that killed me, killed my people, were pillaging the villages, spilling more blood. The scent of it drove me mad, and I gorged myself on it again. Then I discovered desire."

Mya whispered his name, terrified of where this story would lead, but he was lost to the call of his horrible memories.

"There were women in the village that had escaped into the woods, and I-I..."

Mya pushed herself from the bed. In two strides she was beside Erik, her fingers catching the tears that fell from his eyes just as he said, in barely more than a whisper, "I hunted them. I raped them, Mya."

Erik pulled away from her. "You know now what it is to lose yourself to your blood lust. How you are there in your mind but not in control of your body." His Adam's apple bobbled in the lantern light as he swallowed. "I remember their faces. I remember their cries. I remember how many people I killed while lost to my blood lust."

Mya covered her mouth to keep her own cries at bay, as tears—tears for him, for them—streamed down her face.

"This went on for fifty years, Mya. I could not find another vampire or immortal. No one helped me. I tried to talk to the medicine men, the physicians of those times, but they could not help me. I tried to lock myself away, but my chains were never strong enough. I employed pirates, mercenaries, the strongest people I could find in the hopes that they may be able to subdue me. It never worked, and when I freed myself, I killed every one of them. For fifty years I tried to control my blood lust, and failed."

She cupped his cheeks. "What made you stop?"

He looked at her, his eyes drowning in despair. "A little boy who screamed and threw stones at the monster who was raping and butchering his mother. That face—"

Erik shook his head as if he were trying to clear the memory, then pushed away from the table and sat down on the bed, hands clasped between his knees. "That face will haunt me for the rest of my days. When I needed to feed, I used the abhorrence in his expression to make me regain control. I continued to use it until I was able to grasp my limits."

Erik gulped, breathed, and looked down at his hands, as if questioning if they were capable of nothing but destruction. "I have kept track of that boy, the man he became, and the subsequent generations of his family all this time. I have donated whatever they have needed, and I will continue to do so until I am no longer on this planet, but that will still never be enough. I ripped that little boy's life apart in front of him because I could not control myself."

A bitter smile flashed on his face as he looked at her, and it broke her heart. "I am not someone you should trust, Mya. I am not worthy of your love. I am a despicable and horrible person. The things I have done are atrocious. I am no different than the monsters that tried to rape you only a few short days ago."

Mya moved toward him, intent to hold him, to stop his words, but Erik ignored her. "And if you could so foolishly believe in me even after all of this"—his voice broke as more tears streamed from his eyes—"it still would not matter, because I must do the best I can to ensure that you and your brother and your cousin will not go through the same pain that I have. You must understand our metabolisms, our powers, our weaknesses, how we must fight to remain calm, how we must have an outlet for our rage. You must understand everything so that you will never face what I have or do what I have done, so you will never be the monster inside a little boy's story."

Mya braced the chair as she felt her world shift, leaving her spinning and choking under Erik's sea of turmoil.

"Do you understand that if I slack in my duties, if I have a distraction, if anything in our world ever goes wrong, I have failed you all?" Erik pressed at his eyes with his palms, then raked his fingers through his hair. Then he whispered, "And do you understand that even though I know all of this, that I feel all of this, I still want you? That no matter how impossible it should be, you are still there? You are underneath my skin, pumping through my very veins, Mya! I am supposed to be impartial to the three of you, and yet if you, your brother, and your cousin were in peril, I would always come to your aid first, whether I should or not. You are my distraction, my weakness, and I cannot stop it. I cannot control this. I cannot resist *you*. I cannot think or be any other way."

Erik stood in one fluid motion, his eyes flashing. Mya reached for him, but the distance seemed impenetrable.

"I cannot become distracted, Mya. If I do, not only will people die but I could lose all of you. I could lose *you*. And even if you do not die, you may fall into the same peril that rots away at my soul."

He took a deep breath, his eyes telling her of his conclusion before the words could leave his mouth.

"I take care of the people here because I have the power to. I protect them because I should, but I know that nothing I do will ever make amends for the lives I have taken. So, you see, Mya, I am not a good man. I am not right for you."

Mya heard his words. She heard his story, his pain, his

terrible nightmare, and she saw him differently. It was just as Erik said it would be, except instead of a monster she saw him as someone who needed her just as much as she needed him. He needed her heart, her love. He needed her to accept his past, to love him in his present, and to grow with him through his future.

Perhaps she was foolish, or perhaps it was because she remembered how it felt to lose control of herself to her vampire nature, to want to kill, to unleash her rage upon the land. The man Erik had become when he lost himself all those years ago was not the man he was today. But that man, that sad, unfortunate soul, had been forced to carry his sins on his own. She did not want that for him any longer.

Mya approached him. He tried to back away, to create space between them, but she would not let him. When he could go no further, Mya stood on the tips of her toes and wrapped her arms around his shoulders, the position difficult and awkward as Erik stood straight and stiff, a marble statue in her embrace. Then he gripped her arms and tried to remove them, but she refused and tightened her grip. Erik moved his hands down, gripping her sides, pushing her back, but again she refused to move.

"Mya," he croaked, "leave me, please."

"I will not. I will never leave you."

"Mya—"

"Let me love you, Erik. You have spent so long hating your life. Open yourself up to me. Let me comfort you."

"I do not deserve your comfort," he whispered.

"I decide the pieces of me that someone receives, Erik, and I want you to have them all. Just as I hope to one day hold all of yours." She squeezed her arms tighter around his neck, grasping her forearms to keep him close to her. "No one helped you during that dark time, so let me help you now. You told me you could not deny me, so do not try to do so now. Let me share the weight of your burdens and worries. Let me bring you the same peace you have brought me all these years. I am right here with you. I am not going anywhere. I will always be right here by your side. You will never be alone again," she whispered.

A breath left him, and with it he succumbed to her, his final barrier broken. Erik crumbled, his shoulders sagging against her, then his knees. Suddenly they were both on the ground, she within his lap with his arms circling her as they clung to one another. As his head leaned against her shoulder, she thought about her life, and the lives of her brother and her cousin. What would they have endured if Erik had not been with them? What would have happened if they had been turned accidentally too? At least they would have had one another, but Erik had no one.

Mya understood that he had done terrible, despicable things, but she also understood that he would have never committed those atrocities in his right mind. To her, he was not the problem nor the solution; he was as much a victim as the people who had lost their lives to him.

Mya wished that she could wipe away Erik's every fear, every dreadful misdeed, but she could not. Still, from now on she would try as hard as she could to remind him of exactly how she saw him.

She took a deep breath as her hands moved to his back, kneading his muscles. "I know how negatively you think of yourself now, but I need you to know that I do not see you that way."

He tensed, but she continued. "You saved my life. You saved

my family's lives. You were walking through the Black Death searching for people you could save. You were willing to take on the responsibility of another person's life, their choices and mistakes. You were willing to teach them, fend for them, and protect them. You have protected an entire town from hardship and worry."

"But that will never make up for what I have done," he whispered.

Mya nodded. "It does not need to make up for what you have done. The past is the past."

Erik shook his head in her neck. "It is not that simple."

She held him a little closer, a little tighter. "Maybe it can be if you believe you deserve forgiveness. You were a victim too, Erik."

He did not speak again, but his hold on her tightened as he buried his face deeper in her neck. When Erik's breathing had regulated and his muscles had relaxed, Mya kissed his hair and ran her fingers through the strands, working to untangle the ones matted with blood. When she had finished, she kissed his head, his temple, the corner of his eye. She breathed in his scent, basked in his warmth, and even though so much had transpired in such a few short hours, her heart glowed with the knowledge that he here, in her arms.

Erik was her home, and she wanted nothing more than to be the same for him, but she knew she could not give him what he needed most: forgiveness. Her words could never replace those of the people he killed, but perhaps her touch could help soothe his pain, even for a moment.

Mya kissed his head, his temple, the corner of his eye once more, and then followed the contours of his face. She kissed his regal cheek, his straight nose, and slid her lips back and down to his jaw. There she trailed her lips even as the hairs of his beard tickled her mouth.

Erik let out a long breath against her neck, raising goosebumps along her skin. They sat in each other's embrace for minutes, perhaps hours, until the comfort gave way to something darker, hungrier. And even though it was wrong, the feeling was undeniable.

Mya lifted her head, as did Erik. She met his eyes, taking in their depth, their intensity, and then she stared at his lips. She needed to feel them again, *desperately*. She cupped his face, her eyes flickering back to his just once, as if asking for permission. When she realized he would not pull away from her, she kissed him.

His lips were warm, soft and smooth against her own. She meant the kiss to be gentle, something just to taste, to stave off the hunger that had built between them, but then Erik pushed into her, claimed her lips for himself, and she was lost. Her fingers wound in his hair, gripping the strands, keeping him close just as his fingers gripped and pressed into her back.

He kissed her firmly, deeply, as if she were the water that quenched his thirst. This was not like the kiss in the alley. It was too passionate, too thorough, too intimate. It was as if there was nothing separating them—no time, no space, no air. Their bodies moved together, clinging to one another. She scratched his back and pressed her nails there, needing more of him as he moved her closer, pressing her hips against his as he squeezed her waist, her shoulders, then tangled his hand in her hair at her scalp.

Erik angled her head to deepen the kiss, and she moaned into his mouth. The sweep of his tongue lit her aflame, and her hips jerked involuntarily against his own, seeking him, pushing for them to be so close that nothing could separate them, nothing could break them.

Erik pulled at her gown, bunched the material around her waist and gripped her upper thigh. She panted against his mouth as his tongue played with hers. He devoured her, then he spread his legs, forcing her to sink more into his lap. When he gripped her hips once more, she rubbed herself against his erection. Lightning flashed through her body, causing her to moan his name.

Her voice woke them from the spell.

Erik pulled back to look at her, his eyes raking over her face and body like a caress. "We should stop," he croaked.

She nodded, unable to speak, but then he drew her to him and whispered, "One more," before crushing his lips to hers again.

This kiss was forceful, brutish, rough, a mass of lips and teeth and tongues, and she loved it. His fingers played at the laces of her gown as he began to undo them, then his hand slid up her back, skin to skin, while she guided her core against his erection, once, twice, earning a tortured moan.

"No more," he said, his voice hoarse. "No more."

Mya searched his eyes, scanned his face, and then she lifted her hands to his cheeks and caressed them, trying to convey everything she felt but did not know how to say. He grabbed hold of her wrists and brought her hands to his mouth, kissing the insides of her palms. Then he lifted her and carried her to his bed, where he sat her down carefully and looked her over once more. His fingers traced several spots of blood on her gown, and he sighed.

"I apologize for ruining your gown. Let me get you one of my tunics."

Before he could move, Mya grabbed his hand and kissed his palm. "Thank you."

The look he gave her was incredulous, as if she had just procured the known stars in the sky and delivered them to him. Then Erik moved to the wooden chest. Picking out a light-colored tunic, he offered it to her and she stood, accepting the cloth.

He swallowed hard. "Do you require any assistance getting changed?"

She did not—he had already undone the laces, and the five buttons on her gown were ones she had fastened herself that morning—but she would not miss a chance to have Erik's hands on her again. "Yes, please."

Mya turned, and Erik swept her hair over her shoulder. His hands paused on her back for a moment before sliding down slowly. He followed the curve of her spine with a brush of his knuckles, and the cold metal of his ring made her shiver.

He neared the bottom of her laces, undid the first button, and then chuckled. "You could have done this yourself."

She smiled. "I could have, but you so graciously offered."

He undid the last button, and his hands found themselves on her hips. He squeezed her and whispered in her ear, "Do not test me, Mya. You do not know what it will make me do to you."

She tilted her head back to his. "But I have enjoyed everything you have done to me thus far," she said. She caught his gaze and his blazing eyes reignited the fire in her core.

"Get dressed," he commanded before striding outside the cabin, leaving her to grin to herself.

Mya removed her gown and chemise, then changed into Erik's tunic which fell to her knees. For a single moment she stood in the cabin alone, her arms wrapped around her torso as she basked in his scent that was so embedded in the cloth that she was sure it would never completely come out. Then she moved to the hearth and threw her clothes into it.

Her body shook with a mixture of misery and anger when she thought of the night's events. So much life had been lost, so much death had occurred, so much injustice. Although the day had tested her more than she could ever have imagined, Mya felt that she understood Erik on a new level. She felt closer to him, more deeply rooted and connected in an indescribable way.

But she also felt the weight of his history, of his dark past. She shook her head again, took a shaky breath, and rolled her shoulders. It would never happen again. She would not let it. Erik deserved better, and she would do everything she could to make him believe he was worthy of it. He needed to move forward, to let go of the past, and she would show him the way.

Mya moved to the door and opened it, the creak causing Erik to turn around. When he saw her, she watched his eyes begin to light, turning from their normal silver to something unnatural, predatory. It made her blush, and she could feel the tension between them like heat in the air.

"W-Would you like to get changed?"

Erik blinked, clearing away the spell. He looked down at his shirtless body and then nodded sharply. Mya moved onto the porch, but Erik urged her back inside.

"I will change outside."

"But—"

He shook his head. "I will wash the rest of the blood off in the river then change," he said, before gathering a fresh set of clothes for himself.

"Will you toss your bloodied clothes in the hearth? I have

already put my gown there, and I would like to set a fire and burn them to remove any trace of evidence."

Erik's fingers stilled for a moment, then he gave her a smile so dazzling she felt weak at her knees. He stepped before her and dropped a kiss on her head. "That is an excellent plan, *fagr skjaldmær min*. I will be back to you shortly, and we can set a fire then."

When Erik returned, his clothes joined hers in the hearth. They stood together, her arm wrapped around his waist, and his around her shoulder. Erik took a deep breath, filling his lungs with air. Mya watched his eyes flash orange, and when he exhaled, flames shot from his mouth. They filled the hearth, quickly eating away at their bloodied clothing. Mya hoped that one day, much like the clothes which curled and burned to ash under the intensity of the heat, so would the remnants of their negative pasts, never to be seen or experienced again.

7

―――――――

They watched in silence as the fire continued to dance before them, then Mya looked up at Erik, her dark olive eyes meeting his silver.

"Tell me what you did to the men that attacked me. Tell me how much of their blood you spilled."

One breath passed, then another and another as Mya waited for Erik's next words. She watched him, the twinge in his brow, the tightening and relaxing in his jaw, as if he was trying to plan his thoughts in an order that would be respectful to her.

She did not want respect. That form of politeness and modesty did not match her. She wanted brutal honesty, the darkest parts of Erik, because she knew she could digest them. Mya *wanted* to digest them, to steep in them and make them hers, because they called to something in her that could understand them, something that knew them.

Erik met her eyes, reading her desire to create more bonds between them. He was the entry to her exit, the positive to her negative, and she was his. He tightened his grip on her shoulder, then relaxed as if to let her slip away from him should she need to.

She did not. The thought of leaving him would never enter her mind.

"They did not get far from where they attacked you. Walter" —Erik said his name as if it was worse than the Black Plague— "was unconscious, and they were carrying him back to one of their estates."

Erik spun his fingers above the hearth. The fire built, responding to the anger and edge in his tone. "I broke their limbs so they could not walk, then I dragged them into the woods. There I tortured them for information. They had attacked and raped several other women, so I broke a bone for each of them. Then I carved their flesh and tore chunks out of it, making sure not to hit vital organs or veins. I left them to bleed to death, starve, or be eaten––whichever came first. Once they died, I broke their carcasses down and left them to the wolves. What they did not devour, I burned to ash.

"I found the women they attacked and have offered them employment, as well as a guard that will travel with them should they decide to take the position. That, unfortunately, was the best that could be done."

Fury rolled off Erik in waves, and Mya knew he wished he could do more. She squeezed his waist.

"They got what they deserved, and you have done well. I am sure those women will accept your offer. Perhaps they will be able to build a better life for themselves than what they had previously been afforded."

Erik nodded, his gaze on the fire as he said, "You are taking all of this rather well."

She turned to him. "Did you think your brutality would scare me?"

"Not scare you, but give you pause."

"As I said earlier, I wanted them dead. I wanted to know how you killed them to know the depths of your rage, to know what it looks like when it is controlled. I would have not been able to think the way that you did, but perhaps with adequate training I will be able to remove myself from the situation enough to ensure I have covered all my tracks."

Mya took his hand and stepped in between him and the fire. "You are my inspiration, Erik, in many ways. You will never scare me. My trust in you has not wavered, nor will it ever."

His breath hitched. He squeezed her hand, and when he spoke his voice was lower, deeper. "We should go to bed."

She nodded and gave him a small smile as she followed him to the bed. She laid on her side with Erik behind her, but she noticed that he made sure not to touch her in any way.

"Erik?"

"Yes?"

"Hold me the same way you did the other night," she whispered, as she tried to temper her nerves.

He sighed. "You may not be ... comfortable."

"I will be just fine. Come," she said as she patted the bedding draped over her hip.

Erik moved behind her until he was pressed against her back. She lifted her head for his arm, and he shifted her hair to the side. "Would you like me to braid it for you?"

A tiny smile graced her face. "No, unless it will bother you this way?"

"It never bothers me," he breathed. "I have an obsession with your hair. I like how long and wild it is." He ran his fingers through her curls, bunching and twisting them between his fingers before gently sweeping them over her shoulder.

She blushed, happy he could not see her expression as he wrapped his arm around her. Mya intertwined their fingers and pushed back closer to him, wanting to eliminate any space between them. She bent her knees, and he followed the movement, tucking his legs behind her, but as he moved, she felt something hard against her buttocks. She wiggled, trying to understand what it was, when suddenly Erik gripped her hips.

"Stop moving," he said, his tone a warning.

"But what is that?"

"The reason why I said you would be uncomfortable."

"I do not understand." She tried to move back again, to feel the hardness once more, but he held her still.

"I have an erection, Mya."

Her eyes widened and her mouth dropped into an 'O' before she stammered, "Oh, but, well ... why? W-We have not done anything."

He laughed, each breath hot on her neck. "We do not have to do anything. Being near you is enough. It will settle on its own."

His words, his body against hers, and the knowledge that her presence was enough to rile him did something to her. Her nipples became erect, her throat dry, and she had to force herself to swallow multiple times. Then she licked her lips and whispered, "Should I assist you?"

The arm under her head tensed, her only forewarning before he grabbed her by her throat and gripped her hips tight enough that it would have left a bruise if she were human. The move only served to excite her more. She bit her lip, trying to stop the moan before it left her, but he heard it, just as she knew he felt her tilt her head back further to offer him more of her throat.

"I told you not to test me further, Mya. This is the last time I will warn you," he growled, his lips touching her ear with every word. Then he relaxed and withdrew his hand from around her neck, leaving her whimpering at the loss.

"Sleep," he ordered.

She did not think she would be able to, but after several minutes of feeling the rise and fall of his chest and the rhythm of his heartbeat behind her, she fell into a deep, peaceful rest.

WHEN MYA AWOKE, HER HEAD WAS ON ERIK'S CHEST. HER ARM rested on his stomach, and their legs were intertwined. She lifted her head to watch him as he slept, then gently ran her fingers through his hair. She took in his features, looked over his light golden, almost silver eyebrows, the long pale eyelashes that surrounded the orbs she loved to gaze into, his straight nose that narrowed at the bridge before widening in a perfect triangle at his nostrils. She scanned the hairs of his beard, itched to scratch them with her fingernails—

"Are you finished staring at me?"

She nearly jumped out of her skin when her eyes caught his. "I thought you were asleep."

"I was until you woke up." His large hand spread along her back as he stretched, but he made no effort to move away from her. "Did you sleep well?"

She nodded and smiled shyly. "Very. I believe that may have been the best sleep I have ever had."

He met her smile with one of his own. "I am honored to hear that."

Mya hesitated, then decided to take advantage of their position. She gently ran her fingertips through his beard, earning herself a soft moan from him. She did it again, gently scratching the area.

"How did you sleep?" she asked.

"Incredibly well, thanks to you." His eyes closed as she continued to scratch him, and a soft, satisfied rumbling noise started in his chest.

She loved the sound, loved being able to touch him freely like this, so close, so intimately. She wanted this to happen again, every night, forever, and she could not stop herself from speaking her wish out loud. "Perhaps we could do this again?"

He grabbed hold of her wrist and kissed her hand, but the look in his eyes was pained, forlorn. "You know we cannot," he said quietly.

She averted her eyes from his, so he touched her cheek. "Mya..."

A strength borne out of frustration of the unfairness of it all blossomed inside her, and she turned back to him, eyes set ablaze. "I heard what you said. I listened to your story. I understand what you feel, even though your strength of character amazes me."

He opened his mouth to speak, but she refused to hear him deny her.

"Erik, I love you. I have always loved you in the way a woman loves a man."

His mouth dropped open and his eyes widened in surprise. At the look of utter shock on his face at her outburst, she finally realized that Erik did not believe he was capable of love. She was not fighting for them; she was fighting against his guilt.

"I love you," she said again. "In my sea of anger and hatred, the one thing that my heart has never wavered on is you. The only thing I see is you. You are the greatest source of good in my life. My angel, my hero, my protector, my confidant. But you are so much more than that to me."

She touched his lips softly, tracing them with her fingertips. "I know you do not see yourself that way. I know you may believe that my feelings were borne from what you have given me. You have provided for me, kept me fed, warm, and secure. You saved my life. I will not lie to you and say that is not where my love first stemmed from. It did."

She took a deep breath and let it rush out of her, carrying away her fears, her insecurities. She knew he needed to hear her words as much as she needed to say them.

"But that was when I was younger, when I did not know or understand what these feelings were, nor the depths of them. I understand them now. I love you for the man that you are, the vampire you are, for the goodness and darkness that is in you. I ponder you. I am curious of you. You uplift and inspire me. I want to be a better person, not only for myself but to one day be a partner to you."

She bit her lip, swallowing the deep wave of emotions between them. "You are what I want in a husband. You are who I see my future with, and I will not let anything, even you, ruin that image unless I am truly not what you desire."

His eyes were luminous, bold and immaculate as they stared into hers like they could reach the deepest depths of her soul. His chest rose and fell so quickly under her, that his body trembled with each breath. Then his hand cupped her cheek, his palm warm and firm.

"You are everything I desire, *fagr skjaldmær min*. You are everything I dream of so frequently, so often, in fact, that it ruins me when I wake and you are not next to me. My existence revolves around you. My heart beats solely for you. My thoughts are yours. My body is yours. My soul yearns to be tied to yours so strongly that I can hardly bear a moment without you. You are here," he said, pointing to his heart, "at the very core, the essence of my being. You are the air I breathe."

Words failed her under his confession. Her body seemed to fall away until she was nothing more than a heart that hung onto his every word.

"My love for you knows no bounds, no cliffs, no limits. It is immeasurable, endless, and it is because of that love for you that I must protect you."

Mya shook her head, but Erik cupped her cheeks, wiped the tears that had dampened them, and held her to him. "If anything were to ever happen to you, I would never forgive myself. *That* would be my greatest sin. Your safety is of the utmost importance to me, and that includes the safety of your heart, *fagr skjaldmær min.* Too much stands in our way for me to take you the way I dream of, to court you, to ask for your hand in marriage. I wish, oh how I wish it was different, Mya. I so desperately want to be selfish with you."

"Then be selfish with me!" She gripped his wrists, his arms, anything to keep him close, to keep him from slipping away. "Tell me what you need, what *we* need to do to finally obtain that reality."

His fingers rubbed at her temples, then slipped into her hair. "Mya..." he began, as if to tell her it was impossible to believe in such a fate. But then he sighed. "I lost myself to my blood lust. I must be vigilant. I must be ruthless and unyielding in my watch over you and your family."

"But for how long?" she lamented.

"Three hundred years," he said, dropping his eyes from hers as she gasped. "Between a vampire's two hundredth to three hundredth year, they change. Blood lust becomes less catastrophic on the mind. It is easier to control. Cravings for blood become less, allowing the vampire to go longer between feedings, and they receive an ability. I had reached my three hundredth year when I turned your brother. Had I not, I might have killed him when I turned him."

Erik traced her cheek with his thumb in a featherlight caress. "I could never ask you to wait that long, not for me. Perhaps you will find someone else, someone less—"

Anger blazed within her. "Do you truly believe my feelings for you are so fickle that they would fade? That I could ever look at another man the same way I look at you?"

"Mya—"

"Are your feelings for me so little that they could be so easily erased by something as simple as time?"

His eyes narrowed. "Of course not."

"Then do not insult me in such a manner! If you need me to wait three hundred, four hundred, one thousand years for you, Erik, I will do it."

"But that is not fair to you!"

She stroked his beard as she spoke to him softly. "That is where you are mistaken, my love. What is not fair to me, is asking me to spend a single day without you."

He pulled her to him and rested his forehead against her own as they shared the same breath. Yet even with their closeness, her body still trembled, terrified of his rejection. Erik held her, gathered her closer, and she clung to him and let his warmth seep into her bones, her very soul, fighting for any thread of connection they could form to the future they both wanted.

Then, Erik whispered to her, "We will meet here."

She lifted her head from his. "I do not understand."

"I told you I have to protect you, and right now you are so scared I will continue to fight against us that you are trembling like a leaf in the wind." He tucked her hair behind her ear. "I do not want to fight us, *fagr skjaldmær min,* and if it makes you feel this way then I simply cannot."

Her eyes widened in understanding. "Then you mean—"

"You asked me to train you, and I will. Here. After that training, should you allow me, I will court you. I cannot do so publicly," he warned. "England is in a state of unrest from the plague, and nations are still threatening war. We do not know when we may meet another immortal, and if they will be a friend or foe. If they become our enemy, you are the first person they will come after. For your safety, our courtship must stay a secret. But..." He sighed and held her tightly. "May the gods strike me down, I cannot continue to resist you."

Mya threw her arms around him and held him with all her strength as she buried her head in his neck.

"I do not deserve you, Mya. That will never change, but I will spend my entire life trying to be worthy of you."

They met in the middle, lips brushing against one another in a kiss that was both passionate and caring, wild and gentle. It was everything, and in it Mya found a sense of completion.

ERIK KISSED HER HEAD. "WE SHOULD HEAD BACK NOW. YOU NEED to eat."

Mya snuggled closer to him. "I have been drinking extra blood over the last few days, I am fine."

He made a humming noise and she rose from his chest. "Do you need to feed?" she asked.

"No, I still have a week and a half before I will need to."

An idea sparked in her head. She blushed, and although her skin did not pinken, Erik noticed her shyness and touched her cheek. "What are you thinking of?"

Her eyes flickered to his and she bit her lip softly before saying, "Would you like to?"

"What?"

"Feed. From me?" Mya gathered her hair, brushing it to the side to show him her neck.

It was a magnificent thing to see the way she affected him. He had spent so much time hiding it before, but his body was open to her now. His chest rumbled from the shuddered breath he took, and his eyes grew dark. Erik traced her cheek, then slid the backs of his fingers over the side of her exposed neck, making her shiver.

"What an enticing offer. So tempting. So delicious."

His voice grew breathless, and it caused her to pant as if he was stealing the breath from her very body. He kissed her neck, and a bolt of electricity shot straight down to her core. He did it again, trailing his lips over her skin. Each touch unleashed another tendril of desire in her.

"I want to bite you, *fagr skjaldmær min.* I cannot get the taste of you out of my head."

He hummed along her skin and the vibration made her moan. "But I will not bite you here."

"Why?" she asked, her voice husky and wanton.

"Because if I bite you here"—he nibbled her neck, and she jerked forward in surprise as another moan left her lips—"then I will spend the next two days thrusting into you like a possessed man. I will fill you with so much of my seed that you will never be able to rid yourself of me."

Her eyes fluttered closed at the picture of how he would feel inside her. Her hips rocked against his once more and she rubbed herself along his growing erection.

Erik smiled. "You would like that, I see."

Unable to speak, she bit her lip and nodded.

He chuckled. "I will bite you here, instead." He touched the space between her neck and shoulder. "That way I will let you leave this bed, but only after I give you pleasure."

Mya wrapped her arms around him, and Erik drew her close. He grabbed hold of her hips and rolled them once, twice, then widened his legs, forcing her to widen her own and sink down onto his erection. He lifted his hips, and they ground against one another.

Erik captured her lips, her moan, kissing her and taking her over completely, fanning the flames between them as he owned her with his teeth and tongue. She was breathless, shameless, whimpering when he pulled away, surrendering herself to him when he coaxed her mouth open, grinding on him, moving with him, begging for more.

Then he kissed her chin and dragged his lips and tongue down her neck to lave at her clavicle, making the hairs on her body stand on end as every nerve came alive at his touch. Still, he moved her hips, and her core grew wetter. She knew he could smell her desire—she could smell it herself—and she pulsed against him, her entrance throbbing. Mya wished he would slide inside of her, do anything to temper the delirious ache.

"I know," he whispered against her skin.

Mya wondered if she had spoken aloud, or if he knew because he felt it too. He was so hard under her, and at his words he pulled her closer and pushed against the bundle of nerves right above her pulsing lips.

Mya cried out as pleasure snaked through her, making her arch her back. He moved against the same spot, and she moaned again, the sound so lewd and loud.

Erik twitched beneath her. "Beautiful," he purred. "Such a beautiful sound. Cry for me again, *fagr skjaldmær min*. Let me hear what I do to you. Tell me how it feels."

"I—"

He ripped the tunic at her shoulder, and then his teeth pierced her flesh and she screamed his name.

Mya thought she would know what to expect when Erik bit her, but she was unprepared for the sudden, overwhelming surge of pleasure. The small tinge of pain only added to it, and she felt as if she were flying. With each gulp of blood he swallowed, with each brush against her, he sent her higher and higher.

Erik wrapped his hand around her throat and squeezed. The sensation exhilarated her, and she became needy, desperate for the next taste of her high. Mya tore at his tunic, needing to feel his skin, and when she did she clawed at his back. He moaned, and the sound turned her feral, animalistic.

Their movements changed, tinges of violence in their pumping as they ground harder, faster.

Then Erik pulled back, and the sight of his lips coated in her blood made her shiver.

He snaked his hand into her hair and pulled her to him until they were only a breath apart. His eyes blazed into hers, glowing silver and tinged with red at the edges, captivating and magnificent.

Her breath caught in her lungs, and she felt as though she were soaring through the cloud. Suddenly she feared falling, so overwhelmed by pleasure and the tears that began to blur her vision. She clung to him, and he grabbed hold of her, squeezing her behind.

"Erik, it-it is so ... so much. I—" She moaned, but when he rubbed along the spot once more, she cried his name, all other words forgotten.

"Do not be scared, *fagr skjaldmær min*. This is exactly how it should be. Succumb to it. Break for me."

His fingers pressed into her skin as he grasped her tightly, as if he were both commanding her and traveling along this new world with her. Mya knew she was not alone, that Erik could still protect her and keep her safe even in something she did not know.

Then he whispered, "I am right here with you."

At his words she shattered into a million pieces. Her back arched of its own accord, and her legs tightened around his hips while she bucked and thrashed and ground against him, ascending to some higher plane while begging for more. He was the only thing she knew, her anchor, her savior and torturer, and she screamed his name as the feeling flew through her body.

"So glorious," he said, his voice so incredibly deep as he moaned for her. "Your release is such perfection, *fagr skjaldmær min.* I must see it again."

The praise lit a new fire in her, and even though she could barely breathe, she watched him, took in his furrowed brow, the tension on his face, the way he seemed to be losing all control. The elation, the desire, the need to have him pumping through her veins took over and her canines extended.

"Bite me," he ordered, and she did.

The first taste of him was like the legends of ambrosia—pure goodness, pure sin—and the way he threw his head back and surrendered to her gave her a type of power that became an instant addiction.

He cradled her head to his shoulder as she took long, deep gulps, sucking and drinking him in. She was lost in the taste, the feel of him, the sounds that poured from within his throat.

He leaned forward, and Mya adjusted, planting her feet on the bed, spreading her legs open wider, wantonly. The position helped her spread her lips and she moved with Erik, dragging herself against his erection. He was so hard, so long and thick for her that even through the material of their clothes the tip of him rubbed along her opening.

Mya placed her hands on his thighs to lean back and offer herself to him in that way, in any way, in *every* way, but Erik pushed her onto her back, so she wrapped her arms around him, and together they fell back onto the bed. She pulled away from his shoulder and met the crazed look in his eyes with one of her own.

There was no room for words when Erik captured her lips. She squeezed the back of his neck, his shoulders, while he pulled and bunched the material of the tunic above her waist. Then he pressed himself against her once more, and Mya arched her back in response. Her hips came off the bed only to be pressed back down by his own. He weighed her down with his body, and she savored the feel of him.

Their kiss was a battlefield filled with gasps and moans. Erik grabbed both of her wrists and pinned them above her head, and Mya grabbed hold of anything that she could, his thumb, his index finger, squeezing them as he continued to grind against her.

They moved so franticly that the bed rocked back and forth against the wall. Erik spread her legs wider, pushing against her harder, his erection slipping between her folds. The feel of him behind the material drove her wild.

"You are so wet for me," he growled.

"Yes," she hissed, lifting her hips against his again.

He grabbed her, tilted her body to fit his in the way he wanted, and continued to rock against her. "Break for me again, *fagr skjaldmær min.* Break *with* me. Let me see you in ecstasy."

Her eyes closed as pleasure took over. It traveled from her head down to her toes, and she curled them as wave after wave hit her. The waves came closer and closer together, her mind in the throes of ecstasy as a large crescendo flowed through her body. She exploded, crying out, and Erik moved once, twice, before he joined her with his own roar of pleasure.

8

M ya and Erik returned home with blissful smiles on their faces, until they found Gregori waiting for them. Gregori's eyes roamed over her, noting the lack of her dress and how it had been replaced by Erik's tunic. Judging by his expression, he would give them approximately one minute to formulate an explanation or else he would pummel Erik, whether he was an older and thus more powerful vampire or not.

Together they constructed a lie, explaining that her dress had been ruined on her way to the cabin, and Mya sent Erik on his way. She and Gregori had made a deal after all, and the idea of not keeping her promise—especially after lying to him—filled her with guilt. He deserved better.

Telling her brother of her assault was both embarrassing and relieving. He did not judge her or criticize her or think she was weak. Rather, he understood, hugged her, and even through bared teeth he spoke the words that she did not realize she needed to hear.

"I am so proud of you."

Mya had always looked up to her brother, and it seemed she still sought his approval after all these years.

In an effort to be open and vulnerable with him, she told him she would be training with Erik from now on. Her brother believed it was a good idea, even though he made her promise to alert him if she ever believed she was in danger, instead of trying to handle the situation on her own.

Her training lessons with Erik started later that day. Even though she had watched Erik train her brother and cousin for years, it had not prepared her in any way for her own training. He did not take pity on her just because she was a woman, nor because he loved her, something that made her respect and admiration for him grow that much stronger. Over time he taught her how to breathe to execute certain attacks, and how to block incoming ones. Mya was a little over thirty centimeters shorter than Erik, so he taught her how to use her size and lithe form to her advantage. He explained how to take attacks and what they felt like to make sure she would not be surprised, and then he taught her weaponry.

Months of training turned into years. True to his word, after they had cleaned and changed, Erik courted her. He took her on picnics and long walks through the forest. He brought her to a waterfall and taught her how to hunt animals and fish. For the first time in a long time, Mya was happy. Their relationship might have been a secret she kept from her family, but Erik was her joy. She swore to herself that she would always make the most of her moments with him, especially once everything began to change.

Their time of living in England had come to an end. Immortals needed to move often to avoid questions as to why they never seemed to age once they reached adulthood, and if they stayed much longer people would begin to grow suspicious. As such, Erik contacted his friend Miriam who was only too happy to assist them in relocating to France and become their host for a few years.

Mya should have been overjoyed at the chance to leave England, but the thought barely crossed her mind. Instead, she spent far too long being jealous of Erik's friend. Miriam was someone who had been in Erik's life longer than Mya had, someone who had been able to help him, who knew him in a way Mya did not.

And she hated it.

She knew it was foolish. Mya wanted Erik to have support from another immortal, someone he could lean on and share his responsibilities with, but she did not want it to be with another woman, someone he had known for hundreds of years longer than he had known her.

Mya tried to ignore her feelings. When that did not work, she tried to talk herself through them. When that proved fruitless too, she hid them all together. She believed she had been doing an excellent job in that regard, until Erik cornered her by her bedroom door to ask her why she was sulking.

She narrowed her eyes. "I am not sulking."

He turned her to face him and wrapped his arms around her waist. "Ah, we are still playing this game. Pouting then? Do you even have a word for the look on your face?"

Mya rolled her eyes and tried to ignore the thrill of excitement that coursed through her body at his nearness.

"Careful, *fagr skjaldmær min*. The last time you rolled your eyes at me, you were screaming my name."

She gasped and her eyes nearly bulged out of her skull. "Erik! Hush!"

He grinned. "I am simply trying to be helpful. Are you pouting because you would like a repeat performance? I would be happy to give it to you right now."

Mya put her finger to his lips and angrily whispered to him, "Someone will hear you!"

His eyes twinkled with mischief. "No, someone will hear *you.* I have often wondered how loud I could make you scream. I guess now is the time to find out." He bent his head near hers. At the rush of her breath, his grin turned into a full smirk.

"Erik!" she whisper-shouted, but he kept coming closer and closer until his lips brushed hers.

"Tell me," he said, the low timber of his voice making her sigh. Her body heated and she relaxed into him. Mya tilted her head up to meet his lips, but he still would not kiss her, only brush his lips against her own teasingly, seductively.

"Erik," she pleaded.

"Tell me," he said again as his hands followed the curves of her body.

He won what was left of her common sense. The spell was cast, and she abandoned everything to him, including the truth. "I am jealous of Miriam."

Erik pulled back at her words. "Why would you be jealous of her?"

Possibly because I am jealous of everyone who entered your life before me.

She sighed and dropped her chin to avoid his eyes. "She has been with you for a long time. I do not know your relationship—"

"There is not one."

She opened her mouth to interject, but he grabbed her chin and tilted her head up to his, making her meet his eyes. "There is nothing more than friendship between us."

"But—"

"Mya, I had not touched a woman *willingly* until you. Miriam and I are only friends. In truth, she would be more interested in you than me, or any man for that matter."

Mya raised her eyebrow and cocked her head to the side. "I do not understand."

Erik chuckled and ran his thumb across her cheek before tucking her hair behind her ear. "She is only interested in bedding women, my love. Men do nothing for her, and if she is ever linked to a man then she is using them for her own gain."

Mya's jaw dropped. Erik laughed at her, causing her cheeks to grow warm. His eyes still twinkled as he said, "I apologize if I did not explain that correctly to you before, but I will make it clear to you now. There is no one—no woman, man, child, or animal—that I have cared for or will care for in the same way I care for you. You are, and will always have, my heart."

She made a soft whimper as his lips met hers. "I apologize," she said in between their kisses.

"No need," he murmured as he opened the bedroom door behind her and moved her over the threshold. Kicking the door shut, he guided her backward to her bed. "If you mentioned any man with fondness in your voice, I would have felt the same as you. I would have tried to kill him too."

Mya giggled as they tumbled onto the mattress together. Erik spread her legs and fit his hips against her, circling, grinding, drawing a moan from her with the movement she had come to love so much.

"Now, I believe it is time to make you scream, *fagr skjaldmær min.*"

Something was wrong.

One moment they were packing for the start of their new life in France with Miriam, and the next Erik had been called away by a messenger. At first, Mya figured it was nothing more than a small nuance Erik would need to resolve due to his position as lord. It was a common thing, and with the war brewing between England and France, a village needing supplies or townsfolk rioting in the streets would not be surprising.

But he had been gone for far too long.

Mya packed away her last few belongings and set off to find him. Turning into his chambers, she found him pacing. Her heart fluttered knowing he was safe, but the energy pulsating from him twisted her gut.

"What has happened?" she asked.

He sighed when he saw her, then drummed his fingers along the wooden table. "Our path has been cut off by the war."

Mya's eyes widened. "What does that mean? Can we take another path, or will we be unable to leave?"

"We have to go now." Erik began to pace once again. "It is imperative that we leave during the confusion of the battles between England and France. That will be the excuse used for our supposed deaths and why no one will be able to find our bodies. We cannot wait any longer. If the two countries reach another treaty, we may be at peace for too long, and as lord my disappearance, especially with you and your family, will seem suspicious. King Edward would likely hire spies to investigate, and we cannot let them find us. It must be this way," he said, as he ran his hand roughly through his hair.

Mya cocked her hip on the side of a table and folded her hands in her lap. "If that is our only option, then it is exactly what we must do."

"We will be walking through a battlefield, Mya," he said, arms flinging around his body.

"And," she began as she took her hands in his, "we will be just fine."

He sighed at her touch and intertwined his fingers with her own. His shoulders dropped as some of his worry seemed to leave him. "I do not know how you can say that."

She smiled. That such a strong, protective man who could act so easily, so methodically in the heat of the moment, who planned and took care of so many, could doubt what he had taught those around them never failed to surprise her. While Erik had many who trusted him, he still could not trust himself.

"I can say that, my love, because I have spent the majority of my life around you, and you have been training me and my family for years."

"But—"

She shook her head. "I know you are concerned that our blood lust will get the better of us, especially if we are caught in the crosshairs of the battle and are forced to fight. I understand that concern. It is a valid one, but you are forgetting one small thing."

She held her hand to his face, fingers nearly meeting one another to show the measurement. He sighed again at the action, but a small smile ghosted his lips and Mya swore the room brightened.

"And what did I forget, *fagr skjaldmær min?*"

"You. We will not be alone. We will have each other and you."

He opened his mouth to speak but she held a finger to his lips to shush him. "I do not say that to mean we should rely on you, nor are we your responsibility. While we may be young vampires, we are old enough to do better. *You* have taught us to do better, to stay in control."

Mya patted his chest softly and smoothed the fabric of his tunic. Erik made a small *hmm* of pleasure as he gathered her closer.

"I know you will always feel that we are your responsibility, and you will always be there for us to rely on should we need it. But you are a leader, my love. Trust us to know our limits and to share when we feel ourselves reaching them. Lead us, and we will follow you. We are not alone," she said again, "and neither are you."

He dropped a kiss on her forehead as he held her head to his chest. "When did you become so wise?"

She giggled and tightened her hold around him. "I believe I may have learned that from you too."

Erik was right.

The first sign of the war were the empty villages, where the only life seemed to be the crows and small animals scavenging the roads. It appeared that everyone had left in a hurry; furniture lay tossed outside homes, rotting food turning to mush underfoot. At least, Mya hoped, the townspeople had made it to safety.

The next village had not been so lucky. Bodies lay in the roads, their blood lining the streets and seeping into the soil. Erik tried to keep her from witnessing the massacre, but she refused to hide behind their carriage blinds. Mya needed to see the carnage, to be able to stomach that someone once filled with life could now be nothing more than a corpse strewn and discarded like trash. These were the terrors of war, and she knew it would only get worse; she needed to use what she could to prepare for what was to come.

Eventually they could no longer continue by carriage, the roads blocked by bodies of humans and animals alike. They had not traveled as far as Erik had wanted them to, but they had no other choice.

As Mya, Erik, Gregori, and Lucas exited the carriage, they each took a small bag which contained spare sets of clothes, any items that held sentimental value to them, and containers of blood and water. They opened the rest of their luggage and tossed it around the carriage to look like a robbery. Then Erik, Gregori, and Lucas walked back to the closest village to find dead men who would play them in their false tale.

Mya took this time to change. Women were not allowed on the battlefield; her mere image would be enough of an oddity and she would be remembered by anyone who survived. She dressed in Erik's tunic and a pair of Lucas's trousers. Both were far too big for her, so she tucked the tunic into the trousers and tied a piece of fabric around both to keep them from falling. Then she tied her hair at her nape, braided the length, and tucked it into the back of the tunic. She knew the disguise would not stand up to much scrutiny, but her vampire speed would keep anyone from seeing the truth.

When she finished, Mya looked at the carriage one last

time. She felt the bag at her hip and the difference of the clothes that now covered her body, and she was hit by the reality of what would soon occur.

She was not upset about faking her death, nor leaving England, but she had made several of her first, most important memories there: the first time she had felt desire for Erik, their first kiss, their first touch, the first time she had felt free. He, rather than the country, was at the epicenter of so many of her happy memories, yet for all the things she hated about England, she was familiar with it. She knew where the apothecary was. She knew how to get medicine. She had a dedicated space for her experiments, and she knew where to go and what streets to take to access the poor and give them the medicine they had no other means of being able to afford.

Mya also knew she was not the only one who felt this way. Erik had changed so many lives in his reign as lord. He had done so much good, and who was to say the person who fell in line behind him would do the same? What about Gregori? Lucas? What about their memories and hopes and dreams? Leaving England, changing their names, falsifying their deaths—there would be no way to undo any of those decisions.

France would be new: new roads, society, culture, language, people, places. New expectations. There would be so much to learn and experience. Lucas was good at seeing that, at simply enjoying the spectacle of hope, of what was new and fun and spontaneous. He appreciated adventure, while Mya feared it.

But what other choice did they have?

The answer was clear when she watched the men reappear with a body on each shoulder.

They placed each body in the carriage, toppled it over, then in one final act, Erik set the carriage on fire.

They watched it burn together, each caught in their own thoughts, until the footsteps of their armies grew closer. With a sigh they left and traveled through the woods to the open battlefield.

The gunshots were deafening, sending a ringing pain through Mya's ears. She shook her head and remembered this was why Erik had told her they could not use guns. One moment of weakness could give someone—even a human—enough leeway to kill an immortal. All it took was a brain injury, and the new, experimental weaponry the armies were using, were accurate enough now to destroy the complex organ.

Erik ran through the rules once more as they waited in the tree line: Focus on killing the gunmen first, preferably from behind to eliminate risks. Use swords or knives to appear human, instead of relying on your strength. If at any point you feel the need to drink blood, drain the blood in the bags first.

They nodded and stood together, waiting for his signal. Mya knew the moment they leapt forward, everything would change. Whether or not they wanted it to, they were about to make history, to aid England in winning a war regardless of whether they truly believed they deserved to, only because the French army stood in their way. But for their survival, it had to be done.

Erik's fingers brushed her own as if he could feel the grimness in her, and she turned her hand into his and gave it a small squeeze. When they released, he took one breath, then whispered the command.

"Go."

They sped through the air as they fanned out along the field. Mya reached her first man. His gun was leveled at a soldier, and before he took his next breath, she cut off his head.

His body crumpled to the ground as life left him so quickly, so effortlessly. The whole ordeal was over in a second, and it was then she realized she was no different than him.

For just a moment she wondered if he had a family, someone he was fighting for just as she was. But then, she shook her head, regulated her breathing, and reminded herself she could not go down that road. Erik was out there. Her family was out there. She could not fall behind and she could not let this overtake her. After all, this was war, and there would always be sacrifices in war.

Mya killed another man, and another, and another until she lost count. If there was any goodness to be found in this, it was that she made sure they did not feel any pain. She tried to be merciful and killed each man quickly, without hesitation. But in her pathway of death and destruction, she did not notice the gun trained on her from the line of the trees until it was too late.

The shot was so loud it made her head spin, but she forced herself to focus. The bullet would hurt when it hit her shoulder, but she would heal quickly. Then she would be sure to kill that man and anyone else she found hidden away before they could possibly hurt her family.

She prepared for the impact—closed her eyes, took a deep breath to ready herself for the pain—but it did not come. Instead of the expected bullet, she felt a shadow fall over her, and when she looked up, she saw Erik.

He stood in front of her, his back to her, and for a split second she thought he had taken the bullet in her place. Panic gripped her chest. She reached out for him, only to hear him roar. The sound, like a murderous beast, was louder than any gunshot, any scream, any cry of pain.

The temperature rose around them. Mya called to Erik, but her voice was not enough to break him from his spell. She understood the only thing that would do so was the blood of the man who had shot at her, and so she waited behind Erik and allowed him to take vengeance on her behalf.

Flames rippled out of his body, four lines that poured over the battlefield, melting the flesh of the fallen and setting those in its path on fire. The scent of their charred bodies coated the air as their screams echoed around them.

Erik roared again and the flames lifted, floating in the sky before combining. They stilled for a second, then sped toward the man in the trees. The flames burned so hot, so brightly, they vaporized him in an instant.

Erik's hand twitched as he widened the fire, spreading it further and further, burning the trees, the space around them. More men screamed, and their voices were joined by more and more, and more until...

Mya touched Erik's back, molded herself to it, and whispered, "I am right here. You saved me. You protected me. You can stop now."

His powers calmed, but the damage was done. The flames spread along the forest naturally now, burning brush and trees.

"No one harms you, ever," Erik said. His voice was so deep, so dark and commanding that it shook her to her core, then he turned. She felt her breath catch as she took in the blend of silver, red, and orange in his eyes. Before she could say a word, he cupped her cheek and slammed his lips against her own.

He kissed her as if they were not on a battlefield, as if they were not surrounded by death and dismay, as if the scent of his victims did not still hang in the air. His kiss was commanding, all-consuming, refusing to allow any space between them. He was her water, her air, her core, her anchor to this world. Without him she would float away. She kissed him just as hard, just as passionately, giving everything that she was and taking all of him in return.

A large crash sounded behind them, making them break apart, but Erik refused to loosen his hold from her, so she turned to face the new challenge with him.

He relaxed against her slightly as a carriage came into view. The door opened and out stepped a pale woman with long, straight black hair, and dark, almond shaped eyes. She smiled when she saw him, and Erik gave her a tiny smile in return.

"Hello, Miriam."

"It is nice to see you again, Erik. Although next time could you try to rein in your fire? You almost damaged the carriage, and this thing cost a fortune."

He rolled his eyes. "Only you would bring something of high value to a battlefield."

"You will not be complaining when the expensive cushions keep your arse from being sore."

A small hiccup of laughter left Mya's lips, drawing Miriam's gaze.

"Ah, you must be his—"

"Mya," Erik interrupted. "This is Mya."

Miriam paused, and Mya looked between the two, wondering what it was that Erik had stopped her from saying.

"It is lovely to meet you, Mya. I have heard a lot about you."

Mya met her smile with one of her own. "And I, you."

She tried to leave Erik's embrace to properly greet Miriam, but Erik refused to let her go, even when her brother and cousin neared them. When Mya tried to move again, Erik growled.

"Hush," Miriam said with a dismissive wave. "I know she is yours; I will not try to steal her from you. Now, if you are done being territorial, we have a long journey ahead of us, one which I would like to start before your fire blocks our path completely."

Mya giggled under her breath as Erik bristled. After a few seconds he finally conceded and slipped his arms from around her. He gave her a sharp look, but she ignored him and instead took his hand. "You can be territorial later," she whispered.

A grin spread across his lips as he ushered her into the carriage where they were barraged with questions about their relationship by her family and Miriam all the way to France.

9

18TH CENTURY

Mya became a new woman in France.

Miriam was a thief, a charlatan, a seductress, and Mya's self-appointed mentor. According to her, Mya only knew masculine power: how to fight, bear arms, and kill someone. But there was another type of power—feminine power—and it could be just as destructive, just as chaotic, without ever needing to break a sweat.

So, Mya learned how to sing, play the harp, perform, and command a crowd, how to be mysterious, give society a taste of her and leave them wanting more, all while still being comfortable in her own skin. She learned how to take criticisms and rework them to her advantage, how to make a mockery out of stupid men who believed she should be valued less than them for simply being a woman. She learned how to gain money, influence, power, and how to bring men, and even women, to their knees, much to Erik's dismay. He did, however, enjoy that she became bolder and braver around him, especially in the bedroom.

Mya was so fulfilled that she now saw her time in England in a new light. She had even taken to keeping a journal, filled with firsts she'd had with Erik and things she had taken for granted that she was now grateful for. Her life may not have been perfect, but it was hers to live, and every hardship she faced only served to make her a better person.

Their next move was to Spain, a gift from Erik to her and her family. While they couldn't stay in the same village Mya had been born in, they were able to see the resting places of her parents and aunt. Mya spent most of her day with them, only vacating the area to allow her brother and cousin to do the same. She told them about her life and how much it had changed, how much she wished they could have been there to see it.

From Spain they went to Italy, then Switzerland, and it was there that everything fell apart.

The witch trials had been in practice for centuries, and while they had been able to avoid them in the past, this time they could not. Not only had real, practicing witches who belonged to the Magic World—the world in between the human world and the Otherworld—been tried and convicted, but the immortals they worked with had also been killed.

Every immortal knew that they were not invincible, but there had never been such a successful slaughter on their kind. And that was not the only one; there were reports all over Europe of new, young immortals being experimented on, tortured, and killed, especially in Germany and Switzerland. Humans did not seem to know what they were, just that they seemed to be different. Old lore and legends of vampires, werewolves, faeries, elves, mermaids, and more began being whispered in the shadows, and each whisper held far too much truth for their liking.

It was those whispers that made Erik, Mya, and her family finally agree to set sail for America in the hopes that they would be able to build a new, safe life there. They knew America had been stolen from its people, but Gregori and Erik had a plan. They wanted to build a council, a government for immortals. They hoped species who had previously isolated themselves from others would be willing to join them in this new leadership and realize they could have a voice within the Otherworld. With this joining, they hoped that infighting and segregation would stop. Instead of being divided forces against the new threat, they could band together to protect one another. This union offered safety, security, a new life and escape from a torturous death.

They met with Miriam, who had purchased a ship and crew members for their voyage. They gathered their food and supplies and then set sail. During the trip, they matured as vampires and received their first abilities. Gregori gained the ability to control and manipulate energy, and with enough practice he realized that could fortify it, create anything he wanted to with his energy and then use it as a real, tangible object.

Lucas's ability was to become a shadow, something that he enjoyed using to scare the crew. Over time he learned that he could also control shadows in a similar way to Gregori's ability.

But Mya's ability was different. She received the ability to heal her injuries so fast that cuts were gone in a second, broken bones knitted together in a breath, even full appendages returned in the blink of an eye. At first, she was disappointed.

She had wanted something different, something stronger, something that could protect those she loved. But then she realized the power to heal did not have to be hers alone. Through her experiments she found that her healing ability did not just work on her, but also humans. A small cut would heal in a minute, and common diseases disappeared just as quickly.

Then she shared her blood with Erik and found that his own healing ability had strengthened. It was not as strong as hers, but it was enough to make a difference. She gave her blood to her brother and cousin and felt euphoric that she could both help *and* protect others. She could save anyone she wanted to. She could be *useful* in a way no one else could be, and she could fulfill a role no one could take from her—the saving grace of her family.

THE MOMENT THEY ARRIVED IN AMERICA, THEIR PLANS BEGAN.

They received official paperwork, including name changes. Gregori and Lucas were forced to shorten their names, while Miriam changed hers to Lily. From there they purchased several plots of land, including a tavern and inn close to the docks. The location was perfect. Travelers arriving in America would choose to rest at the first inn they saw: theirs. Mya would get them drunk. The alcohol would loosen their lips all while she listened and deftly steered the conversation. Then she took those details and shared them with Erik and Greg. Luke would do something similar, although he seemed to have much more fun by entertaining the women in his private rooms.

It was a simple, unsuspecting con, but it was a fruitful one that yielded valuable information. They had learned local lore and legends of different possible immortals and witch specializations that they never knew existed, murders that may be immortal related, and which immortals had arrived that may be willing to join their cause.

Mya enjoyed her role as spy. While Erik went with Greg to follow new leads and barter meetings for their new council, Mya spent her days training. She pushed her body, wanting to know what her new limitations were, but could not find any. She spent days experimenting, finding out that a single drop of blood held the ability to heal disease, but only if it came from her. She used that knowledge to infuse drinks for those that were sick, those who had made the journey because they were poor and wanted a new life for themselves. She listened to their stories and sympathized with their cause, because she too wanted a better life, somewhere she wouldn't need to hide.

Then, when Erik got back from his excursions with her brother, she spent her nights with him. She enjoyed those nights, not just because of the pleasure she experienced with him but because she could hold him in her arms. At night, they weren't a secret. At night, they were a couple. She called him hers, and he called her his, and that was enough. At night, it was enough. But once the sun rose and she watched him leave, it became ... something else.

That was why Mya worked to keep herself busy. She hoped that if she was constantly moving, constantly striving to learn something new, that her thoughts and the staggering emotions that plagued her would fall to the back of her mind. She hoped that eventually they would go away, but they didn't. Each day she spent occupying herself and each night she spent with Erik seemed to only make them worse.

When would it be enough? When would *she* be enough?

Because even though three hundred years had passed and so much had changed in the world, nothing had changed between them.

Mya now had full control over her blood lust. She had received her first ability. She was helpful and useful to their family. She had proven that she could defend herself and would never be a weakness in war. She had done all these things, everything that she believed should have been enough to make Erik finally claim her, but he had not. Apart from kissing and rubbing against her until they both orgasmed, he had never entered her or taken her the way she wanted him to. She was the secret that he kept from everyone but her family.

She knew that wasn't fair. Erik relied on her, confided in her, trusted her. He made time for her, made sure to start and end his days with her, but she couldn't go with him on his outings with her brother. No one outside of their family and Lily could know they were together. They could not even say they were in a relationship. She understood that, too, understood that the murders of immortals were increasing and no one knew why. She knew Erik and Greg were investigating those crimes to try and learn more, to make sure they could get ahead of it and keep everyone safe, but this council was still up in the air, and a chance at peace, not a guarantee. Mya worried that if it didn't work, their relationship would never progress.

Mya wanted to marry Erik. She wanted to have children with him, walk the streets freely with him in the daylight, where people, immortals, anyone and anything could see. In her opinion she would be a target even if The Council formed. She would always be seen as the weakest link of the family, even if it wasn't true, but she couldn't tell Erik that. If she did, he would—as he always had—prioritize her safety above everything else, even their happiness, and she wasn't sure how much more of that she could take.

THE TAVERN'S PATRONS WERE LOUD, TALKING, DANCING, AND laughing, their spirits high as the drinks flowed endlessly. There were no empty glasses, no wait, no fuss, just joy and easy mirth.

Mya glided behind the counter, watching as the patrons ate, played cards, or left to entertain their partners in the rooms upstairs. The tavern was full to the brim as three ships had docked safely that day, bringing large groups of eager people wanting to celebrate the end of their last voyage and the beginning of their new life.

In all honesty, Mya did not like being around people, but when they were so uninhibited, so free, she found it easier. There was no need to guess what they were thinking, what stories they were spinning or lies they were telling. They were their true selves, something Mya both admired and found easy to take advantage of to help her family's cause.

She'd already heard one tale about blood witches murdering a traveling band of thieves in the next town over— the fifth one this week—and another tale of twinkling lights in the forest that someone believed were faeries. Mya believed both stories, as she knew there was a group of faeries who had come from Europe to America after war had caused the portal to their realm to burn down.

Mya's real concern were the blood witches. The immortals that had been killed had small traces of magic on them, and several had been found with their blood drained. Most of the dead immortals were werewolves, and while the lack of blood made the killings appear to be the work of a vampire, there had not been a war between vampires and shifters for almost a full century.

After further investigation, Greg noticed that the magic signature did not seem to have a limit, like theirs or any other immortals. There was only one answer: it belonged to a witch from the Magic World. They were the only ones who with time, proper casting, spell work, experience, and resources, could grow their powers exponentially.

Then the stories of blood witches began rolling in; witches who had been enslaved by vampires. It was a terrible practice that had started in Europe and continued in America. The abuse and rage the witches had suffered, brought forth a new type of magic, one that rotted away at their souls. They used the very blood in their bodies, and that of their opponent, to fuel their magic, giving them an endless stream of power. They could shift not only their bodies but the very fabric of an immortal's mind.

Mya would've admired them if they hadn't been so dangerous. She understood their need for vengeance and felt that they were justified in killing their captors, but the innocent immortals they now hunted and murdered with glee had done nothing to warrant their death.

Still, as much of a threat as the blood witches were, their attacked served to push immortals to agree to The Council and an eventual alliance, something that had never been done before. Fear could be an excellent motivator for action, and luckily Erik and Greg knew how to wield it to their advantage.

Both men entered the tavern as if her thoughts had summoned them. Greg gave her a nod and smile which she returned. Erik did the same, although his smile was larger, warming his lingering eyes which never left her frame. Even though it was something he routinely did, she still blushed under his attention.

"Aye, wench! Another round of ale!"

Mya snarled at the intrusion. She grabbed two mugs and filled them to the brim, marched over to the demanding man, and poured both glasses directly over his head. He shouted and moved to stand, but she kicked his leg out from underneath him and used his shoulder to slam him back in his seat. The tavern fell silent as all eyes turned to Mya.

"You want ale, you go to the counter and you order it *nicely*. Call me a wench again and I'll break this glass and use it to cut out your tongue."

His face reddened as he tried to stand again. "You b—"

Mya squeezed his clavicle until the bone snapped in two. He opened his mouth to scream, but she shoved his jaw shut. Another man moved behind her to stand, and she narrowed her eyes at him.

"Sit," she ordered.

His eyes grew wide. For a split second he looked at the man she held down, who now had tears streaming down his beet red face, then back at her. Mya could feel the fear radiating off him as he slowly sat down, palms raised in submission.

Mya straightened, her eyes glancing at each man around the table. "When I release your friend, you will help him up. Then, you will leave my tavern or else I will do the same thing to every single one of you. Nod if you understand."

They gulped, and she enjoyed the way they squirmed in their chairs. After a quick look at one another, they all nodded obediently. When she lifted her hand from the man, they propped him up between them and nearly ran out of her establishment.

She sighed as the noise of the tavern returned, the scene now all but forgotten. These were the joys that came when working with people and alcohol, but she couldn't deny the small bit of pleasure she received from having power and control over her domain.

Mya signaled to one of her ladies to clean the table, then moved back behind the counter. She busied herself with serving, all the while being mindful of the man watching her in her peripheral. He continued to study her throughout the night, and she noted that he'd only ordered one drink, which he sipped slowly.

That told Mya that he was here for another reason, and as he began to approach her on sure and stable steps, with a large gait, smirk on his face, and a twinkle in his eye, Mya could tell he wasn't someone who was accustomed to taking no for an answer.

He will be once I'm done with him.

He sidled up to the counter, where he leaned silently against the wood. Mya continued wiping down the surface and ignored him. He seemed to believe she should address him, or that his presence was more important than her tasks. That wasn't how she ran things. It didn't matter if he was one of the gods themselves; he shit just like every other person in this world. If he wanted her assistance and attention, he would need to ask for it.

He stewed for a moment before he finally tipped his hat in her direction and said, "Ma'am."

She set the glass she was cleaning down, flipped her towel

over her shoulder, and nodded to his drink. "Do you need a new cup of ale or something to eat?"

"No, I'm looking for something else," he purred.

She mentally rolled her eyes but did her best to keep her tone light, friendly, and short. "If you're looking for room and board, you could try the inn down the way, we're full."

"I'm not looking for that either." He set his mug down, spread his arms out across the counter and leaned down to invade her space. "What I want is you."

Mya raised her eyebrow. "Excuse me?"

"I saw the way you handled those men. I could use a woman like you. Strong. Smart. Confident. You know how to keep people in line, and you're a fighter. I like that, especially in bed."

She had to swallow the bile that raced up her throat. "I'm sure that might be flattering to someone, but I'm not interested. Move along," she said sharply, waving her hand.

He chuckled, and the laugh grated on her nerves. "It wasn't a request. If you won't come with me willingly, I'll buy you."

Her grip tightened on the counter. "What did you just say?"

"I'll buy you. I have more than enough money, and I always get what I want." His smile broadened. "In all honesty, I was hoping you'd say no. It makes me more excited to take you by force, to break you, to tame you just like I do my mares," he said, his hand inching toward her face.

Mya reared back and hit him square in the chest. She kept her palm open to stop herself from causing any permanent damage, but he still flew across the room and into a table. It broke, and each dish on top of it shattered as it hit the floor.

Time seemed to stop as each person froze and turned to her for the second time that night.

She raised a pitcher in the air and shouted, "Who wants another drink?"

A cheer roared through the room and the festivities started up again.

Mya shook her head as she watched the man leave. Lily was right: men who acted like dogs had simply never been trained. Lucky for her, Mya not only knew how to rectify that issue, she'd become an expert in it.

10

———

Mya smiled as Erik opened the door for her and guided her to walk closer to the buildings. He flanked her side, taking the position nearest to the street. He always ensured her safety. Forever her shield. Her vigilant protector.

He walked her to the back of the tavern in comfortable silence, then led her up the stairs to her room. The moment Mya opened the door, Erik was on her, his lips crashing against her own. She wrapped her arms and legs around him as he lifted her, then kicked the door closed behind them. He all but tossed her on the bed, then stepped away from her to take the dresser and shove it against the door, blocking it from opening.

"What are you doing?"

"You won't be able to stay quiet tonight, and I don't want anyone barging in from all the screaming."

She smiled as he neared her, sitting back on her hands and spreading her legs wide. "You're mighty sure of yourself."

He grabbed the back of her knees and pulled her until she fell back against the bed with a huff. "Are you trying to bait me, *fagr skjaldmær min*?" he asked, his voice low.

She giggled. "Is it working?"

He smirked, and the intensity in his gaze stole her breath and flooded her with heat. "You have no idea what you just started."

She opened her mouth to goad him further, but he shut it with his lips. He laid on top of her, covering her with his body, his warmth. Mya knew she would never get used to the weight of him, never get used to the way it felt to simply hold him like this.

She ran her fingers through his hair. It had grown longer, down to his mid-back now. She loved the length, loved the way he growled into her mouth when she tugged on the strands, and loved it even more when he did the same to her. He tilted her head back until she had no choice but to surrender to him, to let him use her mouth in whatever way he saw fit, to let him pleasure her with his tongue and teeth.

He licked her mouth, delved into its depths, making her moan and writhe against him. He nibbled and bit her lips, sucked them and her tongue, and she whimpered as the action sent pleasure coursing through her body. Her core clenched and throbbed, begging for him to do more than kiss, touch, and squeeze. She longed for him to thrust inside her.

Erik lifted his hips from hers, and when she tried to follow, to rub against him, he surprised her by changing their position.

"Give me your back and put your legs on top of mine," he ordered, and after a moment of shock, she complied.

In the corner of her room was a full-length mirror, one she could now see them in as she sat on his lap, her back to his front. In the reflection, Erik's eyes met hers. They were so dark, the silver blending to a gray so deep it was closer to metallic black. He looked devious, hungry, like a lion ready to feast on its favorite meal, and she shivered under the intensity.

Slowly he pulled on her skirts, sliding the material up her calves, her knees, her thighs, all the while never breaking his stare. She blushed and fidgeted with a need to stop him out of embarrassment, but a deeper curiosity, the desire to see what would happen next, held her still.

Her breath caught in her throat as he gripped her thighs, squeezing her flesh. His hands were so warm against her skin, but the way he held her, digging his fingernails into her flesh as if he owned her, made her shudder.

Then he began to spread his legs, forcing her own legs to follow with his grip. She gasped at the feeling of being stretched, of her body being used as a sacrificial lamb for whatever he wanted, whatever would please him. The feeling was just as freeing and intoxicating as it was overwhelming and terrifying.

"Erik, what are you doing?" Her voice was so husky and breathless that he smirked, knowing just how much he affected her, how much she wanted him.

"Open yourself for me, *fagr skjaldmær min*. Let me see that beautiful cunt. Let me see how wet you are, how badly you *need* me."

His words fanned the flames within her and made her moan, even though he had yet to touch her. There was only him, what he wanted, and the hidden promise afterward. The anticipation was too much, and she spread her legs quickly for him.

She didn't question when he lifted his knees and forced her

to do the same, leaving her legs dangling over the top and side of his. As a reward for her willingness, he wrapped his hand around her throat, tilted her chin up and claimed her lips in a searing kiss. Then he pulled her skirts to her waist, leaving her completely bare and open for him to see and touch. He licked her lips, sucked them into his mouth, then his fingers reached down and stroked the small bud of her core.

She jerked against his hand in surprise, gasping and breaking their kiss. He pushed harder against her, keeping her pinned between his hips and his hand, leaving her barely able to roll her hips against him.

"Use me," he whispered into her ear, and when he kissed the lobe it sent chills down to her toes. "Use me for your pleasure. Go wild for me, *fagr skjaldmær min.*"

She couldn't stop herself as she undulated against his hand, but even as the pleasure sought to overwhelm her, she couldn't meet his gaze in the mirror. Erik had never touched her like this, never put his hand there. She could only imagine what she looked like in the mirror, naked from the waist down, grinding herself on his fingers.

Mya buried her head in his neck. As he rubbed her faster, her moans grew louder. Then he pinched the bundle of nerves, and she cried out as an arch of electricity traveled down her spine.

"Watch yourself in the mirror, Mya."

He was so hard behind her, so tense, and every time he spoke his voice seemed to drop another octave. It was killing her, but she couldn't obey him. She *couldn't.*

"No," she shook her head frantically. "I can't, I can't," and yet she still moaned, still rubbed against him, faster now, getting closer to her release.

"No?" He chuckled in her ear. "You are not in a position to say no to me, *fagr skjaldmær min,*" he warned, and then he pinched her again.

She cried out his name as the pain mixed with pleasure and took her higher.

"Watch," he commanded.

But she still couldn't. It would be so lewd, so wrong to see herself so wanton. And yet she wanted to listen to him, to follow his instructions. She was so caught in between those emotions that she didn't hear his snarl until it was too late.

"You *will* obey me, Mya." He grabbed hold of her throat and forced her head forward, tilting it to the side. "You wanted to play with fire. Now you will know what it's like to get burned," he growled as he sunk his teeth into her neck.

Her eyes flashed open in shock, meeting the image of their reflections. She watched helplessly as he drank from her, her hips circling and grinding against his hand. She couldn't look away at the picture of them, so lost together. Her mouth was open, and each cry he tore from her seemed to reverberate even louder in her own ears. His eyes met hers in the mirror once more and then slid down to where his fingers teased and plucked at her like an instrument crafted just for him.

Erik teased her entrance, and she came. Her release was so strong, so vibrant, that for a moment she saw nothing but colors, bursts of light so bright they blinded her from everything else. Erik held her, anchoring her with his teeth and fingers. He kept moving even after her climax ended.

All she could do was fall into him, relax into his body, and moan his name in high pitched whimpers. Tears fell from her eyes as her pleasure heightened and she became nothing more than sensations and emotions.

He released her from his bite, and she arched her neck back, silently begging, pleading for him to drink from her again.

"Such a bad girl," he murmured in her ear, but his fingers were still touching her, coaxing her.

"Why?" Mya asked, barely able to speak around her moans. She tried to grab hold of his hand so she could focus on his words, but he only quickened the pace.

"What is our one rule, Mya?"

She couldn't think, couldn't answer him.

He nuzzled her cheek with his bearded jaw, then squeezed her breast pinching her nipple. "No man touches you, *ever*. You broke that rule, Mya, and then you disobeyed me," he snarled into her ear. "You deserve to be punished."

She shook her head frantically. "I did—"

He circled her entrance, applying just a bit of pressure as he began to enter her with the tip of his finger. She was so untried that he could barely move within her, and yet every small thrust made her shake.

"I didn't! I swear. Erik ... Erik!" she cried out as he stroked her from within.

"He had plans for you, Mya," he said, as he teased her walls and she quaked around his finger, nearing another orgasm. "That stupid bastard thought he could have you, could own you, that he could make you feel the way I can."

She shook her head, unable to speak to tell him the thought was impossible. She belonged to him, only him.

"I killed him," he hissed, and his anger and fury only added to her pleasure. "And I wanted so badly to come to you, to touch you here, like I'm doing right now." He thumbed her bud while his finger circled and stretched her deeper. "Would you have let me touch you with his blood on my hands? Would you have enjoyed that, *fagr skjaldmær min*?"

Her answer should have been no. His words should not have made her so wet that the bed was now drenched beneath her. It should not have made her nipples harder, her breathing shallower, or her body flush with heat. It was sick. It was twisted. It was exactly what she needed. The orgasm began at the base of her spine, and she felt it travel up her body, roll into her shoulders, expand into her chest—

"Such a bad girl," he purred. "So wicked. So dirty. But I will never let another man touch you, not even his blood. You are *mine*. Every inch, every curve, every cry from your lips, every kiss, every touch, every beat of your heart belongs to *me*."

She came, exploding into a symphony of stars. She traveled along galaxies and saw the vast expanse of the universe. She couldn't stop, and her body continued to spasm as euphoria filled every cell within her.

And then he took her there five more times, his fingers so coated in her juices that he was able to thrust two in and out before he finally turned her around and ground against her until he came.

After he cleaned them, they held one another. Although Mya's entire body was relaxed, her mind was active. She'd enjoyed everything Erik had done to her, but something about his ferociousness, his desperation to remind her who she belonged to when they both knew the answer, made her concerned that something else was weighing on his mind.

She turned in his arms, knowing that he was awake as she

was. Mya ran her hand over his cheek and his eyelids fluttered from her touch. He grabbed her hand and kissed it softly, causing her to sigh.

"Did something happen?" she asked.

When his eyes opened, she knew she didn't need to elaborate. He kissed her hand once more and drew her head to his chest.

"You are my heart. You are the very breath in my body, what completes my soul, and I know that you have been unhappy because of me."

"Erik—"

"Please don't," he whispered. "You have been waiting for such a long time for me. *We* have been waiting for such a long time, and it's not fair to either of us."

He cupped her cheek and tilted her head to his. "You know I want this, don't you? That I want you? I want to shout to the entire world that you are mine. I want to take you with me on trips and to events without having to make an excuse as to why you are there."

"I know," she whispered, squeezing his hand. "And I know why we can't. I just..."

"I wish it could be different too, *fagr skjaldmær min*, and I promise I am trying to make it so. That is why I keep going with your brother to these council meetings. We are so close. If tomorrow's goes well, it will be done."

Her head shot up from his chest. "Really?"

Erik smiled and kissed her forehead. "Yes, and there are so many plans I have made for us, so many surprises that I can't wait to show you. I want to be with you, and this council is going to make it happen. Please, just give me one more day."

She cupped his face. "Erik, I will always wait for you. Even if

I don't like the circumstances, I will never stop waiting for you. I love you."

He kissed her so gently, so tenderly, with so much love and affection that she felt covered in it from her head to her toes. So why did she want to cry?

11

———

Mya was anxious the entire morning. She clung to Erik the moment she woke up, and he held her just as tightly. He promised her that he would come back to her, just as he always had. He told her she had no reason to worry, and when she explained the terrible sense of dread churning in her gut, he assured her he would be safe and everything would be fine. After all, how many battles had they fought together? How many times could the universe have tried to break them apart, and yet they were still standing together?

Mya couldn't argue with that. Logically, he was correct. Time after time, they had always made it through and only grown stronger. Yet the feeling stayed.

After she kissed him goodbye, she busied herself. He told her the meeting that would confirm the formation of The Council would be at 3:00 p.m. The location was only twenty minutes away. By 4:00 p.m. he would walk through the tavern doors, and all of this would be over. She just had to wait until then.

Time moved slowly. Mya checked the tavern clock constantly, thinking an hour had passed when it had only been five minutes. Frustrated, she stopped looking at it altogether and set about doing everything she could to fill her time. She cleaned things that had already been cleaned, then helped to cook items that her staff normally assisted her with.

Finally, it reached 3:00 p.m.

Then 3:15 p.m.

3:30 p.m.

3:35 p.m.

3:45 p.m.

3:55 p.m.

The doors to the tavern swung open, and Mya rushed toward them in delight, only to find her brother. Greg ran to her, picked her up and twirled her around.

"Put me down! Put me down!" she laughed, smacking his shoulders.

"Mya, we got it! We did it! We officially have a council!" Greg said, jumping and twirling around with her, narrowly missing knocking over a table and chairs.

"I am so happy for you!"

"Be happy for all of us! Some things had to change, but this is a start, a huge leap to bringing all immortals to peace."

She hugged him tightly when he set her down, then pinched his cheeks. "You worked so hard on this! I'm so proud of you."

The smile on his face was one of pure glee. "I couldn't have done it on my own."

Mya looked around the tavern for Erik, but she didn't see him. "Where is Erik?"

"He said he had to get something and would be back a little bit later."

Panic raced throughout her body as the sense of dread returned. It was stronger now, and she doubled over, clenching her stomach.

Greg grabbed her. "Mya? Mya? What's wrong?"

"Where's Erik?"

"I don't know—"

"We have to find him! We have to find him! *Now!*" She pulled away from her brother, but he pulled her back.

"Mya, what's happening? Do you know something?"

"Something's wrong! Just please. I need to find him!" she screamed.

"I'll get Luke and go east. You go west. We'll search for an hour, then meet back here. Yes?"

She nodded and they dashed out the door. She only hoped she could find Erik in time.

Mya had only been searching for thirty minutes before she felt it. She didn't know what it was and couldn't describe it as anything other than a feeling. It was as if the dread has suddenly grown stronger, and out of some sick, morbid curiosity, she had to follow where it led.

She paused at an alleyway. At first couldn't understand why she had, until she heard the noise again. Beneath the sound of horses, carriage wheels, and people going about their daily activities, she'd heard moaning and grunting.

She'd ignored the sounds at first—many women had to sell their bodies to eat, gather shelter, and make a name and status for themselves and their families here—but this time she'd heard the male voice, and the sound was *startlingly* familiar.

Mya followed the noise down two more streets. Then she stopped, and she felt the ground fall from under her.

It was Erik. His back was toward her, but Mya knew the width of those shoulders, the strength in those arms, the narrowness in those hips ... hips that had a pair of ankles crossed behind them as he thrusted into another woman.

The woman threw her head back in glee, and Erik groaned, the same noise, the *exact same one* he'd made with her last night. Erik wasn't even drinking from this woman. He was simply enjoying her, fucking her against the wall with the wild abandon that Mya had always wanted, craved, *desired*.

Why?

Why was this happening?

How did everything go wrong?

Why this woman?

What had she done to make him stray from her?

Just last night he had promised to stay with her forever, promised that they would be together after he secured The Council, and now he was screwing another woman against a wall.

None of it made sense.

Something clawed in Mya's gut, and a feeling flickered in her heart. Something about this was all wrong. She took a deep breath and the realization hit her. From here, she could breathe in Erik's scent, but it wasn't right. This ... *thing* didn't smell like Erik, not like his signature scent of pine, ash, smoke and cinnamon. Instead, it smelled faintly of grease, blood, and a large dose of salt.

That's not Erik! It's not Erik!

And then a chill flew down her spine. This wasn't a case of mistaken identity. Someone had done this on purpose. They *wanted* her to think this was Erik, and that made every part of her body burn with rage.

Mya stormed up to the couple, grabbed the impostor by his hair and tugged him off the woman. She threw the man against the wall, and before either of the couple could blink, she had her hand around the man's throat.

His silver eyes grew wide, and for a second, just one second, she wavered. They looked so much like Erik's, down to every sparkle and line that made his eyes uniquely his. They were a perfect replica. But that's all they were, a replica.

Mya tightened her grip on the man's throat and turned to look at the woman. "I'd recommend you leave. *Now.*"

The woman stared at Mya in a mixture of shock and horror before she scrambled to her feet and stumbled out the alley.

Mya turned back to the man and found him smiling.

"What's the matter, *lover*?"

She pulled him back and pushed him into the wall again with so much force his body left an indent in the brick. "Do *not* call me that. You are not *him*," she hissed.

He smirked. "Jealousy doesn't suit you, love."

Mya knew he was baiting her, but she refused to fall for it. "Why did you do this?"

The man's eyes narrowed, and his expression transformed to one of anger. "Because you and your kind encroached on *our* land! Do you know how many of us you've killed? How much you've taken from us? Our women? Our witches—"

His eyes widened as the last word left his mouth, but it was too late.

"What witches?"

His face relaxed and he smiled again. "That's not the question you should be asking, *immortal,*" he said, spitting the word like it was a curse.

Mya opened her mouth to speak, but then she paused and really took in the man in front of her. He wasn't scared of her, even though he knew what she was and knew she could and *would* kill him. In fact, he looked as though he'd won something, like he knew a secret that would break her and bring her to her knees.

The realization hit her square in her chest.

If he was disguising himself as Erik, where was *her* Erik?

Her face must have given her away because the man's expression morphed into one of sick satisfaction. "You've finally figured it out then."

Her eyes narrowed. "Where is he?"

The man had the audacity to shrug. The movement should have been pathetic since he was dangling off the ground, her hand still firmly around his throat, but his nonchalance sent a shiver of fear down her back.

"I might as well tell you. My job here is done. He's at his home. I presume you know where that is, but you won't be able to save him anyway. It's too late for the both of you."

Goosebumps trailed her skin, following the wave of dread that spread throughout her body. In her rage, she tore the man's esophagus out of his body and threw it to the floor, and yet he still died with a smile on his face.

He didn't win, she told herself. *Erik would have never believed...*

But she almost had. And hadn't Erik been worried last

night? Hadn't he seemed to think she was growing tired of waiting? If he had seen…

No.

No!

Mya ran as fast as she could through the alleyways to the edge of the town, then deep into the forest. She dodged trees and flew over streams, then careened up the mountainside to the land Erik had bought when they had first arrived in America.

From what he had told her, Mya was expecting untamed forest. Yet, as she crested the mountain, she found a large area of cleared land where a cabin-style house overlooked a lake. She gasped, and her body slowed to a stop as she approached the door. It reminded her so much of the cabin back in England that it was almost as if she had been transported back there. A million questions formed in her mind, but she shook them away. She would ask Erik about this later, once she knew he was safe.

She could smell his scent all over the property, but it engulfed her when she opened the door. The strength of it told her that he had been there recently, and her heartbeat raced at the thought of being able to see him, to hold him, to put the horrible events of today behind them.

Mya let his scent guide her as she ran through the house, until she ended in a room at the back of the property. It was sparsely furnished with a bed, chair, dresser, mirror, and desk which had a candle that was still burning.

She stepped closer to the desk and her heart plummeted. There, in the center of the desk, was Erik's ring, and underneath a letter addressed to her.

Shakily, she picked up the ring, which was still warm to the touch and opened the letter.

"My dearest fagr skjaldmær min,

I've known for a long time that you were unhappy. You've made the best of our time over the years. You always promised to wait, and I was foolish enough to take advantage of your patience. I am so sorry. I am sorrier than you will ever know. I never wanted to take advantage of you. I only wished to keep you safe, to love you, to cherish you, to marry you and now—

I saw you with him, and even though my heart aches, I cannot blame you. I only wish I'd done better. If I could turn back the hands of time, I would, I swear to you I would. But now what's done is done, and if someone else has your heart then I cannot jeopardize that, for your heart is one of the purest, most beautiful things I have ever known.

I love you, Mya. I will always love you. But if I stay around you, I will take you. I will ruin this for my own selfish needs, and I can't do that. I shouldn't be selfish with you, not anymore.

I wanted so much with you, fagr skjaldmær min. I used to wear this ring to ward off women. When they would ask me about my wife, I would tell them how beautiful she was, how special and radiant. In my heart, in my eyes, you will always be my wife, my mate, the place I run home to, but I understand that I can no longer be those things for you.

I may have squandered my chances, but I hope he gives you what you deserve—marriage, a home, a family—everything you've always wanted. And until then, know that this property is yours. I was building it for us, but even if there is no future for me here, there should be for you. You will find the keys, deed, and all necessary paperwork signed and sealed in the drawer. I have transferred all my assets to you in the hopes that you will live a life without struggle or strife.

This is goodbye, for there is no life without you, fagr skjaldmær min, my beautiful shield maiden, my beautiful warrior. You are one of the fiercest, bravest, most beautiful, most radiant women I have ever known.

With my entire heart and soul; yours forever,
Erik."

Mya clutched the letter and ring to her chest, standing in absolute silence while her heart shattered into a million pieces.

She didn't know how long she stayed like that—frozen into place, barely breathing—but when she came to and saw that the candle was sputtering, she knew there was only one thing she could do. She had to find him and tell him that none of it had been real. They were supposed to be together, live out their lives together. She was going to marry him, bear his children, spend the rest of her life by his side. That had always been their future. She knew it in her soul, which meant this horrible reality that left her heart barren and her entire being ripped to shreds simply could not exist.

No. She would find him. She would show him that what he saw was nothing but a trick, and then they would get retribution, together. They would marry, and the whole heartbreaking ordeal would become nothing more than a bitter memory. That was the only possibility she believed in.

Determined, she made her way through the house, searching for any sign of him. Finding nothing, she moved outside. Following his scent, she called his name while she searched through the forest. When she reached the cliffs, her mouth dropped open at the scene in front of her.

All the trees and brush were gone. In their place were mounds of ash, mixing with the scent of her beloved, her husband. There was nowhere else to go, no other trail to follow and nothing else to search for. His scent stopped by the cliff's edge. The pieces all fit together to create one unbelievable horror in her mind: Erik was gone. Dead. He'd thrown himself over the cliff, committed suicide, all because he'd thought he lost her, because of cruel revenge against someone who had done nothing to deserve it, because she hadn't gotten there in time to stop him, to make him see reason.

If she had just been faster, stronger, listened to the worry that had been weighing her down since that morning, he'd be here now. But she hadn't and now, now he was—

Mya screamed. She screamed louder than the waves that crashed along the cliff, louder than the force of the wind. She screamed so loud that the birds scattered, and she kept screaming as she crashed to her knees in the ash, clutching his letter and ring. She knew nothing else but agony, desperation, and despair. She wanted nothing else but to join him, to give everything up and simply fall away with him, hoping that maybe in another life, another world or dimension, they could have their happy ending. That was the only way to end this pain.

Mya stood slowly, then turned toward the cliff edge. She slipped Erik's ring on her thumb. It was too big, but she curled her fingers over it, pressing the metal into place. She'd keep it close even as she fell and met her death at the rocks deep below.

Then a waft of smoke filled Mya's nostrils, and she turned her head in its direction, searching for the cause.

Her first thought was that it had to be Erik, that he was still alive and she had just overlooked something. She could still be with him, still show him that she loved him. She could still *save* him.

Mya sped toward the scent, but as she drew closer, she found the large house that she hadn't known existed until only a few minutes ago, the place that Erik said he'd built for her, for *them*, was now engulfed in flames, and for the third time that day Mya was powerless to stop the chaos and destruction around her.

This wasn't right. It wasn't *fair!* They hadn't done anything to deserve this! Erik had worked so hard to create a council that would help end all the killings and atrocities of their world. It was supposed to represent everyone, to fix things, but for all his efforts, this is what he'd gotten—what they'd gotten—in return: Tragedy. Heartbreak. Pain.

No.

No more.

Mya would not let it continue. She was going to die. She knew that, she *accepted* it, but she would not go before she got revenge for Erik and before she killed the people who did this to them.

The smell of the fire was overwhelming now, but Erik had taught her how to use her senses, how to keep and control her blood lust. Closing her eyes and rubbing her index finger on the warm metal of Erik's ring, Mya called on her practiced control of ferocious violence.

It wanted blood, and so it sought it out. Mya had scared the animals in the forest with her cries of anguish, so when she searched for the nearest source with the greatest amount of blood, she found exactly who she was looking for—the person who had set fire to their home.

The witch was laughing manically as she twirled around,

droplets of blood flying from her dress. From her spot behind a large oak, Mya saw a slaughtered moose, its blood taken by the woman who now seemed to be celebrating what she'd done.

"One more vampire taken care of! One more gone!" she sang, laughing and jumping and throwing her hands to the sky.

Mya wanted to snap her neck—she even reached out to do so—until she remembered that this blood witch wasn't the only one to blame for what had happened. No, their entire coven was. If Mya wanted to find them and exact her retribution, she would have to wait for this one to lead her to their home. There, she would kill them, every single last one, and only then would she be at peace.

12

Mya followed the blood-drunk witch for two days.

The woman believed she was unstoppable. She used her powers recklessly, performing magic in front of humans only to wipe their minds of it afterward. As Mya watched, she realized just how powerful the witch was, and yet her powers never affected Mya.

Satisfaction pooled in Mya's gut with the knowledge that she was immune to the blood witch's power. If this witch couldn't affect her, it was likely that none of her coven's powers would be able to either. Mya wanted them to be powerless. She wanted them to know that a big, bad monster was coming for them, and nothing they could do would save them. She wanted them to feel the same way she felt, to know the same pain she had known when she lost the only man she had ever and would ever love. Every day, every second that went by was another in which she fed that pain to her anger, her rage, and her soon unavoidable wrath.

Finally, the witch went home, leading Mya to her coven. The house was set back in the poorest section of the city, an old, seemingly abandoned Gothic church. A fitting place for them to die, Mya thought, because there wasn't a single god who could save their worthless souls. Not from her.

Mya knocked on the large wooden door and waited. When it opened, she came face to face with the woman who'd been with Erik's impostor. The witch's eyes grew wide as fear morphed her expression into one of horror, and the reaction made Mya smile. The woman opened her mouth to scream, but before she could make a sound Mya reached forward, grabbed her by her neck and crushed her throat. The woman's eyes bulged before she fell to the ground, dead.

Mya stepped over her body, entering the foyer. Her eyes darted around the room, preparing for an attack, but instead she found four more witches, their mouths also agape in horror. It only made her smile wider.

"You have the gall to look at me as if you don't know why I'm here." Mya's eyes narrowed, and her tone turned bitter. "You took everything from me, and now, I am going to return the favor."

Mya killed them before they could blink, and she killed the next two who entered the room. One of them tried some sort of magic on her, and for that Mya broke her fingers, then her hand, her wrist, and her arm. Mya made the woman scream for even attempting to raise a hand to her, all before she tore her head from her neck and threw it onto the dusty floor.

The commotion brought forth more witches, and Mya killed them savagely. Each drop of their blood fueled her rage, her wrath, her need for vengeance and justice. No matter how many she killed, she could never bring Erik back, so she killed them in his name, in *their* name.

Room by room she slaughtered them. Some, after hearing the screams of their sisters, took up weapons to defend themselves, and a dark, deep part of Mya gained satisfaction after killing them with their own tools. At one time she had held *pity* for these creatures, for the atrocities committed against them, but now? Now they deserved every bit of the killer she'd become.

Mya reached the second to last closed door of the floor she was on. She kicked it open, ready to pounce, but the sight before her turned her blood cold. In the room were a dozen bassinets each containing a tiny, delicate newborn. The babies were mixed, not only human but different immortal species as well. Not a single child made a sound, and as Mya approached them, she felt the sparkle of magic, and knew they must be under some sort of spell.

She sensed a presence behind her and spun, then grabbed the young girl from the doorway and threw her back against the wall.

"Please! Wait!" she begged through broken breaths.

Mya's grip tightened on the girl's throat. "Whose children are these?"

"T-The wit-witches'."

Mya loosened her grip around the girl's neck slightly, then looked her over. She was young, with long blonde hair that was tangled and matted. She had bruises, dirt, and blemishes all over her skin, marring her otherwise cream complexion.

"Please," she begged. "I'm not like them. I'm not, I swear!"

Mya had been fooled before, and no matter how abused this girl might look, she did not want to be fooled again. "Tell me about the children," she ordered, hoisting the girl higher against the wall.

Her eyes bulged, but she made no move to defend herself or remove Mya's hand from around her throat. "They're children the blood witches had with immortals!"

"It's rare for immortals to have children. How are there so many?" she hissed.

The girl shook her head frantically. "These children aren't from normal births. The witches, they do something to immortals, then they sleep with them and kill them. Once they give birth, and the child reaches a certain age, they brand them and teach them blood magic."

The girl held her wrist in front of Mya's face. "Here, this is where they brand those that are taught blood magic. See? I don't have a brand. I'm not like them. Please believe me," she cried.

Mya's eyes narrowed. "And who's to say you're not branded elsewhere and this isn't all a ploy?"

"I know who you are! I know what they did to you, Mya, and to Erik." Her panicked voice dropped to a whisper when Mya tightened her hand around the girl's neck again.

"Do not *ever* mention his name to me. You have no right!" Mya screamed.

The girl whimpered and her hand gripped Mya's begging her to loosen her hold. "I didn't kill him! But I know what they did, and I know why you're here. If you need to kill me or the others, I understand, but please leave the babies. They didn't do anything wrong."

Mya didn't loosen her hold, but she didn't tighten her grasp either. "Others? What others?"

"Th-There are other girls like me who take care of the

babies. We were all shackled, but I was the last one to look over the children, so I was free. None of us are blood witches."

"And after you're done taking care of these children, then what? What do you get out of it?" Mya snarled.

The girl looked down, so Mya shook her, drawing her gaze back.

"Death," she croaked as tears clouded her eyes.

Mya's eyes widened. She let the girl go and watched as she dropped to the ground on her knees. "Explain."

The girl was shaking. Whether it was from fear or weakness, Mya didn't know, but after several gulps of air she finally spoke. "They don't change us into blood witches. They abduct us, normally from traveling colonies, and then they make us take care of their children. Once we've served our purpose, they kill us."

The girl shook her head and looked up at Mya, her big green eyes now filled with determination. "It doesn't matter if you kill me. I'm dead already, but those children didn't do anything."

Mya reached down to the girl, but she shied away, cowering against the wall.

"Please, I-I can give you more. They were going to after your brother, Greg, and Luke. Please believe me!"

Mya drew in a sharp breath. Her heart beat frantically at the thought of losing her brother and cousin. The pounding was so strong it felt as if it would come out of her chest. Her whole world flipped, faded, and crashed on its side.

Get it together! Now isn't the time to fall apart.

Mya grabbed the girl by the chin. The sudden move made her gasp, and Mya leaned over her. "What is your name?"

"E-Elaine."

"Elaine, if you're lying to me about any of this, I will take my time with you. I will break every bone in your body, heal you, and do it all over again. Do you understand?"

Elaine gulped and nodded.

Mya straightened and dropped her hand from her. "Are there any more blood witches?"

"N-No, not here. But there are wards in the cemetery. If any of the witches escaped, they'd go there."

"And do you have what you need here to free the other girls and prepare the children for travel?"

"Y-Yes."

"Then go. Make sure to change your clothes and have the others do the same, then meet me in front of the church."

Elaine blinked for a moment, then stood. Slowly she moved around Mya, constantly checking behind her as if to make sure Mya wouldn't change her mind and kill her, until she finally scurried from the room.

With one last look at the babies, Mya made her way back through the house, over the bodies of the witches she'd killed, and out to the cemetery. There she found five more witches, but she killed them with less vigor than before. Now it wasn't just about Erik; it was about protecting her family. She was more cautious, more precise, and for her efforts she found an additional four witches she would have otherwise missed in her violent haze. Mya picked up their bodies and hauled them into the church.

She had just finished with the women when Elaine met her, as instructed, along with six other young girls. Most held two babies in their arms. The girls themselves looked terrible, covered bruises and cuts like Elaine, but at least they were dressed, and that would be enough for Mya get them to the tavern without too many questions.

Mya gestured for the girls to move back, and then she lit the house on fire. She stood and watched it burn. The fire brought back the picture of Erik's house—their house—and it was as if the flames burned away at Mya's retribution. Suddenly she felt tired, like the weight of the world had finally engulfed her, and the pain she felt went deeper than her skin, her mind, and her heart. It was etched into her very soul.

Someone tapped on her shoulder and Mya spun around, making Elaine gasp.

"I-I just wanted to give this to you. I didn't know your size, but I thought it might help if you changed too."

Mya took the blood red material, trying to keep her hand from shaking. She wiped the blood from her face, hair, and chest, then she pulled off her dress and threw it in the fire. After she'd shucked on the gown Elaine had given her, she gave the girl a curt nod in thanks.

The group walked together until Mya could flag several carriages, paying handsomely for their discretion. Once in the carriage, she grasped her shaking hands tightly, gulping in air and tasting the foul smells of horse shit, blood, filth, and alcohol. They were her reminders that she was here, still alive. She had to be, just for a little bit longer.

They arrived at the tavern, and Greg pulled the door open before Mya could raise her hand. His brows were twisted, his eyes glowing red, and her breath hitched.

"Where have you been? I've been looking all over for you! You were supposed to come right back! Do you have any idea—"

The dam inside her broke open and the tide dragged her under. "Greg," she hiccupped. "He's dead. Erik's dead!" Then the whole world tilted, and she welcomed the endless black.

13

"Your sister killed an entire coven of witches!" Francois, one of the council members, shouted.

"And if she hadn't, we would all be dead!" Greg yelled.

The council meeting had been going on for hours. After Mya collapsed in Greg's arms, he carried her upstairs. Then he took care of Elaine and the rest of the girls. Along with Luke, he set up a nursery for the babies, and when Mya awoke, he held her while she told him everything that had happened.

Mya stayed in that room, staring vacantly at the wall, sitting on the bed she had shared with Erik only a few short days prior. She didn't move, didn't eat, didn't drink, or sleep until Greg told her they had to report what happened to the newly formed council. Mya followed him wordlessly. Now that she had no one to hunt or kill, nothing to investigate and no reason or purpose or fuel for revenge, the fight had left her body. and all she felt was numb.

The fighting started the moment Greg had told The Council

what she had done. Arguments broke out about how unstable she was, how she couldn't be trusted, how she deserved to be punished, and perhaps they were right. After all, she did destroy an entire coven, and she would do it again without a second thought. In fact, she held no remorse for what she'd done. She only wished she'd destroyed them before they had destroyed her, before they had broken her heart and ripped out the very essence of her soul: her beloved, Erik.

"You know our laws," Francois snarled.

"I know them because *I* made them," Greg barked back.

Mya looked at Greg, studying him. For most of the meeting he'd been calm, patient, explanatory, but in the last few minutes he'd become more and more upset, and now he sounded as if he wanted to pounce on the man and tear him limb from limb.

"Then you also know that we cannot make an exception just because this woman is your own flesh and blood."

Greg hissed. "Francois—"

"Do not make an exception for me," Mya said blankly, tired of the arguing, tired of being in this world when Erik was not. "If you must punish me, do so."

Francois's eyes turned to hers, and for a moment she swore she saw delight in them. "Then you admit you should die for what you've done."

Mya's eyes widened in shock, not horror. Francois was offering her exactly what she wanted. Her death would set her free, allow her to pass on from the cruel fate of living here without Erik.

"Mya—" Greg started, only to be interrupted by Francois.

"She savagely destroyed an entire coven of witches. This council was created by you and Erik as a haven for all immortals. If we leave her alive, the message it sends to others is that vampires are still superior and this council will protect them above all others." His eyes narrowed. "We cannot trust that she will not do this again. I vote death as Mya's punishment."

Lily snapped her fan closed. "Francois, you are forgetting why these deaths occurred. The witches killed first—"

"We have no guarantee that Erik is dead. We have not begun an investigation to ensure that he is, which is required *before* any vote for punishment," Greg bit out.

Mya wanted to argue. She opened her mouth to do so, to accept the sweet gift of death, but Francois spoke first.

"And what then? What guarantee do we have that you wouldn't hide your sister to save her?"

Greg took a step forward. "I would never—"

"You have a conflict of interest—"

Lily smacked the table with her fan. "Enough!" she ordered, and everyone fell silent. "Francois is correct. This was genocide, and it is not what we stand for, not anymore."

Greg started. "Mya—"

Lily shot him a look that stalled the rest of his words. "Losing Erik has created a large void for all of us, but no one feels that void stronger than Mya. She is—*was*—his mate."

Mya's head snapped up at the word and she met Lily's gaze. "His mate?"

Lily's eyes widened. "He never told you?" she asked, sighing and pinching her brow as Mya shook her head. "By the gods," she whispered under her breath. "Mya, immortals have mates, partners who they are the most compatible with. It's different for everyone. Some are fated, destined to be together, while others can be rejected. But it is clear from what you felt, from what you've *done*, that Erik was your fated mate."

This knowledge tugged at something in her, something dark and broken. This was just another thing she didn't know, another thing she should have known, another *secret*. "W-What does that mean?" she asked.

"It means that Erik is the only person you would have ever loved or truly been happy with. He's also the only person you could procreate with."

Erik's ring felt warm on her finger, the opposite of the coldness that swept through her body. Mya looked around the room dumbfounded, taking in the faces of sadness, anger, righteousness and pity. Then her gaze landed on Greg and Elaine. "But the blood witches—"

"They tampered with the immortal's fated line," Lily said.

"Which is dangerous," a council member snarled.

"Mya saved us by killing those witches. We could have lost the ability to find our fated mates," another member followed.

"And how will we be able to explain that to the witch council when one of us can extinguish their entire line? When a council member's *sister* has already done so? Do you really believe they wouldn't try to use this as an excuse for war?" Francois said.

Several members of The Council grunted and nodded in agreement.

"I've heard and understand your grievances," Greg said sternly, causing Mya to shift her gaze to his. "I ask that you allow me to investigate Erik's death, as written in our laws."

"There is nothing to investigate! Erik's reaction to believing his fated mate rejected him is understandable, but there has never been a record in all our history of a fated mate committing a massacre because of rejection. Those actions have only ever been committed when the mate has passed. And she said it herself, she tracked him over a cliff!" Francois exclaimed, his pale, powdered skin growing as red as a tomato.

"Regardless," Greg said through clenched teeth, "if we must uphold the law for death then we must uphold the law for investigation."

"And you plan to lead it yourself so you can use your position to hide information and run circles around the rest of us? No, I don't think so," Francois said.

"You're absolutely correct," Greg said, drawing a gasp from everyone, including Mya. "It is not fair that I should run the investigation while being a council member. Until this is adjourned, I will remove myself from the position."

"Greg—" Mya began, but he held up his hand.

"Does that satisfy The Council?" he asked.

"And what guarantee do we have that this will be your top priority?" Francois asked.

"I will provide you with a report once a month."

"Once a week," Francois ordered.

"Fine," Greg said, his body vibrating with tightly controlled fury.

"You will also explain your sister's actions to the witch council. Should she ever do something so horrendous again, you will take her punishment."

Mya called out her brother's name, but Greg threw her a sharp glare before turning back to Francois. "Agreed."

The moment they walked out of the meeting hall, Mya grabbed Greg's arm. "Why did you do that for me?"

"I don't believe Erik's dead," Greg said, ripping his arm from her grasp and marching down the street on furious steps.

His words shocked her, and for a moment she stood still staring at his back, then raced after him.

"He is dead," she whispered at first, but then the raw emotion overwhelmed her and she screamed, "He's gone! Why would you want to investigate his death? Don't you get it? He left. He left me!"

Greg's eyes narrowed, hardened. "And what would you like me to do? Let you die over a possibility?"

"Yes! I would rather be dead. At least then I could be with him!"

His eyes flashed red, and darkness flew at them at such high speed that the wind chilled her. "I will never let that happen," he hissed.

"I wish you would!" Tears clouded her vision and rolled down her cheeks. She looked down at her trembling hands, saw Erik's metal ring, and her heart broke and bled until it was as dead as Erik. "There's nothing for me here. Nothing," she whispered.

Greg didn't say another word.

DAYS AND MONTHS AND YEARS WENT BY, AND MYA DID NOTHING.

She spent most of her time in a catatonic state where she simply stared outside and watched as the sun rose and set. She watched as time went by, as people laughed, ate, grew, fell in love, and died. She watched it all because Erik couldn't, and she knew he'd never see another day beside her.

Greg reminded her to eat. Luke did too, but it was Greg who would force blood down her throat when she got a little too close to the edge of starvation, and it was Greg who took the brunt of her anger every time he made her eat. He also took her anger, her rage and sorrow, every time he stopped her from killing herself.

She tried, by the gods how she'd tried. Her accursed power made it so most things that would at least weaken other vampires did nothing to her. She could go months without blood, direct wounds healed in an instant, and her body rejected poison. Mya tried to hang herself, but the rope broke most of the time, and on the few blessed occasions where it didn't Greg always found her and cut her down. She tried to drown herself; he saved her. She tried to shoot herself; when he realized she owned a gun he removed all the bullets without telling her, and then he removed anything she could use as a weapon until she had no choice but to sit in her misery and endure it.

One day, she watched from her window as someone threw out a hoe. Mya's sunken eyes widened at the chance. She raced downstairs and moved to open the door, only to find her brother. He had the same look on his face as always, a grim glare with a frown at his mouth, as if his disappointment in her was etched onto his skin. Without a word he picked her up and tossed her over his shoulder.

"Let me go!" she screamed, but he remained silent as he carried her upstairs. She pounded on his back, shouted and cried and cursed at him, and yet he still didn't say a word.

He sat her down firmly in her chair before turning to leave.

She yelled so loudly, lost and manic, "Why won't you let me die? Why won't you let me have peace? Why are you being so selfish—"

He laughed, a bitter chuckle that seemed to come from deep inside him, then he turned around to face her with so much fire in her eyes that she drew back for a moment.

"Selfish? I'm selfish? I'm not the one fucking dreaming of killing themselves to try and reunite with a man who might not even be dead!"

Mya rose from her seat. "Don't. Don't you dare say that! He's gone, and the fact that you can't accept that—"

"If that isn't rich coming from you. I can accept that he's gone. I accept it every day that I wake up and breathe this air and have to come to this house to see if today is the day I will find my sister's lifeless body," Greg growled.

Mya threw her arms out as she screamed, "I didn't ask you to take care of me!"

Greg's eyes narrowed. "You're right. You didn't ask me to take care of you, but that's what family does. You may have forgotten we exist in all your grief and pain. You may believe there's nothing left for you here. None of us may matter to you, but I'm not going to give up on you. Hate me all you want, but that will never happen, Mya."

Her eyes stung and his form became blurry under the trail of hot tears as the monster of chaos within her surged to the height of a rogue tidal wave. "Greg—"

He shook his head. With an exasperated sigh, he turned to leave.

"I don't hate you!" she choked, reaching out to him even though she stood stuck, unable to make herself embrace him.

Greg froze.

"I don't hate you," she whispered, "but I have nothing here."

"You have a family, Mya!" Greg shouted so loudly that she swore the whole house shook. "You have a brother and a cousin that love and adore you and want to help protect and save you with every fiber of their beings, but you won't let us! For years all you cared about was Erik!"

"You wouldn't understand!"

"Then make me. Since I don't understand, make me."

The house shook again as Greg's power drew in the energy and shadows around her. The weight of it was so heavy she could barely breathe, barely stand.

"He was my everything, my whole heart, and without him here it feels like it's gone. It feels like my entire heart is vacant, and I can't get that back, Greg. I *can't.*"

Her nails dug into her chest as she tore at where her heart should have been, just as her brother had torn the explanation from her, like each word was cutting through her flesh and bone.

"No, you won't *try* to get it back. There's a difference, Mya. He was your everything and you were his, and the way he was taken from you was a horrific tragedy, but you weren't the only one that lost him! My grief can never compare to yours, and neither can Luke's, but we can understand a fraction of it. Yet, you won't let us. You won't move past your pain. Once upon a time your family meant everything to you, and now we mean *nothing.*"

"Greg, please, no. Don't say that!" Mya cried, but for all her words she still couldn't move to embrace him, to reach out to him and comfort him.

"But it's the truth," he said, and his eyes clouded over with grief. "The moment you lost Erik, we lost you, and we're not enough to pull you back. You won't even let us try!"

She shook her head frantically. That wasn't the truth. How could it be, when watching and listening to his pain hurt her so? And yet, she hadn't shown him anything different. She didn't even know how to, and it sickened her to face the fact that he was correct. She didn't want to try. She wanted the world to forget about her, to let her live in her burdens and misery in peace until she died.

"Greg, just leave me here. Let me live in my pain," she said with a sad smile. "That's all I'm good for—"

"No!" He stormed toward her and bared down on her with such ferocity that she felt as though the world stopped moving. "No. You don't get to say that. I will *not* listen to you sit here and say that. You have a gift, Mya. There is so much you could do, and yet you sit in your fucking chair and squander your life away out of grief. You are worth the sun and the moon. You are my sister, but the woman you've turned into is not the woman I know. Where is the girl who was brave, who would fight, who faced every single adversity? Where did she go?"

Tears rolled down her cheeks as she whispered, "She grew tired. She died."

"No, she gave up. That's what you did, Mya, you gave up."

She snapped. "You act like this is so easy, like I can just flip a switch and become something else. He *died*, Gregori. He died!" she screeched so loudly that spit landed on his face.

Mya pushed him, punched and kicked at him, but he grabbed her and brought her close. She chanted her last words into his chest as her heart broke even further, as she turned raw, drowning in grief and rage and hatred and sorrow. Greg simply rubbed her back, her hair, and comforted her even as she attacked him.

Eventually she grew quiet.

"Do you want a reason to live, to become that woman again? Do you want to have a purpose?" he said into her hair.

"What could I do? What could I be used for?" she murmured into his chest.

"I'll show you."

Over the centuries Greg built his circle—carefully under The Council's watchful eye—and Mya helped him do it.

She helped him turn and trained the new recruits, people who could be trusted like Elaine, Merida, and Dominick. She fought in their battles, their wars, she chased down rogue vampires and killed them. With each person's life she took, she saved another potential mate, another innocent, another person who wouldn't have to face what she had.

Mya learned efficient business practices, coding, how to create official documentation for their companies, how to track, navigate, how to hunt whatever, *whoever,* was her prey that week. She was ruthless because she could afford to be. She fought without conscious, like she had already died, because she had.

A purpose didn't save her. It didn't renew her or bring her back to life, but it gave her something to channel her emotions, her power, and her specific abilities into. But on the days when everything was quiet, when she couldn't sleep, when she watched someone else fall into the deep love she'd once had, she grew cold and fell into her dark misery all over again.

On those days, she hated her purpose.

On those days, she hated her brother even more.

PRESENT DAY

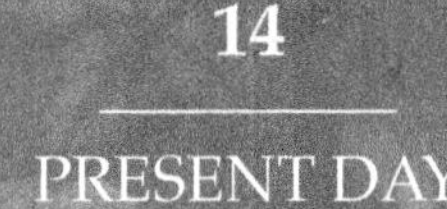

It had been 110,308 days since the last time Mya saw Erik.

She'd mourned him for every single one of those days, until eight months ago when she found out he was still alive. According to Johanna, he *had* to still be alive because an evil bitch named Constance had used him as her own personal guinea pig.

In those eight months, Mya had wrecked the city. She'd turned over every block, every stone, but she still hadn't found him. The only things she had to keep her hopes up were her family and Johanna's word that Constance and her band of minions needed Erik.

Logically, Mya knew that if anyone had gotten their hands on an elder vampire who was now over one thousand years old, they would, of course, keep them alive, if for nothing else than simply the history in their mind and the blood in their veins.

But this was Erik. *Her* Erik. The same man that she had shrines and portraits of in her home so that she didn't forget his face. The same man that she kept memories of in journals, re-writing them as the pages faded. She remembered key moments: the day he saved her life, the first day she felt some-thing different toward him, the first time he'd kissed her, trained her, confessed his love for her. She remembered the day she lost him. Mya would never forget that pain and agony. She'd thought she would never see him again, and now she knew there was a chance she might.

Mya had never been good at having hope or faith, but she would pray to every old and new god if it meant she could see Erik just one more time, if she could hold him in her arms. But eight months of searching had yet to yield anything.

She knew Erik had been alive when they had faced off against Zachariah, and that he had been held in the same area as Johanna before Zachariah had dragged her out. But that cave had been buried under the explosives Zachariah had set, and the mountain was too unstable to explore.

Daniella wanted to use her magic to investigate the area, but it was too risky, especially while she was pregnant. Even though Mya wanted to find Erik, she didn't want it to be at the expense of her friend, unborn niece, and, by extension, her brother. So, she waited, searched, located, and interrogated every rogue vampire she could find, but they were too crazed to give her any answers.

Johanna tried to help as well, but it mostly resulted in rogue vampires coming after her to try and drag her back to Constance. She'd offered to use herself as bait, but everyone, including Mya, had shut the idea down. Even though Mya had mostly ignored Johanna when they first found her—because of how much she reminded her of Erik—she was Luke's mate and she'd become a close friend. Johanna had gone through far too much, and Mya was not willing to subject her to any more.

Johanna enlisted her younger sister, Tamara, who was hiding out in the Fae Realm with her family under Loe's protection, to see if they could help. But even there, with all the powers and resources of the Fae Realm, they couldn't find anything.

It wasn't until Daniella gave birth to Mya's niece, Ruby Adalyn Novak, a beautiful girl with her mother's brown skin tone and her father's hazel eyes, that things changed. Daniella refused to rest, and within days she began investigating the caves.

While Daniella grew tired easily, Johanna's mental ability helped her fortify her strength. Over time they were able to search further and further, until they eventually located the cage Erik had been held in. Based on what Daniella could tell from the vines she used to feel around the bars, it had been broken open from the inside out. When Daniella didn't find any bodies near that entrance, Mya breathed a sigh of relief. Erik had at least made it out on his own, but that didn't answer the question of where he was now.

Daniella pulled several items out of the cave, including a partial map that Mya was now combing over. It was nothing more than lines and dashes, with a few small hand drawn markers. Mya had tried to plot out the distances, but they didn't make sense, and none of the lines, which she figured must be some sort of route system, corresponded to any type of geographical location. She also discovered another partial map in some paperwork Luke had found when he was searching for Johanna. The maps seemed to match, but it was clear there was still a large portion missing. and she hadn't been able to figure it out on her own, nor with the help of any of the databases she had hacked into. There was something there, she knew there was, but she couldn't see it, and it felt as if her heart was breaking all over again with each day that went by without finding Erik.

Mya sighed, her whole body curling into itself over the map. She massaged her temples and closed her eyes. The deep breaths she took should have helped, but they only felt like a waste of time. Mya remembered all the times Greg had tried to beat into her head that she could cause as much chaos as she wanted, but if she couldn't calm the storm when she needed to be mindful and take care of herself, she wouldn't live long enough to find Erik in the first place.

"That bad, huh?"

Mya looked up to see Greg leaning against the doorframe with his daughter in his arms. For a second she wondered if she had manifested him with her thoughts.

No. He probably just has a homing beacon for when I need a dose of reality to kick my ass back into gear.

"Yeah," she confessed.

"When was the last time you took a break?" he asked, walking into the room while gently patting Ruby's back.

"It's been..." She checked her watch and gulped as she realized that over four hours had passed since she'd last moved.

"Thought so. Here, let's trade."

He carefully laid Ruby into Mya's arms and took the maps from her, settling down in the chair across from her. Mya smiled down at her niece's beautiful, scrunched face. She loved her so deeply, so fiercely. It was a type of love she didn't know she could ever feel again, but Ruby also reminded her of all the things she wanted, all the things she once thought she'd have by now.

Ruby cooed, wiggling and kicking her little feet. Realizing she was beginning to fuss, Mya started to softly hum the melody of a song that she'd written one night when she couldn't sleep. It was a heartbreaking song about love and loss, about watching the figure she dreamed of disappearing the moment she opened her eyes.

When Ruby fell asleep, Mya looked to Greg and found him staring back at her.

"I haven't heard you do that in a while."

"What?"

"Hum. Sing. I didn't even know you still did." His hazel eyes looked back at the map as a frown creased his forehead.

Mya fidgeted slightly in the chair, embarrassed. "I do it sometimes when I can't sleep."

"And how often is that?"

"Most nights." She shrugged gently, but she could feel the weight of her brother's stare, the careful assessment of her that he took, as if he could see into her mind, her soul.

Greg flicked a piece of the map, studying it. "I thought that had gotten better."

"It's never really gone away. Some days it's better, some days it's not."

He let out a soft *hmm*, eyes still on the map.

"Greg?" she said, calling his attention. When his eyes met hers, she swallowed down the ball in her throat. She knew it would be hard to say her next words, but she had to. He deserved them. "You were right. You were right about Erik being alive, and you were right when you said I had given up all those years ago."

He looked at her, as if he could tell how much she struggled to start the conversation, but still he said nothing.

"How did you know? About him, I mean. Why did you believe he was still alive?"

He clasped his hands and settled further in the chair. "Because he loved you, Mya. When Erik asked me for my blessing, it was to look after you, take care of you, to keep you as his number one priority. It was never to be *with* you. In all the years we were together, he never took your love for granted. He never expected you to be love him, to *choose* him, and he was willing to force himself to be content with just being by your side if that was what you wanted. Your happiness and safety came first to him, which is the same reason I was willing to give him my blessing."

Tears gathered in Mya's eyes, but she refused to let them fall.

Greg leaned forward and squeezed her arm. "Now that I'm older and I have more experience, I understand mate bonds. I can only try to understand what Erik felt when he thought you rejected him. I believe he wrote the goodbye letter to you because his want, his desperate need to protect you was prevalent in his words, but leaving you? Committing suicide? No."

"Erik was my mentor and my closest friend, but he would never have trusted me to look after you. Even with a broken heart he would have stayed by your side. He would have never left you alone, even if that meant staying in the shadows where you couldn't find him. I'm just sorry that the both of you had to go through this much to end up here."

Mya tried to cover her mouth as sobs began to rack her. She felt her brother take the weight of Ruby from her. She heard him step outside the room, and then he was back, holding her close to his chest.

"I'm sorry," she murmured into his shoulder. "I'm so sorry for all the times that I—"

"I know," he said, his voice laced with pain. "I know there have been times you've hated me, and I know our relationship has never been as good as it once was, but that doesn't make me love you any less, Mya. You'll always be my sister, and I'm sorry for all the times I was hard on you. I know that didn't help."

She wiped at her eyes and shook her head. "No, I deserved that. I needed that. If you had coddled me, I would've stayed in my sorrowful little state and never tried to do anything with my life. Because of you I now have a chance. You fighting with me gave me that."

He smiled, and his warmth broke through some of the darkness surrounding her heart. "If you need someone to fight with or for you, I'm always happy to do so. I love you, Mya, and I will always do anything I can to help you, no matter how difficult you might make it."

"Thank you for always being there, and I love you too."

A soft knock on the open door broke Mya and Greg apart, and Mya smiled as Daniella walked in then and dropped a kiss on Mya's head, then turned to kiss Greg.

"Hey sweetheart," he said as he wrapped his arm around her waist.

"Good morning, love." Daniella smiled at Greg, and there was so much adoration in her eyes that it felt as if Mya were intruding on a special moment between them. It was equally heartwarming and heart-wrenching for Mya to watch. If Gregori was a king, Daniella was his queen. If he was the patriarch, the father of their circle, Daniella was the matriarch, the elemental mother—equally kind, protective, and wrathful of anyone who hurt their family.

She simply fit in a way that was astonishing to witness, and that extended to her place in the entire circle. Daniella had the respect, admiration, and devotion of every single one of their battle officers, warriors who could be difficult to please. She'd become someone they went to for advice, someone who aided them whenever possible, and an incredible fighter that Mya was proud to battle alongside. But even more than that, Daniella had changed Greg.

Mya had seen the same thing with Johanna. Luke was calmer, more positive, serene in a way Mya had never seen before. There were immortals with mates, but the changes she'd watched her family and their other halves go through over the last year were incredible to witness, and Mya had to admit to a small bit of jealousy, of longing. Had she been that way when Erik was around? Was that why his loss was so potent, why it had changed her so? And what would happen when she found him?

What would happen if she didn't?

Mya looked at the maps again with renewed vigor. She had to find him, and once she did, she'd get him to Johanna to restore his memories. She just had to—

"Let me see those," Daniella said, and Mya stood and pulled back her chair to let her sit down.

"There's something there. I can feel it. It's like there's magic I can't see in between the pages," Greg said.

Mya's eyes widened and she moved to look over Daniella's shoulder. She gasped as she realized that she'd been so focused on finding Erik, on making the maps mean something she could understand, that she'd missed the aura surrounding them. It was only a tingle, like static electricity, but it was there.

Daniella fingered the corner of one of the maps. "You won't be able to see it because it isn't meant for you," she said breathlessly.

"The spirits?" Greg asked, rubbing Daniella's back.

She nodded. "We need Johanna and Luke."

***

"What did you find?" Johanna asked when she and Luke approached the table, breathless and still charged of energy from teleporting to them.

"Tell me what you feel," Daniella said, tapping the map.

Johanna ran her fingers over the edges, then gasped, pulling them back. "It's filled with magic. Witch magic."

Mya looked from Greg to Luke, only to find that they seemed to be just as confused as she was. "What are you two talking about?"

"This map is imbued with witch magic, but in a way that no spell or immortal can access." Daniella's eyes touched Mya's then Greg's. "No matter how long either of you spent reviewing it, you would never have been able to see the true contents of the map."

Mya gasped.

Luke stepped forward. "Wait a second, I've never heard of anyone being able to do that."

"It's extremely high-level magic," Greg said, crossing his arms. "Could it be familial?"

Johanna shook her head. "No, a witch's magic is similar to an immortal's. It needs purposeful intention and energy. The fact that this is still emitting magic either means that Constance has touched it recently, which we know couldn't possibly be true, or that it's spelled."

Daniella nodded. "And I believe the way to break the spell is with blood. Your blood, Johanna."

Johanna tilted her head to the side. "My blood?"

"Or Luke's. Both of you have been infected with Constance's blood, and I think this map only reveals its contents to someone who has received her blood."

Johanna and Luke looked at one another. His grip on her waist tightened, and then Johanna asked, "Where do you need it?"

Mya watched as Daniella ran her fingers over the map. Nothing stood out to Mya, nor seemed different from one place to another, but Daniella eventually paused and said, "Here."

Mya edged closer as Johanna pricked her index finger with one of her fangs. She hovered her finger over the spot, then let several drops of blood fall where Daniella had indicated.

At first, nothing seemed to happen, then the aura around the map grew stronger. The air seemed to vibrate as the map began to illuminate. Before Mya's eyes, mountains, forests, and buildings began to appear. Their images grew stronger until the map was colored in rich and vibrant details. When the last of the images had settled, a thick black 'X' appeared, circled over one of the buildings. They all bent closer, scanning the map as best as they could.

Five seconds later, it burned to a crisp. But that didn't matter. For the first time in eight months, they had a lead.

***

The whole thing was a bust.

Mya and her family drove to the spot on the map, where they found a nightclub packed with people. Greg and Luke reluctantly stayed in their cars while Mya, Daniella, and Johanna went inside.

Johanna did a mental scan of the club members and found who they were looking for immediately, but the men recognized them too. Six vampires stood and began to approach them. Mya, Johanna, and Daniella lured them outside to a back alley, and when the nightclub door shut, they killed everyone, save for the leader.

The man refused to speak. Johanna broke into his mind, planning to use her abilities to break the truth out of him, but there was nothing. It was as if his entire mind had been wiped clean. The moment she pulled out, the man's eyes widened and his head exploded, sending bits of matter everywhere. Then the dead vampires' heads did the same, leaving them staring at one another in shock.

Their group searched the immediate area to see if someone nearby had caused the explosions, but they found no one. At a loss, they went home, each with their mate—the other half of their soul—while Mya went home to an empty house.

She didn't blame her family. They had done their best. They tried to help, and they were just as disappointed as she was, but disappointment wasn't all she felt. She was in agony, enraged, and fed up with the entire world. Their lead, their first real lead, had taken them nowhere. They had absolutely nothing. *She* had absolutely nothing.

Mya couldn't sleep. She worked her way through the dark web, searching through forums. She ran background checks on the IDs of the immortals they'd killed, but she came up empty. Each ID was a fake, and the recognition software database she'd hacked into couldn't find anything on them either, not even a Missing Person's Report. It was as if they were ghosts.

Her hands shook, and she knew there was only one thing that could settle her for the night. She changed into black pants, a black tank top, leather jacket and boots. She filled her pockets with her usual weaponry—throwing knives, stars, dust, small containers of alcohol and gasoline, matches, a lighter, a collapsible staff—slipped Erik's ring and the necklace she kept it on into the hidden pocket within her jacket, picked up her sword and headed out to hunt.

***

Mya watched from the skyscraper, scanning the streets for rogue vampires. The wind howled around her and tugged strands of her hair from her braid as she waited. New York City was loud, even at night. The sounds of police sirens, ambulances, and the countless amount of people biking, walking, and talking never ceased. The city never slept, and because of that it was the perfect playground for immortals, whether they were sane or not.

A deep growl mixed with a mocking laugh echoed from her right—the sound of a predator trapping its prey—exactly what she was looking for.

She jumped from building to building, using her vampire speed to fly along the rooftops until she stood above the alleyway. She leaped down from the tall building, carefully timing her fall so that she landed directly onto the rogue vampire's head. Gravity took care of the rest, and his body folded in on itself—tendons snapping, bones breaking—until it resembled a pancake. It made her smile, and the poor human who would have been dead had it not been for Mya, exited the alleyway none the wiser.

Mya took down several other rogue vampires that way, both alone and in groups, but it still didn't ease the frantic beating of her heart. She was beginning to think nothing would, until she came across her third rogue vampire group and noticed that they were stabbing and cutting their victim. They normally preferred to tear their victims limb by limb while they drained them dry.

She sped forward, grabbed the nearest vampire, and pulled their arm back, breaking it in one motion. She moved so quickly that the others hadn't even sensed her presence until the vampire began to howl. He only got out a squeak of the sound before she stabbed him clean through his head.

The other vampires who turned toward her—teeth bared, faces contorted with murderous intent—died within the next two seconds. Then Mya got a look at the man they were trying to disembowel. He was an immortal. His hair was covered in dirt and blood, his face bruised, eyes sunken in, but for a single moment, they met hers, and time stopped.

It was Erik.

She'd found him.

15

Mya did her best to carry Erik through the woods. More rogue vampires had appeared, so she'd been forced to deal with them first before attending to Erik. He'd fallen unconscious after the sixth man she killed. By the twentieth, his breath had become labored. It shouldn't have been possible. Erik was a vampire, an elder vampire at that, and one of the strongest men she'd ever known, but now he was dying on her back.

She wanted to check his wounds, to give him her blood, but she couldn't until she'd made sure they were safe. For that, she had to disguise their tracks. By the time she'd gotten him on her back, four more SUVs of rogue vampires had appeared. Mya could take them all, but each second she spent fighting them was another Erik spent bleeding out, and she would not risk him, *ever*.

She purposefully dragged her steps, letting the weight of him fall into her to make sure the outlines of her shoes were more pronounced. Together they reached the river. Its current was strong, and while she didn't want the added risk, she knew they needed to cross it to help disguise their scent, so she waded through. She bent brush and discarded leaves, doing anything she could to throw them off the trail, but every moment they spent there was a delay. Erik was still unconscious, his blood coating her clothes, and she knew she had to finish this quickly. He didn't have much time left.

Mya found the entrance to a cave, breathing a small sigh of relief. It would serve as the perfect distraction for the vampires she was sure were tracking her, and where there was one cave entrance, there was always another. Hoisting Erik further up her back, Mya leaped onto the side of the mountain, then onto a tree. She traveled through the air until she spotted an opening that would work perfectly for them.

Slipping inside the cave, Mya traveled down the passageway until she reached a large stream of water. She hoped she'd gone deep enough. When she was sure that the cave was empty, she laid Erik down and truly looked at him.

He was nothing like the man she once knew.

His blonde hair had grown long, reaching down his back. Lengths of it were missing, as if it had been caught on something and torn. His face was ashen, his skin paler than she ever remembered it and covered in a layer of soot and blood. She ripped open his shirt to see his wounds and gasped at the deep cuts she found. Her fingers traveled over his chest, and she noted how malnourished he was. It was clear he'd been through hell, and as overjoyed as she was to finally have him in her arms, she was just as angry at his captors for what they'd done to him and at herself for not finding him sooner.

Erik didn't deserve this, but she would fix it. She'd fix it all.

Mya cut into her hand, letting the blade slide up her arm. She needed more blood than usual to cover as many of his wounds as possible at the same time. She held her healing magic back to stop it from sealing her own wound, then lined up her arm with three of the large gashes on his body and let the blood flow. Into it she pushed every ounce of her healing magic.

The wounds began to heal, but it was slower than usual. Too slow. Something must have been wrong with his blood, and because of how much he'd lost Mya couldn't heal both it and his wounds fast enough for him to survive.

There was only one other option; the one thing he had always told her not to do, because, as she now knew, it would trigger their mate bond.

She cut a line down her neck, bent over him, and lifted his lips to the spot. "Drink, please," she whispered. "Don't leave me now that I've found you."

"Don't leave me now that I've found you."

When was the last time Erik had heard words spoken to him with such anguish, with such worry and concern for him? The body pressed against his was warm. Her breasts were soft, like feathered pillows that he wanted to bury his head into, and the smell of her was divine, something of juniper, wildflowers, vanilla, and berries. He wanted to taste her, and that desire was so strong he began to salivate. He swallowed the drool, and then he tasted her blood in his mouth, her essence, and it felt as though the whole world had suddenly sharpened and turned vividly brilliant.

More of her blood slipped into his mouth, and he groaned at the taste.

"Drink, my love," she whispered, her voice like a caress that spread over his skin, chasing away the dark, the cold.

He couldn't deny her. Her throat vibrated against his lips, and he growled. His fangs lengthened and he bit down on her neck. His taste buds exploded as he drank from her, slurped more of her down. He couldn't tear himself away. Each gulp made him feel stronger, more powerful. He was captivated by her, enchanted, drunk on her essence and he needed more.

For the first time in centuries, he *desired* something. Someone. He wanted her etched into the very fabric of his being. He wanted her to coat the inside of his every cell, and he wanted to fuck her while she did it.

He had been held captive, tortured in unimaginable ways and cursed the moment he broke free of his cage. Erik thought freedom was all he wanted, that it was the best he could ever have, but something had always been missing, and now he knew what it was.

Her.

Never had he felt so alive until this moment, so desperate for his craving, so fulfilled by every second that passed by. Never had his heart beaten so fiercely, as if it had found its reason for holding on, and it was all because of her. His partner, his soul, his other half, his *mate.*

He needed to grab her, to hold her close, to roll on top of her and take her. He needed to fill her, to stop the aching desperation that was drowning him, and while he didn't know her, he knew that with absolute certainty, just as he knew she needed it too.

She'd found a way to muffle herself, but he'd heard the soft moans that left her lips when he sucked at her skin, and he felt the way her nipples hardened against his chest. He could feel his hands and arms again. He tested, lifting them, and was pleased when they moved so he could wrap his arms around her.

He pressed his body against hers, and she gasped at the contact. His hands inched up her back, until they became tangled in her leather jacket. He growled in frustration and tore it off her, laying it on the ground. Erik wanted nothing between them and shred the offending material as he rolled her onto her back and climbed on top of her.

He ran his hands over her soft skin, felt the goosebumps as he traced down her neck to her breasts. Erik squeezed them in his hands, rolled his thumbs over her nipples. He heard the sharp intake of her breath, and pleasure ran through him. He wanted to take his time with her, to feel her, stroke her, hear her breathless, melodic cries, but he also wanted to devour her, absorb her, to become one with her.

Erik knew he wasn't worthy of her for so many reasons. But he couldn't stop. He *ached* for her. He wasn't just hungry for her blood or her taste; he hungered for the warmth in her that staved away the emptiness in him, and he would do anything to have it, take everything she had to give, and give all of himself in return.

Her hands roamed his back, pulling him closer as she widened her legs—legs that he fit so perfectly in between. He pressed against her pussy, groaning at the barrier of his pants. She heard him, felt that frustration, and lowered her hand to the band. She fumbled with the closure, and he helped her, sending the button flying somewhere against a wall. Carefully, together, they lowered the zipper.

She took him in her hands, and he swore he saw paradise. Her touch weakened him, made him tremble as he thrust into her small hands. His beautiful mate angled her hips, planning on guiding him inside, but he grabbed her and stopped her. His fingers ran over her stomach, and he heard her breath hitch. Then he slid down, flittering over her pubic hair until he reached her clit. He wanted her to enjoy this, wanted her to know that she was his priority, even if he could barely contain himself from ramming inside her.

Her hips undiluted beneath him, circling, taking the pleasure he gave. His fingers traveled lower, trailed her pussy lips then dipped inside. She shuddered and arched at the intrusion, and he groaned in satisfaction. She was so wet, so ready for him.

"Please," she begged. "Please fuck me. I need you, Erik."

How could he deny her? How, when she said his name so beautifully, when she begged so perfectly?

Erik lifted his mouth from her neck. He licked the blood from the spot, and she shivered. He braced himself on one hand to look down at her. Her eyes were dilated, the dark olive orbs so close to black, glowing as she watched him. Her mouth was parted, each breath shorter than the last. He grasped his cock and guided it to her entrance, ran the tip between her pussy lips to coat it in her wetness, and he watched as her mouth opened wider and she moaned for him. Her eyes flickered from his face down to his cock, and she bit her lip. It made him grin, but the smile died on his face when he couldn't remember her name. He knew her in his soul, felt the love he had for her that was as deep and vast as the ocean, but his couldn't remember a single thing about her, and he refused to take her that way.

Erik opened his mouth to speak but found his throat dry at

the notion of asking her a question that was sure to hurt her, even if he knew he had to. He licked his lips and finally said, "Will you tell me your name?"

Her eyes flew to his. Sadness filled her gaze, but she smiled at him regardless. "Mya."

"Mya," he said, and the name felt so right slipping off his tongue. He swallowed the weight of unknown emotions, and they wrapped around his heart and squeezed. "I'm sorry I—"

"I know you don't remember." She slid her hand to his cheek, cupping it with her palm.

"But how?"

"I know the woman who helped you erase the memories. She's safe now, but she told me what she did, that you asked her to remove your memories to protect me and my family."

He remembered Johanna, bloody and used and flayed open in so many ways that they had to stitch her back together. Erik was happy to know she was safe, to know that she was with the wonderful woman beneath him. Mya had saved his life, activating their mate bond to cure him of the curse that sapped his strength and removed the nutrients he needed from blood. And this beautiful woman, his *mate,* the person who his heart was beating so strongly for, deserved better than a rough fuck against a cave floor.

He moved to get off her, but she wrapped her legs around his hips.

"Mya—"

"No," she said even as her voice shook. "Please, no. We have spent years, *centuries* waiting for the perfect time. I swore that when I found you, we would never wait again, and I would make sure we took advantage of every moment we had together. Please," she whispered, "you left me once. Do not leave me now."

He said her name on a sigh. His fingers brushed the wetness away from her cheek, leaving a small trail of dirt on her skin. "You deserve better than this."

"What I do or don't deserve isn't important. What I want is," she said, cupping his face.

The way she looked up at him as if he was her whole world was undeniable, and his heart screamed in agreement with her. They had waited too long, too many years, and they needed to finally take the opportunity they had to be together.

He sighed again. She was dangerous because he knew with absolute certainty that he would never be able to refuse her. Erik shifted, settled the weight of his body on top of hers again, and growled, "Tell me what you want."

"You," she moaned, arching her back as he ground his pelvis against her clit.

"Then I will give you all of me, all you could ever desire. Now watch me slide my cock into you. Watch how perfectly you take me."

She whimpered at his words. Once more he trailed her entrance with his cock before he slipped the head inside. They both gasped. She arched her back and he watched her every movement: the way she swallowed, the way her hands fisted his biceps as he slid into her. His pace was excruciating slow, but a constant thrust forward, until he felt a small bit of resistance.

His eyes widened. "Mya—"

She planted her feet on the ground and lifted her hips, squeezing the walls of her pussy around him, and he couldn't resist thrusting forward. She cried out in a mix of pain and pleasure, and yet she kept pushing against him. He thrust until he was halfway inside her and had to grind his teeth to keep himself from moving or coming right there on the spot.

"You were..." he bit out, panting.

She nodded frantically, licked her lips, and then she smiled up at him brilliantly. "Yes, I was, and now I'm yours."

He snarled and gripped her hips hard as he slid out of her. "You are mine. Only mine," he said, and then he thrust into her.

Her nails bit into his back as he kept sliding deeper. She cried out his name, and the sound of it leaving her mouth only made him want to fuck her harder so he could hear it again and again. He pushed at her thighs, keeping her spread wide for him until he was fully seated and surrounded by the warmth of her pretty little cunt.

Erik pulled out and thrust back in, and then he did it again and again. The way he felt inside of her was indescribable; so deep, so strong that if he died tomorrow, he would be a happy man. But the way she said his name, squeezed him, and tried to wrap herself around him just to keep him inside her, brought him to the peak of euphoria.

Each thrust was stronger, harder, deeper, his need to never be without her mounting until it fully took him over. He needed to bury himself inside her, he needed to feel her coat his cock with her come while he shot his own within her. His feelings went beyond need, beyond desire, beyond a craving; it was pure, endless madness.

He lifted himself from her, and she wrapped her arms around him..

"Made for me," he moaned as he sat down on the floor with her in his lap.

"Yes," she hissed as he slid himself back inside of her.

He impaled her with his cock, gripped her hips and helped her ride him while he met her with every thrust. They bounced together, her breasts against his chest, her arms clinging to him as his hands ghosted her spine, squeezed her back, because he couldn't stand to be separated from her for even a moment. But it was her eyes, the way they stared into his as if they could see into his very soul, that undid him, and he knew in that very moment that no matter what, even if he had no right to her, even if she grew tired of him, even if he hurt her, even if he perished, it would always be them. They were inseparable, undeniable, inextinguishable.

He would never let her go, never let her have another. He would be whatever she wanted, do whatever she needed him to do, give her whatever she needed to keep her happy, because she had claimed him body, mind, heart, and soul, and he didn't want any of those spaces back. In fact, he wanted her to take them, to fill them, to keep them, just as much as he wanted to steal her own.

"Mine," he growled again, because he couldn't form the words he wished to when her pussy was gripping him, milking his cock.

"Yours," she cried out.

He kissed her with everything in him, trying to convey what she'd done to him, to share and show her all the ways she'd driven him completely delirious with her touch. She whimpered into his mouth, and he cupped her head. His fingers traveled to her scalp, and he gripped the long strands of her hair, keeping their lips fused together.

She moaned louder, her body shaking against his as he picked up the pace. He licked her lips and she opened immediately for his tongue. He could still taste her blood, but now he could taste her as well, the mint from her toothpaste, the coffee with cream and three sugars. He loved exploring her, finding out more about her, but now he wanted to know how she looked when she came for him.

It was that need that made him finally break from her mouth, and they both gasped, breathless and moaning. Erik rested his head against her own and whispered, "I want to watch you come, Mya. I want to see what you look like when you've lost every ounce of control. Lean back on my thighs and take my cock. Take what you need from me."

She obeyed him so eagerly, so happy to please, and leaned back on his legs, riding him with wild abandon. Her head fell back when he grabbed her breast with one hand and drew the nipple of her other in his mouth. He sucked and licked it, moaning at her taste, the feel of her, just as he thrust inside her, and every time she said his name, he grew closer and closer to filling her to the brim.

"It's too much. It's too much!" she whimpered.

He let her nipple go with a *pop*, then took control of her hips again. "Clearly it isn't if you haven't come for me."

"I need ... I *need*..." She trailed off, wrapping her arms around him, and then she latched onto his neck, sinking her fangs into his throat.

His eyes rolled back into his head, and he lost all sense of control. Every drop of blood she drank from him increased the frantic brutality of his thrusts. He was lost to sensation, lost to her, and he was never coming back.

A feeling burned deep within him, one he had not felt in eight months: his ability to create and manipulate fire. Without warning it broke free and slid up and around them, covering them in a wall of liquid warmth. The heat coated every part of their bodies, including his cock, and it caused Mya to scream his name.

Her head tossed back as he poured more of his magic into her. Her thighs shook, her eyes opened wide, she clung to him, squeezed him. If he had been a lesser man then her grip on him might have killed him, but he loved the danger of his mate being consumed by the passion between them.

And then she came, and it triggered his own release. He came so hard he lost all sense of reason, time, space. The air, the ground beneath their bodies ... None of it matter. Nothing existed but her. He continued to ram inside of her until he had filled her, and when his come leaked out of her, he pushed it back in.

16

They walked along the narrow pathway to the abandoned church Erik called home in necessary silence. The church was on the outskirts of the city, hidden from most. It was rumored to be haunted, and had mostly been reclaimed by the forest, but it was still a structure, and there was no telling if Constance's vampires were still looking for him or how close they were. They needed to be quiet, to stay alert and be vigilant in using their senses to alert them of danger.

Time was of the essence, Erik knew that, but he still wished they could have stayed in that cave—in each other's arms—because the moment they separated the distance between them seemed unfathomable. Erik knew it was his fault. It was odd not remembering the person he loved the most—all the times they'd spent together, laughed together, their *history*—and yet still feeling the deep, all-consuming love he had for her. And then there was the grief, the sickness, the hurt and pain he knew he had caused Mya. He wanted to get on his knees and beg for her forgiveness. He had the need to hold her, to tell her it was all going to be okay, that he would never leave her again, and yet he didn't understand why he would have ever left her in the first place.

Missing so many of the pieces left him unsure, off-balance. It was not the first time he'd felt that way. When he'd escaped the cage, he'd felt insurmountable pain. He pushed himself through the journey, self-preservation flooding his body with adrenaline, and managed to escape the cave before everything collapsed. But as he stood outside, free, finally achieving his greatest wish, he realized there was so much he didn't know. The world had changed around him, and he had not seen it as a free man in over two hundred years. He had no idea where to go, what to do, and he had to admit he'd grown complacent.

As Constance's captive he was tortured, bled to within an inch of his life for weeks on end, castrated, branded, dismembered. His body had healed from those instances, regrowing his limbs, keeping him whole, but his mind had come to expect the routine. He lived in constant misery. Now he had hope, he had the ability to live, to feed, to breathe fresh air. It was terrifying, but he'd survived it, just as he'd survived being a punching bag for years.

And yet whatever it was he'd done to Mya caused him more pain and agony than any single one of those instances. All because he'd hurt her. But he would still approach it in the same way, using courage and dedication to push through the fear of possibly losing her. She'd asked him not to leave her, and he promised he wouldn't, but he would not let her leave him either.

He tapped her on her shoulder when it was time to turn, and they traveled over a hill and down into the valley which emptied into the small town. A few steps later, they arrived at the church. Erik guided her to the back and had her wait while he made his way inside, carefully avoiding the traps he'd laid. After reviewing them and confirming that none had been triggered, he opened the door for Mya and led her down to the basement, where the church had a tunnel that led to the other side of the cave system.

Erik lit a torch near the wall, wincing at his surroundings. He had a bed, dresser, mirror, a usable restroom considering he washed himself in the river, but his living arrangements were meager at best. Yet again he found himself not living up to what Mya deserved, and yet again he felt like a failure to her. But when he looked at her, no judgment or criticism clouded her face. Her eyes were downcast, and when he made a move toward her, a shaky breath escaped her lips.

Mya cleared her throat and said, "Do you have anything I can change into?"

They'd managed to make a covering out of the scraps of her clothes, but she needed something that would not threaten to reveal her if she moved the wrong way. He reached into the dresser and pulled out the smallest sizes of clothing he'd stolen. He looked at her, then back at the clothing in his hand and sighed. "I think these will be too big for you, but it's the best I have. I'm sorry."

"No, it's okay. This is just fine." Mya took the clothing from him and fidgeted. "Is there somewhere I can change?"

Right here, with my help.

He shook himself of the thought. "Of course. I'll go upstairs. If you need to clean up, walk this way and make a right," he said, gesturing down the tunnel. "It leads to the river. It's fast moving here, so be careful."

"I will be."

He grabbed the largest shirt he owned and a pair of pants, then he motioned to the door. "If you need help, just call for me."

She gave him a small smile and he left to dress himself upstairs. He had managed to find something that fit his new, healthy form: a black top—a wifebeater, as humans called it, although why they chose that name he would never understand—and a pair of gray sweatpants. He caught a reflection of himself and winced. After cleaning himself up, Erik took a pair of sheers to his hair, evening out the length, changed, and then he waited for Mya.

Eventually the door opened, and Mya stood shyly in front of him. For a moment he just stared at her. She took his breath away every time he looked at her, and his heart beat a little faster as need funneled through his veins.

A small smile graced her lips. Then she drew back, as if snapping out of a trance, and broke the connection between them with a shake of her head. "Do you need to grab anything before we go?"

He knew the plan. They were supposed to come here, get whatever he might need or that might be important to him, then destroy the church and go to Mya's house. From there he would meet Johanna and her partner, Luke—someone Erik apparently knew but could not remember—and restore his memories. It was a good plan, a solid plan, one that would work, but one look at Mya's face told him he couldn't take another second of not trying to broach this distance, to fix what had happened between them. Even if they had a million more important things to do, this was what mattered most—her comfort and nurturing their relationship, whatever she may allow it to be.

Erik tipped his head at the pew in front of him. "I need you to stop and tell me what I did. Tell me how I broke your heart."

Mya shook her head. "We don't have time—"

"Then we will *make* time. Sit down and talk to me, Mya. I know I'll get my memories back, but right now, I need to hear what happened from you. I need to know what you've gone through all these years."

He took a deep breath and stared into her sad eyes. "No more distance. No more protecting my feelings or biding time. If you need to lash out at me, do it. If you need to fight me, do it. If you need to kill me, do it. But let me in, love. Let me ease your soul in whatever way I can."

THERE WAS SO MUCH, *TOO* MUCH, WHEN IT CAME TO THEM AND their history.

Mya knew what would happen when she gave him her blood. She knew it would trigger the mate bond, and she did not regret a moment of their time in that cave, but once everything had ended and the sweat on her skin began to cool, reality hit her. He was there. Erik was back. Every time she opened her eyes, he was in front of her. It wasn't a dream, or a memory, or a nightmare where he would suddenly disappear into the darkness again. No matter how many times she blinked or breathed, his form never changed. He was flesh and bone, and actually real for the first time in three hundred years. The emotions it made her feel were too heavy for her to carry, especially now when she was trying to get him to safety.

For years, all she had ever wanted was to see him, to be with him again, and now that her wish had come true, she felt scared. Her anger had risen to the surface. Questions flooded her mind about where he'd been, why he'd left her, how could he have done this to them, and why couldn't he have believed in her that fateful day?

Mya knew it wasn't fair of her to think those things. He'd been held captive, and she had no idea for how long nor what he had endured. She wasn't even sure what he remembered and what he didn't. She knew she shouldn't blame him, and yet a small part of her still did.

Another part of her blamed the circumstances, that they had let fate constantly get in the way of their relationship. She refused to take that out on Erik. He didn't deserve it, and it was clear that even if he didn't remember the time they'd spent together, he did, at least, feel something for her. But how could she open her heart to him? How could she let down her guard and tell him everything that had happened both before and after he left? And how could she say it in a way that wouldn't hurt him?

Mya sat on the pew in front of him, clenching his ring. It had been a constant symbol of remembrance, a vow she'd taken to never forget him or what they'd shared, and just as it had always done in moments of uncertainty, holding the small trinket made her feel brave.

She licked her dry lips. "Do you remember your last name?"

He shook his head.

"Your name is Erik Haraldsen, and my name is Mya Novak-Haraldsen."

His eyes grew wide in shock. "We're married?"

She smiled sadly as she fiddled with his ring. "No, but we

would have been. You saved me, my brother, Gregori, and my cousin, Lucas, from the Black Plague. Then you became our guardian. You taught us, trained us, and eventually you and I fell in love with one another."

She swallowed through the torrent of emotions threatening to break open her heart. "We were together in secret. You went by the name of Lord Erik Devereux in England, and that made you a target. You were concerned that if you made any enemies and they knew we were together, they would come after me—whether they were human or immortal—and because I was a young vampire, my safety would be at risk. Unfortunately, you were right."

Erik squeezed the wood of pew in his fist. His jaw clenched, but he said nothing.

"We came to America to escape the attacks on immortals in Europe, but they happened here too. We thought the blood witches were behind it, but we didn't know who they were, so you and my brother decided to form The Council to safeguard us all."

She licked her lips again and squeezed the ring so hard she had to remind herself to release it before it broke. "The day all the members agreed to form The Council, I had a horrible feeling. I told you about it that morning, but you promised it would all be okay. You reminded me why we were doing this and said that if we could just cement the idea then we would have no reason to keep our relationship a secret. You told me you wanted to marry me, that you would come back home to *me*."

Mya furiously wiped away a tear and took a shaky breath to try and calm her anger. "But you didn't. I saw you with a woman. You were fucking *her*," she spat, and had to force her rage down once again. "At first, I thought it was you, but the scent was all wrong, and I soon realized it was an imposter. I killed them and ran to where they told me you were, but I got there too late. You had been tricked in the same way I had been, but you hadn't seen through it. You thought I'd rejected you and wrote me a goodbye letter—"

Her voice cracked. Erik stood, but she raised her hand, needing to say this now, to get it out.

"You said you were going to kill yourself and you left me everything you owned. I followed your scent to the cliffs and thought you'd jumped over. Then the blood witches set your house on fire." She scraped the tears from her cheeks. "I followed them, and I killed all of them and burned their house just as they had burned yours."

She stood and stepped in between his legs. When he reached for her, she flinched, and he dropped his hands to his sides. She wanted to apologize, but she didn't know how to form the right words when she was eviscerated by emotion and vulnerable even to the sight of him, so she did the only thing she could. She continued her story.

"For years I was lost without you. I wanted to die. I tried to kill myself, but my brother didn't believe you were dead and fought for me to stay alive. I was angry at him for that, and I was so angry with you for leaving me, for not giving me a chance. I've ... managed through the years. I go out on hunts, and I kill, and it makes me feel a little bit better because whoever I save gets a second chance. I take risks because if I die it doesn't matter, and for three hundred years that's how I've lived."

"Mya—"

She shook her head, and he closed his mouth. "I lived that way until eight months ago, when I found out you were alive and were being held captive. Since that day I've been scouring the city for you. All I wanted to do was find you, and now that I have, I can't believe you're here. I'm scared you're just a ghost that will disappear if I touch you. When I think of what we did in that cave, that I gave my virginity to you, I worry that it's all just a dream, that I'm asleep somewhere right now and when I wake up, I'll have to go back to the horrible reality where you're not standing in front of me. I'm both overjoyed to see you and terrified of losing you every single second that goes by. I've never felt so weak and so scared in my whole life, Erik."

She forced herself to breathe to try to stop the way her body trembled from that fear. "When you left, you took me with you, and now that you're back, I'm forced to reflect on things I never thought I would. I don't want to be distant from you, but I don't want to hurt you with my anger and hostility. I want to love you, but I'm afraid that when you get your memories back and I find out you left me because I was never enough to keep you, it will damage me beyond repair. And even with all of that I want to hope..."

Mya trailed off. She struggled as she took off the necklace and undid the clasp, pulling the ring free and letting the chain drop to the floor. "But it doesn't matter, does it? Because in the end, regardless of what happened, of how many years have gone by, there's only one thing that will always be the truth between us. That I"—she took his hand and slid the ring onto his finger—"much like this ring, will always be yours."

She bit her lip hard and let the small sliver of pain cut through the sadness threatening to take her over. Then she smiled and began to walk away, to hope she could save herself from the torrent of feelings washing through her.

An arm around her waist and stopped her.

"Let me go," she said firmly.

Erik's grip tightened. "No."

"Let me go!" she screamed. "Let me go, let me go, let me go!"

She fought against his embrace, but he just held her. She couldn't break away, and she would have fallen to her knees, defeated, if he hadn't kept her close. He turned her and she sobbed into his chest so hard that she shook them both. He combed his fingers through her hair, and it made her cry even harder, because he'd always loved to do that so she'd kept her hair long in memory of him. Everything she'd done was in his memory, and now he was here. She didn't want to lose him again, didn't want to let him go, didn't want to push him away, but she was torn apart, and her mind told her that she needed to preserve herself, that distance was protection.

"I'm sorry," he whispered into her hair while he stroked her back. "I'm so sorry."

She continued to sob, her tears hot and angry as the pain she'd felt for centuries poured out of her. When at last her grief began to lessen, he squeezed her shoulders.

"I didn't leave you," he said, his voice so strong and sure, but Mya knew he was mistaken.

"You did."

"No, I didn't."

She drew away from him and furiously wiped her face with the back of her hands. "Please don't say that for my benefit. Don't lie to me."

"Mya," he whispered, and the way he said her name like a tormented plea made her pause. He cupped her face and made her look up at him as he said again, "I did not leave you. I swear it."

"And the letter telling me goodbye? What was that then?"

"I don't know—"

She shook her head and tried to pull back from him, but he held her still.

"Stop."

It was not a suggestion but a command, and even after all this time she found herself pathetically listening to it.

"What you said, what happened to you..." He swallowed. "What I *made* happen to you broke my heart, but when you turned to walk away, to hide yourself from me? It shattered me, Mya. I cannot fathom not having you by my side, and I cannot think about not being by yours."

She dropped her eyes from his. "Because we consummated our mate bond."

"No!" he said sharply, and her eyes snapped to his. "No," he said again, running his fingers over her cheeks. "When Johanna takes your memories, it feels like something's missing. It's in the back of your mind but you can't figure out what it is, and your heart can't connect to it. I knew there was something I wanted to get to, something I searched for beyond freedom, but I didn't know what it was or where to find it. I didn't know, until you saved me."

She turned her head from his, but he ever so gently, so carefully pulled it back. She closed her eyes, guarding herself from his expression because she couldn't stand to see the way he begged her to believe him. If she did, if she looked at him now, she would. She'd believe anything he told her, trust his decisiveness, his devotion, as she always had, and in the end, it would only break her further when his memories came back and the truth was revealed.

His lips brushed her eyelids in a gentle kiss that stole her breath. "You are my salvation, Mya. I knew it from the moment I laid eyes on you, just as I know what my heart felt then and what it feels now. There are a lot of things there—despair, concern, sorrow—but there are other things too. Hope. Patience. Compassion. But more than anything, love. I love you. I loved you, and I will always love you, even if you were to leave me today. But if you did, you would take my heart and the entire essence of who I am. I know that now, and I know I knew that before, just like I know it would have been the same way for you. I would have never willingly, *selfishly*, put you through that pain. And when I get my memories back, I will prove it to you. I swear it."

17

Mya's house was deceiving. It sat toward the back of a large, encased piece of land, lined by trees and the lush forest on either side. It was entirely made of stone in a cottage style, but the real brilliance was the interior.

Erik was struck by the space the moment he entered the front door. Several of the walls were lined with large sets of seamless glass doors that led to an open courtyard with trees, hedges, a circular fountain, and flowers. He had never seen anything like it.

Mya locked the door behind him and followed his line of sight. "I like to be alone, so I prefer to spend most of my time here. It's easier when you have a view like this and can bring the outdoors into your home."

"It's beautiful," Erik said, staring right at her.

She blushed, twirling her fingers for a moment before she said, "My cell phone is in my bedroom. I'll call Johanna and let her know we're here. Feel free to take a look around."

She went to move past him, but he grabbed her hands and brought them to his lips. "Thank you for inviting me into your home and sharing your space with me."

His grin grew wider when she blushed again, and with a nod she hurried past him.

Erik ventured deeper into the house. There weren't any personal photos of Mya or her family. Instead, the shelves were covered with plants, books on different subjects, old worn journals, and small trinkets.

He moved to the second floor, where most of the doors were open except for one. Behind it he could smell something burning. Erik pondered for a moment, not wanting to intrude, but also concerned for her property. When he finally decided to open the door, he was shocked by what he saw.

Several tall red candles were lit, giving off a smell of cinnamon and something else he couldn't put a name to. Above the candles was a portrait, and it was like he was looking into a mirror.

"Erik..."

He jumped back and took in the horror etched on her face. "Mya, I'm sorry. I thought—"

She bit her lip and shook her head. Then she cleared her throat. "No, it's okay. It's my fault. I forgot."

He left the room, closed the door gently, and moved toward her. She hugged herself as if to keep her distance from him, but he refused to let her shy away. Instead, he pulled her to his chest. "I'm sorry," he whispered.

Her hands dropped, and after a moment she wrapped her arms around him and breathed him in while she pushed her head further into his chest.

"It's my way of making sure I always remember you. Every

night I light the candles. I change them throughout the day to make sure they're always burning. I used to talk to you ... to your picture, I mean. I'd tell you how much I loved you, how much I missed you. That I hoped you were somewhere safe, born into a better life where you could be happy, and maybe one day I'd get to see you again."

He tilted her face to his. "And now you can."

She nodded and bit her lip. "Now I can."

"Mya..." His gaze roamed hers before settling on her lips. "May I kiss you?"

She gripped his shirt. "Johanna will be here in a couple of minutes and—"

"Just one kiss, please."

Her eyelids closed as she angled her head to his, and he descended slowly, wanting her to know that she could pull away at any time.

"I need to hear it, Mya," he whispered against her lips.

"Yes," she whispered.

He kissed her, and it was as if light had flooded his heart when her lips moved against his. He gathered her closer, and she wrapped her arms around him. It was a kiss of gentle completion, of love and sadness, of hope and despair. It was a kiss that began their path to healing the wound that had been infected and festering for years between them.

Erik pulled away from her soft mouth slowly, then kissed her forehead before running his fingers over her cheek and down her hair. "Thank you for giving me something so precious."

Her eyes opened slowly, and they were so vulnerable his heart skipped a beat. "What have I given you?"

"Your time. Your mind. Your energy. Your love. They are all

of the highest value. Priceless," he said, staring into her eyes, "and I will spend the rest of my life appreciating them and you."

Before she could say anything in response, another presence filled the air. Erik growled low in his throat, and pushed Mya behind him, but she gripped his arm.

"It's okay, Erik. It's just Johanna and Luke."

Erik locked his eyes onto hers. His brow furrowed. "But they didn't come through a door."

She smiled at him. "They don't need to. Come on."

Mya led him downstairs to the living room, where he saw a tall man with golden skin and short brown hair whose mouth dropped open when his green-gray eyes landed on Erik. Several different emotions ran over his face, and Erik wished he remembered him, wished he knew who the man was.

Then his eyes moved to Johanna, and he grinned. Her long blonde hair was shiny, her eyes a vibrant blue glistening like the ocean, and she was no longer marred in cuts and bruises. She looked well taken care of, nourished, and exuded a type of peace that he had never seen from her. There was more there, under the surface, but she was thriving, and it was evident in every single way.

"Erik!" she shouted, running to him and tossing her arms around him. He caught her, laughing as he swung her around before setting her down on the floor. She laughed with him, tears rolling down her cheeks when she cupped his face. "I knew you were alive! I knew it, but it still doesn't seem real!"

He grabbed her arms and pulled back to look at her. "And you as well. You look happy, Johanna, and so incredibly loved. You deserve that."

His eyes slid to man, and Erik realized he must be Luke. For a moment something flickered in his memory. The figures were shadowed. They had no faces, made no gestures or actions, but he could feel the man's loneliness, the void he'd carried inside that he constantly tried to keep at bay. And yet, as Erik looked at Luke now, that void was gone.

"You deserve that too," Erik said.

Luke blinked, uncertain as to how to deal with him, but gave him a small smile. "Thank you."

"You're welcome."

Erik looked for Mya and found her leaning against a console table, her arms crossed. She was trying to appear indifferent, but he could see the jealousy on her face, the uncertainty, and when they locked eyes, she quickly looked away.

Erik turned back to Johanna. "Could you please restore my memories? I have a lifetime of mistakes to make up for with my mate."

Mya's eyes snapped to his, and he gave her a soft smile. "And I'd say with her family, too."

Johanna nodded and gestured to a chair. "Of course. You should sit, though. I took a lot from you, and it will be difficult on your mind to get all the memories back at once."

Erik took a seat, as did Luke and Mya, and then he waited. The fear that coursed through his veins at the thought of getting his memories back made him feel weak. There was time missing between Mya's story and the days of his capture. He didn't know what lie dormant there, but it felt dark, depressive.

He was still certain that he did not leave Mya's side willingly, but in the end it didn't matter. Nothing mattered except her. He had to fix this, all of it—the awkwardness, the distance, the grief and despair. He wasn't foolish enough to believe it could be resolved overnight, or even within a few years, but he wouldn't stop trying until it did. They needed that. They deserved that, and Erik knew Mya needed to see him fight for her, for them. He would fight tooth and nail, and he would conquer every single one of his demons to keep her in his life.

Johanna lifted her fingertips to his temples. He felt heavy, weighed down under a humid fog that filled the room. He struggled under it, trying to catch his breath.

And then it happened.

Mya. Gregori. Lucas. He could see their faces as clear as day. He saw them running, playing, climbing, training, fighting. He felt Mya, their first touch, first embrace. He felt the desperation, the hope that welled inside of him when he confessed his past to her, and he felt her love wash over him. He felt the rolling sea as they traveled to America. He felt the overwhelming joy of finally being able to marry her, to know that she would be protected, and then he felt the betrayal and heartache of being rejected. He felt the death of his heart and the complete obliter-ation of realizing it had all been a trap. He felt the worms that crawled over his skin and the way he'd sat frozen, wishing he could go to Mya when he heard her screams. And then he felt empty, broken, defeated, reduced to nothing as time passed by, until he saw the sky again and was taken captive by Constance.

When Erik came to, he was on the floor of Mya's living room. The light was too bright, the faces of those peering down at him blurry. He closed and opened his eyes multiple times before he could clearly see, and the first face that came into his vision was the one he'd always wished for, the one he missed most, the only one his heart had ever and would ever beat for.

Mya.

He reached for her, sat up and hugged her. He clung to her tightly and swore that nothing would ever separate them again.

Johanna and Luke moved to help him, but he gathered them in his arms just as the tears gathered in his eyes.

THEY SAID THEIR GOODBYES, AND MYA AND ERIK WATCHED AS Johanna teleported away with Luke. But even such a marvel didn't distract Erik from what he had to do next.

Mya was hurting and so was he, but they needed this conversation for him to right his wrongs, for healing to begin.

"Mya?" he started.

She looked up at him, and for a moment he couldn't speak. He was lost in the deep, wild forest that lived in her eyes, mesmerized by the shades of green yellowed by sunlight that danced every time she blinked. They were so magical, so majestic, and he had never thought he'd see them again.

He licked his lips and bared his heart to her.

"I used to dream of your eyes. I dreamed of them for years when I was alone."

His voice sounded haunted, even to his own ears, but he swallowed the feeling. He sat down on the couch, gesturing for her to join him. "Sometimes I wondered if I forgot a shade or hue. Were they darker, lighter, more golden, greener? That was..."

He licked his lips, his throat dry, and swallowed again. "That was the most terrifying part of everything—knowing how many years had gone by and wondering if I had forgotten something about you. But I never truly forgot them. For years, I would stare at the trees when we would transfer locations. I did the same after I escaped. I'd walk through the forest aimlessly. It would feel like something was crushing my heart into pieces, but I didn't know what it was."

He drew in a deep breath. "It was you, love. I was always searching for you, always hoping to find you."

Tears clouded her beautiful eyes, and she choked out his name.

"May I hold you? I know I have no right to ask but—"

"Always, *please*," she croaked and all but jumped into his lap.

He wrapped his arms around her, cradling her to him as he'd done many times when they were together. She fit so perfectly, and he missed her, a type of desolation that he had no name for. He felt her hopelessness as strongly as he felt his own. They'd survived years without one another, but they hadn't lived since the last time they touched, and he mourned all the time he lost with her.

"I'm sorry," he whispered into her hair while he ran his fingers through the silky strands, realizing how much he'd missed that too. "Your hair had become a vice for me. Without it I would fidget endlessly in that church, and nothing would sate that need. Now I know why."

She whimpered into his shoulder and squeezed her arms around his neck, clinging to him.

He kissed her head, her temple, her cheek, her neck, and she tilted for him, opened herself to him. She gave him access, gave him permission, and though he longed to take it, he couldn't until he gave her the answers she needed. She'd told him she thought she wasn't enough to keep him with her, to make him believe in their love, when that could not be further from the truth.

"I have made you cry so many tears for me, my sweet *fagr*

skjaldmær min, my beautiful warrior. I do not want to make you cry anymore, but I need to tell you what happened."

She pulled back to look at him, then cupped his cheek, her warmth seeping into his skin as she smiled sadly. "It's okay. We need this."

He kissed her hand. "We do," he said, and took a deep breath. "The day we received the final approval for The Council, I told Greg I needed to get something for you. It was a ring … an engagement ring."

Her eyes widened and a small gasp escaped her lips.

"I was going to ask you to marry me, immediately. I didn't want to wait another second. I'd been planning to for months. I had the perfect stone picked out, and the jeweler had finally finished crafting the ring. It was as if everything had perfectly aligned." He cupped her cheek, tucking her hair behind her ear. "I couldn't wait to get back to you, but on the way there…"

He trailed off as the image of her with that man flooded his memory, taking him back to the nightmare of his past. His whole body shook until Mya brought him back with a soft squeeze of his cheeks.

"I know," she whispered.

He closed his eyes, took several deep breaths to calm and refocus himself. When he spoke, his voice cracked. "I was devastated. You were, and still are, my everything, and believing I had lost you destroyed me. I kept walking, and I suddenly found myself in front of the house I'd built for us. I knew I couldn't live there. Everywhere I looked, I saw you, because that's how I'd built the house. Every room, every finish, it was all for you."

Erik swallowed. "I wrote the letter. I gathered all the documents, and then I left the house and walked along the cliff. I felt empty. Your ring was still in my pocket. I thought about throwing it over, but I couldn't. I couldn't let you go."

He cupped her cheeks, lifted her head to his and stared into her eyes. "I. Couldn't. Let. You. Go."

She bit her lip, and he ran his thumb over it, pulling it from her teeth. "I didn't leave you. I was going to go back to the tavern to see if there was some way to reclaim your heart, but I didn't get the chance. The blood witches had finished their ritual by then, and I was too late."

Mya clung to him and squeezed his shoulders as they trembled together.

"That's why they tricked us, *fagr skjaldmær min*. They needed a way into our minds. We had never ingested their blood and were so careful about what we ate and how we fed, so they used grief and heartbreak instead. The emotions gave them a way to control us..." He looked down. "A way to control me. Your ability to heal made your blood, mind, and heart stronger. Their magic did not affect you. Since I had your blood in my system, I was able to break free of their spell, but not before most of the damage had already been done."

He closed his eyes to shake off the feeling of weakness, the darkness that plagued him. "They casted a paralysis spell on me. The only reason they didn't kill me was because I was the closest to an elder vampire they'd ever gotten their hands on. Their spell removed my ability to use any of my powers once they forced their blood inside of me. Then they buried me alive in the same spot you went to."

Mya's eyes were full of horror, her skin now ashen and pale.

"I heard you scream. You were right above me, but I couldn't get to you. I smelled the smoke of the house burning. I listened as the world changed, and all I wanted was to get back to you, but I failed. I failed you. One hundred years went by underneath that soil, and the next time I saw the sun was when Constance made me her slave. I'm sorry, *fagr skjaldmær min.* I'm so sorry I wasn't strong enough," he whispered and shook his head to clear it from the memories of his captivity.

Mya's eyes suddenly hardened. A fire lit in them, and her nails pressed into his back as she squeezed him to her, making him hiss.

"Mya?"

"Finish the story," she commanded.

He smiled at her gently, sadly. "There are some things you don't need to know, *fagr skjaldmær min.*"

"No. You have had to carry your burdens for years. You asked me to tell you what happened to me, and I did. I told you everything, in full detail, even the things I regret, the things I am not proud of. I want to know everything that happened to you."

"Mya—"

"*Everything,* Erik. I will not let you carry that weight by yourself. Talk to me, just like you asked me to talk to you. Please, my love."

He took in her face, the fight in her eyes, the softness of her cheeks, the decadence of her mouth, and found his thumb rubbing along its softness. Her mouth opened for him, and he sighed.

"Will you still want me when you know what happened?"

He didn't realize he'd spoken aloud until she answered, "Nothing could ever stop me from wanting you. I won't look at you differently, Erik. I promise you."

He tilted her head and kissed her forehead because he

couldn't muster the courage to look her in the eye. "Constance is a blood witch."

"*Impossible*," she hissed. "I killed them all."

"She is one. I'm not sure if she was born one, found a grimoire, or obtained their spells and rituals some other way, but she is a blood witch. Her goal is children. She's obsessed with having a family, with having immortal children who are strong and powerful."

Mya drew back. "Erik, did you—"

"No!" he shouted, the simple thought of touching anyone other than Mya, disgusting to him. "No, I never touched her. She tried to get me to father a child with her, but I could not. I couldn't even get hard for her, so she tried to break our mate bond."

Mya's mouth dropped open, frozen, speechless.

"She couldn't because I'd already met you. I was already in love with you, and that emotion was too strong for the spell to work, so she took delight in torturing me instead. She..."

He forced another deep breath through his body. It was easier to think the thoughts himself than say them to her, to possibly face her judgment. He didn't want her to see how weak he had been in those moments. But Mya didn't speak or push for more. She waited patiently for him, and that gave him the courage to continue.

"She castrated me," he said in a barely audible whisper. "Multiple times."

Erik couldn't look at her, embarrassed by the trauma he'd endured. "I don't know if it's because your blood was in my system for so long or because of the paralysis spell, but I received the ability to adapt to wounds and pain. I heal faster, and once an injury has happened to my body, it takes longer for the same wound to manifest again. One strike of a sword took off my cock or my arm or my foot. In a week it would grow back. She would go to strike me again, but it would take two, three, four times before she could get through the bone, and instead of it taking a week to grow back it would take three days, two, a few hours at most."

"When that stopped working, she tried other things—fire, branding, sodomy. I was a toy for her to play with, and later an experiment. She drained me of my blood and kept me in a barely alive state while she tried to manifest my ability in her other vampires, but it never worked. When the cave system began to collapse and I escaped, she cursed me with the inability to retain the nutrients I need from blood to heal. That's why you found me the way you did. Your blood cured me and—"

He felt a tremor. At first, Erik thought that he was the one trembling, so he pushed on and on. He rushed through his story as to not get lost in it, so he could be honest and open with Mya, to give her the things she'd asked to know. If he said all the horrible things just this once, perhaps he'd never have to say them again, never have think of them again. Perhaps he could lock those memories in the past with so many other things he wished he could be rid of.

But he was not the one trembling. Mya was.

Erik marveled at the expression on her face. The rage and anger he expected was in her eyes, but there was so much more in them too. For a moment, he was scared she would pity him, that she would see him as less of a man, a coward, not the man she knew or had looked up to all those years ago. But her green orbs showed empathy, compassion, and a type of misery that matched the deepest depths of his soul.

"I'm sorry," she whimpered. "I'm so sorry, Erik. I'm so sorry."

She hugged him, squeezed him, molded her body to his own as if she could hold him back from all the demons that had dug their claws into him, and in that moment he wished she could. She cried for him, wailed and sobbed and screamed for the pain he'd experienced, and he held her just as tightly. In every sound, expression, and movement she broke another barrier in his mind and soul.

Erik clung to her. He let her take his turmoil, his darkness, and expunge it in a way he did not know how to do. He let her tears be the gateway to his own, and for the first time he realized that they did not only need to heal the trauma that had happened between them, but the trauma that was present in themselves as well.

18

They talked throughout the night, wanting to reconnect, to fill in the spaces between the people they were three hundred years ago and who they were today.

Erik felt incredibly lucky and thankful to be by Mya's side again. She'd overwhelmed him with not only her care now, but the things she'd done to keep his memory alive over the centuries, not only emotionally, but logically and financially. Mya had worked with her family and Lily to forge the documentation that had burned in his house. By doing so, Mya had gained access to his savings and the insurance policy. She'd filed a claim and received the payment for his home, and allocated the money into a mirage of accounts, including high yield savings accounts, certificates of deposits, bonds and stocks. She'd even allocated him a 401K through her family's company when it was first established. The result of her efforts made him one of the wealthiest men in the world. If he wanted to buy an island, even build and monopolize one, he could and would still have money to spare. She'd also found the name of the family member he'd harmed when his blood rage was out of control and had continued to pay the man's descendants.

Mya had done anything and everything to honor him. That was her love for him, and Erik felt guilty for ever questioning it. He'd always believed he didn't deserve her, that she could and should do better, but she didn't want anything else but him. It was time he accepted and respected that. One conversation would not resolve the years of heartache they'd been through, but he was grateful for the chance to try again with her.

As the night went on, they moved to her bedroom where they could lie in one another's arms, at some point his eyes closed, and he was surprised to see the sun when he opened them again. It had been years since he'd last slept, and he knew it had only been possible because of her, because of the peace she gave his soul.

Her phone vibrated again, and she grumbled as she rolled over to answer it. She read the message and sighed. "It's my brother. He wants us to come over. Are you ready to see him?"

Greg had been Erik's closest friend, someone he trusted and enjoyed mentoring, but he was also Mya's older brother, and Erik had hurt her. He wasn't sure how Greg would react to him, whether it would be with open arms, a stoic expression, or a punch to his jaw. But regardless of what might happen, Erik wanted to see him, to begin mending that bridge as well, so he nodded.

They dressed and moved downstairs, but as Mya went to open the door, Erik pulled her behind him. Stepping forward, he grasped the doorknob in his hand and flung the door open, where they were greeted by twenty-five men on her property, seven cars, and eight more driving up the road.

Mya pulled out her knife, and Erik saw pure fury and murder in her eyes.

"No, love," he said softly, "You've fought more than enough battles for me. Let me fight this one for you."

A growl tumbled out of her chest, and he chuckled at her fierceness. The dragon's nest had been disturbed, and his beautiful warrior was ready and willing to massacre anyone who trespassed on her land or threatened him. Erik had never found her to be more perfect than in that moment.

She opened her mouth to say something, but he grasped her chin, bent down to her height, and kissed her. When he finally pulled away as their adversaries grew closer, she grasped his shirt.

"You get five seconds. *Five*," she warned. "And I'm only giving them to you because I feel like you need this. If they're not dead by then, I will be out of this door with you."

"And I will throw you over my shoulder and spank that beautiful ass of yours," he said with a grin.

She batted her eyelashes at him and said, "Careful. I might like that."

He trailed his fingers over her cheek and down her neck, where he grasped her throat, making her gasp. "You have to learn to stop teasing me, especially during a fight." He held out his hand for a weapon and she gave him a dagger, handle side first.

"Not in this lifetime or the next, my love. Now go. Five."

He rolled his eyes at her and chuckled again, then took a step out of the door. His eyes narrowed as he faced Constance's army, and his annoyance grew. They had no right to be here on Mya's property, to sully her soil with even a single one of their footprints. But there was another question that he had to ask:

How had they found them? Her house was far enough away that they shouldn't have been able to track them, unless there was something in him that had led them there.

He bared his teeth. The rogues moved, but they were not fast enough. Erik was an elder, and with his strength and powers restored, a small army would be nothing to him. He used the sun's rays to superpower his fire ability, and those that were hit disintegrated immediately. Then he threw balls of burning fire at the cars, exploding those nearest to them. For the few that were still alive, he dashed toward them and stabbed them clean through their brains, killing them all before the first body had even dropped to the ground.

He walked back to Mya and wiped the blood from the dagger on his pants. She greeted him at the front door, dragging his face to hers. He picked her up and crushed his lips to hers. Kissing Mya was like coming home, like finding peace and sanctuary. It was passionate, wanton. It was *right.*

"You were cutting it close," she whispered, her tone low and husky when they separated, and his heart beat a little faster at the sound.

"I'll make sure to kill them faster next time, my queen." He nuzzled her neck and put her down before they turned back to the scene. "Mya—"

"I know. I'm calling a cleaning crew and letting Greg know what happened. He has a lot of contacts. Maybe one of them can figure out how they found us."

Walking through Greg's house brought back a lot of memories for Erik. The vase displayed in the alcove was from a dig they'd joined in Spain, another trinket on a shelf was from an Indian man they'd saved in England, and there were several other pieces from the time they'd spent together over the centuries.

Erik didn't know it at the time but saving Greg had opened the door to his happiest memories. It had given him the family he'd lost so many years ago, and he hoped he could reclaim a piece of that family again.

When he walked into Greg's kitchen and found him cooking with his wife and mate, Daniella, Erik was struck by how much he had changed. The Gregori he knew had only ever been focused on taking care of others. He'd been the brains of their operation, a leader in his own right, far better at it than Erik. But he had never, ever seemed so relaxed, so carefree, so jovial. It made Erik immediately like Daniella and the effect she had on him, and he liked her even more when she gave Mya the tightest hug and he saw the smile that lit up her face. She meant something to Mya, and Erik was happy to see her friends, her family, people who she could share her heart with.

Then Daniella came over to him, and he could feel her assessing him in her mind before she threw open her arms to hug him. "It's nice to finally meet you, Erik. I've heard a lot about you."

"You too," he said as he hugged her back.

Greg lifted a tray of hors d'oeuvres out of the oven. As if it was a sign, Daniella grabbed Mya's arm and began to pull her of the kitchen.

"W-What are you doing?" she asked, laughing as she stumbled along with her friend.

"Giving the boys their privacy. Come say goodbye to Ruby before Elaine takes her for the night, and catch me up on all the details," Daniella said, winking at Greg before leaving them alone.

Erik waited patiently as Greg moved around the kitchen. He gave Erik a single look, but otherwise didn't acknowledge him as he mixed a batch of items together and put another tray in the oven.

It wasn't that Erik was afraid of Greg. It was a matter of respect. If the tables were turned and Greg had hurt someone Erik loved, especially a sibling, Erik wasn't sure what he would feel if he saw him again. Greg was the reason Mya was still here today. He had stopped her from taking her life multiple times, and while Mya now knew Erik never left her, Greg did not.

"It's been a long time, old friend," Erik said finally.

Greg sighed and turned to him. "It has been. It's good to see you."

Erik's eyes widened. "Really?"

Greg nodded. "I wasn't sure how I'd feel seeing you standing in front of me. I thought I'd be angry."

"You'd have every right to be."

"Perhaps, but I never believed you had actually left Mya. Am I right about that?"

Erik's jaw ticked at the thought and he nodded. "You are. I would never leave her. She's my everything."

"Then there isn't a reason for me to be angry."

Greg grabbed several dirty dishes and brought them to the sink. Erik followed suit, grabbing the remaining items and bringing them to Greg, who smiled in thanks.

"You don't want to know what happened? You don't ... need me to tell you?"

"No."

For the second time in less than five minutes, Greg had shocked him.

"You've always been brooding. Quiet. Stoic, even, but now you're unsure," Greg said, and Erik averted his gaze. "I don't mean that in an embarrassing way. I just mean that it's clear to me you've been through a lot, and it isn't just that you've been missing for so many years."

Greg turned away from the sink and leaned back against it. "I know trying to get your bearings after so long is going to be difficult, and I'm certain you weren't being fed expensive cheese and wine during your time with Constance. You've gone through enough, and honestly, I'm just happy to have you back."

Greg looked toward the door and Erik followed his line of sight, watching Mya talk to Daniella, Luke, and Johanna. She was smiling, laughing, and it filled his heart with joy.

"I haven't seen her like that since before you ... since you've been gone. She'll laugh, and she'll smile, but it's—"

"Weighed down," Erik answered, remembering the smile she gave him at the church before they'd spoken.

Greg looked at him then, his gaze hard. "You took that smile off her face when you left, and you've brought it back now that you're here. I need you to fight for her, Erik, for the *both* of you, because you deserve it." He crossed his arms and glared at him. "If you leave again, you better stay gone or else I will kill you myself."

Erik's gaze never wavered from Greg's as he said, "I'd do it myself if I left her."

"Then we have an understanding. Come here." Greg stepped forward and gave him a hug with a pat on his back.

Erik returned the embrace and couldn't help but smile. "Thank you."

"Of course. And I called some friends who wanted to see you."

Erik tilted his head to the side, "Who—"

"Well, if you're not a sight for sore eyes."

He turned to see Lily coming through the door. She had a huge smile on her face that crinkled her eyelids, and he laughed while he gave her a tight hug. She gave his arms a squeeze, then stepped back and rested her hands on the shoulders of a woman who had appeared beside her. "Erik, I'd like to introduce you to my wife, Oaklynn."

Oaklynn was short—likely under five feet tall—with long reddish-brown hair and brown eyes. She reminded Erik of a firecracker, and he knew immediately that she was Lily's perfect match.

"It's nice to meet you," she said, holding out her hand, which Erik shook.

"You as well."

Greg gave Lily and Oaklynn a hug in greeting as well. "Technically they're not supposed to be here since Lily is still part of The Council, and that makes it a conflict of interest but—"

"We couldn't stay away once we found out you were alive," Oaklynn said with a smile.

"You've been missed, Erik," Lily said, her expression softening as her eyes began to glisten.

Daniella poked her head around the door frame, and Greg clapped his hand on Erik's shoulder. "Well, now that we're all here it's time for us to get started."

ERIK SHARED EVERYTHING HE KNEW THUS FAR, INCLUDING THAT Constance's army had found him at Mya's house earlier that day.

"Have they ever found you so easily before?" Merida asked, one of Greg's seconds-in-command.

"Yes, but I thought it was something I had done. Clothing, where I was staying wasn't secure enough, and so on," Erik said.

Mya laced her fingers through his. "But that wasn't the case with my house. We burned the church, got rid of anything Erik had before except for the clothes he has on now, and if they had some sort of tracking device on those—"

"Then they would have grabbed him then, not waited for you to come along," Greg finished.

Mya nodded.

"It could be a magical locator spell. Have you ever ingested Constance's blood?" Oaklynn asked.

Erik grimaced, then nodded.

"That would be enough." Oaklynn fished for her bag, and pulled out an old leather book, crackling with power.

Luke's eyes grew wide. "Is that..."

"Yes," Oaklynn said with a nod. "It's a blood witch grimoire. Not all of us are evil." Her eyes touched every person in the room as her words hung in the air.

"Oaklynn is the reason we were able to create blood banks and extract platelets that specifically aid vampires. She's a pathologist, as well as a blood witch." Lily said, as she squeezed Oaklynn's leg and smiled at her with pride.

"I know blood witches have caused immortals a lot of

heartache over the centuries, but there's more than just one side to us. Our abilities can heal, and we can do a lot of good. The blood witches you've met were turned to the magic, not naturally born, and that turning makes them crazy. Much like a rogue vampire."

"What does that mean?" Johanna asked.

"Essentially, the magic those blood witches use is a type of curse. It can only be triggered by extreme trauma and will quite, literally drive them crazy. There's no saving them from that madness. They will fixate on one specific theme, likely what caused them to gain access to that magic in the first place, and they will continue down that path until they die."

Oaklynn turned another page from the grimoire. "I'm not saying that because I sympathize with them. What they've done is inexcusable and they deserve to die but knowing what they're fixated on may help us to better understand why they've done what they've done. Once we know that, we might know how to stop them."

"Children."

Everyone's gaze shifted to Erik, and Mya squeezed his hand, anchoring him to the present and keeping his mind from slipping into the past.

"Constance's focus is on children," he said.

"Could she have lost a child?" Merida asked.

Oaklynn leaned back against the couch, flicking through the pages of the book. "If that's the case she's going to want to make more, and fast. She'd capture powerful immortals to father her new children."

"But we've never found any children at any of the places we've infiltrated," Greg said, crossing his arms.

"Maybe children are too difficult for her," Daniella said,

drawing their gaze. "Maybe she wants children, but she can't be a mother, and that's why she's kidnapped and turned so many humans so she can have the family she's always wanted without having to raise them."

"It would explain why she's so focused on making them stronger," Erik said, and several of their group nodded in agreement.

"That would also explain why she's focused on you. You're the current key to her strengthening her family," Merida said, her expression apologetic.

Erik could feel Mya's annoyance rising at the thought, so he squeezed her hand and then wrapped his arm around her shoulders.

"I've found the locator spell," Oaklynn said, looking up from the book. "It's not a permanent solution for her. She can only use it for as long as she has your blood and for as long as you have hers in your system. Mya said that you were under a curse when she found you?"

"Yes," Erik said. "It kept me from absorbing the nutrients we need in blood and stopped me from using my powers."

Oaklynn made a soft humming sound. "I have an idea of what she did to you. That spell, even after being broken, lasts for three days. That's the connection she has with you. Her magic is still in your blood, and that's what she's using to power the locator spell."

"Which means she's going to come after me with everything she can," Erik said, and Oaklynn nodded.

Erik watched as Greg and Daniella shared a look. It told him that they had a plan, and he wasn't going to like it.

Greg cleared his throat. "Then we need to use that while we still can."

Mya's head snapped and she glared at her brother. "What are you saying, Gregori?"

"Mya," he said softly, "we have the opportunity to catch her right in front of us." His gaze moved to Erik. "We need to discuss taking it."

"*What* are you saying," she bit out again.

"We may need to use Erik as bait."

"No!" She rushed to her feet. "How could you even suggest that? Erik..." She stared at him, a look of horror crossing her face. "You ... Tell me you don't agree with this."

"My love—" He reached for her, but she smacked his hands away.

"I just got you back. I *just* got you back after so long. How could you? How could you want to do this when I may never see you again?"

"Mya, please—"

"No!" she screeched, and before he could move, she ran from the room.

19

___

ya felt Erik's presence from the hallway. She wished
she could stand to be away from him, but she couldn't.
When he opened the door, all she could mutter was a weak,
"Leave me alone," even while her body begged for his touch, for
him to sweep her into his arms and promise he wasn't leaving.

Erik closed the door gently behind him. She could feel him
at her back, and when he wrapped his arms around her, she
sunk into his warmth as though he had pulled her out of the
freezing cold.

His tone was so soft, so broken as he said, "*Fagr skjaldmær
min,* please don't run away from me. It breaks my heart to watch
you walk away, or for you to tell me to leave you. I will never
leave you. I promised I wouldn't."

The thought of him leaving cut through her like a knife of
betrayal, and she spun out of his embrace. "That's right, you
promised, but that's exactly what you're wanting me to watch
you do, leave."

"My love—"

"Would you be okay if it was me? Would you be fine with letting me go out there and be the *bait?*" she snapped, fully knowing the answer.

His eyes narrowed and filled with fury.

"That's what I thought."

Erik took a deep breath, then tilted her chin up to his. "You're right, *fagr skjaldmær min,* but there's a difference between you and me. You do not have a locator spell that turns you into a giant beacon for the enemy."

She bit her lip.

"My love, I dealt with them easily today, but that wasn't even a quarter of Constance's army. Who knows how much they've grown since I've been free. You heard Oaklynn. They had three days to find me. One day has already passed. They could find me *anywhere*: at your house, here. What happens if Greg and Daniella are here alone with Ruby?"

Mya shook her head, but the image of Greg and Dani fighting, of any possible danger coming to her niece, was still there. She averted her eyes from Erik's and tried to steady her tone even though she felt like she was drowning. "Th-They could handle it. We could plan for it."

Erik stroked her cheek, drawing her gaze. "Gregori is the same age I was when they buried me alive. I believe in him and his wife's abilities, but when they would also have to protect their child ... It's selfish to put them through that, and you, my love, have never been selfish."

Mya's knees shook at the thought of losing her brother, or Dani and Ruby, but her heart was breaking at the thought of losing Erik again, of something going wrong, of him truly dying this time.

"I don't want to lose you," she whispered.

"You won't," he said as he tucked her hair behind her ear.

"How do you know? Why are you so calm? How are you so certain?" she asked, fisting his shirt in her hands.

"Because I was alone before. Now I have you. Even if I cannot believe in myself, I will always believe and have faith in you. Always."

Mya grasped the strands of Erik's hair as he kissed her, twirling them in her fists to try to keep him close to her. And he held her as if she were his whole world, the key to his entire being.

When they broke apart, she whispered, "I'm sorry for walking away from you, and for being so..." She looked down and mumbled, "difficult."

He grasped her chin, leaving her no way to retreat from him, and said with a smile on his face, "You are not difficult. You were scared and hurt. I understand that. I understand you, and I always will."

Erik rested his forehead against hers and for a moment they simply shared their breath.

"*Fagr skjaldmær min,* will you let me do this? I can't without you, not without your permission and your faith in me."

She gulped and held him tighter. "Promise me you'll come back."

"I promise. We have a lifetime to heal and live through together, and I refuse to waste a single moment of it."

She nodded and they kissed once more. He reached down and took one of her hands in his, and together they opened the door and returned to the rest of the group.

Mya looked at them, saw the empathy in their eyes, and it made her shy. "I'm—"

"Mya and I have discussed it. I am willing to bait the enemy so we can finish this war once and for all, but only if every possible protective measure has been taken."

Erik's tone was authoritative, and she straightened as some of her fear melted away.

"I'm sure you all know that I have been kept away from Mya for the last three hundred years. I'm not willing to spend another second without her. This plan must work. I will not move forward if there is even a slight probability of me not returning to her side at the end of this. Does anyone here have any objections to that?" Erik asked, then turned to her and smiled.

Mya nestled into his side, wrapping an arm his waist as she watched her own family and friends smile and shake their heads.

"Then let us end this war once and for all."

THERE WERE SEVERAL STEPS TO THEIR PLAN.

The first involved Oaklynn casting her own locator spell on Erik. To do so she needed to share her blood with him, and she shared a drop with everyone else who would be fighting alongside them as a precaution.

Oaklynn had also confirmed Mya's healing ability extended beyond physical ailments to abilities, spells, and curses that affected her mental or emotional states. Knowing Constance wouldn't give up the chance to try and take control of a single member of their group, Oaklynn and Astrid created an enhancement with Mya's blood that would temporarily act as a cure should any of them begin to fall under Constance's magic. It would only work once, so they had to act with caution. Since Astrid had created threads between them, they would be able to feel the mental slip in one of their comrades and get them to safety before they lost them all together.

Then they ran through different scenarios. Erik estimated that Constance had at least two hundred vampires when he'd last seen her at the cave, so for safety they doubled those numbers. Neither Johanna nor Erik remembered there being any older vampires, meaning they would be newly turned and weak. Daniella would use her ability to boil each vampire's blood, which, due to their connection to Constance, would at least weaken and distract her while Oaklynn would work to drain Constance's power and stop her from being able to cast stronger magic.

While it seemed things should go in their favor, Oaklynn warned they needed to keep as much of Constance's army alive as they could. If they outright killed them, Constance would be able to use their blood for more powerful and dangerous spells.

They each had their roles and weapons, so all that was left was for Oaklynn to cast a spell which would make Erik appear to still be under Constance's curse. He would then make his way to the old church to be kidnapped and delivered back to their enemy.

Mya hated it all. No matter how hard she tried, she couldn't let go of the fear that was eating away at her heart.

Erik placed his hand on her chest, right over the beating organ. "The day they took me away from you, you had a bad feeling. You warned me of it several times and I didn't listen to you when I should have. If you have that feeling right now, this all ends. I won't go and we'll find another way. Do you?"

She took a deep breath, but she already knew the answer. "No, I don't."

The corner of his lip tipped up in a half smile. "And you told me Daniella's spirits tell her things. She hasn't warned us away from this, correct?"

Mya looked down. "No, she hasn't."

He tipped her head back up to meet his eyes. "You are my mate. You are my wife. I am going to build a home with you, in your house or somewhere else if you like, and I am going to fill that delicious cunt of yours with my come so often, that I'll keep your beautiful belly round with our children, no matter many you want. We'll have our home, our family, and all of this, all our pain and strife and the chaos we've gone through will fade away. This is the last part of that chapter of our lives, *fagr skjaldmær min*. Trust me."

Erik cupped her cheek and she leaned into his hand, feeling his warmth. Mya parted her lips on a sigh when he bent down and kissed her, and she kissed him back with every part of her being.

"If you don't come back to me, I will find you and drag you back from the deepest pits of Tartarus only to kill you again myself."

He grinned proudly, squeezing her hand. "There's my queen." He kissed her once more and squeezed her hand. "It's time to go."

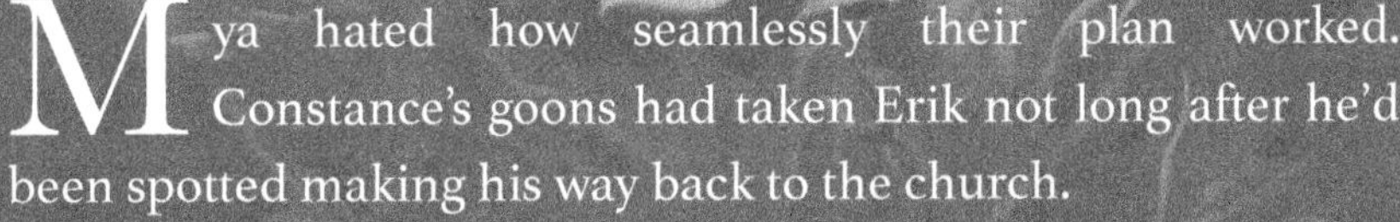

20

Mya hated how seamlessly their plan worked. Constance's goons had taken Erik not long after he'd been spotted making his way back to the church.

She'd had to watch them kick and punch him, and sit by while they dragged him back to their car and drove away. Mya wanted to go after them, to wage war against them for even *daring* to lay one finger on him, but Greg had put a hand on her tightly balled fist and reminded her that this would all be over soon. No matter how much it killed her, she had to see this through.

She'd been silent the entire time they'd followed the car, caught between the fear that they would somehow lose him and the rationale that she had to believe in him, that they'd done everything to make sure he'd be safe. Mya, along with her family, Greg's seconds-in-command, Merida and Dominick, Lily, Oaklynn, Astrid, and the rest of the battle officers watched from the forest as Erik was led down an old mine shaft tunnel.

Then they saw the signal: Erik's fire flashing brightly outside of the entrance. Mya ran to meet him, and when she laid her eyes on him, she felt as though she could finally breathe again.

"Hi," she said softly, reaching out her hand to his.

Erik clasped her hand and smiled. "I missed you too, *fagr skjaldmær min.*"

"Have you run into anyone?" Greg asked.

"No, but I'm certain that explosion will bring someone our way," Erik said, before turning and walking with the group through the tunnel.

He was proven right two minutes later when a stampede of footsteps dashed toward them. Erik shot out his fire and incinerated them, leaving ash in their wake.

As they continued walking, Merida whispered, "I don't like this. It's too easy."

"Do you think she's testing us?" Dominick, her husband, asked.

"We just brought a bunch of strong immortals *to* her. It's what I would do," Merida said.

Greg nodded. "Everyone, stay on guard and keep your distance for as long as possible. Fight magic with magic until we know what we're dealing wi—"

"Stop!" Merida shouted. "Lily, check the walls."

Lily moved forward and held up a hand. The air vibrated for a moment as she used her power over metal, and then a crack sounded on either side of the wall before two angled metal sheets fell not even a foot in front of the group, their sharpness cutting through the air. If they had been standing under them, they would have been sliced in half.

Merida had been right. Constance either knew they were

there or had been expecting them to find Erik. She'd prepared for them. The trap would have left them defenseless until their organs and limbs grew back, a process that would take weeks without necessary care. That meant Constance's aim was to capture, not kill.

They walked on slowly, methodically checking for traps and using their magic to kill the few groups of enemies that rushed toward them. But Mya knew it was all part of Constance's plan; their slow pace gave her time to fortify herself against them.

But there was only one outcome here, one destiny for that bitch, and it was to be impaled by one of their swords. That *would* happen. They would end this war today, and they would be *victorious*.

They finally entered the main area of the mine shaft, and as if summoned by her thoughts, Mya laid her eyes on the woman with long red hair, blue-green eyes, and an air that reeked of malice. Mya had to grind her teeth to stop herself from throwing a sword right at her head. She felt Erik's hand stroke the back of hers, tempering her fury, and she returned the action to comfort him as well.

Constance clapped her hands together and stood from a makeshift throne. At her movement, hundreds of vampires flanked her sides. Mya's ears twitched as she heard more vampires waiting in the numerous tunnels that sprawled out from the main cave. By her estimate, they were up against almost five hundred vampires.

Constance's eyes scanned the group, and when they landed on Greg, she snarled. "You have killed so many of my family. You've attacked and raided my houses and tried at every chance to break apart my kingdom. You are a *traitor* to your own kind and unfit of being a ruler."

Greg shrugged, a smirk playing on his lips. "I would offer my condolences, but I truly don't give a shit."

Constance's eyes glowed red momentarily, but then she shook herself from her blood lust. She stood straighter, angled her head back, and glared at Greg. "Bow before me. Beg for my forgiveness and acknowledge me as your queen"—Constance licked her lips, her eyes glazing over with desire—"and I will let your family live here with me. We could be one. We could stop all these wars and let vampires rule the world as we were meant to. Our children would be safe."

Daniella's jaw ticked. "You say you are a queen"—she rotated her wrist, cracking it before taking out her sword and pointing it at Constance—"then as a queen, know that you will die tonight watching your kingdom burn to the ground."

Constance screeched, and they attacked.

Daniella unleashed her power, and it hit their enemies like a shockwave. The vampires in the cave staggered, as did Constance, but even Daniella couldn't take on five hundred at one time. In tandem, Johanna slipped into their minds to send them to sleep, but it was a trap. Every single vampire's head exploded, sending chunks of their brains through the air as their blood coated the walls and pooled on the floor.

Erik took over, using his power to navigate the tunnels and incinerate the bodies he found, but Constance's army just kept coming, and now he was the target.

"They're backing us into a corner," Mya growled.

"Fight. We'll clean up as we go," Greg said, and that was all she needed to hear to launch into action. Mya dashed from vampire to vampire, cutting off their heads with ease, but there were still too many of them. They needed to slow them down.

A loud crash echoed through the tunnel, and Mya turned

back to see that Daniella and Johanna were using their abilities to block the entrances, sending rock and dirt tumbling onto their enemies. It wouldn't hold them forever, but it would help for now.

Then Mya heard the unmistakable click of a guns. Dozens of them.

"Get behind me, now!" Greg yelled.

The group formed behind him, and Greg pulled in the darkness, molding it into matter that he used as a giant shield. But it wouldn't be enough to hold off the military grade weapons for long.

Daniella erected a large wall of earth, then fed her power of darkness into Greg's to make his shield stronger for the attack. She wavered but kept pouring in her power, and it was then Mya realized what was truly happening. Constance was trying to wear Daniella out. Without her, they would suffer a massive hit to both their offense and defense. The same would've happened if Johanna had gotten caught in the mental traps Constance had set.

The guns went off, and Mya made her way to Daniella. Her magic held for the first round, but the second round began to make it through, and Daniella groaned. She staggered to the side, but Mya caught her before she could hit the ground.

"Luke, feed Greg your shadows! They're trying to take Dani down!"

Luke shifted his focus, blending his shadows into the darkness to help reinforce Greg's shield against the attack while Mya cut at her wrist and held it to Daniella's mouth.

"Drink," she ordered.

Daniella bit down, and Mya rushed her healing power into her.

"Oaklynn, we need to kill them. We don't have any more time to waste!" Dom said.

"Dom's right!" Merida called from her husband's side. "The vampires are starting to climb out of the rubble. We're going to be sitting ducks!"

"Then we'll have to end this fast. If Constance reclaims their blood, we're fucked," Oaklynn said.

Mya watched as Johanna nodded. The air grew humid around them, then she shouted, "Go now! I've frozen the vampires in place, so they won't be able to shoot!"

"Turn their guns on them! Kill everyone you can. I'm going after Constance," Greg said. He lowered the shield at the same time Lily turned the guns on the vampires and fired, shooting them in their heads. A bullet grazed Constance's arm before she ducked, and Greg dashed toward her.

The group worked their way through the hordes of vampires. Mya cut another one down, then paused and watched as his blood began to move as if it had a life of its own. Turning, she saw that the same thing was happening to all vampires she'd killed, their blood gathering, then traveling away from their bodies as if being drawn toward something.

"What the—"

"Stop!" Oaklynn screamed, causing Mya and Erik to look up at the large red shield Constance had erected. "You have to kill Constance, *now!* She's casting a reanimation spell!"

"What?" Erik shouted and blasted another array of fire at his targets before they rushed back to Oaklynn.

"Reanimation allows her to raise her fallen enemies' bodies and control them. And with how many we've slain..." Oaklynn trailed off, her mouth open in horror.

"How do we kill them?" Mya asked, twirling her sword and decapitating another vampire.

"You won't be able to! We have to stop her, right now!" Oaklynn screamed.

But Mya and Erik couldn't stop killing the vampires. If they did, they'd be overrun. Mya looked around to see most of their group in the same predicament, while Greg fought to both defend himself from vampires and break through a shield of magic Constance erected.

"Take care of the vampires. I have to help Greg!" Daniella reached down to the ground, and her eyes glowed red as she pulled in more power from the earth. The boulders from the rubble lifted and she slammed them at Constance's shield, but to no avail.

"Astrid, Oaklynn, Dani, we need to link our powers!" Johanna yelled.

Astrid stood in the center of the four of women. The threads she'd woven between each member began to manifest and glow, sending purple sparks through the room before they dimmed to the four shared between them. Daniella and Johanna shared a knowing look before Daniella began to issue orders.

"Oaklynn, see if you can bind yourself into her blood magic so I can work through you. Astrid and Luke, try to find cracks in her shield. We just need one for Johanna to do what she needs to. Erik, you're the strongest of us. Try to smash that shield."

They tried. The tried with all their magic and abilities and might to break the shield, but nothing was working. Mya was growing increasingly frustrated, and when she gestured to the others that the dead vampires had begun to twitch, they knew they were running out of time.

In a last-ditch effort, Daniella used her power to break the ground beneath Constance. It buckled, and for one single moment, her concentration slipped and the shield cracked. Seeing the opening, Luke slipped his shadows inside and tied Constance's legs and arms, while wrapping a shadow around her neck.

Johanna used her power to break into Constance's mind, and froze her mouth mid-sentence, ending her chant. Then Greg struck at the shield again and finally, it fell away.

In one glorious last stroke, Erik lifted his sword and decapitated Constance, sending her head flying before it hit the ground with a hard *thump*.

The battle still raged on, but they were on the winning side now. They pushed back at Constance's minions, easily defeating them even in their large numbers, until they were the only ones left standing.

But instead of celebrating the end of their century long battle, Greg issued an order. "Split up and move out. I want this place searched top to bottom."

"What's wrong?" Mya asked.

"Something doesn't add up. Did it look like we just fought a maniac to you?" Greg said, grabbing one of the guns off the ground and checking the chamber.

"No," Erik said, sliding his sword back in its sheath as he moved to stand beside Mya.

"Exactly. Constance planned for us, and she shouldn't have known we were coming. Erik killed everyone who appeared at your house. No one ever came to ours, so how did she know?" Greg asked.

Merida sheathed her weapons as she added, "And then

there were our powers. I understand Dani's and Jo's from previous battles, but..."

Greg nodded. "She knew I wouldn't be able to hold off that many guns forever, and that's information not many outside of our battle officers know."

Greg grabbed Daniella's hand and the two led the group down one of the passageways.

"We need to find paperwork, clues, a computer, anything that can provide insight as to how Constance knew so much about us," Greg instructed.

As they walked, they disarmed traps and found several cages coated in the blood, skin, and organs of Constance's victims. Then they came across a metal door with a digital keyless lock. Mya moved to the front of the group and disarmed the lock, then Greg threw open the door. Once his gaze swept through the room, he signaled it was safe for them to enter.

They filed out into the room, each taking up a section to survey and comb through. Mya spotted a computer and sat down, using her hacking software to break into the system. Greg stood beside her and flipped through several pieces of paper he'd retrieved from a bookcase. "Shipping details, inventory, it's all here. They got this all in last night."

A loud crash called their attention, and they turned to see Daniella staring at the back of the picture that she'd pulled out of a frame. "Who is Katherine Martin?" she asked.

Greg and Lily moved toward Daniella, and she handed them the picture, pointing to the back.

"I don't know—"

Lily snatched the photo from him, flipping from the front to the back of the picture repeatedly. Then a look of shock came over her and she gasped. "Katherine Martin was Francois's daughter. He reported her missing three hundred years ago. The investigation was never closed."

Greg's eyes narrowed and he leveled his gaze at her. "Lily, the only people outside of my circle who knew we were coming here today was The Council."

She staggered back. "Greg, Francois is an ass, but he wouldn't go this far—"

"Actually, he would," Mya said, her voice shaking, and the group circled around her.

"I traced the routing number that's been funding Constance's operation. It goes through a lot of shell companies and offshore accounts, but I was able to hack into their system. The account is registered to The Diamond Group, of which Francois is the CEO."

Lily shook her head. "But that's not enough to prove that it's him. It could be anyone."

"Except he emailed Constance this list." Mya brought up the secure document and scrolled to the bottom slowly. It was a list of several hundred names, most of which were crossed off. At the bottom were theirs, along with their powers and weaknesses and all the other data they had been forced to share with The Council.

Erik's eyes grew wide. "Francois was the last person to be approved to join The Council. He's who we saw the day I disappeared."

It was Mya's turn to gasp. "But why? What would getting you out of the picture do?"

"It would give him control of The Council," Greg said. "I was going to be the leader. If anything happened to me then it would then go to Erik, and then the next strongest person, Francois. I think Francois knew you were Erik's mate, Mya. He knew if he pushed you hard enough you would kill the blood witches for him, and if you didn't then they'd kill us."

Lily nodded. "And with Greg giving up his seat to save your life, Francois would be free to lead The Council until Greg had concluded his investigation into Erik's supposed death."

"But with the wars..." Mya's eyes widened.

"Exactly. I've been too busy to investigate Erik's whereabouts, meaning Francois has been able to gain power and replace our seats as he sees fit," Greg said, slamming his fist onto the desk.

Mya turned to Erik and found his face and eyes brimming with anger. The man they trusted, the man their *people* had trusted, was a traitor responsible for centuries of their pain.

Greg dialed a number on his phone and put it to his ear. "This ends tonight."

21

———

Francois was just on the other side of this door.

Erik could imagine Francois sitting down with a smile on his face, likely overjoyed that Erik and possibly several members of Mya's family—maybe even Mya herself—were dead. Erik wanted to rip the man apart.

Not only was Francois behind his capture, but Mya had found the incriminating information they needed to prove he was the one enslaving witches. Francois had been the original cause of the blood witches. He had supplied them with the immortals to target. He was behind the deaths of hundreds, the torture of thousands. Erik remembered the faces of the women Zachariah and Constance had stolen, raped, and brutalized, the men they'd forced to change into immortals and driven so mad that killing them was a mercy.

Francois was the reason why Greg had almost lost Daniella, why Johanna was still attending therapy for the scars he'd left on her psyche. He was why she had to be guarded and hidden from the public or else she'd be hunted down and captured again, why her family had to hide in the Fae Realm. But worst of all was that Francois was the reason for Mya's pain, for the healing they would need to work through together, for the days, years and centuries that had been stolen from them. They had no idea what other secrets he had hidden or who else he'd hurt since the time of being acting leader of The Council. But they would, *very* soon.

Finally, it was time for the meeting to begin. Greg, Erik, and Luke walked into the room, and Francois's face fell. Erik noticed that the faces of several other members did as well, while others averted their eyes in mock shame.

Francois wasn't working alone. There was more corruption here they still had to uncover, and from the way Greg's stance had changed, he'd noticed it too.

"Council, I come before you with incredible news. As you can see, Erik is alive." Greg's eyes narrowed as he stared right at Francois. "Much as I had expected."

Francois donned a mask of surprise as he stood. "My god," he gasped. "I can't believe it! Where have you been? Where did they find you, Erik? Why did you leave The Council?"

Erik's jaw ticked, but he swallowed back his anger and smiled. "I was captured by blood witches."

Several of The Council members gasped, then whispered to themselves.

"For all this time?" Francois asked.

"I thought they were all gone!" a member exclaimed.

"If they could capture him, they could capture us!" another member said, and several others murmured in agreement.

"They must be made our top priority!" Francois said.

Erik, Greg, and Luke all shared a look. Misdirection? The man was incredulous.

"I believe there are other matters that must be dealt with first," Greg said.

"Nothing is more important than the safety of vampires, *Gregori,*" Francois hissed.

"I've had enough of this, shut up," Luke barked.

Francois drew back. "How dare you—"

Greg pushed a button and the projection screen behind them came to life.

"Oh, we dare," Greg said bitterly. "Just like you dared to be the mastermind behind this entire war, Francois!"

Greg opened the bundle of documents and they spread across the screen, displaying all of Francois's crimes. The man's eyes grew wide, his jaw falling open in horror.

Then he ran.

Francois reached the door and threw it open, only to come face to face with Mya. She grabbed him by his neck, hoisted him into the air and slammed him onto the ground. Then she buried her knee against his throat and growled, "You're not going anywhere."

The Council guards arrived a moment later and took Francois away. Erik and Mya shared a look of adoration and love before she slipped back out the door.

Greg smirked. "Now, I believe there are several orders of business we need to attend to."

The meeting ended with Erik and Greg reinstated as members of The Council, and Greg reclaiming the role of leader. Their next order of business was to find out everything Francois had done. They raided his office and sent battle officers to his home. Once they had their hands on every piece of evidence they could find, Erik, Greg, and Luke took Francois to a secret location and tortured him for hours.

It didn't take much to get him to reveal all the things he'd done and the people he'd worked with, including some of guards and council members, just as they suspected. Then Erik had gotten the pleasure of killing him, *slowly*.

The evening was both chaotic and cathartic. It had been a long time since Erik had gotten the opportunity to work with Greg and Luke, and at moments it brought him back to the past. He was proud of the men he'd spent so much of his life with. He was especially proud of who they'd become and how they'd gone on to grow without him, and he felt honored to be able to share a space in their lives once more.

They each changed into a new pair of clothes, and Erik burned their old ones along with Francois's body before they left and made their way to Greg's car.

"It's been a ... wild couple of days," Luke said, sliding into the back seat.

"It has been, but at least now everything is as it should be." Greg's eyes flickered to Erik's as he turned on the ignition. "Now, let's go home."

An idea formed in Erik's mind at Greg's words. "Can we stop off somewhere first? There's something I need to check."

MYA RAN A HAND THROUGH HER LONG CURLY HAIR.

She'd kept herself busy while Erik was gone. She'd tidied

the house, changed the sheets, did everything she could possibly think of to keep her mind busy until she'd passed by the room she'd made Erik's shrine for the fifth time. Then she blew out a harsh breath and decided it was time.

For years the shrine had been all she'd had left of him, but now she could touch him, hold him. If she wanted to start moving forward and building a life with Erik, she'd need to get rid of her old vice first.

She stared at his eyes in the picture, looked over his long blonde hair, his frame, and realized that although this portrait was exact in its likeness to him, it was missing his spark the liveliness in his eyes. It was something no one could capture, not even the greatest artist or sculptor. Erik was a masterpiece all on his own, and this replica and all the time she spent using it as a way to keep her connection to him was no longer needed.

Decided, she pulled it down from the wall with a large sigh and felt a weight lift off her shoulders. Then she stared at the empty spot. The portrait had been there for so long that the wall was discolored around it. Mya wiped away the dust, threw away the candles and decided to move the console to the entry way. She rested his picture there. Perhaps in time they would take others, make a family wall out of it. She smiled as the feeling of bliss settled within her.

A family, with him.

She'd wanted that for so long, and to know it was finally obtainable meant everything to her. That thought spiraled through her and led her to check the front door once more to see if Erik was back. A lance of fear sliced through her heart, and she wondered if that would ever go away, if she would ever stop worrying every time he was away from her.

Then she heard Greg's car door slam, and she smiled. Mya

opened the front door, her grin growing as Erik took long, sure steps toward her. When he reached the threshold, she tilted her head up to his.

"Hello, love."

"Hello, *fagr skjaldmær min,*" he said, smiling back at her. Then she was in the air, wrapping her legs around him while he kissed her and kicked the door closed behind them. He nuzzled her neck as he set her back down, then turned and looked at the changes she'd made.

"The real thing is much better to look at," she said breathlessly.

Erik cupped her cheek and she leaned into his touch, her eyes fluttering closed.

"Mya," he croaked, and her eyes flew open to meet his.

He paused, and she squeezed his arms. "Erik, what is it?"

"No, it's just..." He trailed off, and she tilted her head in confusion. He frowned before clearing his throat. "This is harder than I thought it would be."

"What is it? Just tell me what you need to say. I can take it, I swear," she said, even as a million horrible thoughts flashed through her mind.

Erik took her hands and kissed them. He seemed to relax at simply being able to touch her, and then he fell to one knee.

"Erik?" she gasped.

He slipped something out of his back pocket, and in between his fingers stood a white gold ring. Its prongs were shaped like leaves, and in each of them stood a green diamond. The metal twisted and turned like stems, all coming to surround another large green diamond at the center.

Her eyes widened. "Erik, is that...?"

He smiled. "Yes, I went back and I was able to find it." He swallowed. "Mya—"

"Yes!"

He stared at her in a mixture of shock and awe. "...what?"

She fell to her knees and wrapped her arms around him. "Yes! Yes!" she repeated, basking in his scent, his breath, the feel of his skin against her own.

Erik laughed, and each rumble shook her body. Tears of joy poured from her eyes. He kissed every inch of her skin, then they broke away just enough for her to watch as he slipped the ring onto her finger.

"You didn't even let me finish my proposal," he said, in mock sadness.

"I didn't need to. My answer was yes. It has always been yes, and it always will be."

Erik cupped her cheeks and kissed her like she was his everything, and she kissed him back just as intensely, just as passionately. His arms went around her waist while hers went around his neck, then he lifted her until she was pinned against the wall. Mya wrapped her legs around him and he pressed further into her. She could feel his erection hard and thick against her stomach, and she moaned, her hips tilting, core pulsing at the thought of having him inside her again.

"May I touch you?" he whispered against her lips.

"*Please*," she begged, pushing his blazer off his body and onto the floor.

"I'll be rough with you," he murmured as he trailed his lips over her skin. "I *have* to be rough with you."

"I can take it," she whispered. "I won't break."

He shifted, tilting his body from hers and sliding his thigh between her legs. His hands went to her ass and he squeezed her tightly, then he ground his thigh against her clit, and she moaned.

"Yes, you will, *fagr skjaldmær min.* You will take it. You will take everything I give you and you will beg for more. You will break for me." He licked her neck. "You always break so beautifully for me."

Her nipples grew so hard that every time they brushed against her shirt it was too much. Electricity and chills raced over each part of her body, setting her aflame. She was so sensitive for him, so turned on, so desperate to have all of him that she knew he was right; she would take him, would do whatever he wanted, would please him in whatever way he needed, as long as he made her come.

He hoisted her higher, forcing her to widen her legs and seat herself fully on his thigh. The pressure made her cry out, as his hand wound into her hair and tugged her head back against the wall. His eyes were so dilated, the irises nearly fully black, and when he inhaled, she knew he could smell her desire.

"Is that for me?" he growled.

"Yes," she whimpered, her hips grinding against him of their own accord, chasing her release.

"Good girl," he murmured against her temple, kissing the spot, and she moaned at his praise. "That's my good, precious girl. Always so happy to please me."

"Yes," she cried as he pushed against her harder. She squeezed his biceps and together they fell into a rhythm that was theirs, would forever be only theirs, and he took her higher and higher.

"I can feel it," he growled into her ear, tracing the lobe with his tongue, sending goosebumps all the way down to her toes. "I can feel how wet your pretty little cunt is for me."

She groaned, embarrassed at how true his words were and how they made her even wetter. Mya turned her head away from him even as she continued to grind against his thigh, the movement as necessary to her as breathing.

"I can *hear* it," he groaned. "It's like music to my ears. But you know what I want, *fagr skjaldmær min*, so give it to me." He licked the pulse of her neck. "Give me your cries. Sing for me, my beautiful queen."

His teeth slipped into her neck, and she cried out in pleasure. She ripped at his shirt, needing to feel his skin, to press her nails into his back as she continued to buck against him. He moaned at the taste of her, at her noises, her cries, and then her head tilted back against the wall and she came for him. She broke apart for him, just as he had sworn she would.

Mya clung to Erik through her orgasm, but he kept drinking from her, kept pressing against her, and soon he began to work her to another one. He kissed her, the taste of her blood still on his lips as he bit, licked, and sucked her mouth. She slid her hands down to his belt and managed to undo the clasp before he ripped it out of the loops and wrapped it around her wrists. Then he tore at her clothes, ripping them until they were nothing but shreds that fell to the floor.

He pinned her hands above her head and tied the belt around her wrists, his eyes roaming over her body.

"Erik?" she panted.

"I'm well aware that you can get out of this. Don't, and I won't punish you." He said, then he lifted her, sliding her body up the wall while he trailed hot kisses over her skin. He licked and nibbled her collarbone, slid down to her breasts and sucked at one while he toyed with the other.

She arched her back, offering every inch of herself to him, and he smiled, sucking her harder. Mya wrapped her bound hands in his hair, holding his head to her chest as his hand slid over her stomach and down. After coating a finger in her wetness, Erik began to rub her clit in circles that had her undulating against him, her body begging for his touch, begging for him to use her however he wanted.

He pulled away from her nipple and slid his hand down to her thighs. He spread her open, then lifted her legs over his shoulders. She gasped. She was five-foot seven-inches tall, and Erik was a foot taller than her. At this height, she could touch the ceiling.

"Erik?" she said, her voice husky and breathless.

He stared up to her, his head between her thighs, face so close to her pussy that every breath he exhaled gave her chills. "I've wanted to taste this for so long. I've dreamed about it."

She blushed. "Erik, you don't—"

He smacked her clit, and the sudden flash of pain and pleasure making her whimper and buck against his hand for more. "You won't deny me this, Mya. I need it, just like I need you. I need to know what you like, how you like it, how you taste, how you move when I kiss you here"—he ran his thumb over her clit—"or here"—he slid his thumb down, spreading her pussy lips—"or even here," he said, sliding his thumb over her asshole and making her breath hitch and her eyes widen. "I need to know every piece of you, and by the end of tonight there won't be a place I haven't touched, licked, or sucked."

Then he spread her folds, and she watched helplessly as he licked her pussy. The cry that left her lips was loud, and she was dripping with unabashed need, but it was the pleasure on his face that did her in, the way he closed his eyes and moaned at the taste of her.

"My own ambrosia, the sweetest nectar of the gods."

"Erik," she moaned his name as he gave her a long, deep, slow lick, making her body quiver.

"You are my goddess, Mya. I prayed for you. I pray to you, and now I will worship you until we are both sated." His eyes burned bright, silver glowing with red. "Don't deny me, my goddess. Show me what you like, and when I get it right, reward me with your cream."

He ate her. He devoured her. He sucked, and nibbled, and licked her in every way possible until her back arched, her hips bucked, and she rode his tongue while her thighs shook. She came all over his face, and then he did it again, and again, and again. He sucked her clit until her eyes rolled back into her head. Then he slapped her pussy, slid three fingers inside of her, and curled them to reach a spot that had her screaming his name once more.

He bit her thigh while he pumped his fingers, rubbing her clit with his thumb until she felt an odd sensation, something new. She both chased it and ran away from it, grabbing Erik's hair and tugging him against her one moment, then trying to push him away the next. Before she could stop herself, she came so hard she squirted all over his hand.

His eyes glazed over with lust as he cleaned her with his tongue, then drew some of the wetness down to her asshole. It shouldn't have felt good for him to rub her there, for his thumb to slide over the rim of her hole, but it did, by the gods it did. It felt so good that she came again from his touch, from the way he sucked her clit, from the way he worked against her asshole. When his hand wrapped around her throat, she screamed his name and saw stars.

He pulled her back from the wall, lowering her slowly until she was on the floor. "Hold onto me," he ordered, and she did, half delirious as he broke open the closure of his pants.

His cock sprang free and she moaned at the sight of it, so swollen, red, and dripping pre-cum all for her. Erik squeezed the back of her leg, throwing it over his forearm. The position caused her hips to tilt to the side as he continued to spread her, then he pressed his cock to her pussy and rammed all the way to the base.

She screamed out, her voice growing higher in pitch as he slammed into her. He was brutal with her, possessive, grasping her neck and forcing her to watch him, to stare into his eyes as he undid her with his every stroke. He was in her, around her, taking her, claiming her, fucking her with wild abandon, but when they came together it felt like nothing else. Her pussy clamped down on him, begging for every single drop of come in his balls, and he gave it all to her.

When Erik pulled out of her, she thought they were done, but then he spun her around, pulled her ass back and ground against her. "This hungry little cunt is going to take me again," he whispered into her ear.

"Erik," she groaned, her nipples rubbing against the wall with his every move. "It's too much, I can't ... I *can't.*"

He smacked her ass, angled her hips, and thrust in so deep she cried out.

"You can." *Thrust.* "You will." *Thrust.* "You want this." *Thrust.* "You want me," he growled.

She screamed his name as he spanked her ass over and over, then she pushed back against him, spreading her legs, wanting to feel him deeper inside her, wanting to take him harder.

"Beg for it," he groaned, nails pressing into her ass cheeks as he pulled her back.

Tears of pleasure poured from her eyes as she turned her head to his. "Please!"

"Please, *what?*" he commanded, fucking her harder, pushing her closer to the edge.

"More. I need more. Harder. Deeper. I need ... I need you, don't stop, don't stop, *don't stop!*"

"Good girl," Erik purred, then he bit her neck, and she came. Liquid rolled over her thighs but she didn't care, too lost in her orgasm and the way he continued to fuck her. She ripped the belt apart, her hand grabbing his hair to hold him against her as he continued to use her pussy, to pound into her with utter abandon.

They came once more. Then he took her on the floor. He made her ride him on the couch, bent her over the chair, then ate her as if she was his favorite meal on the dining room table, before he took her again. They washed each other in the shower, and Erik ate her once more. He drew her a bath to ease her body, but she had moved past the point of no return, and when he neared the bathtub, she took his cock into her mouth and sucked him until he came, swallowing it all.

They relaxed for an hour together in one another's arms, until he moved them to the bed, where he gently took her again and again. She slept for hours afterward, naked and basking in the warmth of his body until mid-afternoon, when he brought her breakfast and made her come once more.

Every word, every caress, every time he slid inside her was a reclaiming of her heart and her soul, and she would stay by his side until the day time stood still.

EPILOGUE

The corruption they'd uncovered implicated six other members of The Council. Erik and Mya were part of the teams that hunted down the perpetrators, tortured them, and uncovered their secrets.

They did their best to find those that had been harmed and get them justice, but Erik also had to fill his seat on The Council. At Greg's, Dani's, Johanna's and Mya's urging, Luke finally agreed to take one of the open seats. Merida took another, and they eventually filled the remaining seats with good, dedicated people who wanted a better world for vampires and all immortals.

The answer was to create The Agency, a place where anyone, even humans, who had suffered at the hands of an immortal could go for help. The Agency was the answer against war, against the darkness and tragedy they had suffered. It was how they planned to create a better world for their future generations.

Generations like Mya and Erik's double set of twins, and the baby currently kicking in her stomach. It had taken years of therapy and vulnerability to get to this point, and even then, Erik sometimes found himself absorbed in the bleakness of his world, reliving all those years without Mya.

But they were happy, and when he looked at her, when he felt their unborn child kicking in her stomach, when he saw the wedding band on her finger, the wall of photos of their family, when he heard the laughter of their children, even their fighting and tantrums, it all made sense. It was all worth it. And if he had to, he would do it all again, go through every moment of suffering, just to get to this brilliant, beautiful space with her.

His wife.

His queen.

His goddess.

The mother of his children.

The other half of his soul.

Fagr skjaldmær min.

Want to read about a mafia queen who doesn't need anyone and the mafia king who will kill to stand by her side? Scan the QR code below!

Not ready to say goodbye to these amazing characters? Turn the page for a few never before published bonus scenes!

BONUS SCENES

DELETED SCENE (GREGORI AND DANIELLA)

For the first time in what felt like days, when Daniella opened her eyes, she saw light. Between the whirlwind of yesterday and the early morning, she was exhausted.

She groaned against the sun's intrusion and closed her eyes again, planning to fall back asleep against the warm body beside her. Unfortunately for the both of them, that delectable body was missing.

She frowned at the disturbance of his absent form, and got up, planning to express her complaint to Greg once she found him. Daniella searched for him, checking the next few rooms. Soft banging and the mouth-watering scent of bacon drew her to the left. She loved Greg. She really did. But there was something about watching him move around the stove, shirtless, the muscles of his tan skin rolling as he flipped her favorite maple sugar bacon. It brought forth a hunger that had nothing to do with food.

He tilted his head to the side, turning as she approached

with a cocky grin, while lifting several strips out of the pan. "I never knew food could turn you on."

She should have been embarrassed that his vampire senses gave her away. But she was too hungry, sleepy, and now horny, to care. "It's not the food."

Before she could blink, he lifted her and placed her on the counter. Greg settled himself between her legs. The contrast of the cold surface and his warm body made her shiver, and then his lips were on hers.

She moaned, wove her hands around him and into his hair, grasping at the strands to keep him firmly pressed against her. He answered her call by pulling her hips closer, and she sighed in delight. The motion opened her mouth to his. He slipped his tongue inside, once, twice, teasing her until she followed him back, then they intertwined with one another, dancing in passion and desire.

When he pulled away, she was panting. He chuckled, but his voice was low, his laugh breathless.

Greg grabbed a bacon strip and held it in front of her mouth. She allowed him to feed it to her and couldn't resist giving his finger a soft lick in thanks.

His eyes darkened, but a loud pop interrupted the moment. Greg dropped a kiss on her head, before turning to check the bacon. "Good morning to you too, love."

Daniella's eyes widened at the endearment. She stared at his back, watching his muscles stretch and release as he moved about, pouring pancake batter into a pan. "You've never called me that before." She whispered.

"Does it bother you?"

"He's hiding." The voices were internal now. She still hadn't

told Greg about them, only because she wasn't sure how to put it into words, but in moments like this, it was useful.

Jumping from the counter, she came to his side and placed her hand on his arm, giving it a soft squeeze. "It doesn't bother me. I like it."

"Then I'll do it more often."

Daniella stood on her tiptoes and kiss his cheek. He gave her a blissful smile that pulled at her soul, making her feel light, joyful, exuberant. "Do I have enough time to take a shower before the pancakes are done?"

"Mm," he tapped his chin, "I suppose. But you should be quick. I can't guarantee I won't eat them if you're gone for too long."

"Does food even satisfy a vampire's hunger?"

"No, but I make great pancakes and I'm not against eating them all."

"Well, I've got some cake you can try instead." She giggled and spun, smacking her ass cheeks hard enough to make them shake.

His warning growl made her dash toward the door, laughing all the way upstairs.

THE STATE OF THE ROOM SHOCKED DANIELLA. IN LESS THAN A few hours, Greg had repaired most of the broken items.

I suppose being a vampire comes in handy for these types of things.

Other than a few dents in the honey wood furniture, the room seemed as good as new. The floor was clean, no hint of debris, and the window replaced. He had even hung soft pink and cream curtains.

Several articles of her clothing hung in the closet, enough to keep her comfortable for a week if not two, and within the bathroom she'd found all her necessary toiletries, including her rose scented body wash and her exfoliating luffa.

Things weren't perfect. She knew that. If it were anyone else, she would have never given them a second chance. Trust was not something she gave easily. Her upbringing had made sure of that, and knowing that Greg lied to her, hurt. But he was trying, and it was clear he was trying hard, even before she'd discovered the truth. If it weren't for that, things would have been different. But if he were willing to meet her halfway, then she was willing to do her best, too.

She sighed. Who was she kidding? She'd been half in love with the man from the start, and breaking down this last barrier made her feel like she was flying. This was an entirely different side of Greg, one that she craved desperately. It made her feel at home, and that was dangerous. She had to stay objective.

The eyes staring back at her from the mirror told her that ship had sailed. She was in too deep, had always been, and she couldn't imagine feeling any different. All she could do was try to be honest, even if her heart had already betrayed her head.

She took a shower and donned a white blouse, which she half tucked into a pair of light-colored jean shorts, Daniella made her way back downstairs and waded into the kitchen.

"Is it safe to come in?"

Greg sat on a barstool eating a raspberry. He gave her a slow once over and when he met her eyes, he grinned. "I think I can behave, for now."

She took a seat on the barstool beside him, grabbing a plate of eggs, bacon, and pancakes. "This was really sweet of you, thank you."

"You're welcome." He kissed her temple, and then took a bite.

Looking around the kitchen, she tilted her head. "Where do you keep the blood?"

He choked, coughing as he tried to swallow, hitting his chest with a fist.

She patted his back as he took a large gulp of water. "Are you okay?"

"Ella, what did you just ask me?"

"Well, you did all of this for me, but it doesn't really nourish you in the same way. So, I thought the least I could do was get you something that would. Aren't you hungry or—"

He cut her off by tucking her hair behind her ear, his fingers lingering on her neck. "Oh, I'm hungry all right, but you mentioning blood right now is not the best idea. I'm a little too close to taking it as an invitation."

Her skin heated at the thought. This was not the first time she'd wondered what feeding him would feel like.

His phone rang, and with a sigh, he answered.

Daniella turned back to her meal, trying her best not to listen to the conversation.

After a few quick words, Greg ended the call. "That was Astrid. She's the person who can help you understand your new abilities. She said we can meet her at 11:00. Let me go get ready and then we can head out."

Daniella nodded. "Thank you again for your help."

"You're welcome, and Ella?"

She tilted her head to acknowledge him, only to be stopped

as he settled behind her. The warmth of his chest radiated through her thin blouse and against her back.

His arm came to rest beside her on the counter, while his fingers curled around her hip.

"Stop teasing me." He whispered, his lips brushing against her ear with every word. "I only have so much restraint." With a squeeze of her hip, he let go and walked out of the kitchen.

She bit her lip and then she smiled mischievously. *I look forward to breaking it.*

BONUS SCENE (GREGORI AND DANIELLA)

Daniella awoke to something moving over her body. The woven towel brushed her stomach delicately, both damp and warm, causing goosebumps to pucker along her skin. Then Greg's lips followed, the heat of his mouth, the slickness of his tongue trailed over each bump making her shiver and moan.

Her eyes slid open to find Greg's head dangerously close to her core, making it pulse in need. "What are you doing?"

His gaze held hers for a moment before sliding over her entrance, dark and hungry. "I was just cleaning you up. Seems I made quite the mess."

Her skin heated at the memory and a fresh wave of wetness gathered between her thighs.

Greg's eyes blazed. Dropping a kiss on her knee, he brought the towel between her legs, spreading them further, and wiped the junction slowly, getting closer and closer to her pussy. "I want to play with you," he whispered.

"Play?" She rasped.

"Yes. You see…I want to know everything about you. Everything you like. I fear I may have become a little obsessed with your moans, the way your body writhes, the way you feel, your screams, and so I want to know everything." He leaned forward, his thumb tracing her folds. "I want to take you higher, I want to feel your cream around my cock again."

She couldn't speak, could barely breathe.

Greg dipped his finger inside of her, making her cry out. He trailed the digit up to her clit, circling the nub as he whispered. "Will you let me?"

"Yes." Daniella hissed, her hips lifting in unabashed need.

"Get on all fours, baby."

She adjusted her position, and turned back to look at him. His eyes raked over her form and he let out a sound, a vibration that started in his chest and traveled over her body. It was a growl of pleasure, of damnation, and she felt it all the way down to her toes.

Greg's lips curled into a smile, his fangs bit into his lower lip and all she could think about was how badly she wanted them in her neck again.

He shifted, grabbing the satin tie of her robe. "Close your eyes."

She did and a shiver coursed over her skin as she became hyper aware of him. Daniella listened as he moved from behind her, and then covered her eyes with the sash, tying it securely behind her head. Her nipples tightened and her hands curled into fists as anticipation raced through her.

Greg's touch was featherlight as it roamed the contours of her body. He caressed her skin down to the curve of her ass where he squeezed her flesh.

"You are so incredibly beautiful." He said, his voice husky and low.

She blushed. "Thank you—"

Daniella gasped as Greg grabbed hold of her hips, and pulled her down. Something pointed brushed against her clit sending an arc of electricity through her body.

Greg inhaled, and the vacuum of air made her realize it was his nose. He sniffed her and she blushed again, but then he ran his tongue from her clit down to her folds and back up in long, sensuous licks and she was lost. She moaned, jerked her hips at the action and he chuckled beneath her. Greg did the motion again, then spread her folds and speared her with his tongue.

He rolled the sides of his tongue and thrust it in and out of her pussy, making her cry out. Greg licked up, flicking her clit with his tongue before taking it in his mouth and sucking, hard. The action made her buck forward, lifting off his face enough for him to ram two fingers inside of her.

Her moans grew louder as he ate her. Reaching behind her, she tried to touch him but he grabbed both of her wrists in his hand and held them behind her back, restricting her. The position forced her to tilt her hips against his mouth and surrender to him. She writhed on top of him, circling, sliding over his mouth and tongue, and his throaty moans urged her on.

Without warning, he released her hands and smacked her ass. The sudden motion, combined with her new freedom, made her fall forward with a yelp. He grasped her thighs, helping to catch her fall until she planted her hands on the floor. Then he spread her legs wider and suddenly disappeared.

"Greg?" She panted.

"Shh, don't worry I'm still here." His body pressed against hers, his chest to her back, and he cupped her face.

"Let me give you a taste." Greg crushed his lips against hers and she moaned tasting his saliva, both of their orgasms on his tongue. Then she cried into his mouth as he rammed inside of her and filled her with his cock.

She fell forward from the surprise, catching her weight on her elbow, and he grabbed a hold of her, holding them both upright while he continued to pound, so slow, but so deep. His tongue tangled with hers as they moaned into one another's mouths, and when he pulled away she could feel the beads of saliva connecting between them.

"Fuck," he groaned, sucking her bottom lip into his mouth before kissing down to his neck. "I could do this for days, for weeks."

She moaned, tried to formulate words, but he trailed his fangs along her neck, causing her to gasp while he continued the same sinful pace.

His voice dipped as he whispered into her ear. "I can't get enough of you. I can never be full of you." His fingers slid around her hips, down to her clit as he circled the bud.

Her head dropped forward as pleasure coasted through her body. Sweat beaded along her skin and she leaned down, pressing her chest into the ground, the angle driving him deeper, allowing her to push back into his hips and hands harder, faster.

Greg groaned, the hand on her hip sliding up her back, caressing her spine as it reached the back of her hair. "I wish you could see yourself right now. See how good you look taking my cock."

She bit her lip as that thought spurred another tendril of desire loose within her and her pussy grew wetter, hotter around him.

He gripped her hair, pulling her head back, tearing a moan from her lips. "The things you do to me, Daniella." He moaned, and then his body fell down upon hers. The hairs of his chest, brushed her back, and she writhed, every inch of her body alive and desperate for his.

He gripped her neck, and whispered in his ear. "You've changed me." He moaned, slamming his hips into hers, making her cry out. "Your scent is in my nostrils, your taste in my mouth. Your heartbeat, it's so loud." Greg gripped her breast, twisting the nipple in his hand and she arched into his touch.

"Your skin, your pussy, the way it grips me." He moved faster, harder. "I'm gone, Ella. Completely consumed by you." Greg surged forward, his thrusts powerful, brutal, unrestrained, and she loved every single second of it.

Daniella clenched her fists around the rug, the fibers stroking her skin as Greg ground her body against it. He was so warm against her back. She felt every ripple of muscle, every stretch of his tendons as he buried himself inside of her over and over again and her body clenched to take him.

Greg traced his tongue along her neck, and he pounded into her cunt like a wild man. All she could do was surrender to him, to the force of his thrusts, the ministrations on her clit. She trembled beneath him, turned her head into the rug to muffle her screams while saliva drooled from her mouth.

Then his hand moved back to her throat. She turned her head and he captured her lips in a searing kiss before he moaned her name. "Fill my ears with your screams baby, give that to me. Let me see you come undone for me. Give me your cream."

She broke apart. The orgasm had her clenching her toes as it soared up her body. Her pussy fluttered around his cock, but it wasn't enough for him. She was still flying, still meeting heavenly bliss when he pulled her up. Greg grabbed a hold of her arms, forced them behind her back and thrust so hard she lost all sense of reason. There was only him, only this, only him taking control of her entire being. His squeezed her throat again before his fangs slid into her neck and she slipped into madness.

Daniella bucked against his hips as he hit her g-spot. Tears ran down her face, the wetness leaking down her chin as he continued to take her.

"Mine. All fucking *mine!*" He growled.

She tilted her head to the side, and his next bite was deeper, harder, and she came again. She came so hard cream dripped from her pussy down between their thighs. Greg's hands left her arms, grabbing her hips as he buried himself deep. Then he was coming, roaring as filled her, as he clung to her, curved her body into his so she would be forced to take every drop of him. And she did, she wanted to, begged him, pleaded in her mindlessness for him not to stop, wiggled her hips to force him deeper until he was spent.

DELETED SCENE (JOHANNA AND DANIELLA)

"He *what?*" Dani shrilled.

Johanna jumped from her seat on the couch. She rushed to cover the speaker and yelled to her friend in a hushed tone, "Shut up!"

It had the opposite effect. Dani cackled, then fell into a full laugh, which only served to further Johanna's embarrassment.

"I'm never telling you anything again!" Johanna said.

"I'm sorry, I'm sorry, it's just too good. Please continue." Dani said, still laughing.

Johanna huffed. "Absolutely not."

"If you don't tell me, I can't help you." Dani said in a mocking sing-song voice.

Johanna sighed. Dani was right, *unfortunately*. Every time she called, Dani would check on Luke and Johanna's relationship. Sometimes she offered little tidbits, or an outside perspective that Johanna treasured, but this time the topic was …

uncomfortable. Still, Johanna needed the advice and didn't have anyone else to turn to.

"Fine." Johanna sighed again, closing her eyes as if she could block herself from her own embarrassment.

"Alright, alright. So you two kissed and uh ... had *fun* at the beach, and then?" Dani asked.

"Nothing."

"What do you mean nothing?"

"Absolutely, nothing!" Johanna threw her hand in the air and then let it land with a loud *slap* on her thigh. "He hasn't touched me all week, and we haven't talked about what happened. When we go to bed we just cuddle, that's it."

"What the hell?"

"Now you see my dilemma." Johanna said, leaning her head back against the couch.

There was a slight ruffle on the line, before Dani spoke. "Okay, let's start from the top. Tell me what happened one more time."

"He told me he loved me, I kissed him, he kissed me back, and then we ... you know." Silence greeted her. "If you start laughing again, I'm hanging up."

"No, no. But you have to see it from my point of view. The two of you are better than reality television."

Johanna rolled her eyes at that.

"Okay, so he told you he loved you. Did you say it back?" Dani asked.

Johanna paused, then squeezed the bridge of her nose. "No ... I just reacted."

"That's not the worse thing in the world. If you weren't ready to say it—"

"I was! I mean, I am." Johanna took a deep breath and let it out slowly. "I love him, Dani. I love him so much."

The pitch of Dani's voice elevated slightly, and she sounded like she was smiling. "Okay, that's good. Are you sure there's nothing else?"

"Well..." she gulped. "There were things Luke said he wanted."

"Oh? What things?"

Johanna remembered in *vivid* detail what Luke had said, the exact list, word for word of what he wanted from her, and she also knew she could *never* say those things out loud.

"Me," she said finally, pulling at her shirt. Johanna fanned her chest as the memory heated her skin and set a surge of wetness to her core. "He said he wanted me, and I've since told him *multiple* times that he has me, but he still won't touch me, and I don't know what else to do."

Dani groaned. "It will never stop to amaze me how dense the two of you are."

"Hey!"

"It's the truth. You used to think it was impossible for anyone to love you, *truly* love you after they got to know you. You're better with that now, but it's still a daily struggle, and Luke is the same way. The only difference is he still blames himself for what happened to you." Dani said.

"He does?"

"Yes he does." Dani said, a note of disappointment in her tone. "He hasn't said anything to me about it, but the both of you are stubborn. Once either of you get an idea in your head it takes a long time for you to let go of it, unless you have irrefutable proof."

Johanna opened her mouth to reject that idea, then paused. Dani was right. "What do I do?"

"I think even if you had told Luke you loved him, he wouldn't believe you, not at first anyway. So if he won't believe you when you say it, show him. The same goes for this whole, possessive, 'I'm yours' thing."

Johanna bit her lip as she fussed with the material of her shirt again. It was a good idea and it wasn't something she had tried, but that was a new world for her. "How do I show him?"

Dani made a soft hiccup of delight, then said, "Ah, my friend. Let me teach you the art of seduction."

DELETED SCENE (MYA)

Mya opened the double doors and stepped into her courtyard. The night was calm, peaceful, the opposite of her erratically beating heart. She walked down the stone path to the terrace, and sat on the bench, pulling her harp in front of her.

She closed her eyes and let her fingers begin to play. The melody was sad and dark, speaking to the loneliness, the melancholy nature of her soul. And then she began to sing.

You were my everything,
And without you I am cold.
I no longer see color,
I close my eyes and wonder,
Where have you been?
What have you seen?
Is there a piece of you that still longs for me?

Do you cry for me, would you breathe for me if you
were still beside me?
I dream of you,
I call for you,
I miss you,
Come back to me, please.

ACKNOWLEDGMENTS

To you. Yes! You! Thank you so much for reading my novel. Knowing that you took the the time to read it is beyond amazing to me. You help every author to move forward, to write their next book, to publish, to celebrate. That's all you. So thank you again, take care, and I can't wait for you to read my next book!

ABOUT THE AUTHOR

Melissa had a difficult time speaking as a child, and thus writing became her best friend. There she learned the power of emotion, how to communicate heartbreak, sadness, tragedy, and still hope for something better: the happy ever after.

She loves to write imperfect, possessive heroes, that will risk their lives for those they love, strong heroines that can hold their own, and steamy scenes that grab you by the throat and bring you to your knees.

Melissa lives in a small town off the coast of Egypt, and is a huge mythology buff, with a love of all things magical, supernatural, paranormal, and steeped in lore and fantasy. When she is not writing Melissa can be found singing and dancing her heart out, or up, late at night, contemplating space and the universe with a large cup of tea.

facebook.com/MelissaCumminsAuthor

instagram.com/melissacumminsauthor

patreon.com/melissacummins

9 781958 769102